I0746929

THE LAST GUARDSMAN

ALSO BY RHONDA CHANDLER

The Ritornello Game

(Book 1 of the Marlonburg Series)

The Fires of Autumn

(Historical Fiction)

THE LAST GUARDSMAN

RHONDA CHANDLER

STAIRCASE
BOOKS

THE LAST GUARDSMAN

Copyright © 2021 by Rhonda Chandler

www.rhondachandler.com

All rights reserved. No part of this book may be reproduced or transmitted in any form or by any means, electronic or mechanical, including photocopying, recording, or by any information storage and retrieval system, except for brief quotations in book reviews, without the written permission of the publisher, except where permitted by law.

This is a work of fiction. Names, characters, events, and incidents are entirely the product of the author's imagination. Any resemblance to actual persons, living or dead, is purely coincidental.

Cover design by Kristen Langefeld

ISBN 978-1-7325797-6-7 (paperback)

ISBN 978-1-7325797-7-4 (large print)

ISBN 978-1-7325797-8-1 (ebook)

Published by Staircase Books

Staircase Books

1111 S. Lincoln Ave. #465

O'Fallon, IL 62269-9998

United States of America

To

Kristen, Jennifer, and Adrienne

with love always

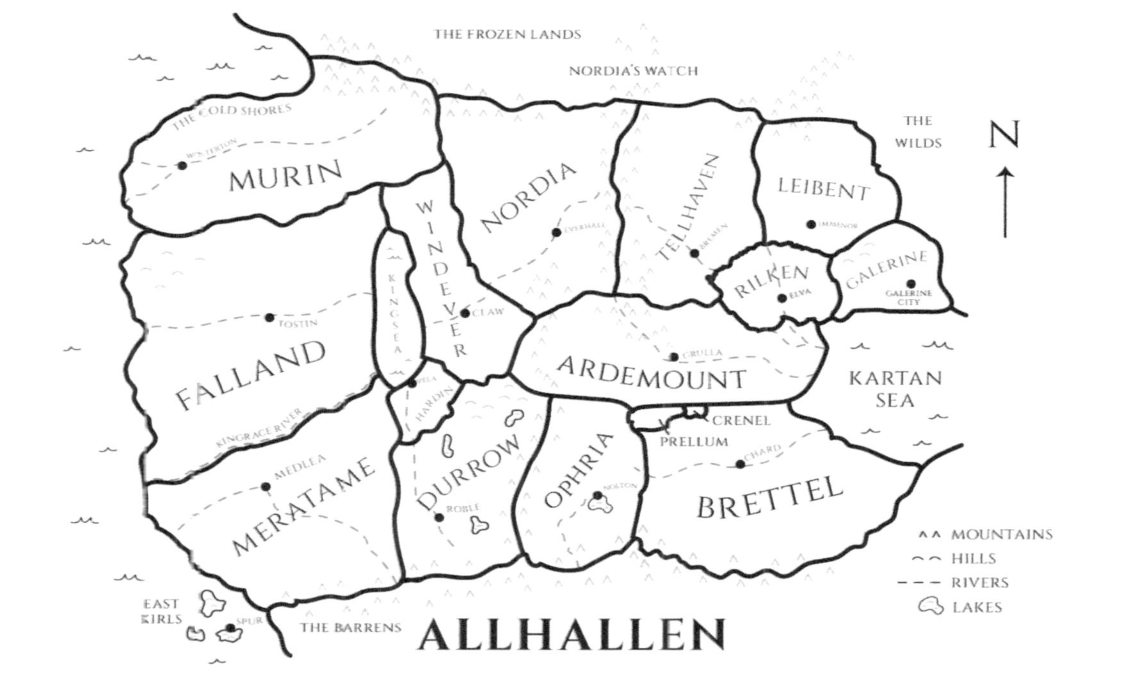

THE FROZEN LANDS
NORDIA'S WATCH
THE WILDS
N
THE COLD SHORES
WESTERTON
MURIN
NORDIA
EVERHALL
TELLHAVEN
BRUMEN
LEIBENT
EMMENOR
RILKEN
ELVA
GALERINE
GALERINE CITY
WINDEVER
CLAW
KINGSEA
FALLAND
TOSTIN
CRULLA
ARDEMOUNT
KARTAN SEA
PELA
HARDIN
KINGRACE RIVER
CRENEL
PRELLUM
CHARD
MEDLEA
DURROW
ROBLE
OPHRIA
NOLTON
BRETTEL
MERATAME
EAST KIRLS
SPUR
THE BARRENS
ALLHALLEN
MOUNTAINS
HILLS
RIVERS
LAKES

TELLHAVEN
LEIBENT
GALERINE
ARDEMOUNT
KARTAN SEA
RILKEN
ELVA
POLTA RIVER
TELLMAN RIVER
NORTHWEST ROAD
NORTH ROAD
SOUTH ROAD
WEST ROAD
EAST ROAD
POLTA RIVER
TELLMAN RIVER
N
WHERE THE KING FELL
THE GRUMPY RABBIT
BALLROOM BY THE SEA
FOREST   FARM LAND

TABLE OF CONTENTS

1
———

The Forest Road

The bear waited in the small ravine near the road, where the trunks of the trees were thickest. He could smell the soldiers—the metallic tang of their half armor, the sweat of their horses—long before the sound of hooves thudded and echoed on the road. And he knew the men were afraid. Afraid and reluctant to retrace their steps.

The sound of their progress slowed as the road dipped and began its turn toward the place where the bear watched. The smell of fear grew stronger and the hoofbeats slowed even more to a cautious walk.

A beast of a man came riding into view between the trees, tall and broad in the shoulder, his massive body half-hidden by the great shield he carried at his side.

After him came a hawk-nosed, black-bearded man with hard eyes, a rich mantle of deep green draped around him. He raised his arm and the whole company halted.

"What's this?" the hawk-nosed man cried out. "Who has done this?!"

The soldiers on the road raised their shields and turned their mounts. In some places they could see past leafless trees, but the dense branches of the evergreens were impenetrable.

It did not matter. They would see no one. The bear smelled no other men but these for miles.

The hawk-nosed man stared at the roadside, bewildered. "This is not what I expected, Mago."

The beast-man got off his horse and silently gazed at the sight which awaited them on the road bank.

After a few moments' hesitation, the hawk-nosed man dismounted too. "Who could have done this?"

"I smell bear," said Mago, the beast-man.

"Of *course* you do," the other cried with impatience. "The bears have been all over here. But bears wouldn't do *this*."

The hawk-nose took in the whole scene. A row of dead men lay there. Not mauled by bear claws and teeth, but pierced by the arrows and spears of men. One of them numerous times. Nevertheless, they had been laid out with great care, as if with great honor, side by side. A group of travel-weary horses, horses which should have fled in fear from both bear and spear, instead waited sorrowfully by the men who had ridden them.

The bear crouched down and took a few steps closer,

up the side of the ravine toward the road. His front paw brushed a dry, winter-killed bush, making it crackle.

The hawk-nosed man whirled around at the sound. His eyes searched the forest where the ground sloped downward away from him. But he saw nothing.

"You there!" He pointed at the soldiers still on their mounts. "Get down here and lash these bodies to the horses. Quick! We must get them to Elva!"

The soldiers obeyed, but the smell of their fear increased, assaulting the bear's nose.

Mago studied the ground. "Are they all here, my lord?"

The hawk-nosed man held tight to his own horse's reins as he peered through the trees, looking deeply into the forest. "They have to be."

Mago circled the ground where the bodies lay. It was lightly damp from an early spring rain, and littered with the remains of some winter leaves. "Dallen got away."

The hawk-nose swore. Violently. "He can't be running wild in the forest. The bears must have gotten him. They *must*. No one could have survived those brutes. That's the only possible explanation for it."

Mago nodded slowly. "If the men had been alive, they wouldn't have left their horses behind. Dallen's horse is still here. All the horses are still here." The forest drew his eyes again. "We'll have to search for them, for their bodies."

"The necessary but troublesome proof." Hawk-nose frowned. "Very well. Send out your searchers when you can. But *we* must get to Elva quickly."

Hawk-nose climbed back onto his horse, his scent

uneasy yet his voice spoke with command. "One way to seize power from an enemy, Mago, is to speak first. Ride with me. I'll tell you what to say to the people about this when we return to the castle. No one would dare challenge you."

The beast-man grunted, mounted his horse, and took his place next to the other on the road. Meanwhile, the soldiers made a sloppy job of fastening the bodies to the saddles of the waiting horses, and the horses were fast losing their calm.

The bear inched forward through the trees as the men scrambled to finish their work, roping the horses with the dead to those with the living. The bodies shifted and slid as the horses moved. Soldiers cursed, dismounted, and tied them tighter. At last their work was finished and the group of them readied to ride.

The bear emerged from the trees. A growl formed deep in his chest and rumbled through his throat, flinging itself out into the forest air. The horses circled around, close to panic at the sound.

The beast-man turned back, hefted his spear and hurled it with precision and strength at the bear's head. The point struck the bear near his throat, but bounced off, falling to the ground. The men stared in horror as the bear stepped fully out onto the road. It stood on its back feet, towering over them. Another man threw a spear. Then another. Arrows flew from hastily-grabbed bows. All fell back onto the road, scattering like the discarded toys of children.

Cries of dismay rang out. The soldiers spurred their

horses to flee. The roped ones, lurching with the frantic motion, almost lost their lifeless burdens.

The bear stood in the road and lifted his head high. Another roar resounded through the trees, chasing the men in their flight.

It was a roar of grief. A grief so strong that it pulled sorrow from the surrounding trees.

But it was also a roar of anger.

Anger for the inglorious way the king of Rilken was being transported to his capital city of Elva.

2

____

A Noise in the Street

I knew that Zilla only wanted to talk about the
bears. She was my mother's good friend and our
neighbor in the area of Elva that everyone calls
Guardstown. Her stout, stone house was similar to ours.
Her interests and her need to stitch and sew, the same as
ours. Her husband was also a Guardsman, one of the
honored thirty who protect the king's person at all times.

The difference was that Zilla's husband Drony was
currently in Guardstown, while my father was out on
duty with the king, traveling from the country of Tellhaven on their way back home to Elva. And that is why
Zilla struggled to keep the concerns I saw in her eyes
from slipping off her tongue.

Mama was also aware of Zilla's struggle. I could see it in the way she tilted slightly toward her friend even while her fingers plied the embroidery needle that was decorating the collar of Papa's shirt for his return surprise. Mama's eyebrows lowered slightly, and she kept sending Zilla understanding looks, even though she seemed to hope that Zilla would be able to restrain herself.

The wives of the Guardsmen have this unspoken promise between them. They do not speak with fear on their breath. Do not voice what *might* happen, or *could* happen. Those fears are useless. They eat the heart and soul out of one. They take the strength that is meant for other things.

The children of the Guardsmen whisper their fears into safe ears. Ears that will send a whisper of encouragement back. But nothing had caused such whispers for a long time.

Yet something gave Zilla a need to talk today. She was being careful in choosing her words, careful because the king's path led through those very northwest woods where the bears had been sighted.

So Zilla talked and Mama let her, because Mama never hid from hard things, although she always thought first of protecting us.

"The bears are larger than most, Tara. Drony has spotted one." Zilla poked her needle firmly into the fabric she held. Too fiercely, I thought. That stitch would pull too tight. I wondered what Drony had said.

She went on. "We hear they are unusual too, in that

they travel together. They're not solitary like most bears are."

"Well then," Mama replied, "it sounds like these bears are almost as wise as the Guardsmen. For they, too, always travel together."

I knew Mama said this for our benefit, so I met her concerned glance with a reassuring smile. A smile that tried to remind her I was not seven years old, but seventeen, and my sister Rosabel less than two years younger. Mama returned my smile with a friendly nod.

Rosie wasn't listening or she would have had plenty to say. She was in agony trying to make her own embroidery needle perform well. So she had tried for ten years. I was mending a torn skirt, and my fingers could work without much guidance.

"Could these bears be the Guardians of Rilken, Mama?" I asked. "The ones that come at urgent need?"

Zilla answered instead. "Those are stories, Silvie, stories we're proud of in Rilken, but only stories after all. Today we trust in the Guardsmen and the walls of Elva. If Elva stands, Rilken stands. And, there's no *urgent need* or danger for the Guardsmen," she added quickly, with exaggerated calm. "Or for the king. The Guardsmen have sighted the bears a number of times, and the bears have not attacked anyone at all.

"But you know, Tara," she said, turning back to my mother, "it's good to be aware of what is happening in the vast western forests."

This last sounded as if it was meant to be Zilla's justification for herself, for her inability to be silent about a fearful subject. She pulled her last stitch too tightly, making the material pucker, reached for Mama's scissors and snipped the dangling thread without knotting it first. Yes, Zilla was deeply concerned about the bears.

"The western forests or the eastern plains. The Guardsmen are aware of all of it," Mama said mildly. She glanced over at us and noticed Rosabel's sturdy concentration. "Is your thread misbehaving, Rosie?"

Rosie sighed. "No, my fingers are. I just can't make my stitches look like Silvie's."

"I hope not," I said, trying to dodge the comparison. I held up the mended skirt. "These straight stitches alone would make a very boring pattern."

"I don't mean *those*," answered Rosie. "I mean the flowers you stitched on your white sash. The beautiful roses." She held out the square of linen she was practicing stitches on. "This looks like a lettuce."

I protested. "That looks like the middle of a very nice rose. You have to keep adding the petals around it. Don't you think so, Mama?"

Mama took the piece in her hands and studied it. "You might have better luck if you made your stitches smaller, Rosie. The curved lines of the flower will stay in control that way."

"What if I drop the curved stitches altogether?" Rosie suggested. "What if I made only straight lines? I can make stars using straight lines. I could become famous as the girl who put stars on everything! Of course," she hesitated, "the straight lines would really have to *be* straight and that is hard to do too."

"I'll find some gold thread for your stars," I told her.

She laughed, stretched her arms, and went to look out the front window.

I searched through the thread box, pushing my long hair back so I could see clearly, but it kept sliding off my shoulders, making a white-blond veil that was hard to see through. As I did so, I felt Zilla's gaze rest on me.

I looked up, gave her a quick smile, and busied myself with the thread box. In that short moment, I had seen what I didn't like to see. Both pride and hope were in Zilla's gaze. She would be thinking again that I would make a fine bride for her son Ross.

I knew that Ross agreed with his mother. He went still as a statue whenever he saw me, his face flushing red like a cherry. But I felt there was something missing in Ross. Something I hoped for in a husband that I could not see in him. I usually can find words for what I think and feel, but I couldn't come up with the right ones to explain to myself what it was that was lacking.

Not that I would need to explain to anyone else, because Mama and Papa had made it clear that they would not let either of their daughters go for several years yet. Papa called us his roses. Rose White and Rose Red. Rose White because of my pale hair, which was almost the color of snow, just like his. And Rose Red for Rosabel's red curls, which were an even brighter red than Mama's.

"When do you go visit your mother next?" Mama asked Zilla.

This pulled Zilla from whatever she was imagining about me, and she bent to her own work again. "Next week. We'll go visit when Drony takes his turn as guard."

She thrust her needle into the shirt she was mending and looked up at Mama. "Could I borrow the carry sack you made this winter? The dark blue one with the Elva roses on it? I'd like to show it to my mother. She loves seeing your work."

"Of course," Mama replied. "And it could be useful to you and carry things as well."

"Oh, no! I could never use it. I'll fold it very carefully so it doesn't get hurt."

"Silvie, could you get the rose bag for Zilla?"

I put down the thread box and went over to the chest that Grampy had made of maple wood as a gift for Mama the year I was born. I lifted the lid while Zilla talked on.

"Thank you so much, Tara. You have such a gift with the needle. I can imitate you, but I can't seem to think of things like you do."

I knew Mama felt uncomfortable when Zilla talked like this. She hated compliments that came with slights to the giver. So I hurried with the rose bag. But then Zilla had to spread out the bag and finger the stitching.

"It's beautiful, Tara."

Before Zilla could say more, Mama said matter-of-factly, "You're welcome to it. Just tuck it in your work bag and—"

"Mama, do you hear that?" Rosie was staring down the street.

Mama listened a moment. "I don't hear anything. Why—"

"Everyone's coming out of their doors, chanting. Has the king returned?" Rosie pressed her face eagerly against the glass pane to see better.

Mama and Zilla stared at each other for a moment, in a way that made my heart pick up speed. I forgot all about the embroidery thread. Mama gathered up the folds of Papa's shirt, pinned the needle into the collar, and put the shirt into her work bag. Zilla was at the window before her. I came just behind and reached for Mama's arm.

"Do you hear that now?" Rosie asked. "What is it?"

"I don't *see* anything yet," said Zilla, softly. The blue door of the house opposite opened, and tall, thin Erinne stepped out into the street, her hand holding tight to her young son, her face white against the black of her hair.

I glanced at Mama and the fear on her face startled me. I saw her struggle to steady herself. Saw determination move in where fear had been.

"I must step outside now," she said. "You girls stay here." She kissed both of us quickly while I could do nothing but stare open-mouthed at her.

Zilla opened the door and squeezed Mama's shoulder. Mama grabbed her shawl, and they stepped out into the street. Rosie took my hand and held on tight as we stood in the doorway, feeling the chill of the early spring air.

"Can you hear it now?" I whispered to Rosie. "It's the Oath of the Guardsmen."

Rosie turned to me, wide-eyed. "Which means—"

She didn't finish her sentence. She didn't need to.

We both remembered what had been told among us as children. The people of Guardstown only come out to chant the oath when one of the Guardsmen has been killed.

TARA STOOD TALL, and spoke the words that she knew as thoroughly as Bevan did. She and Bevan had done this before, for other fallen Guardsmen. It had been long ago, when their girls were small, but this was the first time Tara had to step out of her house and chant the words alone.

I am valor for my Valor, the King.
I am strength for my Strength, the King.

All up and down the street, women and men emerged from their homes, stood in respect, and mouthed the chant.

I am truth for my Truth, the King.

Heads turned and eyes searched down the street to where the chanting was loudest.

From around the bend, a horseman came into view. Tara recognized Captain Mago from the palace. He sat tall in the saddle, bare-headed. One arm cradled his helmet, the other gripped the reins. His horse walked solemnly, purposefully.

Two more horsemen appeared, riding side by side, following the captain in slow, mournful procession.

I give my life for my Life, the King.

More horsemen came, but none were wearing the green-on-green of the King's Guardsmen. All wore the dark blue of the palace. And in the distance she could see a chestnut horse. Without a rider.

Tara could not keep the tears from wetting her eyes. She chanted even louder.

I am valor for my Valor, the King...

She recognized the horse. It belonged to Gunn. His wife stood outside a house not three doors down from where Tara stood. Gunn's wife stepped out into the street, looking hard. She covered her face with her hands. Tara's breath caught in her throat. *Oh, Bevan, just come around that corner riding your horse. We will face whatever happened together. Just come around that corner!*

Instead, another riderless horse came. A white horse with a silver-grey mane. Tara felt her stomach tighten. It drew nearer. Across the street, Erinne lifted her young son into her arms. Her mouth gaped open, but no sound came out.

A third riderless horse. Then a fourth. Neither was Bevan's dun. The chant faltered along the street. Sobs replaced words as horror grew.

I give my life for my Life, the King.

Tara made herself say the words firmly. Had all the Guardsmen fallen? Six of the elite guards surrounded the king at all times, and after them more soldiers also. *What could have happened?*

A fifth riderless horse came in procession. A shriek echoed in the stone street, followed by a long, moaning cry. Tara looked around for Zilla. She had her arm around a woman bent double with crying, but cast a worried look Tara's way.

Where was Bevan? Where was his horse? She thought of the news of the wild bears. None of the horses in front of her had been attacked. No claw marks slashed their flanks. Bears had not done this. But what had?

Captain Mago led the procession just past Tara's house to where the street widened then ended in a flat front of houses side by side. He turned his horse, circled back, and came to a halt, his soldiers assembling in formation behind him. All the soldiers and horses were clearly visible, but Tara could not see any sign of her husband. Five. Five horses. Where was the sixth?

She pulled her shawl tightly around her and crossed the cobbles to look up at Mago. "Captain? Where is Bevan? Where is his horse?"

Mago stared coldly down at her, his face hard like living armor, and something in his look made Tara step back.

"We do not honor the bodies or the horses of traitors," he said in a harsh voice.

Tara gasped, but Mago turned away. He raised his hand in the air, and signaled for silence.

"Hear me, people of Guardstown!" His voice buffeted the houses and echoed off the stone walls. "King Adare of Rilken has been killed, murdered on the forest road before he and his company could gain the safety of Elva's walls!"

The crowd moaned. *The king? The king is dead?* Words poured around her, while Tara stood stupefied.

"The bodies of your brave, fallen men are in Elva Castle," Mago called out, "being prepared for burial with all the honor due them."

His eyes found Tara's. Hatred burned inside them. He lifted his hand and pointed at her.

"Today I proclaim that Bevan the Guardsman is both traitor and murderer. The killer of his fellows *and his king*. He broke his oath to king and people, committing the worst crime possible under heaven. May his body rot forever!"

Tara could not keep herself from crying out. "*No!* That didn't happen! Bevan wouldn't *do* that! He *loved* his king. He loved his fellows." She glanced around, trying to meet the eyes of her neighbors. Erinne. Sally. Zilla. Erinne stared back, blindly.

"Bevan is not a traitor!" Tara pleaded. "You've lived near him for years. You *know* he would never do such a thing! He'd never break his vow!"

"Woman!" Mago bellowed in rage. He moved his horse closer to where she stood. The people of Guardstown melted back as he approached. "Do you say I *lie?*"

Tara should have seen the threat, should have taken warning, but all she could think of was Bevan. She glared at the captain.

"I am saying the words you use do not tell the truth."

Mago's fist moved swiftly. Tara staggered for a moment under the blow, then fell to the ground.

$$3$$

The Gray Cart

We stood in the doorway of our house—Rosie holding tightly to my arm—and saw the blow that felled our mother to the cobblestones. Heard her head hit the ground like a pumpkin.

We bolted from the door in an instant, darted between the bystanders, and—heedless of the palace guard—dropped to our knees on either side of her crumpled form. Rosie grabbed one of her hands and rubbed it, while I gently touched her shoulder. But Captain Mago hadn't finished. His words rained down like hailstones.

"You have a quarter hour to gather your things and leave Elva. The law keeps me from killing you now. But if I ever see you in Elva again, no law will stay my hand."

He raised his head and looked around at the people of Guardstown. "Hear me again, all of you! This Bevan *is* traitor to his king! By his own hand he broke his vow and murdered the one to whom he owed all. *Never* let his name be spoken again!"

The people of Guardstown nodded their heads in obedience. But I did not. Inside my head, I screamed my fury at him.

I will not obey you, Mago, because you are lying! My father knew he could no longer trust you.

You are the one who struck down an innocent woman!

Something my father would never do. And he would never strike down his king or his fellows!

THE PALACE GUARD moved back down the street, leaving misery in their wake. The leg of one horse brushed Rosie's back. We both hunched forward, protecting Mama, until they were past.

"Mama," I whispered in her ear. "Can you hear me? We've got to get you out of the street."

I looked around instinctively for someone who might come to our aid. Blank faces backed away, shooting furtive glances at the retreating figures of the palace guard. Some stood there, numb with their own burden of sorrow, statues of people we had once known.

Mama stirred.

"Can you sit up?" I asked urgently. "You have to sit up! Help me, Rosie."

We pulled her as gently as we could into a sitting position and held her securely there.

"Take deep breaths, Mama," Rosie said. "We have to make it to the door. At least get that far. That's all."

Mama took a breath. That was something. I looked across at Rosie. "All our strength. Ready?" Rosie nodded.

Together we lifted, staggering with the awkwardness of it, but with our arms firmly around and under Mama's. I kept my eyes on the ground right in front of me as we crossed the cobbles, hoping I wouldn't trip on the skirt that swirled around my ankles.

Mama tried to bear her own weight, but the injury was too new. She could barely hold herself upright. I was grateful for Rosie's strength. After many stumbling steps, we finally gained the door.

We guided Mama to the chair she had just been sewing in, and eased her down. I closed the door firmly, and slid the bolt across.

Mama leaned on the table, her head on her arms. Thick waves of dark red hair splayed across the tabletop. Rosie patted her shoulder, and looked up at me with scared eyes.

"What was Mago saying?" she asked, in a small voice so unlike her.

"It doesn't matter what he was saying. Mago is a liar. Papa didn't trust him." My voice shook, but what I said was true. The Guardsmen often worked with the palace guard, and lately Papa had been wary of Mago.

"Why is this happening, Silvie?" Rosie asked, almost in a whisper.

"I don't know, but we have less than a quarter hour

now, and we will have to gather what we need quickly." I went to the maple wood chest on the wall and raised the lid. "We'll need cloaks, walking shoes, the tinder box, money, clothes, food—"

"The sewing," said Mama, her voice muffled from the table.

I glanced at my sister. Hope rose in both of us at the sound of Mama's voice. "Yes, the sewing." I pulled it from the chest and fought to think clearly. "If we could fit everything we need in two carry bags each, wearing our cloaks and shoes, that could work."

I laid out the carry bags on the floor and gathered things as I spoke. "Rosie, get skirts and stockings for all of us. And walking boots. We'll wear those and put our other shoes in the bags."

She ran up the stairs while I opened the pantry cupboard. Cheeses, bread, dried fruits, walnuts. I stuffed them all hurriedly into a bag. I reached only for those things that didn't need cooking, for where would we find a hearth? And grains and dried beans were too heavy to carry.

"Take the dried meat," Mama's voice came heavy and slow. "Put candles in the tinder box."

Rosie clambered down the narrow stairs from the bedrooms above, her arms filled with clothing. "I grabbed all our favorites, mine and yours and Mama's. And sweaters and underclothes too."

"Fold them quickly and put them in the bags." I pointed to the line on the floor.

I darted up the stairs to our parents' room, found the leather pouch that contained paper and pen and ink, then eyed the small chest that contained our family savings. I turned the key in the lock and studied the coins. We would have to divide up the money. If thieves beset us and found it, we would lose all we had. And I knew we would be a target for thieves. I slid all the coins into a thick woolen sock of Papa's and hurried down the stairs.

"Put some of this in your sock, Rosie, and some in Mama's pouch, then—" I stopped, stunned. "Mama!" I cried. Tears filled my eyes.

Mama was sitting up and blinking slowly, her beautiful face grotesquely swollen. Blood streaked her face and matted her hair. The gashes on her forehead bled dark and slow. One eye struggled to open. Her puffy mouth formed indistinct words. "Bring me water and a rag, Silvie. Keep packing. Hand me the mirror, Rosie."

I continued to gather and fold, tuck and pack, but glanced constantly at Mama as she dipped the rag in the water bowl and dabbed at her face.

Rosie couldn't take her eyes away. She stood by the table watching Mama. "If Mago would have been wearing his mail glove, he would have killed you," she said.

Mama nodded slowly, her open eye staring into the small mirror. "Yes, he would have. But he didn't." She dabbed at her face again. "Get me the linen for a bandage, Rosie, then help your sister. I hear the wheels of a wagon."

I ducked under the table, pulled off Mama's day shoes, and slid the sturdier walking shoes on her feet. The day shoes went into her carry bag. I draped her cloak over her shoulders and thought frantically. *What have we forgotten?*

"Our caps," Rosie cried, running to the drawer. "And mittens!"

"Hairbrush and comb!" I called out. We gathered the last of the things together, buttoned the bags, and hauled them to the door.

"Help me with this," Mama said. We wound clean linen around her forehead and across her face. The linen hid some of the grotesqueness, but as we tied the bandage in place allowing her good eye to see out, blood spots already showed through.

"He didn't break my nose, at least," Mama said, wryly.

"A favor he didn't mean to grant," Rosie replied.

A loud thump at the door made me jump.

"Come out now!" a harsh voice called.

Mama stood slowly, holding onto the table. "Open the door, Silvie," she said quietly. "If you can take my bags for now, I will try to manage myself at least."

There wasn't time to say any kind of goodbye to our home. I allowed myself one more glance at Grampy's wood chest against the far wall, then opened the door.

A GRAY CART stood outside with a large, shaggy workhorse harnessed to it. It was the kind used to transport prisoners like murderers and thieves, and I instantly felt its humiliation. The driver opened the door of the cart, but made no move to assist us with our bags or help us climb in.

I made Rosie go in first so she could help Mama from the front, while I helped from behind. Then I handed our bags up to Rosie and climbed in last. One stiff, silent figure sat on horseback just beyond the cart. His eyes were covered in the half helmet Guardsmen often wore, but I could see the shape of his chin. Drony. Zilla's husband.

The cart lurched forward before I could settle myself, and I sat down hard on the wooden ledge that counted as a seat. I wrapped my arm around Mama's and held tight.

No sound came from the square or the street that led from it. But I knew we were being watched. Eyes peered from the windows. A few people stood and glared in the open air.

We had not gone far when a voice cried out. "Stop! Wait!" Anger was in the words.

Zilla strode from her house, her face flushed red. I shrank from the look in her eyes and hoped Mama wouldn't be able to see it.

"I won't have anything belonging to a traitor in my house!" Zilla threw something into the cart and Rosie clutched at it. Zilla turned away without looking at our faces, and I heard the slam of her door.

"It's the rose carry bag," Rosie whispered.

Mama's bandaged face showed no expression. She did not move at all. I reached for her hand and squeezed it.

Just beyond Zilla's house lay the borders of Guardstown. A group of city boys I did not know were watching from a street corner. But I caught sight of Ross standing in front of a house nearby, that tuft of brown hair that he could never comb down, sticking straight up. He, too, stared at us, and I slid lower in the cart. *Couldn't the horse move any faster?* I held Mama's arm tightly and took a deep breath.

That was when the first mud clod flew.

It struck Mama's knee, making her cry out in surprise. And, of course, Rosie picked it up and threw it right back into the group of boys. Rosie, who struggled to keep her stitches even, could throw a rock at any target and never miss. She didn't miss now. A yelp went up from the center of the crowd, and Rosie ducked as more mud flew in response.

The silent Guardsman came to life. He banged his shield with his mailed hand. "Away now! Or I'll lock you all up!"

The crowd hurried away. No one ever argues with a Guardsman. I dug a clod of sticky mud from my hair and dropped it over the side of the cart.

"I got the tall one right in the forehead," Rosie said grimly. "He didn't expect that—the brute!" She brushed the dirt off the front of her skirt. "At least Zilla returned your favorite bag, Mama," she said in a consoling tone. "Oh. Wait—"

Rosie unbuttoned the bag and stared into it. She leaned closer to us and spoke in the low voice of a secret longing to be shared.

"Zilla put food in the bag."

4

—————

Decision at the City Gate

The cart finally stopped just outside the city gate of Elva. The driver got off his horse and jerked open the cart door. "Hurry up, now. Get out."

Tara's face throbbed, her head ached, and she could barely see. After the long cart ride, her legs and back felt completely bruised. But in response to the driver's words, her daughters gripped her arms and guided her out of the cart.

Rosie passed the bags down to Silvie while Tara stood by. People jostled her as they pushed through the busy gate, muttering in their annoyance. She took a deep breath and fought the urge to panic. Instead, she concentrated on Rosie and Silvie.

They were her courage. They always had been. Daughters to work for, plan for, and defend. She had become a different person when they were born. A better person. Just the sight of them now gave her strength and purpose. They needed to get to someplace safe. Somewhere they could rest and heal and think.

As soon as the last bag had been passed, Rosie jumped down. The cart pulled away, disappearing into the throngs of people. But the Guardsman lingered.

Tara shifted the bandage on her face so she could catch a glimpse of him. "Thank you, Drony. Please— please, tell Zilla goodbye."

She thought he gave a quick nod, but she couldn't be sure. Then he too turned his horse and joined the flow of movement pushing into Elva.

Tara took a deep breath. She felt incredibly dizzy. "Girls, let's get away from the gate. Silvie, you go first. Let me rest my hand on your shoulder."

"We've got the bags, Mama. Don't worry about them." Silvie moved ahead slowly, laden like a pack horse, while Tara gripped her shoulder. Rosie, carrying all her bags, followed behind.

"What a lot of people there are," Rosie exclaimed. "I've never seen so many people!"

"Yes, you have, Rosie," Silvie replied. "On festival days."

"Well, maybe."

They struggled through, pushing forward and down the road, until the crush of people eased somewhat.

"Get to the side of the road when you can, Silvie,"

Tara said, close to her ear. "We'll need to talk about what to do next."

Silvie led them over to a place away from the stone road, and Tara gladly sank down into the soft grass. The girls sat next to her, careful to keep their bags between them, so no traveler could easily snatch them.

Both girls were looking closely at her with sober expressions and she wondered what they saw. The glimpse of her own face in the small mirror had frightened her enough. She pushed the image from her mind.

"We're outside Elva's west gate." Rosie sounded worried. "But Grampy and Gramma live far to the east. If we're not allowed to be in the city, we'll have to walk *miles* around it. They could have at least asked us which gate to stop at."

Silvie pulled a piece of grass through her fingers. "I don't think they cared much. The cart took us to the closest gate and that was all. I'm glad it did. I wouldn't want to be paraded around Elva in that thing."

"But Grampy—" began Rosie.

"It doesn't matter, Rosie," said Tara. "I don't think we'll be going to Grampy's."

Rosie stared. "Not go there?"

"We can't." Tara searched her mind to find the right words, but her mind seemed strangely slow to provide them. "If we go to them, as we are, looking—looking—like we do, and tell them the reason, we would be bringing this lie—this horrible lie about their son to them. I cannot do that."

"It would kill them," Silvie added.

"Yes, it would."

"That means we can't go to your sisters either," said Rosie, "because they live so close that of course Grampy and Gramma would find out."

"I want to be around someone who loved Papa like we do," Silvie said quietly. "Not someone who was jealous of him. And who might use that jealousy to take Mago's side. That would kill *us*."

Tara turned toward her eldest. "I have never talked about this with you," she said, quietly.

"You didn't need to," Silvie replied. "It was on your sisters' faces."

"We could see it everywhere," said Rosie.

"When did you girls gain such understanding?"

Rosie plucked at the grass with her fingers. "Silvie's always had it. I'm just catching up."

"But it explains why we will not walk around the city tonight," Silvie said.

"Or tomorrow," said Rosie.

All three of them looked down the road toward the lowering sun.

"I've never been west of Elva," Silvie said. "What's it like?"

"Mostly woods and forests," Tara replied. "Filled with hunters and woodsmen. I haven't been there very much either. The king's domain extends miles into the western forests, and his hunters search through the trees every day to bring in game for the royal table. The northwest road and this one, the west road, cut completely through the forested lands to the borders of Rilken."

"Then Tellhaven must be at the end of this road,"

said Silvie.

Rosie let out a little gasp. "Is this the road Papa was traveling on?" She peered down the road again, and it was impossible not to feel waves of sudden hope coming from her. The nonsensical hope that if she looked hard enough she would somehow see her father riding down the road toward them.

Tara answered quickly. "No. He took the northwest road out of Elva. The one that leads to the heart of Tell-haven and to its capital city. This one leads to the southern end of Tellhaven, and Ardemount."

"Oh," Rosie said, in a small voice.

"But this road has a good deal of travelers and inns and maybe towns and villages. And we might find...we might find..." Tara found it hard to keep talking. "Some-place," she said at last.

Silvie pointed down the road. "The sun is lowering."

"Yes," said Tara. "We must get walking."

They got to their feet and gathered their things. Tara carried the rose bag in one hand and rested her other hand on Silvie's shoulder as before. Every step was hard and brought on dizziness. All she wanted to do was lie down and sleep. She tried to fight through it, concen-trating on each step, but it was hard work, and she felt she would collapse at any moment. *One more step. One more step. One more step.*

The chant in her head urged her feet forward, until an ominous sound made them all stop in their tracks.

A huge bell rang out from the citadel of Elva behind them. A deep-throated bell, its voice full of majesty, of beauty. Of sorrow. Its sound poured out in waves through the sky, reverberating down the broad road. Throbbing with the pain in Tara's head.

They turned to look back at the walled city, at the red roofs that covered the towers and halls of Elva Castle. At the flags that flew from its pinnacles.

Other travelers stopped too. Horses were reined in. Wagons halted. Passengers twisted around in their seats to stare. She could imagine what every one of them was wondering. *What does this mean?*

"What flags do you see, Silvie?" Tara asked. "Which are still flying?"

"The Duke's flag is there, and those for the two princes, and..."

"And what? What do you see?"

Silvie's voice wavered. "They are lowering the King's flag. They are lowering the green-on-green."

Tara could see it in her mind's eye. The flag of rich field green—the color of the vast pasture and crop lands of east Rilken—crossed with the darker green which represented the west lands of trees and forests. The two halves of Rilken united in the flag. Under one king. His colors. And the colors of his Guardsmen.

A woman seated on a wagon aimed toward Elva suddenly shrieked. "The king is *dead?* King Adare is dead!!" A sob of despair. *"Sender, help us!"*

Horses slowed, wheels creaked, until nothing moved on the road. Travelers, one and all, seemed stricken. Their silence broken only by cries of alarm as understanding came to them. The mourning bell tolled on and on. Relentless in the news it had to tell.

"The flag is gone, Mama," Silvie whispered in her ear. "There is no green-on-green above the castle now."

"Go, Silvie," Tara whispered back. "We must keep moving. I won't be able to stand much longer."

The pealing of the bell followed them down the road. The sorrow of Elva—of all Rilken—dogged their steps. When they had finally come to a place where the traffic was thin, Rosie moved closer and spoke in a low voice filled with pain.

"He didn't do it."

Rosie must be thinking of Mago's proclamation. His horrible lie. Tara shook her head firmly, then winced at a fresh throb of pain. "No, Rosie. We know your father's heart. He did not—and *never* could—lift his hand against his king."

"Never!" said Silvie.

Tara had spoken low and urgently, not wanting to be heard by anyone else. But what needed to be said, had been said openly between them. The confession stirred their strength. They gathered their determination and went slowly on their way.

5

One Thousand Burning Candles

Prince Ravelin stood alone in the center of the large, round room and stared at the unearthly sight. His father, draped in robes of white brocade, lay on a bier before him. A gold circlet crowned his father's dark hair. The sword of ceremony —polished so bright—rested on the bier at his side. As if at any moment the king could reach out, grab it, and leap to life again.

But the king, his father, did not move.

One thousand burning candles circled the room, lining the white marble walls in tiered rows. King and son, alone together in the middle of them. Ravelin could not bear to look at the dull, lifeless face. So, he stared at the brilliant sword as it reflected the candle fire.

In the eerie stillness, Ravelin spoke low.

I wanted to go with you on your travels.

But you were afraid that I had not completely healed from the sickness that plagued me this winter, that it might return. So you said, "not this time."

To cheer me, you said this was only a trip for armor fitting. You promised I could come, instead, to see you set off to join the King of Tellhaven and the Duke of Nordia. That I could see your honor as you rode with the Hosts of the North, rode with them into legend. Into every man's dream. To return with triumphant glory.

Now you will not have that great honor.

I grieve for you, my father.

That you who gave me life found death on that road instead.

If you had given way to my begging, would I be lying on a bier next to you now? I almost wish I were.

Because I thought you would always live.

THE FLICKERING of the candles and the glare of the sword hurt his eyes. He bowed his head and covered his eyes with his hand. But he could not leave his father's side.

He felt he would remain, all his life long, standing in this hushed room, bowing before his father's sword, while the surrounding candles whispered a thousand requiems.

A rap sounded on the door, echoing in the hard stillness. His uncle, the Duke of Elva, entered. Ravelin raised his head then quickly looked down again.

Studied his father's swollen hand where it lay next to the sword. He wished his uncle away, but the man walked to the other side of the bier so Ravelin could not help but see him. See his father's brother, born just a year behind him, but so unlike in every way.

"What happened to the Guardsman who did this?" Ravelin asked.

The Duke cleared his throat. "My men shot him, your highness. He has paid for his crime."

"Not enough."

The Duke bowed.

"And what of my brother? What news of Dallen? Has he returned yet?"

His uncle sighed. "My dear nephew, I tried to explain to you in the gentlest way I knew that your brother must have been killed by the same madman that took your father's life. If not by him, then by the bears that set upon us immediately after."

Ravelin stared across at the Duke. "And which do you believe it was? The bears or the madman?"

The Duke looked uncertain. As Ravelin watched his face, waiting for him to continue, he thought how very much his uncle's features resembled a bird of prey. The candlelight accentuated the curve of his nose and the darkness of his eyes.

"I believe it was the madman," the Duke said. "I saw him pull Dallen from his horse just before the bears attacked us." He met Ravelin's gaze and his eyes seemed to soften. "I would spare you these details—"

"How many bearskins did you bring back?"

"What—"

"How many bearskins did you take in payment for their treachery? How many did your men kill?"

The Duke's dark eyes narrowed. He blinked several times, frowning. When he spoke, it was with a patronizing tone, a tone meant to placate a child much, much younger than Ravelin.

"My dear boy, you do not understand, but then you could not. You have had no experience with these bears. The Guardsmen have been on watch for them this past year. If these were ordinary bears, their pelts would be lining the Great Hall at this moment. But no arrow, sword, or spear of man can kill these beasts. I do not think they can be natural to this world."

Ravelin could not keep the questions from spilling out. "Do you think the Sender sent them? Would he send such as these to us?"

"Oh, no. Surely not. We know that the Sender sends all things *good*." The Duke was soothing a child again. His words held a hint of mockery. "So they *assuredly* are not from him."

"Where are they from then? Are they some of the monsters that the Hosts of the North defend us from?"

"My dear Ravelin, if I knew, I would tell you. But until we can find out who or what they really are, it is useless to guess."

"So this great evil, this evil that felled my father, has not been answered by anything that was noble or true? My father is killed like a dog in the road and all that is good or right in heaven remains silent?" He felt almost wild as he asked the questions.

"What could it do now anyway?" The Duke replied.

He walked around the bier and reached out an arm to Ravelin, resting a hand on his shoulder. "This has been the worst of days, Your Highness," he said gently. "My only consolation is that your dear mother didn't live to see this awful day."

Ravelin did not answer.

The Duke kept talking. "Go to your room now and rest. Find what comfort you can. The days ahead will be hard for all of us. Go now. Rest."

His uncle's presence was the only thing that could force him from his father's side. Ravelin left the marble room. He walked down the castle corridors and climbed the stairs toward his chambers, not looking for anyone and not seeing anyone. Only once did he pause. In the hallway outside his brother's door. He gazed for several moments at the dark, silent wood, until he could endure no more.

He reached for the handle and pushed the door open. A man was standing in the middle of the floor, boxes and bags piled around him. Ravelin's heart leapt, irrationally. The man raised his head and looked at him, mourning in his eyes. Ravelin's hope sank again. It was Olif, Dallen's personal attendant.

"What did you see, Olif? What can you tell me about the forest?"

"I can tell you nothing." Olif's deep voice rumbled slowly. "Nothing, Your Highness. I was not with them. The king's party left the inn very early in great haste. It was some four hours before the rest of the company could be ready to follow."

"Was there no sign of anything on the road?"

Olif nodded. "Where the road runs across Vallenro's land, we found a scattering of weapons. Some spears. A few swords. Damaged shields. I recognized none of them as Prince Dallen's."

"What did you do with them?"

"The armor boys gathered them and we made all speed for Elva. In the stables I found the prince's horse in his stall."

"But no sign of Dallen?"

"No, sir."

Ravelin could think of nothing more to say. He stood there, dumbly, and silence fell between them. At last, he nodded his thanks to Olif, and left.

He entered his own room and strode directly to the window, pushing the heavy drapes aside.

His servant approached quietly. "Your Highness," he said gently, "may I get—"

"Leave me, Wells. I would be alone."

"Certainly, sir. But I will be near when you call."

The door closed without a sound and Ravelin sighed. He looked out the window, into the fading light. Elva Castle sat on the highest ground in the city. From his chamber window, situated as it was on a hall two flights of stairs above the main reception hall, Ravelin could see evidence of the northwest road. The gash it made as it first cut through the forests, before it blurred into the distance.

Dallen, where are you? You can't leave me like this!

He stared at the dark line that curved through the trees until he gave it up and pressed his hands against his eyes.

6

By a Stream

Tara, Silvie, and Rosabel trudged down the west road into the last light of day. Behind them the darkness grew quickly, filling the gaps in the forest on either side of the road, and finally darkening the road itself.

They rested often for Tara's sake, so their progress was slow. She carried the rose bag, while the girls carried three apiece, and she kept one hand on Silvie's shoulder. But they would have to stop somewhere very soon.

Tara hoped for an inn. It would be worth spending a few of their coins for one night's rest in a bed and the chance for a meal and a washing. She wanted to clean all the dried blood out of her hair.

And a good night's sleep would give them the space they needed to think. Because beyond this, she didn't know what they should do. Where they should go.

A lie had banished them from Elva, cut them off from friends and family, and sent them on this journey into darkness. And Bevan? If she even began to think about what might have happened to him, she would collapse right when her girls needed her the most.

Silvie slowed her step. "Mama, can you see all the lights ahead? Up there on the left? Is that an inn? What else could be so bright with torchlight and so close to the road?"

Tara's eye teared as she looked and the light ahead blurred. Nothing was clear. "It must be," she said quietly.

"I hope so!" Rosie sighed. "I'm so tired I'm ready to drop."

They moved forward again, the possibility of relief giving purpose to their steps, until, at last, they reached the inn.

Long stretches of blurry light meant the inn was large, a long building with at least two floors. Tara could smell cooking—roast meat and warm bread. Sounds of activity with horses and carriages seemed to come from everywhere.

Silvie stopped abruptly and Tara ran into her.

"Mama, Rosie...we can't stay here."

"Why not?" said Rosie, with the sharpness that weariness brings.

"The palace guard is here. See the colors on the

horses under that stable light? They must have just arrived."

"Captain Mago?" Rosie asked in a hushed voice.

Tara shuddered, but her understanding of palace movements calmed her at the same time. "I don't see how it could be," she said, "unless he left Elva before we did. And with the king's death, I think—I think the Duke would keep Mago by his side."

They stood and looked at the stables. "There are a hundred men in the palace guard," Tara said. "Silvie's right. With the palace guard about, we cannot stay here. We're bound to recognize some of them, and they us."

Heartsick, and ready to weep from weariness, nevertheless, they moved to the other side of the road and plodded on. After a long time in silence, Tara said, "Here, Silvie. We'll have to turn into the trees and find what shelter we can. We can't go on any more tonight."

"I'm so tired I could sleep on a stump," said Rosie.

"Well, that's good," Silvie replied. "We're likely to find just that kind of bed."

Tara remembered one of the things Bevan had told her from his travels. "This forest to the right is still in the king's domain. So, rough though the underbrush may be, it will have been tended some for the sake of the hunters. It won't be like a completely wild forest."

"What if we go in here?" Silvie asked. "Between these two trees? Rosie, come up here with me and help me find a way."

Rosie moved next to Silvie. Tara looped the strap of her carry bag over one arm and put one hand on Rosie's shoulder and the other on Silvie's. The girls held their hands out in front of them, and cautiously stepped into the forest darkness.

"How far off the road should we go, Mama?" Silvie asked.

"Far enough so no one can see us," Tara replied.

They moved cautiously through the opening in the trees that Silvie had selected, testing the ground with their feet before putting their weight on it. And at the same time straining to see in the dark, straining to hear every sound. It was hard going. In the gloom, unseen branches and twigs caught at their skirts and poked at their faces. They inched forward in this manner for some time until Silvie said, "Wait."

"What is it?" Tara asked.

"Do you hear that? Running water. There must be a creek nearby."

They moved forward slowly, craving every bit of light from the half moon that made its way through the leafless trees, craving the light like crumbs from a far-off feast.

"There's a break in the trees here, and the land seems to slope down," said Rosie.

A few more steps and Silvie said, "We've found the stream, and it's bigger than I thought. See how it reflects the moonlight in places?" She took Tara's arm. "There's a big tree right here at the top of the bank. What if we lean against it for the night? I don't think we can find a better place in the dark."

Rosie felt the ground at the base of the tree. "It's dry here." The girls lowered their burdens.

"Our clothes bags will cushion the ground at least," Tara said, "and make it easier to sleep."

They nestled themselves under the tree. Tara leaned against a soft bag, pulled her cloak around her, and closed her eyes, feeling the pounding of her head. A rummaging sound came to her ears.

"What is it, Rosie?" Silvie asked.

"I'm trying to see what Zilla put in the bag. Oh! Bless her! It smells like her raisin cake."

"And that's a block of cheese," Silvie joined in.

"Dried pepper meat."

"Bread loaves."

"A water flask."

Tara held out her hands in the dark. Her daughters found them and set cake and cheese and meat in them. The food tasted *so* good. Zilla was an excellent cook, and this sign of friendship made tears prick Tara's eyes.

Zilla and Drony. They had to act their obedience to the Duke's captain, as everyone would have had to, no matter what they believed. She could not find out now what they truly thought.

After the meal, they leaned against the tree, their bags, and each other, settling into a half-sitting position to sleep. Tara took a deep breath and made herself listen to the forest. It was so different from the broad open fields and pastures where she grew up. What might this strange woodland be saying in the night? Would there be anything comforting, anything familiar?

An owl called, a throaty, rhythmic cry. Far away another owl seemed to answer. Light rustling came from the branches high above them. Some animal? Or a wind?

"I know what I forgot to pack," Silvie whispered, leaning against Tara's right shoulder. "Soap." She let out a sigh of regret.

"It's all right. We'll find some somewhere," Tara whispered back.

Rosie lay against a plump bag, facing the stream's small reflection. The night was getting colder.

Tara shivered, closed her eyes and took another deep, slow breath. Now that she wasn't struggling to walk anymore, the pain of Guardstown filled her head.

Mago's accusation. Something unusual had been in his eye when he spoke it. But before she could work it out, his blow and the fall to the cobblestones had confused everything in her head. *Truth.* Part of the Guardsman Oath. *I am truth for my Truth, the King.*

Bevan first said that oath years ago, kneeling before King Adare's throne in the Audience Hall. She could still hear the firmness in Bevan's voice as he carefully spoke each word. *Where was truth now?* What had truly happened to Bevan? To the king?

Fear suddenly threatened to choke her. But Silvie held onto one of her arms, and on the other side of her lay brave Rosabel, ready to defend them all with one mud clod.

The girls should be sleeping in their warm feather bed with pillows. Behind sturdy walls and barred doors. With friendly neighbors on either side of them. That was all they had ever known. Until now.

She turned her mind to think of something safe.

Sewing.

She forced her mind's eye to imagine a needle piercing a linen cloth, dragging a rich, red thread behind it. When the thread was taut, up the needle came, like a diver returning to the land of air and life. She pictured moving the point of the needle, selecting a place, and pushing it down through the cloth again.

"Mama," Rosie said softly. "This river makes me think of the Mourner. I feel so sad that I think the River Mourner must be flowing nearby."

Tara reached out her hand and touched Rosie's hair.

Silvie sat up and leaned closer to both of them. "I'm glad only the Sender can see the Mourner. I don't think any human being could endure it. Surely not I."

Rosie sat up and reached for Tara's hand in the dark as thoughts of the Mourner seemed to fill all of them. The invisible river that coursed its way through all the lands of AllHallen, carrying the blood that spilled anywhere on earth to its honor in the Sender's Hall.

"Your Papa said that the Mourner gave him courage. He knew that if he fell in battle, or while guarding the king, the Mourner would carry his blood to the Sender." Tara remembered the look on Bevan's face, his earnestness when he spoke of it.

The girls fell silent, but Tara could feel their unasked questions. *What truly happened on that forest road? Is Papa really dead? Was his body left to the wild animals? What are we going to do?* Tomorrow they would talk about these things. If they could brave them.

Tara picked up her imaginary stitching again when Rosie's grip tightened on her hand. She knew what

Rosie was going to say. Rosie would ask if Papa's blood was passing by them in the Mourner right now, and Tara did not want to answer.

But Rosie did not ask that question. "There's a bear across the stream," she said, in a low voice. "Silvie, look. I think it's watching us."

7

As Smoke into the Darkness

I craned my neck to look past Mama and over the top of Rosie's head. Moonlight caught part of a huge dark shape. The front half of it was standing in the stream. A large head turned toward us. The eyes blazed a fierce yellow light.

I stifled a gasp.

The monstrous creature moved.

I heard the plash of a foot stepping into the stream, heard the low growl. *Had our end come?*

We couldn't run in the dark. We could barely see. We had no weapons and Mama was so injured already. The bear surely smelled the food in our bags.

The sound of another plash.

The bear was crossing the stream.

Calm strength, Silvie. At the first encounter with an enemy, a Guardsman always communicates the greatness of his strength in a calm manner.

The words sounded so clearly in my mind. As if Papa were speaking them now instead of last summer in the garden.

Calm strength.

I stood up and cautiously stepped over to Rosie. "Stand up next to me," I said softly. "If we raise our arms and move them slowly together, it might think that we are a bigger animal than we are."

Together we faced the bear and the stream, moving our arms slowly, hoping that with our cloaks we looked like a large animal in the dark. The bear stopped and stood up on his hind feet in the shallow water on his side of the river.

"Please, bear," Rosie whispered, while she moved her arms. "Please think we are not worth your interest."

The bear dropped to all fours, making a bigger splash. He lowered his head and moved steadily toward us. I thought I heard the rumble of a growl. This was not a bear from the Rilken stories. This was a huge animal looking for food.

"Mama, he's coming!" I cried.

Behind us, Mama called out. "Sender, defend us, or we are lost!" Her voice broke. "We have no one, Sender. *Please help us!*"

Mama's cry disappeared as smoke into the darkness. The bear paused in Silve stream for just a moment reconsidering.

I wished for safety. For protecting stone walls. For

Papa's quick spear. For a friend to come at our call. But, it was as Mama said. We had no one.

The bear began to move toward us again, with purpose. Rosie bent and grabbed large stones from the riverbank. She thrust several into my hands, and they felt smooth and wet. "Get behind that other tree. Then aim for its nose and head. It might not want to take on two enemies."

I did as she said. Rosie let a stone fly and the bear yelped. Even in the shadows Rosie could find her mark. She threw and I threw. The best I could do was confuse the bear. Rosie's perfect aim made the bear retreat to the shallows back on his side of the water.

"Well done, Rosie!" I called softly.

"But he's still there. He's not leaving."

The yellow eyes surveyed us. I stepped out from behind my tree and gathered more stones, not daring to do more than glance away from those eyes. I took my position again.

And there we stood for long terrible moments. Me behind my tree. Rosie in front of Mama by the original tree. The bear in the open river with baleful eyes. The bear opened its mouth and let out an angry roar.

Oh, Sender, I whispered, but I never finished my prayer.

"Look in the sky!" Rosie called.

It was an odd thing to say at such a time. But I glanced up. Flying up the riverbed toward us, was an immense bird. Its belly glowed like burning embers. A fire in the night. As it flew, it came lower and lower until the river's reflection made it look like there were flames in the water.

With a loud, hasty splash, the bear disappeared into the trees on the far side of the river. I put the stones in my pocket and scrambled over to Rosie and Mama.

The bird landed on a tree next to our small camp. It folded its dark gray wings and perched on a branch looking down, shining like a torch on a city wall.

"Oh my," Rosie said with a breath.

"What is this?" I whispered. "It feels like something I've read once. An old story from an old, old book." I sank down at the base of our tree and stared up at it.

"I'm not sure," Mama said in a hushed voice. She lowered herself to sit beside me. "I've heard that the country of Falland sees great birds. Messengers..." Her voice trailed off.

I felt unbelievably drowsy. As if the presence of the great bird brought a stubborn and immovable rest. Rosie leaned against the pile of soft bags she had made. Mama leaned against Rosie, and I curled up at Mama's side.

The night birds stilled. The breeze hushed. Only the water continued to run gently over the stones. And the last thing I saw before my eyes closed in heavy slumber, was that the bird was still there.

8

———

Pate the Useful

Night descended. Prince Ravelin sat at his desk in his chambers. Wells, his servant, had lit every candle in the room and clustered a number on the desk to illuminate Ravelin's work. But it was work Ravelin did not want to do. Though Lord Kendall, his tutor, insisted it be done now.

Ravelin laid down his pen and stared at the paper he had marred in his attempts at writing. "My ink is cold, Kendall," he said to the robed man who sat in a chair nearby. "It is freezing the page. The words will not warm to me."

Kendall squinted at the paper and frowned at the marked out passages. "You *must* stay after it, Your Highness. Make the pen obey you." He reached for Ravelin's pen and wiped the glass tip carefully, almost lovingly, then laid it across the paper and moved the inkwell an inch closer to Ravelin.

Ravelin refused the hint. "The fault is not in the pen. It agrees with me perfectly. I do not want to write *this*. I cannot say what my uncle wants me to say."

"It is not your uncle's wish alone," Kendall replied. "This is what every heir to a throne must do on the death of the previous king. The country must hear from its new ruler right away. Must know every moment that it is firmly governed. Otherwise there will be fear, terror, upheaval, even insurrections!"

Kendall's face was etched with the horror those words carried. "Unless you speak right away and forcefully, the rule of Rilken will slip from your family's grasp. The nobles will fight for Rilken, tear it apart. Many a war has come from the slowness of a king."

Ravelin looked away. "I am *not* the king of Rilken. Dallen is."

Kendall leaned back in the chair and gazed at him with sorrowful eyes. "The palace guard is searching for your brother's body even now. Night will not stop them. The forest will be filled with torches and lanterns. They will not cease until your brother's body lies safely in the round room next to your father."

Ravelin shrank inwardly. He did not want to see his brother lying next to his father in that room. Not ever.

"They are searching even now, you say?" He got up and went to the window. Wells quickly pulled the heavy curtain aside for him. "They should be. Because from what my uncle said, no one saw my brother die."

Ravelin stepped to the glass and peered into the night. "How strange. I see nothing from here. No lanterns or torches. No flashes of light. Nothing at all shines in the forest."

Kendall came to the window and stood next to him. "It's at least fifteen miles away that your father fell. You could not possibly see that far. And the road turns. You know it does."

Kendall used the same tone that his uncle had. The tone that said—more than words could—that Ravelin was acting like a child. Asking childish questions. Insisting that hope could be true when grown men knew it was false. Yet Ravelin could not help saying what was foremost in his mind.

"I will help the searchers. I can go to the forest and look too. In fact, I must. Staying here and waiting will drain the life from me."

Kendall gasped and put his hand on Ravelin's arm. "But—but, that is what you must *not* do, my prince! The forest is too dangerous. You are the only member of your family left. You *must* stay here in Elva Castle. Besides," his voice dropped, "you cannot possibly want to join the searchers. Such a gruesome task. They are not likely to find your brother's body whole, you know. More like a foot, or a hand, something the bears left behind—"

Wells cleared his throat forcefully and stepped toward the window, drawing the curtains across it again. He turned toward Ravelin.

"Are you thirsty, sir? Would you like some refreshment?"

The attendant's voice was kind, but determined. Wells had a look in his eye that quelled Kendall's flow of speech. The tutor turned away with a frown, sat down by the desk again, and made a show of arranging papers and wiping pens.

Ravelin did not join him. Could not. His body was rigid. Muscles stiff. His blood frozen like the ink in his pen. He was in the forest with the searchers, seeing what they were seeing, and his heart threatened to fail him. He tried with effort to push the images Kendall had called up out of his mind, images of Dallen's body in pieces scattered in the underbrush. Wells gently cleared his throat again, calling Ravelin back to himself.

"I—I do not know, Wells." Ravelin felt in a daze. He glanced back at the closed curtain.

"Then sit by the fire, sir. Let me stir it for you. Writing is hard work," Wells added. He ushered Ravelin to the comfortable armchair by the fire.

"The prince has *not* been writing," Kendall said, in an aggrieved voice.

"Not writing is hard work too," said Wells. He poked a log into place with a flurry of sparks.

"You are interfering, Wells," said Kendall. "The prince has work to do and he must do it tonight. Royalty cannot waste precious time on grief."

A loud knock sounded at the door and Kendall swore. But Ravelin was grateful for the interruption. "See who it is, Wells."

Wells opened the door, then stepped aside with a smile. A young blond-haired man, short of stature, held a large tray filled with covered dishes. At the sight of him, Ravelin felt a surge of relief. He waved him in, but Kendall groaned and rolled his eyes.

"Well, if it isn't Pate the Useful," Kendall said with a sarcastic tone.

"Actually, it is," said Pate. "And I *am* being useful." He set the tray on a table at Ravelin's side.

"Here is a mountain of food made for our good prince by the hands of the castle cook himself. He would let no other cook or assistant put their hands in it. And, I must say..." Pate cast a serious glance at Ravelin and he spoke quietly, "he had a hard enough time keeping his tears out of it."

Pate lifted the covers off the dishes and his voice became animated again. "Cook says you requested your beef done just this way for your seventh birthday. And this was your favorite bread when you were ten. The stewed fruit with cinnamon is a regular choice of yours, so he tells me, and this cake is exactly like the one he made for your sixteenth birthday. The whole kitchen was drooling at the aroma it gave off when it was baking. The chocolate sauce alone..." Pate looked upward in gratitude.

"Pate!" Kendall rose from his chair and looked sternly at him. "The prince has an important task to do, and you are IN-TER-RUP-TING."

"What task?" Pate asked lightly, looking at Ravelin.

"I have to write a speech for tomorrow morning," Ravelin answered. "For all the court and the castle."

Pate put on an expression of mock gravity. "I *know* the kind of speech you must write. *Very* daunting. The kind that will be copied most assiduously by the best of scribes as every word falls from your mouth. It will then be sent by swift riders to the four winds. One north, one south, one west, one east...

> *Where the sun will rise,*
> *and the ships will set*
> *far across the Kartan Sea,*
> *Where Molly Drake*
> *that girl by the lake*
> *will smile her best at me—"*

"Pate!"

"You called, Master Kendall?"

"Enough of this prattle!"

"Yes, sir! At once, sir! 'Prattle? Enough! You are trying the patience of our Master Tutor.'"

Kendall rolled his eyes. "You may go now, Pate."

"Nonsense," said Pate, drawing up a stool for himself and sitting down on it. "I am under strict orders to watch the prince eat and to bring reports of every mouthful to the kitchen."

"The Duke has ordered this be done tonight," Kendall replied.

Pate immediately took on the demeanor of a kind father. "And it will be, Lord Kendall. We shall see that it is done. As for the Duke, I believe that at this moment he is up to his cheekbones in spice pudding. So we must not deny our prince sustenance, must we?"

Kendall shook his head and glowered. "If you were not such a privileged young pup..." The tutor left the rest of his sentence unsaid.

Ravelin was glad to see that Kendall's look had no effect on Pate's cheerful countenance. The young man swiveled on his stool. "But I work hard for my privilege, as do you, Master Tutor."

Kendall opened his mouth to say something, but Pate rushed on. "However, I know that the kitchen is open late tonight for anyone who could use the kind of comfort that good food brings.

"The cooks are working through their sorrow by cooking. The rest of the court by eating. I have no doubt you will find your favorites among the offerings. Was it the wine pie? You will have good company. Lord Locke, Tibbett, and the chamberlain were in the dining room when I went by just now."

Kendall looked thoughtful at this. "Well. Perhaps—my prince—if I return in an hour?"

Ravelin nodded. "An hour or two would be fine."

"Very well, then." Kendall bowed and went out.

As the door closed, all mockery disappeared from Pate's face. He looked with concern at Ravelin.

"I would ask how you are, but I think I can see."

Ravelin nodded slowly and stared at the fire.

Pate sighed. "Kendall has been spreading fear and gloom throughout the castle. And when I heard he was with you, I came as soon as I could. Unfortunately, Cook was just beginning to ice the cake. Was Master Kendall working his dark magic here also? I can see by the look on Wells' face that he was."

Pate clasped his hands around one knee and leaned back, balancing carefully on his stool. "Master Kendall is the most knowledgeable and yet most thoroughly unwise person I know. He has learned his subjects well, but they haven't learned him. He can craft a speech in perfect form, but at the same time have no understanding of what people need to hear."

"Yes," said Ravelin, roused by this thought. "Or what my own heart and mind need to say also."

"I was sure it was something like that," said Pate. "Do you know what you need to say, or has our intimidating Kendall driven it all away?"

"I think I know." Ravelin rubbed his hands together. They felt icy like the pen. He held them out towards the fire. "My father always seemed to know."

"Then," said Pate. "I propose that after taking some of this fabulous beef dish—for I think Cook has outdone himself—and having in your own stomach the aid and good wishes of your people, after that, what if you sit down at your desk and write out exactly what you need to say? What you want to tell Cook. And me. And Wells here. And especially, what you want to tell Dallen, wherever he is."

Ravelin's heart leapt at this idea, but he shook his head. "Kendall and my uncle would never let me say what I wish. They are looking for a very formal, very clear, assumption of power. I am king in name. My uncle the regent for the next two years. But I cannot say those words. For the life of me, I cannot do that." His eyes filled and he turned towards the fire.

"You have a very long night ahead of you then," said Pate.

Ravelin sighed. "Yes, and at the end of it, my uncle will win."

Would he continue to win every day of Ravelin's life? How differently his father would deal with this! How he always invited discussion, made room for thought. While the Duke chafed at the need to just get things done. Yet, somehow, Ravelin could not think of anything important his father had left undone.

"There is a way..." Pate had a mischievous look on his face. He dropped his foot to the floor, turned on his stool, and faced Ravelin squarely.

"What if you write your speech now—saying just what *you* want to say—before Kendall comes back. Then, set it aside. When he comes, ask him to write the speech for you. Beg this humble favor of him. If I know Master Kendall, he will be eager to do it. But then tomorrow, read your speech instead. I have no doubt that yours will be worthy of those swift riders heading to the four winds, and that Kendall's will not."

Ravelin studied him, drawing courage from his friend's audacity and from the humor in his eye. Then, the humor faded, and Pate was all seriousness.

"Because, my prince, what your people really want in their deep, deep sorrow, is to hear—not from the Duke, and most certainly not from your tutor, but— from you."

9

———

In the Woods

A refreshing spring breeze, the kind Tara loved, flowed through the bedroom window in the morning. It smelled of new warmth after the cold of winter, of woods and fields beginning to wake, and she thought it odd that the city of Elva smelled so good. The breeze touched Tara gently and stirred her hair. And she awoke.

Not to the feather bed in its beautifully carved frame. Not to the warmth of Bevan stretched out, sleeping peacefully beside her.

But to rough bark, lumpy tree roots, and the damp of forest dew clinging to her cloak and stockings, turning the ground she sat on into the beginnings of mud.

She sat up slowly, painfully stiff. Her face and head

throbbed with this change in position, and she let out a small groan.

"Does it hurt badly today, Mama?" Silvie knelt beside her and studied her closely, a worried look on her face.

"I think one of my eyes is swollen completely shut. Could you take off this bandage?"

"Rosie, bring the water flask," Silvie said.

Tara leaned forward and tilted her head up. The cool water dribbled down her face. A gentle tug and Silvie pulled the bandage off. "I wish I didn't have to say this, Mama, but it looks much worse."

"Injuries always do look worse on the second day," Tara said as lightly as she could. She didn't want them to know how much it hurt. And, just as she thought, she couldn't open her injured eye.

"They look worse on the third and fourth days too," put in Rosie. She and Silvie both eyed her carefully, their earnest faces close to hers. "Remember when I fell on the stone step?" said Rosie. "It took my elbow a week to start looking right."

"Do you want to put the bandage back on?" asked Silvie.

"Not right away," Tara answered. "The air feels good on my face."

Silvie went to wash the linen bandage in the river while Rosie dug in their bags for food.

"The bread won't last long in this dampness, Rosie," Tara said. "We'd better eat it first."

Rosie handed her a generous chunk of the bread.

Even though it was no longer fresh, it tasted so good.

Like the taste of their home blended with the smells of the forest. Tara tore off small bits and chewed slowly because every movement pulled at her swollen face. Silvie returned and draped the wet bandage over a bare tree limb before taking the bread Rosie held out to her. They ate in silence for awhile, thoughts turned inward, until Rosie spoke.

"I didn't just dream of that large flaming bird, did I?" She gazed at the tree where the bird had perched.

"Not unless I had the same dream," Silvie answered. "I think the Sender heard your prayer, Mama. He sent something to protect us."

"That deep sleep was as much a miracle as the bird of fire," Tara said.

"He sees us," said Silvie thoughtfully. "He let us know that he is watching out for us."

Strength flowed into Tara's limbs with that realization. She took a deep slow breath and felt better for it.

Silvie passed the cheese around. While they were eating it, Rosie asked, "What do we do now, Mama? Go back to the road?"

"If we can find it," said Silvie. "I don't know what direction we came from in the dark."

"Maybe we can listen for it like we did the stream," said Rosie.

They all held still for a long while, listening, but no manmade sound came to them. Only the chattering of the morning birds and the scurrying of squirrels, scrabbling up the trunks of trees and flinging themselves from branch to branch.

"It might be too early for travelers," said Tara.

"There were a lot of people at that inn," Silvie said. "They have to make some kind of noise in the morning. Maybe we walked farther last night than we thought."

"Or in a direction we didn't realize," Rosie added.

Tara finished her bread at last and brushed the crumbs from her hands. "I think I'll need some help standing up, girls. I've never felt so sore in my life."

"More than just your head hit the cobbles, Mama," Silvie said, as she took Tara's hand. Rosie took hold of the other, and they pulled gently, but firmly, as Tara got to her feet.

Her head throbbed even more and she ached all over, but after a few dizzy moments, her mind cleared. That was some relief. She took off her cloak and Silvie shook it out for her. After putting it back on, Tara brushed off her skirts with her hands. Both girls stood waiting, watching her.

"I don't think we need to try for the road again," she said. "We are as safe here as we could be on the road. The palace guard is not likely to come through this wood. And we do have this stream. We can follow it, going the way it came from. It must flow into the Polta River near Elva, so we don't want to go that way. Every village needs a water supply, so we're sure to come across houses and people somewhere if we walk alongside the stream."

They washed their hands and faces in the stream, brushed and tied back their hair before gathering up their bags. Tara folded the drying bandage and set it inside her carry bag. She noticed that Rosie put some of the river rocks into the pockets of her green cloak.

"In case we meet another bear," Rosie said. "Or anything else."

A small, narrow path ran along the top of the riverbank. It looked like an animal track, the kind that crossed the wild meadows in East Rilken. Silvie started along it, carrying her bundles. Tara followed with the rose bag. Rosie came last. They did not make quick progress, but they moved steadily along. It was good to be doing something, Tara felt. Going somewhere, even if they didn't know where.

The sun rose higher, and its rays pierced the forest. Along the river, budded trees had yet to release spring's first leaves. A breeze stirred the branches far above them, making them creak. Glancing up, Tara thought of the huge bird that had lit the night and driven away the bear.

"Thank you," she whispered. "Thank you so much."

Ahead of her, Silvie's voice continually came back to them like a good guide.

"Watch out for that stump!"

"Fallen tree!"

"Mud hole!"

Silvie would glance back to make sure they had heard. And Tara and Rosie would carefully move around or climb over them.

If only Bevan were with them.

The memory of that last morning came to her. Bevan dressed and ready for travel though the sun had not risen. Bending over his daughters' bed and kissing them goodbye while they gave him drowsy hugs. Downstairs she had held the lantern for him as he gathered his pack.

"It will be long months away, Tara," he had said. "The rest of the winter and possibly into spring. But you know where my heart will be. And look here, I've tied the gift you made for me on my belt." He pointed, and there was the small brown pouch she had stitched for him, covered with a pattern of tiny roses blended with the cabbages of his parents' farm.

"I will think of you every moment," she replied. "And I will have a surprise waiting for you at your return." That's what kept her cheered through his every absence, making a gift for his return.

He held her tightly, a hug she could still feel. A hug for remembering. She had stepped out in the cold dark, holding the small oil lantern. Across the street, Erinne was doing the same for her husband.

Bevan climbed up on his dun-colored horse and smiled down at her. "Take care, my love." Then he turned his horse streetward. And as he turned, his face set in the way it always did. A man ready for duty to his king.

Tears pricked her eyes, and she took a deep breath. She couldn't give way to sorrow now. She had to keep moving.

At that moment, Rosie began to sing.

Oh, sing me high
And sing me low,
And sing me where
The wind blows.

I'll listen high,
I'll listen low,
And find you where
The wind blows.

Rosie often sang when she worked in the house, scrubbing or sweeping, or even weeding in their garden behind the kitchen. Her voice was clear and bright. A familiar loveliness as they walked through these strange woods. And yet, in its loveliness, it became a poignant reminder of all the good they had lost.

Oh, sing me out
And sing me in,
And sing me where
My heart's been.
I'll listen out
And listen in,
And tell you where
My heart's been.

Oh, if only by some miracle, Bevan were alive and whole again! Tara thought of the wonderlight in his eyes when he held Silvie for the first time. His patient, encouraging voice when he taught a very young Rosie to aim her throws. The sound of that voice and the strength of his arms had been Tara's whole true life.

Oh, sing me near
And sing me far,
And sing me to

A bright star.
I'll listen near
And listen far,
And find you at
The bright star.

The song flowed on around her memories until she heard Silvie call out. "Rosie, stop! Mama's crying."

Silvie led her to a fallen tree, and they all lowered their bags and perched on it. There they gave vent to the tears that had been demanding release for so long. They did not talk. They just cried, sobbed, wiped their faces, and took deep breaths. After some time, by a hidden common agreement, they rose to their feet, picked up their bags, and went on.

LATE THAT MORNING, Silvie surprised a bird too close to its nest. It flew at her and struck at the arms she could barely lift, weighted as they were with bags, to protect her head. Rosie threw rocks to scare the bird away. They fled into the woods, getting scraped and poked by branches and thorns. Only after making a wide arc around the bird's nesting place could they return to the river path again.

Rosie found some berries on a wild bush and picked a handful before Tara could get a close look at them and make her fling the poisonous things away. Rosie scrubbed her hands thoroughly in the river while Silvie again bemoaned the absence of soap.

They had been walking for hours, but had seen no village or homes or a single human being. The land sloped upward, which made walking harder. But there was nothing to do except grip their bags tighter and continue on their way.

10

Let There Be No Envy or Ill Will

When Ravelin followed his uncle into the great hall of the castle, he felt over-whelmed by the number of people that filled it. Rows of seated courtiers rose instantly and bowed. Behind them, all the rest of the castle residents already stood, shoulder to shoulder, their bows a ripple of color, of movement, which made them look all together like one single living thing.

But they were individuals. And distinctive. He could tell by their clothing who they were—the pale linen of the cooks and their assistants, the browns of the tutors, the grays of the artists and even darker gray of the architects in charge of reconstructing the oldest wing of the castle. The dark blue of the university scholars. The velvet robes of nobility edged with ornate embroidery. Maids, groomsmen, tailors, teachers, writers, mapmakers, hunters, gardeners, and more than he could recognize at the moment. All of the people who made this castle a living, breathing place.

But along the walls—the soldiers.

Palace guard to the left, attired in their midnight blue, a color created just for them. The elite Guardsmen of the king to the right.

Ravelin could not take his eyes from the Guardsmen.

Treachery and murder had come from their ranks. Yet, here they stood. Half-armored, swords at their side, their shoulders draped in the green-on-green. Solemn and still. As if nothing horrific had occurred.

His heart raced faster.

The Duke led him to the one chair that sat on a dais facing the audience. A chair with gold arms. With a back and seat intricately embroidered in red and blue, green and gold, a green drape across its back. A chair that rested on a raised floor of white marble. A chair he had sat in only once, when he was eight years old and impishly teasing his father. Long before he could begin to imagine the burdens of the man who sat there.

The Duke stopped at the foot of the stairs that led to the throne and motioned to Ravelin to climb them. Ravelin hesitated a moment, but realized there was nothing else he could do. So he climbed them, then turned around and stood on the top step.

The Duke looked up at him and frowned. He stepped up and spoke low into Ravelin's ear. "They cannot sit down if you do not. No one can sit in the presence of a standing king."

Ravelin nodded. He obediently perched on the edge of the chair. To his relief, the nobility took their seats. He immediately stood again and held out his hands before they could do the same.

"Please, stay seated, honored lords and ladies, you who served my father so well. I, myself, will stand because I can see all your faces so much better if I do."

His uncle had taken a place standing on the first step to Ravelin's right. Ravelin saw the side of the Duke's face tighten as he spoke. Which meant the Duke was displeased by this.

Ravelin unrolled the paper in his hand and read the preamble Kendall had written, a preamble which spent some long minutes addressing every nobleman and every kind of person gathered in the hall.

Pate was standing at the end of the last row of chairs, listening intently. Kendall was on the other side of the room, standing directly behind Lord Vallenro.

Kendall was nodding and appeared to be mouthing the words of the speech along with Ravelin. At the end of the preamble, Kendall's lips stopped moving and a perplexed look came into his eyes. Ravelin turned his gaze towards the back of the hall and took courage from Wells' loyal face.

"This morning we gather together to grieve. Indeed, we will be grieving together for many months, many years to come. How can we not feel the loss of such an able king, such a good father as he was to me and to you all?

"We will say much more of him at the day set aside for his praise in a week's time. And if I started now, those of you standing would not be able to bear up long before I had finished. Because none of us at this moment can begin to comprehend the greatness of our loss.

"We sorrow together, good people, but I ask you this. Do not be afraid of what the future might bring.

"In my brother's absence, I will take over the duties that would have fallen to him. I have youth, but my uncle and Lord Locke and my father's wise advisors remain, guiding this great country as they have always done.

"The motto of my family's house in the found tongue is this, *Absit invidia.* 'Let there be no envy or ill will.' When Dallen returns, I will gladly step aside and place him on the throne that belongs to him.

"But I, Ravelin, will not be king and I will *never* be king—" He could feel dismay stir through the crowd, so he spoke louder and with more determination. "—and I will tell you why.

"I refuse to accept a title given to me by a murderer's hand. Even if, by the will of the Sender, I rule this country I love so well, I will rule as 'Prince' always.

"The Princedom of Rilken will continue to be strong and peaceful and prosperous, astonishing our larger neighbors and drawing their admiration as it has in the past, just as my good and honored father intended.

"We cannot but sorrow at the evils that have befallen us, but I ask you again, my good people, my *dear* people, let us move on without fear."

. . .

His words ran out. He did not remember having written more. He hoped he could do what he was asking the people to do. And his eyes were so full that he could not see the paper in his hand. He blinked rapidly and lowered his arm.

A loud cry came from the back of the room. "The Sender love you, dear prince!" It was repeated again and again until he could not distinguish the voice from the echo. Tears glistened on faces. Applause rose in the hall like a wave and rushed forward to break over him.

Pate discreetly held one hand palm down in front of his chest. He was making the fingers of the other hand gallop over the first like swift horses carrying a speech to the four corners of the country. The perplexed look had not left Kendall's face.

Lord Locke, his father's secretary, had risen and clapped while tears ran down his fleshy cheeks. The lords and ladies around him rose also.

Ravelin was not sure what to do next. He bowed his head briefly to the audience then stepped down and escaped through the side door.

He took a deep breath and let it out slowly. He had done it. He had given the speech he wanted to give. It was over.

His uncle followed him through the side door, and shut it firmly after him. "Ravelin!" The Duke was angry. "You foolish, foolish boy!"

11

A Clearing in the Forest

In the afternoon, the path along the top of the riverbank widened. I almost missed that sign and what it could mean because I was concerned about Mama. She was having a hard time staying on the small track. Whenever I glanced back, her feet would be partially in the brush on the river side of the path, or she would have strayed off onto the forest side.

"Are you all right, Mama?" I asked.

"I'm all right, Silvie," she answered, as she stepped off the path again. Rosie's eyes met mine, and I saw concern in them, too.

"Why don't we rest on the riverbank for awhile?" I said. We picked a dry grassy spot on its slope and sat in a row. Rosie passed the water flask and I broke off pieces of Zilla's cake. Then I told them what I noticed about the path.

"Animals wouldn't make a broader path, would they?" I asked. "Doesn't that mean men have been here? We could be getting closer to someone's home."

"We have to be," said Rosie. "Every path leads somewhere."

It was time to ask the question that had bothered me for some time. "Then what should we say about ourselves to the people we meet? People in villages can be suspicious of strangers. You always said that about villages in East Rilken, Mama."

Mama swallowed her cake and brushed the crumbs from her fingers. "I don't want to tell anyone something untrue," she said slowly, "but the complete story of our circumstances may not gain us any friends. And it could make things harder for us."

Rosie looked somber at this. "Can we say we're just poor people looking for work?"

"No, not poor," I said. "People will see the style and cut of our dresses, dirty though they are, and know that we've come from Elva."

"Silvie's right," Mama said. "Country people don't dress quite like this. I didn't until we moved to Elva."

"So, we could still just say that we're looking for work," Rosie replied.

"And when they ask where we've come from?" Mama asked.

I had a sudden thought. "We could tell them our

bigger story." I looked at Mama. "Tell them that you were born and raised on a farm in East Rilken. You were married there, and we were born there. We lived in Elva for awhile, but don't like the city. It is a dangerous place, and you were attacked. We have heard good things about the people in the woods of West Rilken and hope to find work and a home there."

"What if they ask about Papa?" Rosie said quietly.

"There we continue to tell them the truth," I said, staring at the river water flowing around the stones in its way. "We tell them it's too painful to talk about, and it makes us very sad."

"That is the truth," Mama whispered.

I put my head on Mama's shoulder and took her hand. Rosie hugged her other arm and kissed the uninjured side of her face.

"How can we find out what really happened to Papa?" Rosie asked quietly.

"It must have taken place miles from here," I said.

"As much as I can guess, it did," said Mama. "We will talk about this more later, but now we must see what we can find before nightfall."

We gathered our bags and continued on for what seemed like another half hour, when the path turned abruptly away from the little river. I stopped and stared at it.

"What is it?" Mama asked.

"The path turns into the woods here." I pointed. "Should we follow it?"

"It still has to be going somewhere," said Rosie.

"We can follow it a little longer and see," said Mama,

"but, Rosie, fill our water flask first, before we leave the stream too far behind."

We waited while Rosie did that, then followed the path into the trees. In only a few minutes, it emptied out into a large clearing mostly surrounded by tall leafless trees. On the far side of the clearing, a wall of rock jutted up out of the ground. Backed up against the rock face, stood a small, low building made of stone with a dark slate roof. The wooden shutters and door had carving on them, a pattern of gentle vines growing upwards. Had we come to the edge of some rich estate?

Rosie called across the clearing. "Is anyone here?"

No answer came. I glanced at Mama, and she motioned me forward.

Rosie took the lead and knocked loudly on the door. There was still no answer.

"There can't be anyone here," Rosie said. She pushed on the door handle and the door swung open. All was dark inside.

"Hiya!" Rosie called from the doorstep. But no sound came from within.

"Why is the door unlocked?" I asked warily.

"I wonder..." said Mama.

"What?" asked Rosie.

"This could be one of the king's hunting stations. Your father talked about them. They are scattered all over the king's domains as a place for the king or his hunters to rest. That could explain why, even though it is a simple building, it is well made. See the chimney and the tile roof. This building was made to last. That means we're still on the king's domain."

"That also means we can't eat a single animal here or we'll be accused of stealing," I said.

"That's true of any land belonging to someone else," Mama replied. "But an empty hunting station could be a decent shelter for the night."

"What if any hunters come?" said Rosie.

Mama didn't answer right away, and when she did she seemed to be thinking hard. "They might not," she said at last. "At least not just yet. The king has vast lands, and the hunters do not stay in the same place for long. If they take all the game in one region, there will be no animals left to produce more. If they hunted in this area last year, they may not be back this year."

"We've been in these woods all day," said Rosie, "and we didn't see any animals, did we?"

"Just some squirrels, a few birds, and that bear," I replied. "We could just see what it's like, Mama. Rest awhile. Stay here one night if we could."

"I would love to put these bags down for a while," said Rosie.

"First, let's see if we can open those shuttered windows," said Mama, "and get a good look at the place."

The hunting station turned out to be a simple one-room building, longer than it was deep. One window opened onto its face, along with the door. Another window opened on a narrow side, and a fireplace topped with a chimney sat at the other end.

The shuttered windows opened easily from the inside, which agreed with Mama's guess that this section of forest was recently hunted. The whole place would have been well-tended last autumn. The floor, instead of being dirt as I expected, was made of slate, and it was fairly level.

"The king liked to hunt," I said. "And the Guardsmen would go with him, wouldn't they? I wonder if Papa ever came here."

"He could have," said Mama.

"That makes me feel better about being here," said Rosie.

The station was simply furnished. A long table with two long benches on either side of it, a wooden chair, and a wooden stool. Another bench stood across the end of the room underneath the window, and in the far corner, a cupboard.

Everything was covered with a thick layer of dust, which made me strangely hopeful. If this building had been left undisturbed for a few months, then maybe nothing would disturb us if we dared to sleep here tonight.

Rosie went immediately to the fireplace. "Here's a tall stack of wood. And it's dry." She sounded pleased. She bent to examine a box of fire tools which sat next to the fireplace opening.

"The chimney looks tall enough to draw well," said Mama. "Smoke shouldn't come back into the room."

Mama had always been particular about chimneys. Had always said she could not endure a smoky house. This ordinary practical matter comforted me. I turned and studied the rest of the room.

A broom stood in the corner nearby. A row of hooks

dotted the wall behind the door. The whole space was simple, spare, and orderly.

"Let's get rid of this dust first," I suggested. "Then we can have a real rest. Here, Mama." I lifted the wood chair, carried it outside, and brushed off its seat. "You sit here while Rosie and I clean."

It felt strange to have Mama quietly obey me. She was always the active one in any task that had to be done in our home. Rosie and I usually moved like two little moons around the greater warmth of her sun. But she accepted the chair and I saw her settled. I couldn't heal her poor face, but Rosie and I could clean the station for her. I went back inside.

"I need a rag," said Rosie.

"What about the cloth I used to wrap the hairbrush in?"

"Should we sweep first?"

"First and last. Hang up the bags on the hooks there so we don't get them dusty."

"They have dirt from the forest on them in places."

"We can brush them off and shake them out when we're through."

Rosie wiped the table and I swept. It felt good to be doing something so normal. To hear the rhythm of the broom brushing across the slate floor. I glanced out the window. Mama was still sitting in the chair. Her head was turned as if she were gazing at the trees on one particular side of the clearing.

"I'm glad the stream is not far away," I told Rosie.

She was vigorously rubbing down the benches. "I'm

glad that the water we've drunk from it hasn't made us ill."

I swept the dirt from one half of the room out the open door. Mama wasn't in her chair. She had walked over to what looked like the beginning of another path on the other side of the clearing and was standing there looking at something. I turned to sweep the second half of the room.

Rosie started singing, because singing is something Rosie often does. A nonsense song about a courting frog and a cat pretending to be a queen. Her voice was missing its usual exuberance, but she was trying. I swept another dirt pile out the door. Mama was standing at a different place, but still looking into the trees.

Together, Rosie and I wiped the floor on our hands and knees. We worked quickly, eager to get Mama inside and to make us all comfortable. I rolled up my sleeves and was surprised to see bruises on my arm. Until I remembered the bird attack. I shook my head at the thought and busied myself with the floor.

Once that was done, I took our bags outside and brushed the dirt off of them before replacing them on their hooks. Rosie got to work building a fire. Mama was still standing by the edge of the clearing when I finished.

Twilight was coming on. I stepped out into the clearing and walked over to where Mama stood. The air was getting colder, and I pulled my sleeves back down. As I got closer to her, I could hear her voice. Her back was to me, but she was speaking aloud. I paused and waited.

"Sender, please hear me. You could not have watched over us last night if you meant for us to die now. Please, show us what to do!" She bowed her head. "I—I cannot protect my girls as you can. Our only hope for their future is in you. Please. Please give them something. Anything. Something from you that will help them before we starve." She bowed her head and held silent for a time.

I wondered if I should tell her of my presence, when she raised her head. "Please, Sender of all good, show me—show me what to do." At that, I crossed the rest of the clearing and put my arms around her.

The shadows were deepening, but Rosie had been working with the tinder box. With a supply of twigs and small dead branches, she had managed to start a small but neat fire on the hearth. Two short logs from the stack sat on top of it. The long room began to be a little cheerful.

We put a chair close to the fire for Mama. Then Rosie and I went to the stream to refill the flask before night fell and it would be too dark to see. I brought a bowl we had found on the shelves and filled that too. We sang as we went so Mama could hear where we were. Afterwards, Rosie and I gathered another pile of twigs and broken branches from what was immediately around the clearing, and put them next to the stacked wood.

When those tasks were done, we took a serious look at the food we had left. I laid everything out on the table in front of us. Cheeses—two small and one larger round the size of a hand. A bag of dried fruit. Walnuts. Zilla's dried pepper meat, and the last of her bread as well.

"We dare not eat all of this right now," I said. "I should have taken more from home when I had the chance."

Mama placed a gentle hand on my shoulder. "You took all you could at the time, Silvie. You did well."

We divided up one of the small cheeses, ate a handful of walnuts each, a strip of pepper meat, and a few bites of Zilla's bread. It didn't feel like enough, but it was something.

Mama said to turn the long benches over for beds. The supports and braces at either end acted like headboards and footboards and the wood of the seat upside down was broad enough to make a narrow bed.

"At least we won't be sleeping on the cold floor," she said.

We put most of our extra clothing on, layering stockings and underclothing for warmth. Spring nights are still very cold in Rilken. Then Rosie and I stuffed the clothing that remained into three of our carry bags for pillows.

Night had come. Owls hooted from somewhere in the trees around us. Rosie and I shoved the table in front of the door for safety, closed and locked the shutters, and slid the three bench beds as close to the sparking fire as wisdom would allow.

The three of us hugged and kissed each other goodnight, just as we would have done before climbing the stairs in our home and crawling into our feather beds in

Guardstown. I laid my head on my pillow bag, tried not to feel the hardness of the bench, and gazed at the fire.

Last night, under the tree by the river, I had fallen asleep gazing at fire too. The fire in the belly of a miraculous bird. The Sender's bird. A bird who watched us all night. Now, as I could barely keep my eyes open, I felt that the one who sent the bird was still watching.

12

The Aunt and the Nephew

Olivia, Duchess of Elva, gratefully extended her hand to the footman who helped her emerge from the coach at the base of the castle steps. She felt horribly stiff and sore from long hours in a swiftly moving, bouncing and swaying coach, and the night air was chill. Her daughter Petronia climbed out after her.

"I am going right to my room for a long bath," Petronia announced, and without another word went through the castle doors that led most directly to the rooms used by the royal family.

After giving instructions to the servants about their things, Olivia followed her, but instead chose the corridor that led toward the large apartment which housed her husband's study and receiving room. She would have loved to change her clothing and relax, but the tragic news brought by the messenger they met on the road made her want to see her husband right away.

His servant greeted her with a look of surprise that masterfully and quickly altered into a look of welcome. He ushered her to a comfortable chair in the Duke's receiving room, but she didn't sit down.

"Who is with the Duke at this late hour? I hear voices from the study."

"The Duke is speaking with Lord Vallenro, Your Grace. I will let His Highness know that you are here." The last statement sounded more like a question.

Olivia pulled off her gloves thoughtfully. "Do not disturb him now, Harmon. I will come back later."

"Yes, ma'am. Is there any other message?"

"Tell him I am very, very sorry."

"Yes, ma'am."

This time Olivia went in the direction of the family apartments. For there was one person in the castle who would be suffering more than her husband.

She found her nephew sitting alone in a chair by his fire, a half-eaten tray of food at his side. He rose to his feet when he saw her. She hugged him tightly, then released him.

"Oh, Ravelin, what great sorrow," she said gently, gazing at her nephew's face.

He looked away. "It would be easier to bear if Dallen were here."

"Yes. It would." She wasn't sure what else to say about this. The messenger's words had been confusing.

Wells brought a chair for her, and she joined Ravelin in front of the fire. He stared at the flames while she waited.

Ravelin frowned. "My uncle is angry with me."

"How could he be?" Surely anger was out of place in a grieving household. Yet Allard could be unpredictable.

"I was supposed to make an accession speech this morning, to read what Kendall had written out for me according to the Duke's instructions. But I read what I wanted to say instead. And my uncle was furious."

Olivia knew well the temperament of her husband. Could almost imagine the scene. Her heart sank.

"Could I read your speech, Ravelin? Would you mind?"

Wells brought it to her and set a candelabra on the table nearby to brighten the page. She had read only a few lines when tears filled her eyes. She had to wipe them away so she could finish.

"You wrote this yourself?"

"Yes." He had been watching her as she read, a hopeful expression on his face.

"It is beautiful." She handed it to him. "And very moving."

"It is what I think. What I feel."

"I can see that." She studied his face as he folded the paper in his hands, hoping he would say more. After a few quiet moments he spoke.

"My uncle called me a foolish boy."

Olivia cringed inwardly at this, but kept her demeanor calm. "Did he say why?"

Ravelin sighed. "He said that I had lowered the status of my country in the world. That the people would not accept being reduced to a princedom. That I had been sentimental and foolish."

Those were hard things to say to a boy who had just lost his father and most likely his brother too. How often she wished Allard had Adare's restraint, but that was a useless wish. Especially now.

She glanced toward Wells, who was standing unobtrusively against the wall, waiting to be of service. "Wells, were you there? How did the people respond?"

"You would not have believed how great the applause was, Your Grace, unless you had heard it yourself. All I saw was the outpouring of love from the people to our prince."

"I am glad to hear it." These were the words she said, but in her heart she knew applause could be false. And that court tears and court cheers changed quickly into less desirable things.

So, here were two conflicting, irreconcilable responses to Ravelin's speech. But right now, right next to her, sat Ravelin. She reached out and touched his shoulder.

"I'm glad you saw that. I'm glad you saw the people's response to your speech. As for the rest, and as for your uncle, let's see what the next days and weeks will bring. Until then we need to fill these unendurable days with some occupation that will help us get through them."

She leaned back in her chair and watched him. The firelight brought out hidden colors in his brown hair. The same color his mother's had been. His kind, kind mother. He was so young when he lost her, and his face looked so very young now. How alone he must feel!

"Can I tell you about one of my first memories of your father?" she asked gently.

He raised his head and turned to her. "Please do."

"It was just after the marriage treaties had been signed, the ones that betrothed me to your uncle. The royal house of Rilken was invited to be guests of honor at Falland's famous autumnal dances, and I was invited to go as well. These dances last for seven nights and are filled with all sorts of customs and traditions. Every night a different style of clothing is required, and the artistic effect is just beautiful.

"It happened on either the second or the third night. The custom for a particular dance was that men were supposed to choose a lady they were especially fond of for their partner. You know how your uncle throws himself so deeply into politics. He chose for his dance a wealthy and powerful Falland countess while I just watched.

"Oh, Ravelin, courts can be merciless places. I felt the eyes of people on me, could almost hear the judgments in their thoughts when I was passed over. Several pulled back from me as I skirted the room. I tried to find a place where I could watch without being noticed.

"Your father wasn't dancing then because your mother had been slow in regaining her strength after

Dallen's birth. And even though she had made the long trip, she spent much of the time resting and did not attend the dances.

"Well. I finally found my watching place, half-hidden against a wall. I saw your father studying his brother, and then I saw the king's gaze turn to where I stood. And then, Ravelin, your father did a most marvelous thing."

"What did he do?"

"He strode down the side of the ballroom, courtiers bowing and melting back as he passed, came right up to me, and held out his hand with a great smile on his face. 'Come, my new sister. This is good music for dancing.' He led me onto the ballroom floor with a great flourish, while the courtiers clapped and Allard looked around to see what was happening.

"They say that every woman has some particular dances in her life that she will never forget. And that is one of mine. Not just because of your father's grace of person, but because of his grace of heart."

Tears wet both of their faces now, but they were shared tears. And they did not need to be wiped away so quickly.

They sat for a few moments in silence until Olivia remembered something. "I bought some books for you on my travels. Books for both you and Dallen. I know how you like to add to your libraries. Can I give you his books as well, to keep for his return?"

He looked directly at her after she said this, and she saw a faint smile on his face.

"Thank you, Aunt Olivia."

She smiled fully back at him, wishing she could do so much more. She pressed his shoulder with her hand, and rose to go.

"I will have my servant bring them to you right away."

13

The Duchess and the Duke

Olivia stopped in her own rooms long enough to leave her cloak, adjust her hair, and change her traveling boots for more comfortable shoes. Then, after giving directions for Ravelin's books, she once again made her way to the door of her husband's business chambers.

"How is the Duke, Harmon?" she asked as the attendant ushered her inside.

"Enduring, Your Grace," he replied. "But it has been very hard."

She sat down in the chair Harmon offered her, picked up the wine goblet he placed on the table at her side, leaned back, and listened.

"Who is with him now?"

"Still Lord Vallenro, ma'am. He has been here for quite a while."

It was not difficult to hear her husband's voice when he was angry, or when he was intensely concerned about something. Now, he was forceful in the way he was talking to Vallenro, and she felt for the poor man. For a few moments she could hear every word clearly as Harmon opened the door to the Duke's study to tell him of her arrival.

"How could you not have found any trace of him by now?" the Duke was saying. "Don't you know your own land?"

She could not hear Vallenro's answer, but it was enough to make her husband moderate his tone.

"Of course, I don't blame you. Of course not, Vallenro, but if only you had known of the bears' presence before the king's party had passed through, we could have warned them. And to have heard nothing more of—"

Again Vallenro spoke.

Again the Duke's voice changed. Olivia was relieved to hear it more concerned, more conciliatory.

"I will send you more help. The palace guard will need to return to Elva, but I have many sharp-sighted men at my disposal. You will hear from me soon."

The door opened wide and Lord Vallenro emerged. A tall, gray-haired man, he seemed unusually bent and did not attempt to hide the tears on his face. He came over to her and bowed, but did not return her greeting.

Instead he said, "It was on *my* land, Your Grace. I will never forgive myself!"

Olivia felt bewildered at such emotion. "My dear Lord Vallenro!" She gave him her hand and searched for any words that might help. "We trust you completely. Be assured of this."

He bowed over her hand, but was too affected to say anything more before he left the room.

A SMALL SOUND made her turn. Her husband had come out of his study, and she was struck by the lines on his face.

"Allard!" She went to him, but he held up his hand as if to block her. "Please. No tears. I have seen more than I can endure."

"Of course." She stopped where she was. "I understand."

She had been away too many months; she could feel the distance between them. And even now she had returned unexpectedly early. Allard did not like unexpected things.

"Come, sit with me, Allard. You look so worn. What burdens you must be carrying right now!"

He followed her to a cushioned couch, near where she had been sitting before. They sat down, side by side. She studied his face for clues that might tell her how to proceed.

After a few moments, he said, "I did not expect you for a long time yet."

There was a certain tone in his voice, a certain tightness, that told her he wished her away. She took a brave breath and pretended she was wanted.

"Petronia did not want to wait for the duke's son to return from his hunting trip. It seemed he would be away some weeks, and there would be nothing much for her to do in his absence. So we said our farewells and left the same day he did."

"So Ophria is already tired of her? Ready to send her back?"

Olivia stared at him. "No! Not at all! The duke's son enjoyed Petronia's company *very* much. The Ophrian court was certainly ready to admire her. I believe their wedding is almost a certainty. And as for his hunting trip—you know as well as anyone that a hunter must go when and where the game are running."

He had been sitting still, his head bent, his eyes on the hand of hers that he held politely between his on his lap. At this, he stirred.

"Of course," he said absently. "One must go where the prey is." He shook his head at some internal thought. "How is Petronia?"

"Exhausted as only hours in a jostling coach can make you. She was heading for her bath when I left her."

He raised his head and seemed to really see her for the first time. "You're still in your traveling dress?"

"I couldn't wait to see you," she replied, trying to smile at him. There was no responding smile on his face or in his eyes.

"I am so sorry, Allard. I feel the horror of this terrible news."

"You don't know all of it yet. The king was murdered on the road by one of his own Guardsmen."

"That's impossible!"

He let go of her hand and pulled away. Olivia put her hands in her lap.

"Impossible?" he said. "That is what everyone thinks, I'm sure. I was coming to greet him with the palace guard, but we arrived too late. Adare and Dallen were both gone."

"Dallen? Dallen too?"

"Yes. Assuredly. Killed either by that villain or by wild animals. Unfortunately, there is no sign of his body at all, which makes everything so much harder. Ravelin won't accept his loss. He keeps expecting his brother to return miraculously."

"Poor Ravelin," Olivia said softly. "What a terrifying thing for him. It is natural that he can't accept it. The loss of his father is hard enough." She would not dare to give her husband advice, but Ravelin needed her to defend him.

"Give him time, Allard. Give him time." She worked to keep her voice gentle. "You of all people would understand how he feels right now. The loss of a brother..."

He did not respond, but gazed down at the carpet at their feet.

"Adare gone," she said quietly. "I never thought I would see this day."

"And never wanted to either, I'm sure." He raised his head to look at her, and his eyes were hard.

"Of course not!"

"You would be willing to make him a legend, just like everyone else."

She stared at him, not knowing how to answer this. If it would even be safe to answer this. She was so very tired, and Allard was being more difficult than usual. She tried to distract him.

"I see you've made some changes in this reception hall since I left. You've brought in a new mirror?"

She left the couch and walked over to where a large framed mirror was mounted in the center of the far wall. The mirror reached almost from floor to ceiling and was just as wide as it was tall.

She turned back to look at him. "*Is* this a new mirror? It looks like the one from the manor."

He got up and came toward her. "It is the one from the manor. I find this wall fits it so much better. Look." He walked ahead of her and pointed into the depths of the mirror. "It reflects much more light on *this* wall, don't you think so?"

She looked where Allard wanted her to look. Tried to ease his anger, and what surely must be his own sorrow, by giving him all the kindness he needed. Yes, the mirror glowed beautifully, and she told him so.

"The Galerine mirror-makers have never had such an enthusiastic patron," she added. "Lucky for them when you visited their city."

He rubbed his hands together and smiled at this. "You have been very patient with my mirror collection," he said, suddenly gracious. "Even though I know you have not cared for it. In truth, I am buying a new mirror for the manor and moved this one here."

Allard was right. She had never cared for his mirrors. Once she even had a nightmare about this particular mirror. That it had a face of its own looking out at her. The face had been ghastly and hostile, but she would never tell him of it.

"I think this is my favorite mirror of them all," he said proudly. "Come, Olivia, I won't tire you much longer. Here, look deeply into it and you can see the handiwork of the artisan, the layers that are hidden in place of your reflection. Don't you think this mirror is the most beautiful one you've ever seen?"

She was exhausted, but he had just lost his brother. So she gazed into the mirror as he directed and found herself astonished.

Somehow, beyond everything in the room that was barely reflected in the mirror, beyond the ivory-gold embroidered furnishings, and the sight of her tired face, beyond them she could see the mirror for itself. A white, pearlish light seemed to flow from it, and she gasped.

"It *is* beautiful, Allard. It's stunning!"

He came over to her, took her in his arms, and actually kissed her.

"Thank you, my love. I'm glad you see it as I do. I don't think those artisans could create any mirror more beautiful than this."

"Nor I," she agreed.

"Now, follow your daughter's example, and go refresh yourself."

· · ·

A DIFFERENT ALLARD came to her chambers that night an hour before midnight. She was still awake. Even though she had longed for her bed when she climbed out of the coach hours ago, her heart needed to spend time sitting in the candlelit room alongside Adare's bier. Sitting with him for awhile. Saying goodbye to her brother-in-law and king. She had just returned to her room, and Menta, her maid, readied her for bed.

Somehow Allard had heard that she had visited Ravelin and was intensely interested in everything Ravelin had said to her and she to him. She sat on the sofa at the foot of her bed, feeling her husband's growing displeasure as she talked. He strode back and forth in front of her fireplace, and his steps quickened with her words.

"He thinks I'm furious, does he? Of course, I'm furious!" He stopped his pacing and wheeled around to face her. "We have proudly carried the title of kingdom for eighty years. Think, Olivia. Eighty years! And with one stroke that fool wants to wipe it away! A princedom, indeed!

"Who does he think he is in doing this? I am a prince of the land just as he is. Younger son of the heir just like he. The Council of Nobles will not let him get away with this."

"Could Dallen change things when he comes?" she ventured.

He threw his arms up into the air and looked to heaven. Then he brought them down, slapping his thighs sharply, startling her.

"Dallen." He shook his head. "Did you not hear me

earlier? Dallen will not return. He is assuredly *dead.* When you told Ravelin to keep Dallen's books for him, you were encouraging that boy in a lie, Olivia. That was a witless thing to do. You forget that I was there."

"The message was not clear—" she began.

He stepped closer to where she sat, his eyes almost desperate in his anger. "I was there," he repeated. "I saw this madman drag Dallen from his horse. If the rest did not survive, how could Dallen have survived?"

He turned his back on her and walked briskly to the door.

"I'm sorry, Allard." She was on her feet. "So sorry!"

Before she could reach him, he had gone through the doorway and shut the door firmly behind him. She stood for a moment, staring at the closed door, listening to the sound of his footsteps walking across the outer chamber and hearing that door shut just as firmly.

She turned slowly and walked unsteadily to her bed. It seemed to take much effort to lift the coverings and crawl in. She lay there, oblivious to the softness of the pillows, the silkiness of the bedding, the crackling of the fire, and closed her eyes, trying to blot out her husband's anger.

Images flashed in her mind. Vallenro's face contorted in his grief. King Adare's still body. Ravelin's hollow eyes as he stared into the fire.

And Dallen when she had last seen him.

It was the summer day she and Petronia had left for Ophria. Dallen had bounded energetically down the grand staircase to hand them into the coach and wish them safe journeys. She had been struck then, like always, by his demeanor. His face so perpetually alive, aware, and confident. And beneath the dark hair that mimicked his father's, a pair of grey eyes seemed to take in everything. Were those eyes seeing anything now? Or was Dallen truly gone forever?

14

Changes in the Night

I woke early. At least, I thought it was early. The fire had gone out, and everything was dark in the hunting station. My eyes searched the gloom until I found a thin line of gray light where the shutter edge met the stone wall. Dawn was on the way.

I held still, listening for other sounds. Only gentle breathing. Rosie, right next to me, and Mama, just beyond her, were still asleep. I closed my eyes and tried to fall asleep again, but I couldn't.

All day yesterday through our long hike in the woods, dark thoughts had hounded me. Sorrow and fears pulled at my hair and my cloak, but I had to keep moving, keep watching for obstacles, keep encouraging the others. For Mama's sake. For Rosie's sake. Now, in the dark before morning, with everything still, I could lie here and think. I took a deep breath.

What I had done yesterday—leading with the welfare of the others in mind—had felt so natural. Because it was what Papa had always done. What he had always taught us to do simply by doing it himself. It was part of the Guardsman's Oath, but Mama claimed that it had been part of Papa long before he ever swore it.

> *I am valor for my Valor, the King.*
> *I am strength for my Strength, the King.*
> *I am truth for my Truth, the King.*
> *I give my life for my Life, the King.*

The words of the oath made me proud when I was a child. Rosie and I would make our dolls say them. Later, the words confused me, and I questioned them openly, puzzling over the words, especially the truth part.

One afternoon, a few years ago, when Papa and I were walking home from the castle, after a ceremony for new Guardsmen, I asked him about them. I didn't want simple answers, the ones I had already known. I wanted deeper answers. Mama and Rosie had gone to help with a new baby, so Papa and I had time alone together to talk.

"Why do you swear these things?" I asked. "Why truth? I understand making a vow to never lie, but to swear to *be* truth?"

"Do you know that many Guardsmen consider this the hardest part of the vow?"

This surprised me, and Papa went on to explain.

"We swear it because truth protects, Silvie. It is truth's nature. Truth protects life. And love. Truth protects growth and all things good. It is the foundation for a people so they can soar. It is the pillar of a glorious kingship. That is why we swear to be truth.

"Lies and deception always destroy. They twist people's understandings and the way they shape their thoughts and decisions. Look at it this way. Truth is to the mind and soul what strength is to the body. A Guardsman must always be discerning and searching out the truth."

This last comparison I could understand and told him so. I could see truth as the cornerstone of soul strength. But truth and lies were often hard to distinguish from each other. And the actions of physical strength were so much easier to detect.

As we turned the corner and crossed the cobbled street towards our part of Elva, I bemoaned the nature of mankind.

"I wish strength would always be used for good, Papa. But there are so many cruel men and women in the world. Like the robbers who tried to attack the king on the road to Leibent. I wish people never used their strength to hurt others, but they do. Strength is used to destroy what matters to other people. To kill. To do all manner of evil things."

He took my hand gently as if trying to ease my despair over the world. "That doesn't change the truth of what strength was always meant to do. A person's power, however great or small, was always and only meant to be used at the direction of Love. Never forget that, Silvie. But also remember this. Love is one of the most powerful weapons on earth."

I nodded my head then and believed his firm words. Utterly and completely. Because all the training and all the building of strength that my papa worked on every week with the Guardsmen was designed to protect. Protect their families, their neighborhood, their city, their castle, and their king. They protected everything they loved. Love protects.

As I thought about this, lying on a hard bench in the cold dark of the hunting station, another memory caught at me, and I finally realized what I had suspected before. I saw clearly now what Zilla's son Ross lacked. *Strength works in the service of love*, Papa taught. Yet, at the moment of my great need—when we were being attacked with the mud clods—Ross had only watched. He had used his strength to do nothing. His father had intervened, but Ross? Ross did not have a Guardsman's heart.

My papa had a Guardsman's heart. And a Guardsman's strength. And a Guardsman's love.

My heart squeezed tight in my chest. I gulped for air as tears shuddered out of me. I was not crying for Ross. I was crying because the protecting walls of my world had all fallen down, and the Strength of my life, my papa, was gone.

AFTER A LONG WHILE, I wiped my face with my hands and sat up in the darkness. The bench beds were not comfortable at all, no matter how we had tried to pad them. And the room was so cold. I reached over and patted Rosie's shoulder.

"Rosie?" I whispered. "Help me move the table without waking Mama. I have to go outside."

Rosie sat up abruptly, like she often did. "It's freezing in here," she whispered back.

I stood up and walked cautiously toward the door. "Over here, Rosie," I whispered.

We pivoted the table out of the doorway just enough so I could slip outside. The sky was lighter now. The sun would be up soon. I looked around the clearing and rubbed my arms fearfully. There were no birds in sight, but I could hear them in the trees singing to the dawn.

I tried not to be nervous. I was only going around the side of the station to a short path that led to the "necessary" Rosie had discovered yesterday. The king's builders had provided for everything, even cleanliness for the regular needs of human beings. But this forest spread out for miles in every direction, and there were spiders in the woods, and attacking birds, and death-dealing bears.

Silvie, stop it!

It wasn't like me to be fearful. I hadn't been—in Guardstown. But now we were out in the unwalled lands.

I finished at the necessary, hating the cold, and made my way numbly back to the station, watching the trees with suspicious eyes. I bore bruises from yesterday's bird attack, and the soreness had made sleeping more diffi-cult. I held my arms tightly to myself as I went. Mama had known about birds protecting their nests. It felt odd to think about it now, but Mama had grown up without a wall.

Across the clearing, a bright red bird sat on a branch. I could see it easily amongst the browns and pale greens. For some strange reason, I felt it was watching me. And that it was somehow...unsure.

I made a rush for the door but the bird lifted from its branch and flew straight toward me.

"Oh, go back!" I cried, spinning around and covering my head with my arms.

Immediately, the bird turned in midair and went back to the branch it had been sitting on.

I lowered my arms and stared at it. Yes, it *was* watching me. I glanced around at the surrounding trees, then back at the red bird.

"I'm not near your nest, am I?" It felt strange to speak the words out loud in the empty clearing.

The bird shifted its feet on the thin branch and chirped twice at me.

"Oh, good." As soon as I said this, I marveled at it. *What had just happened?*

The bird had clearly chirped to tell me that I was at the right distance, or good distance. Actually, I thought it said "comfortable place," which immediately conveyed that it was not threatened by where I was, and yet, *how could I possibly know that?*

I stared at the bird. Its scarlet head moved constantly, tilting this way and that, yet I knew its attention was mainly directed at me. And that...it was friendly.

I took a deep breath and rubbed my arms. This was not a dream. It couldn't be. Yet, there was the bird. Silent. Waiting. I gazed at it and felt strangely comforted.

"Thanks, friend!" I called softly.

The bird chirped again and my mouth dropped open in astonishment. How could it answer me unless it understood what I said? It was shocking enough to realize I understood it, but that it could answer me and *did* answer me was something I couldn't quite grasp.

"You *understand* me?"

A trio of chirps. Happy satisfaction in response. Which was a bird's way of saying yes. It did understand me.

Dazedly, I turned toward the door of the hunting station and froze.

ROSIE LEFT the door open so she could listen for Silvie and so the light would help her locate the tinderbox. The room was too cold to be comfortable in. Or to try to sleep again. A new fire must be laid first.

The hunting station had its own tinderbox mounted on the wall, but Rosie felt it would be stealing to use it. *Only if we get desperate*, she told herself.

The striking of the flint woke Mama. Rosie could hear her stir.

"Stay there, Mama. Stay warm until I get the fire started."

Rosie set to work, hearing as she always did, every time she struck the flint, her father's voice.

That's the way, Rosie. That's the way. You've got the right vigor for the job. You can kindle a fire as fast as any Guardsman.

And she always heard the smile in his words.

It took some minutes to get the fire going, but at last she was satisfied with a smart little blaze. She used the bellows to make it blaze higher, then held her hands out to it.

"Thank you, Rosie," Mama said in a sleepy voice from her bench bed.

"I love making fires. I love making things warm." Rosie admired her work for awhile then said, "I think I'll go check on Silvie."

She opened the door and stepped outside into the morning air. Silvie was standing right there. Not moving. As still as stone. Like the statue in the fountain of Guardstown Square.

Rosie grabbed Silvie's shoulders. "Silvie! What *is* it? What's wrong?"

Silvie blinked and pointed.

"Rosie," she said in a shaky voice. "I cleaned the doorstep. I know those weren't here yesterday."

Rosie whirled around and gasped.

Tara got up from her bed as quickly as she could in response to the girls' cries—her heart instantly racing. She slid around the table that half-blocked the doorway, and stepped outside. They both looked whole and unharmed. She blinked hard, wishing her injured eye would open all the way.

"What's the matter?"

"Look, Mama." Silvie pointed with a hesitant hand. "Roses. How did they get here?"

Tara looked, and wonder filled her. Where only bare ground had been before, two rosebushes flanked the door of the hunting station. Mature bushes, well-leafed with green, as if it were midsummer instead of the beginning of spring.

One of the bushes was filled with blooms the color of pale cream. The other with fiery red flowers, an orange glow deep in their petals. Soft beads of morning dew dotted the leaves and blooms, and a gentle fragrance filled the air around them.

"Mama, who could have done this?" asked Silvie. "Did someone come here in the night while we were sleeping and plant them?"

"No one plants mature bushes," said Tara. "Spring is for cuttings and seedlings."

She got to her knees and peered under the lowest branches. "The soil is undisturbed. These bushes think that it's high summer and that they have always been here. Look how dark their leaves are compared to everything around us. Darker than most rose leaves, I think."

Then she gasped. How could she not have seen it immediately?

"They are Rose White and Rose Red," she said slowly. "For Silvia and Rosabel. They're the colors of your hair."

"Oh my," said Rosie quietly.

"Yes, the colors are familiar, Mama, but even more." Silvie reached out and gently lifted a rose bloom with her fingers. "Imagine these roses against a dark blue background. Your blue carry bag. The one Zilla filled with food. Mama, you could have stitched these. Yet these are real!"

Tara's mouth dropped open. She touched a fiery bloom with her fingertips. It was true. The curve of these petals felt familiar. Her fingers remembered the feel of the needle as it went up and down, tracing the outlines and filling in the colors. *The leaves!*

"I—I didn't have the right color for rose leaves," she said. "So I had to use a slightly darker color. Just like this."

Rosie darted inside and came back with the rose carry bag. A cream rosebush filled one side of the bag. An orange-red rosebush covered the other side. The colors and shapes matched perfectly.

"Your embroidery came to life, Mama," Silvie said, helping her to her feet.

"But what does this mean?" asked Rosie.

Tara gazed at the bushes. "I don't know. But I think the Sender means to give us courage."

"It's like that bird by the stream who was a night candle for us," said Rosie. "Oh! I wish there were someone to tell about this, because I would be telling everyone I could right now!"

"There may be something else." Silvie spoke hesitantly.

Tara turned to look at her. "What else?"

"Maybe I just imagined it. If I did, it won't work." Silvie took a few steps away from them into the clearing. She held out her arm and called, "Would you come here, please, friend?"

As if in reply, a small, bright red bird flew out of a tree and landed on Silvie's sleeve.

Tara gaped at it. "Oh, my goodness."

"Just before I saw the bushes, I found I could understand this little bird. That it was talking to me, and that it could understand me too."

Rosie was all excitement. "And look, Silvie, it brought you a present!"

Silvie held out her other hand, and the bird opened its beak and dropped a small leaf into it.

Rosie took it out of Silvie's hand and looked closely at it. "That's a new hawthorn leaf. We can eat those!"

Tara caught Rosie's arm, ready to keep her from poisoning herself again. Then she gasped. It *was* a hawthorn leaf. She recognized its shape.

"Rosabel, just yesterday you were ready to eat poison berries. How do you know this is a hawthorn tree? They don't grow in Elva."

Rosie's exuberance faded, and bewilderment filled her eyes. "I—I don't know. It's like it told me. That it was safe." Rosie pointed at the ground beneath a group of trees. "Look, Mama. Isn't that wild fennel?"

Tara looked. Yes. It was. Rosie hurried toward it.

Tara glanced at Silvie. The red bird was now perched on her shoulder and they seemed to be carrying on a conversation. Rosie returned, holding the fennel in her hands so Tara could examine it.

"Rosie, is this really happening? Silvie is talking to a bird, and you suddenly know plants and trees? And fully grown roses have appeared outside our door, according to some—some pattern? This is not because I struck my head, is it? Just some dizzy imagining?"

Rosie put an arm around her shoulders. "No, Mama, because we're *all* experiencing this. We all saw the bear and the flaming bird the other night. We all see the roses now."

Tara shook her head slowly, wanting to laugh and cry at the same time.

"It's like you said," Rosie continued. "The Sender is giving us courage."

"It's more than that, Rosie." Tara took a deep breath, and as she spoke the words she knew they were true. "The Sender Himself will be our Guardsman."

15

Griefs and Wonders

All three of us were still in a daze of wonder when I spread out our breakfast on the freshly cleaned table. I could not help but see how little food we had left, but I did not feel so hopeless now. We ate fennel with our cheese and dried meat, savoring the flavors. Rosie wanted to let the hawthorn leaves grow larger before we picked any.

"Mama, do you think we should stay here again tonight?" Rosie asked.

I watched Mama closely. The swollen side of her face was turning darker purple in some places. And the eye had just begun to open again. I thought of her trouble keeping to the path as we walked. She needed to rest and heal from her injuries so badly, but I was afraid she would tell us to pack up and get ready to travel again, in spite of what she needed.

"I don't know," she said. "I'm not sure what to do next."

This made me feel uneasy. Mama had always been sure.

"Do you think those rosebushes have something else to say?" I asked.

"What do you mean?" said Rosie.

"They are so firmly planted in the soil outside. Does that mean we are to stay here, or be planted here too?"

It was hard to read Mama's expression because of the swelling on her face. She appeared to be thinking. When she didn't answer me, even after a long while, I said, "Mama, why don't you lie down and rest again? Rosie and I can unpack, and we can show you what we brought."

She agreed, so we cushioned her bench bed with our pillow bags, helped her get as comfortable as she could, then unpacked the remaining bags that had been waiting on the wall hooks.

We held up things for her to see before placing them neatly on the table. Every single thing felt like an old familiar friend, and I had to blink back sudden tears.

Rosie surprised me. She had grabbed a small cook pot, for something useful, she said. And a long metal cooking spoon. "Although I wasn't thinking of cooking," she admitted. "I was thinking that I could hit someone with it if I needed to." She had also grabbed her favorite book of Nordian tales. I loved that.

I had brought all the knitting and the sewing. Every

needle, every skein of embroidery thread we owned. And all of our half-done projects. Including Papa's shirt. Mama held out her hands for the shirt and laid it on the pillow next to her. Rosie and I sorted our few belongings in an orderly way, grouping some on the table, the cook pot and the spoon by the fire, and our sewing in a bag of its own. When I glanced at Mama, she had already fallen asleep, her hand resting on Papa's shirt.

I MOTIONED to Rosie and the two of us stepped outside. Rosie flopped down on a patch of the long unruly grass, and I sat down next to her. She was waiting for me to speak, but there was so much in my mind that the words collided inside my head. I couldn't think how to begin.

"What is it?" Rosie asked. "I saw you looking through the food bag and you were frowning."

"There's not much left in there," I replied. "I thought I packed so much, but..." I shook my head slowly.

"When I think of Papa and the king and Guard-stown, I want to despair, Rosie. I want to give myself wholly to limp limbs and dire thoughts that have no future good in them. But, Rosie, how *can* I?

"A bird *talked* to me! You know things about plants that you never knew before. So we can eat them safely. Mama stitched rosebushes for a place she had never *seen* before. Think of that! And they came to life! And a huge flaming bird protected us from a bear! I mean, I mean—I don't *know* what I mean."

As I said this, the little red bird flew from a thicket of trees and landed on the ground nearby. "We're surrounded with griefs, Rosie, but we're also surrounded with wonders that lift our souls."

Rosie leaned back on her hands and looked around the clearing. "Yes. Wonders." A look of awe was on her face.

After a few moments, I asked, "Are the trees telling you something? Do they speak in voices?"

Rosie shook her head. "It's more like a sense of knowing. In an instant they become familiar to me. As if I had grown up with them. I look at one and then the next, and even though I've never seen their leaves before or the shape they make against the sky, it's like I've *always* known them. What they are. And—though this sounds strange—*who* they are."

I would never in my life have considered a tree as a *who* instead of a *what*. Until Rosie said this.

Rosie eyed the little red bird hopping around us. "The Sender must have done all this."

"Yes." I watched the red bird poke through the clumps of grass. "How do I know that this little bird is not worried at all? The forest has plenty of food, and the nest she helped build this year is the best she's ever built."

Rosie's eyes widened. "She's really telling you that?"

I held out my arm, and the bird hopped onto my sleeve, being careful with its claws. "No. And yes. It's like I've always known this bird, like you've always known the trees."

"But we *haven't* always known," said Rosie. "Only just today."

The bird hopped to the ground again, then suddenly flew up into a tree.

"What's she telling you now, Silvie?"

I stood up, brushed my skirts off, and looked in the direction of the stream. "A dog is coming. One she's seen before, but she prefers to be safe in the trees all the same."

A dog trotted awkwardly into the clearing and stopped short, studying us. It lifted its nose and cocked its russet ears. Russet spotted its dirty white coat and the tip of its tail. But I saw the ribs standing out on its sides.

"It only has three legs!" Rosie cried, in a voice filled with pity.

I walked slowly toward it. The dog tilted its head and looked at me. In his eyes I could see his story. I wasn't imagining it or making it up. The dog was telling me!

"It's a hunting dog," I said to Rosie. "His name is Tike. He was turned out from his home after he lost his leg. The master couldn't afford to keep a dog that can't hunt."

"How long has he been on his own?"

"Through the winter."

Rosie was staring at me. "Try asking him to come."

"Come here, Tike," I called gently.

The dog crossed the clearing with an awkward kind of walk, and Rosie and I reached out immediately to pet him. He was so hungry that I could feel the pain in his stomach.

"Wait here," I said to the dog. I slipped quietly indoors and felt inside our food bag. When I returned, I held out a half strip of dried meat to the dog. He snapped up the meat eagerly.

"Silvie," said Rosie. "The animals don't just understand you and you them. They also *obey* you. That bird, now this dog—they did what you said the moment you asked them to. And," she added, "you just gave it some of the last of our meat."

"I know." An idea came into my mind. It could be foolish, but who would ever believe anything that was happening to us right now.

I turned to the dog. "Do you know where there is any food *we* can eat?.... You've seen eggs? What kind of eggs?.... Chickens? Are they wild chickens without nests? We can't take eggs that belong to someone else.... All right."

I looked at Rosie. "He says the chickens are wild and they lay eggs in tufts of grass, under rocks, all over the hillside. A little wild flock. And they are not very far away. He was just going there himself."

"Are you going to go get the eggs?" Rosie looked alarmed. "You'll have to sing so I can hear you. I can't leave Mama. If she wakes up, she'd be terrified."

"I don't feel like singing, but I'll sing," I promised.

TIKE LED me around the chimney side of the station, where the forest sloped downward. He was right; the eggs weren't far. All the while I sang a song of the traveling river and everything it saw on its way to the sea. The dog never left my side. He carefully nosed out eggs for me, and after he had eaten what he needed, I had six.

When I returned, Mama woke up. She marveled over the dog and the finding of the eggs. We cooked them over the fire, one at a time, using the large flat spoon as a griddle. As soon as they cooled we ate them right off the spoon with our fingers. Tike came inside and curled up next to the fire while Rosie held the cooking spoon over the flames.

After we had eaten, we just sat together in the fire's warmth. Tike put his head on my lap and I stroked it gently. I wished for pillows and real beds and softness, and for bowls and spoons and more food, yet I felt comforted in this moment, looking at Mama and Rosie's faces in the firelight. Even looking at the way the light reflected on the rust patches of the dog's coat.

Though we didn't discuss it again, I knew we were going to stay here, in this station, for at least awhile. Then fear crept in. Fear of losing even this small moment of quiet comfort.

"Mama," I said, "the king's servants are going to find us here sometime. Maybe soon. What do we tell them?"

Mama looked thoughtful.

"I know what to say," said Rosie. "We tell them that we are tending this corner of the king's domain for the king. That we are his servants too."

Mama and I stared at her. Rosie shrugged her shoulders. "Papa always spoke of guarding the king's interests," she said. "I heard it so often that I felt we were *all* doing that anyway. So it feels natural to think that we are still guarding the king's interests, even here in these woods."

I nodded my head in agreement. Tike shifted and I waited until he had settled again before stroking his back.

Rosie poked the fire and added small branches to it, then a larger log from the stack. "Who is king now?" she asked, in a more subdued voice.

"Dallen, of course," Mama answered. "He is the Prince of the Crown. From all reports, he has all the good qualities his father had. Your papa thought highly of Dallen."

Something troubled me. "When Mago made the—the announcement in Guardstown, he didn't say anything about Dallen. Didn't Prince Dallen go to the armor fitting at Tellhaven too?"

"I thought he did," said Mama. "Perhaps he stayed in Tellhaven and wasn't in the forest."

"Then he would get the news of his father's death by messenger and could even now be on his way back to be crowned king." And Dallen too would be told Mago's lie. The thought felt like a blow.

"I've been thinking," said Rosie. "What if another Guardsman killed the king while Papa was trying to protect him?"

"That would never happen, Rosie," said Mama. "We know those men too. None of the Guardsmen would kill their king. And no one could make them want to do it. It's impossible."

"Just like it's impossible that Papa would have."

"Yes, like that."

Rosie bent a twig in her hands until it broke. "But someone *did* kill the king," she said.

"It doesn't help to think of what I'm thinking," I said, "but I can't help it." Both Mama and Rosie turned toward me.

"If Captain Hurd hadn't come down with the winter fever, *he* would have been the one to go to Tellhaven. Papa would not have had to take his place."

Mama's eyes looked so sad, I couldn't bring myself to finish. But Rosie couldn't see Mama's eyes from where she was.

"And Papa would still be alive," she said.

16

———

One Last Look

It was the morning of the People's Farewell, a Rilken tradition from beyond memory. Today the doors of Elva Castle would be opened wide from noon until sunset, so that anyone who wished could file through the candle-filled room and say goodbye to their beloved king.

Lines formed at the castle gate shortly after sunrise, and maids from the castle kitchen offered drinks and "king rolls" to those who were willing to stand for hours, waiting for the opportunity to have a last look at King Adare.

It would be Ravelin's last look too. After sunset, his father's body would be placed in his coffin and sealed there, to await his funeral several days hence. Then, after the funeral, there would be months of visits from the rulers of neighboring countries, bringing gifts of honor to the old king and gifts of honor to the new.

Today Ravelin hoped to stay in the round room and greet the people for as long as he could. He remembered doing the same when his mother had died. But then his father and brother had been with him.

Pate and Wells would accompany him today. Ravelin had other friends among the nobility, but the presence of any of them at his side would make the others jealous. So he had chosen his servant Wells, the son of a knight long dead, and Pate the Useful, whom everyone treated as a son of the castle. No one could feel ousted from a place of honor then. For in their minds, Pate and Wells would be invisible, and it would be understood that their future ruler wished to bear his sorrow alone.

Ravelin had stayed in his chambers since the day his father died, emerging only once to make his speech. So when he stepped out into the castle corridor shortly before noon, he received a shock that almost made him stumble. Six Guardsmen stood in the hallway, half-armored as they usually were, but nevertheless at rigid attention, with swords and other weapons close at hand.

He did not feel safe.

His father had always shown appreciation for the Guardsmen. Had given each a gift for every year they served him. He knew their names. Knew about their families.

Yet, one of them had decided to kill him.

Ravelin walked swiftly past the Guardsmen, and when Pate caught up to him, Ravelin spoke into his ear.

"What are they doing here? Why are they following me?"

Pate looked surprised for a moment, then his face returned to its usual light-hearted demeanor.

"That's what you pay them to do, Your Highness. That's why you train them and house them and provide them with horses and weapons. Just so they can follow you around."

Ravelin didn't respond. He knew all this, of course. But now he didn't want the Guardsmen anywhere near him. Only the palace guard. They would be enough.

Would he be allowed to send the Guardsmen away? Could he? They had taken vows to protect the sacred and inviolable person of the king. But a vow that can be broken is no vow at all.

Pate walked quickly at his side, matching him step for step, though Ravelin was four inches taller than he.

"I know this group of Guardsmen, sir. My father trained all of them. You have Drony and Lunn. Parry and Ben. Adam and Coll. I'd swear they are good men, all of them. And Drony's wife makes the most heavenly raisin cake. Every year on Gifting Day she gives whole cakes to her neighbors. My father praises the taste of it."

For just a moment, Ravelin wondered if the madman's wife had also made cakes, then he allowed Pate's words to calm him. Because now he had to focus on the Farewell. It was the last act he could do for his father before his burial, and he wanted to acquit it with dignity.

When he entered the round room, his uncle, aunt, and cousin Petronia were already there, seated in the velvet armchairs that had been placed in a row at the head of the bier for the use of the royal family. They rose when he entered and gave him solemn bows and curtseys.

Then Aunt Olivia hugged him and kissed his cheek. "Dear Ravelin, how are you?"

He didn't know how to answer this, especially with his uncle looking on, so he simply said, "I am here."

She nodded and stepped out of his way so he could take his seat. Unfortunately the Duke's chair was next to his. It had to be because he was the king's brother, but Ravelin avoided his eyes and wished him far away. Pate and Wells took up positions behind his chair. The doormen unlatched the tall, gilded doors at the far end of the room, and the first of the people came in.

Their faces were sober and sad. Many wept unashamed, men with their hats in their hands, and women wiping their eyes on their shawls. In the few moments they had to look at their former king, Ravelin studied their faces. Stricken faces, openly grieving. Strangely, this heartened him. After their moment with the king, they moved toward him and bowed, while he dipped his head in acknowledgment.

God bless you, my prince. Sender bless you. God love you, my prince.

These words or something like them were murmured continually. And the gifts—he had forgotten about the gifts. Flowers and more flowers, which Pate and Wells took for him. Gifts of wine and jars of honey. Knitted caps and scarves. They all brought things as a gift to the new king. And by tradition, the Guardsmen—yes, the Guardsmen—took it all and gave it to the poor.

The hours passed quickly, and from noon to sundown, Ravelin never left the People's Farewell. He was enthralled by the faces he saw—their respect, their sorrow. It was the faces of his people that held him in the holiness of the day.

He tried to look into the eyes of each as they spoke to him, tried to receive their homage as graciously as his father would have. By looking at them he was able to forget his uncle at his side. Too soon the sun set and the double doors at the far end of the room closed. Those who had not been able to enter, left their gifts in the hall outside.

After all the crowds, the room now felt strangely intimate. The back doors opened and the great black coffin was carried in.

Now the whole room stilled. Watching him. Waiting for him. As silent and motionless as the Guardsmen positioned by the chairs, by the doors. What would *they* be thinking at this moment?

Ravelin walked up to the bier and gazed at his father's face. He looked at the closed eyes and whispered, "I love you. And I promise I will always try to do what's right and good."

He bent and kissed his father's forehead. It was cold. His father was no longer there.

One last look. Ravelin took a deep breath, and turned away.

17

Dusk

T he sun had set. Darkness settled on the fields north of the capital city.

The bear loped along, keeping to the hedges and ditches. He ignored the dogs that barked, riled by his scent. And the people who glimpsed him as he ran. People who would take up hatchets and clubs for protection, and then urgently survey the livestock, crops, and property allotted to them.

But they would find everything unharmed.

The bear paused before entering the woods and looked back. Lanterns bobbed here and there across the shallow valley behind him. He could hear the shouts of men and the fear-filled cries of animals. Soon their alarm and concern would be just another story to tell. For everyone would find everything as it should be. Everyone.

Except one.

The bear turned and plunged into the forest.

18

———

An Interrupted Meal

"Well, I'm glad that's over! What an exhausting day." His uncle took a seat at the table in the private dining room. Six chairs used to sit around the rather large oval. Now there were only four.

Aunt Olivia caught Ravelin's eye and smiled as he took a chair at the far end from his uncle. He had come only because Olivia had wanted him to. His uncle and cousin had made no such entreaties.

Petronia seated herself in her usual chair, which was to Ravelin's right, but because of the length of the table, much more than a few feet away. She played with the spoon that had been set at her place. The look in her eye told him that she wished she were elsewhere.

That sentiment was the only thing he shared with his cousin.

She looked so much like her father. Dark hair and dark eyes, but had her mother's pale skin. She also had all of Olivia's grace of movement, but her behavior and conduct were more like the Duke's. And everyone knew that father and daughter were not the best of friends.

As the soup was served to them, Ravelin hoped there would not be much conversation tonight, that he would not have to constantly think of words that would please those gathered here. Instead, he wanted to think of the people who had loved his father. He wanted to remember their faces.

The family ate their soup in silence. No one spoke until Aunt Olivia laid down her spoon and said, "That was a beautiful tribute to Adare." Her voice was gentle. "He always had the love of his people."

"He knew how to get it too," said the Duke. His tone was not complimentary.

Ravelin lowered his spoon. He caught Olivia's eye, and she gave a slight shake of her head, as if to say, "It will do no good to reply." He looked down at his bowl. Spring onion soup. It had been one of his mother's favorites. Grief filled him and his stomach felt sick.

He stirred the soup slowly and watched the thin liquid slide over the bowl of his spoon. Again and again. The people of Rilken—those honest, open faces—had shared his sadness. Here, in a room with his closest relations, he felt horribly alone.

At least for the moment they were caught up in their own thoughts, and he had relief from his uncle's dictates. However, when the meat course was served—the mutton and pigeon and beef—his uncle seemed to come fully alert again.

"Petronia," he said, "I noticed you were holding your spoon in a different manner tonight. And now your knife?" Disapproval apparent.

Petronia raised her head and met her father's look. "I'm eating in the Ophrian style. I think it is *most* elegant. My hair is also done in the fashion of their court. My maid practiced for days and now she can do it correctly."

The Duke glanced at her head. "I noticed that. I thought your maid must have sprained her wrist." With a snort, he turned his attention to his beef.

Petronia's mouth tightened. She watched him for a moment and picked up her knife.

"They use more than just a knife and spoon in Ophria," she said, with an effort at lightness. "They also use something like a small spear with two points. It's called a balancer, and a person can eat quite prettily with it."

She looked at Ravelin. "Imagine not having to put your fingers in the plate, or having to maneuver an unreliable piece of bread. You spear your meat like this," she used the end of her spoon to demonstrate, "and then cut it with your knife, like this. What do you think, Ravelin?"

"Very elegant," he replied.

She looked to her father, but the Duke ignored her. This did not deter Petronia. She continued to eat ostentatiously in the Ophrian style and added to this by talking of the Ophrian style of dress, and how fond of music the court was. In fact, music seemed to fill the castle at Nollton. Petronia spoke of flutes at breakfast, singers in the castle gardens, and plays at night with actors and musicians.

"Oh, it's a court filled with so much—so much *life!*" Petronia looked around the table, pleading in her eyes. Ravelin felt sorry for her and didn't know how to help her.

"No doubt, they were trying to impress you, my dear," said the Duke.

"No, no, they weren't. It's like that all the time. The duchess herself is an accomplished singer. Isn't she, Mother?"

"Yes," said Olivia. "She has a beautiful soprano voice."

"And loves to have a court that will do nothing but listen to her," the Duke said, with sarcasm.

"Well, assuredly," said Petronia. "But who wouldn't want to listen to her?"

"Do you think they will listen to you in your turn, Petronia?" The Duke scowled. "You sing like a frog."

Petronia reddened at this. Olivia stared down at her plate, her knife motionless, waiting.

Finally, Petronia lifted her chin. "Maybe they will listen to me for other reasons."

Her father took a gulp of his wine. "No, they won't. They won't listen to you for any reason at all."

Petronia put down her knife, pushed her plate away, and glared at him. "How can you say that? You don't know that. You've only visited there. I've lived there for months!"

"She worked very hard when she was at their court, Allard." Olivia spoke in conciliatory tones. "You would have been proud of the way she conducted herself."

The Duke seemed not to hear this. He also stopped eating, but instead of being angry, faced Petronia with a benign expression.

The look made Ravelin uneasy. He exchanged a quick glance with Olivia. She appeared nervous too.

"I can say that, Petronia." The Duke spoke slowly and deliberately. "Because you will not be going back to Ophria. Ever again. There will be no need to."

Petronia paled. "What do you mean?" She sent an anxious look to her mother.

"I mean," said the Duke, "that you are going to stay in Rilken and marry your cousin." The Duke nodded towards Ravelin.

"I what?" Petronia raised her voice. "I *what?*"

"You will marry your cousin Ravelin."

"But I don't want to!"

"You are a royal daughter. You were born solely to be of use to the crown. It doesn't matter what you want."

Petronia sat rigidly, looking at no one, twisting her handcloth in her lap. "So now I have a new king to obey?" Her voice was small and tight. "I have to do everything Ravelin says as well as everything you say?"

"No," said Ravelin. "I have no plans for marrying at present."

"But you will," said the Duke, in a voice like fencing steel.

Ravelin did not answer.

The Duke turned back to his daughter. "You were aiming to be the bride of a future duke—a ruling duke, yes, but a duke nonetheless. Here in Rilken, you will be a queen. Although, if your cousin has his way, you won't have that honor. Princess would be the highest title you could hope for."

"That is what I already am," Petronia said angrily. "And it is a title you do not want me to use."

"Out of deference to my brother the king and his princely sons, yes, I chose to use my ducal title. But I have always been Prince Allard of Rilken. And you are Lady and Princess."

"But what does any of it matter?" Petronia spoke loudly. "Ophria is so much bigger than Rilken. And my uncle the king wanted that alliance. And I agreed with him!" She looked defiantly at her father. Ravelin was afraid for her.

The Duke's face darkened and his eyes hardened like stone. He opened his mouth, but before he could say anything, an urgent knocking sounded on the door.

Almost a pounding.

"Enter!" the Duke called out angrily.

The door opened, and a footman stepped into the room. He bowed to Ravelin and then to the Duke. "Your Majesty, Your Highnesses, please pardon the interruption, but an important message has just come for Duke Allard."

"Well, hand it to me, man, and be off," said the Duke.

The footman hesitated. "It is your steward who begs to speak with you."

"Then send him in. He may speak openly here. I hide nothing from my *king*."

Ravelin's face grew hot at this mockery. He laid down his knife and spoon and considered leaving. But the message that had come seemed important. And it could have something to do with Dallen.

The steward entered, brown-cloaked and brown-bearded. He grabbed his hat from his head and bowed deeply.

The Duke got to his feet, scowling. "Maynard, what are you doing here? Why have you left the manor to interrupt my dinner?"

The steward hesitated, looking from Ravelin to the Duke. Ravelin motioned for him to come closer. This was the man that controlled the large properties his uncle had north of Elva. Yet, his demeanor did not show him to be the proud overseer, second to few in Rilken. Instead, Maynard looked like he was gathering courage to say something.

"Your Highness—"

"Yes," snapped the Duke, "what *is* it?"

"I have the unfortunate duty of telling you that your manor has been, has been—not attacked—but, well, things have been marred. Defaced. Ruined. And, yes, insulted. That is what happened. I came to tell you that your manor has been insulted."

The Duke threw his handcloth on the table and approached the steward. "What are you babbling about, man? Tell me plainly what has happened, or I'll replace you!"

The steward steadied himself. "The rows of carved columns at either side of the grand entrance to the manor have been slashed, repeatedly. The woodwork outside the manor has been thoroughly defaced. Not a piece of carving has escaped. The iron gates at the head of the drive have been twisted off their pivots." He stopped abruptly, staring at his lord.

The Duke's look was fierce enough to wither any man.

"Who *dared* to do this?!" cried the Duke.

"It was—it appears to be— it must have been—"

"Who?!" the Duke roared.

Maynard took one step back. "A bear, sir."

An extraordinary change came over the Duke's face. The anger, the boldness, the fierce command that was his uncle, melted away. It wasn't that he paled—that would have been impossible for a man of his disposition. It was that something in him suddenly...evaporated. Ravelin stared at him.

The steward, too, waited for the Duke's response. "And—" The man glanced at the Duke, looking for permission to continue. The Duke remained motionless.

"And there was a large—well, *very* large—pile of bear droppings outside your study window, sir."

"Bear droppings?" It was Olivia who answered him.

"Yes, ma'am," he replied, bowing to her. "The head gamekeeper says they were unmistakable."

Ravelin's eyes were drawn to the silver salt cellar that

had been placed on the tabletop near his plate. This cellar was in the shape of a bear. But that was not unusual. Bears filled Rilken's folk tales. Bears had been woven into tapestries by Rilken's artisans. A small bear head was even part of his father's coat of arms. And yet, recently bears had been so frightening—had attacked—on the forest road. He picked up the silver bear and looked at it closely.

"Was anything else destroyed, Maynard?" Olivia spoke in a voice meant to calm.

The man looked to her with relief. "No, ma'am. No more than what I have told you. In daylight we will be able to search more thoroughly, but lantern light showed us this much."

The Duke finally found his voice. "And no one saw this—this *fiend?* Not a single person? And he had the leisure to destroy all these things while you were sitting around and doing what?"

Maynard lowered his head. "No one saw him, sir. I was in the records room going over the accounts, when one of the men came in and said he saw a strange shadow run from the manor across the fields. It was heading toward the woods and set all the dogs to barking. So the gamekeeper and his men and the house guards took lanterns and went out to look. They found what I have reported to you."

"Could this have been done by the bears you were telling me about, Uncle?" asked Ravelin. "The ones you said were not natural to this world?"

The Duke shuddered once, then strode from the room.

"Mago!" he bellowed as he went. "Get me Mago!"

The steward remained standing awkwardly where he was until Ravelin gave him a nod. He bowed quickly in response, then followed the Duke out.

The horrible family dinner was over. What Ravelin remembered most about its ending was not Olivia covering her face with her hands. Or Petronia's mocking bow to him when she left. But the look on his uncle's face when he first understood that the attack had been made by a bear.

A look Ravelin had never seen on him before. A look that told him his uncle was afraid. No. Not afraid.

Terrified.

19

A Stranger in the Woods

Morning dawned over the hunting station and with it came all the concerns of the day. Mere handfuls of food remained in our bags, and Mama seemed exhausted. Too tired to get up or move much from her bed, hard and uncomfortable though it was. I felt more and more that it must have been a miracle she had been able to walk so far through the woods. Maybe now she could begin to heal. Really heal. She always told us that good rest brings healing just like good work brings joy. But, still, what were we to do?

Tike helped me find more eggs, and we cooked them over the fire as we had done before. Again I took Rosie outside to talk while Mama slept. The minute we stepped out the door, a worried look appeared on Rosie's face.

"We won't have any food but forest food tomorrow, Silvie, and Mama just sleeps."

"She won't always sleep, Rosie, but she does now because she needs it now."

I looked at the trees surrounding us, at the light blue spring sky above, and listened to the chirping of the birds. "I think we are to use the gifts the Sender gave us. That's what he must have meant for us to do."

"Then I'll plant a garden," said Rosie impulsively. "I can use the fire tools to prepare the ground and gather wild plants and bring them here. It won't provide food right away, but over time it will."

"And I can search out the animals and learn about the forest from them," I said. A thought struck me. "The river! Rosie, could we make some sort of net to fish with? There must be fish in the river."

Her eyes lit up. "Let me hunt through the under-growth. I'll see what I can come up with." She moved off quickly with her usual eagerness.

Something like a white flag waved from a tree branch a little way into the woods. I moved cautiously forward to look. A squirrel was flicking its tail rapidly. Not just any squirrel. This one was completely white from the top of its pale pink nose to the dusty white of its tail. And it was watching me approach.

"Well met, friend," I said quietly. "We will not hurt you. Neither this dog, nor I. His name is Tike."

The tail slowed. The squirrel scrambled down to a thicker branch and stood up on its hind feet to look at me. We gazed into each other's eyes, and somehow, like with the red bird and with Tike, I knew her. In her eyes I saw her family, her tree home, the acorns and nuts she had buried in the winter, her ability for speed, and her quick understanding.

Knowing her brought a sense of restfulness. This little squirrel was so far removed from the pain of Elva, so unaffected by it. Her life was of the forest and the stability of the trees. Suddenly I became aware of more squirrels, of mice, foxes, and rabbits. Of one doe about twenty paces distant. Of larger birds circling high above and dozens of smaller birds scattered through the finger limbs of the trees. The animals were aware of me too, and yet, they weren't afraid of me. Was this also part of the Sender's gift?

"Rosie, do you see this squirrel?" I turned my head. "Rosie?" The clearing was empty. She must be browsing and gathering materials for a fish net.

I turned all the way around, scanning the trees. No brilliant red hair stood out in any direction, which surprised me. My sister's hair stands out in a crowd; I should be able to see it in a predominantly brown forest.

She couldn't have gone far. But I had no idea how long I had been standing there, my thoughts wholly on the animals.

Fear threatened instantly. Fear of losing my sister. I took a deep breath and swallowed it down. The squirrel was watching me with a curious eye. I tried to speak calmly.

"Did you see the red-haired girl who was here with

me? Do you know where she went? Could you find her and call to me when you do?"

Like a streak of white, the squirrel scrambled up the tree and jumped to the next one. I saw it leap from branch to branch and tree to tree, pausing before each determined spring, leaving branches shaking wildly as it passed.

Tike nudged my leg. We stepped out into the clearing, and I stroked his back while we waited. Suddenly, a wild chittering came from behind the chimney side of the hunting station, where the land sloped downward. I hurried toward it, Tike at my heels.

Rosie came through the trees, her hands full of twigs and plant stems. "What is going on with that squirrel? It scared me half to death! And now it's herding me like I'm a lost sheep or something."

Relief flooded me. "The squirrel found you for me. I couldn't see you, so I sent her to find you and she did!"

The white squirrel returned and was watching us. Rosie's exasperation changed into curious interest. She looked at the squirrel closely.

"Thank you, squirrel," I said, putting my arm around Rosie. "This is my sister. She has to gather plants for nets and a garden all over the woods. Would you watch out for her? You and your family? If she gets lost, bring her right back here. Will you do this?"

The squirrel waved its tail twice and gave a trio of deep chirrups.

"Oh, thank you!" I cried.

Rosie stared at me, a puzzled look on her face. "What just happened?"

"You now have a bodyguard," I said proudly. "And—she loves your hair!"

I saw the look on Rosie's face, and it heartened me. If we hadn't been moving in such sorrow, my sister would have laughed out loud.

THE BEAR HAD EXPECTED THIS. Men wearing the Duke's colors combed through the woods, armed with useless spears, carrying useless arrows.

But there were so many.

They were accompanied by a dozen or more Rilken dwarf spies. Men who by nature walked low to the ground and could find tracks and signs that other men missed. The dwarf spies also had keener sight and a keener sense of smell than other men.

The bear did not fear them. He did not fear any man. But he had no wish to fight with any of them.

So he ran to the west, deeper into the greenwood. Without thought or purpose beyond running.

ROSIE at last had enough stems and winter-killed brush to make an attempt at weaving some sort of net. She sat on the doorstep of the station between the rosebushes with a pile in front of her. The white squirrel sat on the ground not far away, watching her.

"Do you want my help?" I asked.

"Not yet," she said, bending a young tree shoot she

had uprooted into an oval shape. "I'm going to test the strength of some of these first. If they break the minute they feel the current of the river, the net will be of no use to us."

"I'd like to see where that path leads." I pointed to the side of the clearing away from the river, where the land fell away and the opening of a path beckoned. "I won't go far. I'll take Tike and stay on the path. If you think I've been gone too long, whistle and the squirrel will come get me. If I need you, I'll have Tike bark. But who knows? Maybe that path will lead us to food too."

Rosie looked toward the path. "All right. Don't be gone long."

"I won't."

I crossed the clearing, Tike following with his limping walk, and looked down the slope. The path was broad enough for two people to walk together, which meant it was a path that expected to be used. The packed earth led downward, then turned at a sharp angle to go down again, weaving its way down the side of the forested hill.

A sound came from Tike's throat, and I looked closely at him. "There are people down there?" I wanted to see who and what they were. I waved at Rosie and started down.

I walked slowly for Tike's sake and came to the place where the path turned back on itself. There in the middle of the next length down, stood a rabbit—a large, brown rabbit who didn't want to be seen by me. But not for the usual reasons that rabbits hide from humans.

"Stop," I said, before it could disappear into the underbrush.

It stopped, with overwhelming reluctance. Tike nudged my hand and I felt the damp of his nose on my fingers. Something about this animal made Tike seek comfort.

The rabbit hid its eyes from me. But that didn't matter. Because of the Sender's gift, I knew what the animal didn't want to reveal. That blood was often in its claws and teeth. And that it liked hearing the painful cries of other rabbits.

"You will not harm another living thing ever again."

It shuddered at this, as if trying to cast my words away.

"You will not," I repeated, firmly. "Now leave this region and seek your food elsewhere, so the rabbits here don't have to live in fear of you."

The rabbit darted off the path at once and scurried down between the trees until it was out of sight.

I took a deep breath and considered what this meant. Animals, like the little red bird, the white squirrel, and Tike had obeyed me gladly. This rabbit had obeyed me too, even though he preferred to live his life of malice.

I walked on, lost in thought, as the path wound its way down the side of the hill. I felt the enormous responsibility of one who has to be obeyed, and it scared me. *Sender, give me wisdom!*

At the next turn of the path, I caught sight of something below us. I crouched down to peer through the trees. It appeared to be a good-sized inn. Smaller than the one we passed on the west road, but busy enough.

Smoke poured from the chimneys all down the line of the long building. I could see stables off to the side and a scattering of small buildings behind. A chicken coop. A large outdoor washing tub. And people. A woman stirred something in the tub with a long wooden paddle. A man led a horse out of the stables, followed by a boy.

I heard a rumbling in Tike's chest and rubbed his head immediately.

"I will not let that boy throw rocks at you again. We won't go any farther today, but thank you for showing this to me."

A brindled cat crept up the hill toward us.

"Are you from the inn?" I asked. The question wasn't strictly necessary, because I could sense that she wasn't. She had been on her own for several years, but remembered a life among people and missed it.

"You can come back with us if you want to," I said. "My mama loves cats."

Tike and I started up the hillside, and when I looked back, the cat was following us.

When I came out into the clearing again, Mama was sitting outside on a chair watching Rosie weave her net. The weaving didn't seem to be going well and Rosie looked frustrated. The cat immediately jumped up on Mama's lap and settled herself there.

"Where did you find this cat, Silvie?" Mama sounded pleased as she stroked the soft fur.

"She found us on the side of the hill, and it looks like she's happy she did."

I sat down on the grass by Mama's side, plucked a blade of it, and pulled it through my fingers. "There's a large inn at the bottom of the hill path," I said. "Maybe we could buy bread there." Rosie glanced up at this, a hopeful look in her eye.

"I'm sure we could," said Mama. "I can't think of an inn that wouldn't sell bread to a traveler."

"Could we work there?" asked Rosie. "Silvie and I could find paying work until you are well, Mama."

"We don't know what kind of place it is," Mama answered. "Or what kind of people they are. We'll need to find that out first. And it would be best to ask for work one at a time. If they are not sure about us, they would more quickly refuse three people than one."

"If *I* can work there," Mama continued, "I could learn of the place and then suggest your help. But only if we need to. My work might be enough for us. I would rather you two stay here."

I wasn't sure what I thought of this plan, at first. Then I realized that Mama was starting to sound like herself again. With relief, I reached up and patted her knee. "How are you feeling now?"

"A little less tired. Maybe tomorrow afternoon I can visit the inn."

Mama saw the concern on my face. "But only after I wash my hair and face," she said, "and you girls help me look as presentable as possible."

Rosie put down her half-woven net and leaned back on her hands. "We can do that, Mama."

"There's a place on the path where we can see the inn easily," I said. "We could wait for you and watch for you there."

I was about to ask what kind of work Mama was hoping to get, when Tike began to growl. The cat got to her feet, jumped down, and arched her back. The white squirrel leapt onto Rosie's shoulder, taking her by surprise.

"They smell bear," I said.

I stood up and peered through the trees across the clearing. "Where is it coming from?" I called.

A frenzied chirping came in reply.

"From the stream," I told Mama and Rosie.

"We don't need to be alarmed this time," said Rosie, getting to her feet. "Because it will obey you, like all the other animals. It will, won't it?"

I thought of the rabbit on the path. "I think so," I said slowly. "I think because of the Sender it might have to." I took a few steps away from the station in the direction of the stream.

"Mama, go back inside," I said over my shoulder.

"If you are out here, I am out here," came the firm reply.

I took a few more steps and waited. White Squirrel called to her family. Redbird called to her friends. A chorus of squirrel chirps and bird calls told me exactly where the animal was. Tike stood close by my side.

I heard the crackling of brush. Something large, something powerful, pushed through the undergrowth. Then the beast emerged into the clearing. I instinctively stepped back and wished for my father, for his presence, his shield and his spear.

The beast was the color of tree trunks and larger than I could have imagined. Much larger than the bear who had challenged us on the river at night. It stood on all fours, motionless for a moment, then lifted its great head and regarded me.

"What is it telling you?" Rosie called softly from behind me.

I reached for Tike with my fingertips, steadying myself with the touch of his back while my thoughts whirled. Every animal I had met after the Sender's gift, I had known at once. Had understood at once. Had seen with eyes more than my own.

Not this one.

I studied it, waiting for some sort of understanding to come.

This animal made me feel blind.

Moments passed and still we stood. I stared at the bear's eyes, trying with all my might to see what was inside them, but I could not. No story came to me. No awareness. Nothing I could comprehend. *Sender, what does this mean?*

"Silvie," Rosie's voice sounded nervous behind me. "What's wrong?"

Understanding came, but it brought no comfort. Without taking my eyes from the animal, I answered her.

"This is not a bear."

. . .

Rosie gasped and I doubted myself. Was I losing my mind? The great animal *clearly* was a bear. It had bear fur, a bear build, and bear claws. And that shaggy head, and those teeth! But then—a real bear would be revealed to me by the Sender's gift.

So what was this—or *who* was this?

Rosie appeared at my side holding a fire iron. I was barely aware of her. The bear looked directly at me, with sorrowful eyes. My chest tightened. I had to say something, but I didn't know what to say.

"If you are looking for food," I called, "I'm sorry that we have none to give you. We have barely any left for ourselves except for wild plants. And the forest has enough of those for you and for us."

The bear moved its head from side to side, sniffing the air. Was this its way of studying us? Then it turned and ambled down the path toward the stream until its hind end disappeared through the trees.

I felt a strange sense of loss.

20

The Errand of Pate the Useful

It was late afternoon, the day after the People's Farewell, when Pate the Useful left the castle, wrapping his cloak around him for protection against the cold spring wind, and made his way down into the streets of Guardstown. He knew the streets well and did not have far to go before he stopped to knock on a dark red door, then, turning the handle, went inside.

A woman hurried briskly down the hallway toward him. "Pate!" she exclaimed.

"I got away as soon as I could, Mother."

She hugged him tightly. "It's good medicine to see you."

"Would that I could cure all that ails us," he replied, as he hugged her in kind.

"Pate—your father—he's never been so low before. It's beyond grief, Pate."

"I can understand that. It's the death of two things he spent his life loving and protecting. His king and his Guardsmen."

"It's exactly that. How are things with the prince?"

He gave a sad smile. "Exactly what you would expect."

She nodded soberly. "Poor boy. Poor, poor boy. Is there still no news of Dallen?"

"None."

"And Avelyn? How is she?"

"I haven't been able to see her for days. She's hard at work on the new mural in the hallway with the other artists."

"Give her my greeting when you see her."

His mother had a special light in her eyes when she spoke of Avelyn. A light that went straight to his own heart. "I will, Mother. Thank you. Is Father upstairs?"

"In his room. I'm so glad you've come. He could use a good talk with you."

Pate took the stairs two at a time, but slowed before knocking on his father's door. A voice called out, "Come!"

His father was sitting in his wood-carved armchair by the window, looking out over the streets of Guardstown. His white hair was neatly combed, his white beard well-trimmed, but his face and eyes were those of a man in the midst of a great sorrow.

"I saw you coming down the street."

"I thought you would," said Pate, taking off his cloak

and tossing it over another chair. He grabbed his preferred stool and placed it near the window next to his father. Now they could both watch the streets together.

"You had more than your usual purpose in your step."

Pate nodded. "I did. I come with a commission for you from our new monarch."

A wry look came over the weathered face. "And what would the Duke of Elva want with me?"

"Ah. Interesting response that, Father. I actually came from your true ruler, from Prince Ravelin."

His father's look softened.

"But before I tell you what he wanted, I need to tell you why. Our new and already beloved ruler is trapped like a hunted animal. He faces daily coercion from his uncle to believe and behave as if Dallen were dead. His uncle has charged the tutor Kendall with continuing the pressure whenever the Duke can't coerce in person. Ravelin cannot give up hope for Dallen, so he stays in his room, refusing the tutor whenever he can."

"He doesn't have to stay in his room, a strong, young man like he is."

"But he does," said Pate, more soberly. "His grief is heavy upon him. And, even if he would leave his room, he can't. Because outside his room, stand six of the King's Guardsmen. And Ravelin is terrified of them."

A look of pain filled his father's eyes, and Pate knew the reason why.

His father turned to the window, and his gaze seemed to search for something far beyond the rooftops.

"For eighty years the Guardsmen have protected their monarchs," he said, quietly. "Eighty faithful years. Whether they were the King's Guardsmen or the Queen's, they have spent their lives in training, in sacrifice, in watchfulness, in devotion. Not one ruler was ever successfully attacked when the Guardsmen were near. Until..."

Pate's eyes were instinctively drawn to his father's left hand. Three fingers remained of the five. Evidence of the sacrifice one Guardsman had made to protect the king he served. And this comfortable home was evidence of the gratitude that King Adare, at the time just a little older than Dallen, had felt toward the man who preserved his life.

The look on his father's face showed that he wasn't seeing the streets of Guardstown. In his mind he was on the forest road, imagining every angle, every possibility, every move that armed men could or should have made, and feeling the anger of ignorance and helplessness.

"Do you see how it could have been done, Father?"

"I go over it and over it in my mind, Pate, and I can't. I heard what Mago said on the street that day. No one could help but hear it. That one Guardsman somehow defeated five of his comrades and killed the king? It cannot happen. Because of training, the instincts of one of them, are the same as the instincts of all of them. I could stretch my imagination to accept that one Guardsman could fool another one. But not five. *Never five.*"

Pate leaned back on his stool and grabbed one knee for balance. "I've been thinking. If it all took place the way Mago said it did, this man, Bevan, was it? He must have had help of some kind. What if this crime had been planned for years? What if this man had been carefully selected, by, if not some renegade recruiter, by someone outside of the Guardsmen? Some noble perhaps, who put pressure on a recruiter..." His voice trailed off, because his father was already shaking his head vigorously.

"No, Pate. That too is impossible."

Pate tried not to show irritation at his father's fervent belief in the Guardsman system. "How can you know that? You don't think that could happen either?"

"I'm not saying it *couldn't* happen. I'm saying it *didn't*. Make no mistake. I know the material men are made of. Many of them are corruptible. But in this case, no. It was not the recruiter."

"You're sure?"

His father nodded slowly. "Because I recruited him myself. I'm the one who found Bevan in his eastern farm village. His gifts of physicality, speed, and accuracy were already apparent. And he was known among his people for his loyalty and integrity. His young wife was just the kind of woman for Guardstown too. Smart, sensible, and as true as her husband. I sponsored his training myself. He passed the final tests with ease."

The old man stared out the window again. "If I had been on the street that day, I would have been tempted to call Mago a liar."

Pate was glad his father hadn't been. Though his father still had much of his strength and the keen sight that had once made him a superior Guardsman, Mago was something else. Mago was the kind of fierce soldier that bad mothers told their children stories about, to threaten them into obedience. And give them nightmares.

"She did though."

The words confused Pate for a moment, and he tried to think of what his father could mean. "Who did? Who did what?"

"The man's wife. Bevan's wife. She stood up to Mago and called him a liar in front of everyone."

Pate leaned forward, aghast. "What did he do?"

His father met his gaze. "He struck her down in the middle of the street, and after he paraded away, no one came to help her. By the time I got down the street, her daughters had managed to get her inside."

Moisture grew in his father's eyes. "Shame upon shame has come to the Guardsmen this week. Deaths. Accusations. And then for Guardsmen to stand idly by while a palace guard nearly kills one of our own..." He bent his head and wiped his face with his hand.

When he raised his head again, anger was in his eyes. "Since when does the palace guard *dare* claim authority over the Guardsmen? We should have handled it! But that was taken away from us, and now, not only are the Guardsmen suspicious of each other, they have lost their courage. And they have been shamed and accused before the whole country."

He rubbed his face fiercely. "Prince Ravelin did not even come to their burial. So these good men who lost their lives were placed in the ground without the honor and blessing of their sovereign."

Pate cleared his throat. "Ravelin did not come because he is afraid that another Guardsman is waiting for opportunity to kill him." His father's piercing blue eyes were on him. "The Duke has been telling him that Bevan killed both his father and brother. Ravelin believes he is next. He sees his own death in the tips of their spears, on the points of every dagger."

His father was listening closely.

"Which brings us back to his commission. It would ease our prince's mind greatly if you and I would accompany him when he must leave the castle. Be right at his side. I think he might accept the presence of the Guardsmen if you and I were there too. He said he will trust the man who saved his father's life once."

His father looked out the window again as if he were looking back into memory. "*I am valor for my Valor, the King...*" he whispered.

"Will you come, Father, for Ravelin's sake?"

"Yes." His voice was firm now. "And for the sake of the Guardsmen, too."

Pate got up from the stool and reached for his cloak. "What finally happened to the man's wife and daughters?"

"They were forced from their home, put in a prisoner's cart, and taken to the city gates. Exiled from Elva. And as they left, young thugs threw mud at them. Afterwards, their house was plundered. Beds, cupboards, clothing, dishes—people took whatever they wanted. I have never seen the people of Guardstown act so disgracefully."

The words wrung Pate's heart. After a long silence,

he shook himself and reached for his cloak. "I must get back to the castle, but I will see you there tomorrow, Father, and together we will work to lift that disgrace."

"Wait." His father looked up at him. "You know, Pate, you've never fooled me for a moment. I know you never took to the tools of my trade. Never cared for arrows and swords and marksmanship. You had your own tools, your words and your wit. But you have always had the watchful gift. The eye of the Guardsman. Ever since you were a little pup. "

He got to his feet and came over to Pate, resting his hands on Pate's shoulders. Pate felt the strong weight of them, and the keenness of his father's penetrating gaze.

"The castle is swimming with lies right now and wisdom will be your only protection. My son, take great care. As watchful as you are, know that others are watching you. I give you the advice I would give a new Guardsman. *Never look where the enemy wants you to look.* Do you understand? Never."

"Yes, Father. I understand."

"Take great care, son," he said again.

"Yes, Father."

The strong hands tightened on his shoulders for one moment, then Pate went down the stairs and out into the street, full of thoughts.

21
___

The Smell of Fish

"I think," said Mama, "that until we know more about this animal, we better stay inside." We returned to the station, shuttered the windows, and pushed the table in front of the door.

"It's not enough to keep such a great bear out if he really wants to get in," said Rosie.

"We do what we can do," said Mama, wedging a bench against a table leg.

The shuttered windows made the room dark, so we naturally drew near the fire. Mama sat on the chair. Since we had used all the benches to brace the table, I sat on the floor. Rosie, like always, worked to arrange the fire until it was just the way she wanted it. When she finished, she sat on the floor next to me.

"So, what do we do now?" she asked.

"I don't know," I replied.

"Do you think he will come back, Silvie?" said Mama.

They were both looking at me, thinking I might know something they didn't.

"He's not a real bear," I said. "If he were, I would know who he was, which would give me some idea of what he might do. But..." I shook my head slowly. "I can't even guess."

I kept thinking of the bear's eyes. What had I seen in them? Had I seen darkness—that horrible darkness that stole from the world's light?

No. Not that.

Emptiness? No, something was definitely present there. Something impassably present.

The only thing I was sure of was that I had witnessed great sorrow and great strength combined.

Should we be afraid of this bear? Somehow, I couldn't bring myself to fear it. At the same time, I felt that wisdom would wait. And watch.

"How long do we stay inside?" asked Rosie.

"Redbird said she would tell us when the bear was safely far away."

"What a help it is to have animal spies," Rosie replied.

"Yes," I agreed. But I was distracted, thinking about the bear. I had not told it to leave the clearing. I had not told it to do anything. It left of its own accord.

The three of us, standing with a dog and a squirrel— oh, yes, and Rosie's fire iron—had not frightened it away. Frightening this beast would be almost impossible. No, it left because it wanted to. There could be no other reason. *But why had it come?*

We sat there listening, waiting for a long time. I opened the shutter once to hear Redbird say that the bear was still at the stream. It had been at the stream for a good while. The waiting was becoming tedious.

"Silvie, would you read to us?" Mama asked. "It would help to pass the time."

Rosie had been peeking through a narrow crack in the shuttered window at the far end of the room. At Mama's request, she searched through one of the hanging bags and pulled out the book she brought from home and handed it to me. *Tales from Nordia.*

I turned the pages. "Which do you want to hear?" I said absently, my mind still on the bear at the stream. "*The Host of the North. Isle of the Kings. The End of Winter. Orphan Lost—*"

"That one," said Rosie. "*Orphan Lost.*"

I moved nearer the fire and tilted the open book to catch the firelight. It would be so much easier to see the page if we unshuttered at least half a window. But what if I was wrong about the beast?

The thought of its head and shoulders pushing through the opening made me glad enough to sit in the dark. Yet, the feeling of being imprisoned was oppressive. I took a deep breath and forced myself to concentrate on the words on the page. "*Orphan Lost.*

"*In a country to the west of Nordia, there lived a troubled man. His father, on oath, had promised that one of his sons would marry the only daughter of his cousin. No one knew why the father had made such an oath, for he distrusted the cousin, and the cousin's family was coarse in manner, coarse in heart, and coarse in deed.*

"One by one the young man's older brothers married the women they chose, until the youngest brother was the only one left to fulfill his father's oath.

"'You must,' the older ones insisted. 'Else our cousin will use secret means to ruin our whole family and you will never escape in the end.'

"So the young man was engaged to the cousin's daughter. Every moment he spent in her company was wretched. For it did not take long to find that she was a spiteful, vindictive woman. She ranted and raved about everyone who had wronged her, and took no delight in anything, but stirring up strife. And though she was only nineteen, she was angry at all the older brothers for not choosing her, and angry at this last for his reluctance.

"All peace left the young man's soul. He was duty-bound to marry a woman who hated him, and he dreaded the approach of his wedding day as his final doom.

"Now a certain earl had done great service for the king of Falland. The king rewarded him by making him overlord of a large area of land. The young man's mother had left him some property in what was now the earl's domain. As the earl wanted to meet the landholders under him, the young man journeyed south and was cordially received by the earl on his own estate.

"The earl took a liking to the young man, approving of his interests, character, and temperament, and decided he would be the perfect groom for his young ward—a gentle girl with weak lungs, but a kind and lively heart."

Vaguely, I heard the sound of birds, but I was deep into my favorite part of the story.

"The earl asked the king's permission for the marriage, and—as the will of a king surpasses the claims of a cousin— the two were happily wed. The young man could not believe his good fortune. But the angry cousin came to the wedding and cast dark looks all around—"

Whump!

I startled. The book fell from my hand.

"That was at the door," Mama said.

The cat leapt from her lap and went to the door, nose in the air. There was no mistaking the meaning of her meow. Tike got to his feet and barked. I could barely believe it.

"They smell fish," I said.

"Fish??" Rosie and Mama cried together.

"Fish." I got to my feet, went to the window, and put my hand on the shutter. "Red?" I called through the crack. "Where is the bear?"

A series of chirps sounded, and I spoke their meaning out loud. "It's on the far side of the clearing, watching the station from the edge of the trees."

More chirps. *What?*

"The bear brought the fish to our door!"

Rosie reached for the shutter. "Let's open it just a little and see."

"Just a little," added Mama, quickly.

I peered out. The bear was standing under the first of the trees directly across from the hunting station. Its nose was lifted, reading messages from the air. The brindled cat put a paw on the door and meowed loudly. Tike barked again. I wasn't sure what to do.

"I think the bear is trying to show us that he's not a threat. Didn't Papa say something like that? If someone gave you room and had no weapon? Do you think he's staying back on purpose?"

"We can move the table," said Rosie, "then open the door and grab that fish before the bear can charge across the clearing."

I studied the bear without responding.

Rosie began to pull the bracing benches away from the table. "I'm so hungry." After hesitating a few moments, Mama helped her.

"We'll do it quickly, Silvie," Rosie said as they shoved the table away from the door. "You keep your eye on that bear. Or whatever it is." She reached for the door handle.

"Wait!" I took one last look out the window. "Rosie, you grab the fish. I want to talk to the bear."

"All right," said Rosie.

"Don't go far from the doorway, Silvie," said Mama. "Papa also said to always have your escape ready. We'll shove this table against the door again if the bear begins to move toward you."

A table and a door would be nothing against this bear, but I did not argue. If the bear had wanted to attack us, it would have already done so. But Mama and Rosie were truly scared, so I agreed to their plan.

Mama took up a position by the table edge. Rosie crouched down on the side of the doorway.

"Animals, stay back," I ordered. "Out of the way."

Tike and the cat retreated, but they were tense and alert. The white squirrel stayed near Rosie.

"Okay, then." I took a deep breath and opened the door.

I STEPPED through the doorway keeping my eyes on the bear. Rosie snatched quickly at the fish on the threshold.

The bear shifted the weight on its front feet, first to one, then the other, and back again. Its head turned slightly from side to side. It was studying me. Us. The whole hunting station. I was sure of it.

I felt an overwhelming desire to talk to it. The long claws on its paws made trust impossible. But, it had understood me before when I said we didn't have food. Why else would it have brought the fish? If only I could understand it.

"Did you bring the fish?" I called, knowing, of course, that it had.

The bear held perfectly still. A flicker of red moved from one tree to the next, high up in the branches above the bear.

"Are you baiting us?" I asked.

The bear turned its head to the side.

Was that a no? Half a no?

"Can you understand me? The things I say? Because why did you bring the fish unless you knew we were hungry?"

The bear began to move, but not toward me. Back and forth. Four steps in one direction, then wheeling around to take the same amount of steps in the other direction. Like the pacing of a frustrated human. Back and forth. Forward and back.

"Thank you for the fish," I said, making sure my words could carry across the clearing. "Thank you."

The bear growled. Or half-growled. A rumble, a throat-clearing. Words formed in the air, and goosebumps rose on my arms.

"You're welcome," it said.

Rosie had been hovering just inside the doorway. At this, she gasped.

"Silvie!" she whispered excitedly. "Even *I* heard that!"

"You can understand me?" I cried. "You have understood everything I've said?"

This time the bear clearly nodded its head. My heart leapt.

It stopped pacing and faced me again. "Who are you?" it said.

I hesitated. "A family. Who are you?"

"A bear."

"I think you are more than that."

The bear ignored this. "What are you doing here? Are you from the inn?" Each word came low and steady. "Inn people cannot come into the king's domain."

"We came from Elva. We are caretakers of this hunting station, keeping it for King Adare, I mean, King Dallen. Why did you bring the fish?"

The bear's head drooped for a moment, then it lifted. "As you said, you were hungry. Did you plant the roses? They weren't here before."

"We didn't plant them. The Sender did."

"Why?"

"Mama prayed and the flowers appeared."

"Your mother prayed for flowers?"

It felt *so* absurd. Having a conversation with a bear who was not a bear about flowers which were not normal flowers. Beyond strange. But I kept on.

"No. The Sender sent the flowers because he is our Guardsman."

The bear had started to pace again, but at this it stopped abruptly. It looked uncertain for a moment.

"Tell me who you are," I said. I took several steps farther into the clearing.

"I'm a bear."

"If you were, I would know."

"I am a bear."

"Now the bear *is* baiting me. All right, then."

I surveyed the woods, and my eye seized on a pair of pointed ears and a pointed black nose. "Fox, come!" I cried.

Immediately a tawny fox ran into the clearing and up to my side.

"Weasel, come! Rabbit, come! Hawk, come!" I had never called animals like this before, but I felt the bear's challenge.

Instantly, the animals emerged from the woods and hurried toward me. A hawk swooped from the sky and dropped to the ground nearby, giving no attention to the rabbit.

I looked across the clearing and took a deep breath. "Bear, come!"

It did not move.

"The gift the Sender has given me includes all animals, but somehow not you. Why?"

It looked away, swinging its large muzzle, then looked back at me. I gazed into its eyes. I could not understand the beast like these animals at my feet, but whatever it was, the eyes told of great pain. Sorrow broke over me like a wave. And with it came the answer.

"You are a man in the form of a bear, are you not?"

The answer came with reluctance and—*did I just imagine it*—relief. "Yes."

Before I could reply, the bear swung around and disappeared into the woods.

22

———————

What the Hunters Found

Ravelin stepped out of his apartments on the morning of his father's funeral, dressed formally in the royal green-on-green. Guardsmen stood in the hall as usual, but Pate's father was in front of them, and Pate was at his side.

The company of them went down the dark marble steps that emptied into the great hall. His uncle was waiting there next to a long oak table, his hand resting on the lid of a wooden box. He motioned Ravelin over and spoke close into his ear.

"The hunters found something last night. They believe it belongs to Dallen." He thrust the box into Ravelin's hands.

Ravelin stared at it a moment, then lifted the lid.

Inside, curled and torn, lay a bloodied glove. Dallen's glove. He knew it was Dallen's, because he had a pair just like it.

"Of course," his uncle went on, "you'll insist that the finding of this doesn't prove anything one way or another—whether Dallen is alive or dead. Perhaps he cast aside his own glove before he met his end—"

His uncle's lips kept moving, but Ravelin could no longer attend to his words. Trembling began deep inside his bones, a trembling he could not control and feared to show.

"Still," his uncle was saying, "we can have a funeral for Dallen whenever you are ready. It would be the proper thing to do for a brother."

Ravelin nodded, or thought he did. His uncle took the box away from him and returned it to the table. Ravelin stared at the box, seeing its grisly contents through the walls, until Pate touched his arm and quietly said, "Your Highness, it is time to go."

Ravelin came to himself and looked around. Aunt Olivia and Petronia stood in the center of the hall waiting for him. Petronia looked sullen. His uncle had gone as far as the door and turned back with impatience. From somewhere came energy enough to move. Ravelin walked through the hall and out the doorway without looking at any of them again.

He rode his horse through the streets of Elva, following the long cart draped in green velvet that carried his father's coffin. By right and honor, six of the King's Guardsmen rode beside the coffin, guarding their king by oath even now. Ravelin found it ironic. The

Guardsmen by their might and by their failure were the reason their king was dead.

Pate and his father rode on either side of Ravelin as he had asked, stationing themselves between him and the six who were assigned to him today. Ravelin stole glances at his own Guardsmen. From the waist up they wore full armor; breastplates and helmets gleamed in the sunlight. They looked inhuman. Metal beings that no one could control, whose thoughts were hidden from all.

Ravelin's heart began to race. He took a deep breath to calm it, and then another. Crowds lined the streets. Weeping. Wailing. Throwing flowers underneath the wheels of the cart that carried his father's body. He looked around wildly. Yes, Pate was still here. And Wells was riding right behind him. Pate's father rode on Ravelin's left, silent and watchful.

"May I get something for you, sir?" Pate asked. "We are almost to the Grave Hall. Just a turn down the next street now. This way is longer, but we'll take the shorter way back to the castle."

Ravelin could hear in his voice that Pate was trying to calm him. Pate was seven years older than he was, and had been his friend all his life. His friend, and Dallen's.

Dallen.

Ravelin took another deep breath. The bloody glove hovered in his mind, beckoning to him. He tried to shake it out of his head.

"Here we are, Your Highness," said Pate.

Looming before them was the magnificent stone

facade that marked the burial place of generations of Rilken's royalty. Pate's father held the horse's head, while Ravelin dismounted. Wells appeared and from somewhere handed him a goblet of light wine. Ravelin drank half of it obediently, then turned toward the hall.

Guardsmen lifted his father's coffin from the cart and carried it inside. The carriage containing the Duke's family opened its doors and his aunt walked into the hall beside him, Petronia and his uncle following. Solemn horns and stringed instruments filled the hall with music of veneration and sorrow.

Ravelin took his place in the front row of chairs, with all the nobility and the city officials that were able to fit in the grieving room seated behind him. Outside, standing in the walkways or sitting on the grass, crowds of people waited, silent and still, ready to hear the eulogies in King Adare's honor.

Lord Locke spoke first. He moved ponderously, but with dignity, and his words did the same. He told of coming to the castle years ago as cousin to Ravelin's mother, and ending up friend and secretary to the king. His praise for Adare was detailed and sincere, and after he had finished, applause filled the room and poured in through the windows. Locke came over to Ravelin, bowed deeply before him, and when Ravelin stood up, gave him a hearty, fatherly hug.

Lord Vallenro was next, and the thin, gray man struggled to get his words out. His speech praised the king, but also apologized to the dead man and to everyone else with a guilt that Ravelin felt was unreasonable. Vallenro broke down and sobbed in the middle of it and could not finish. Locke took him by the arm and graciously escorted him back to his seat.

The Duke of Elva told stories of his brother the king as a youth, of boyish escapades the two had had together. Climbing the turret roof of Elva Castle. Racing on foot from one end of the city to the other. But it seemed that in the pretense of praise, every story had the subtle effect of showing his father as the lesser and the Duke as the greater.

Gentle laughter broke out from time to time. Scattered clapping also. But Ravelin did not join in either. He felt uneasy. Did anyone else notice the artful deflection of praise? Olivia sat on his right. Pate to his left. On the faces beyond he could detect nothing except the usual attentiveness.

When the Duke's finish was met with loud applause, Ravelin turned to Pate who was clapping.

"Do you think that was truly in praise of my father?" he said quietly. "Do you approve?"

Pate shook his head no, then leaned over to whisper in Ravelin's ear. "But I've found that when men of great power speak, it's always best to clap."

Ravelin nodded dumbly. It was his turn now. He stood and walked to the platform. The audience stood with him and clapped more vigorously than they had for his uncle. Cries of *Ravelin! Ravelin! Our prince, our king!* came from the grounds outside, and he felt heartened.

He had prepared a simple speech with stories that showed his father's wisdom and his love, first for his wife and sons, then for Elva and all Rilken. He included a copy of the letter of praise from the Duke of Nordia stating why the King of Rilken had been chosen to ride with the Hosts of the North, something the earlier speeches had failed to mention. And he had been able to prepare all this without interference from Kendall or his uncle. Now Ravelin would be able to honor his father before the people of the land, great and small.

He held up his hands for silence. Wondered if he should ask everyone to sit down. Remembered his uncle's words that no one could sit down in the presence of a standing king. And so, in a state of flustered uncertainty, began.

He read the words on the page in front of him, working to make his voice carry to the far ends of the room, but he had a strange sense of being absent from himself, of watching someone else speak the words.

His uncle had an irritating habit of playing with his gloves when he was bored. Taking one off and curling it in a ball. Then straightening it out and pulling on each of the fingertips. Repeating this over and over. He was doing this now and Ravelin found himself staring at him. Staring at his glove. Or was it Dallen's glove, the very one that he had seen this morning? Dallen had just lost his glove, hadn't he? He couldn't be dead.

Pate coughed. Twice.

Ravelin blinked and realized that he hadn't been speaking for some time. That somewhere along the page he had fallen silent, but he didn't know where it had been. *What had he said and what had he not said?*

He read the letter from the Duke of Nordia, then took his seat, conscious that his speech had not been well done. That he had probably omitted things that he had wanted to say, but when he lost his place feared repeating. And now he would never be able to do it again. His chest hurt with the realization. He had wanted the speech to be so good for his father's honor.

The applause was graciously loud. His uncle came over to where he was sitting, took his hand, and led him to the front of the room to receive the applause of the people again. Then he was led outside to remount his horse.

The Duke said, "You do not look well. Would you prefer to ride in the carriage with us?"

In answer, Ravelin put his foot in the stirrup and swung his other leg over his horse's back. Pate and his father and Wells took up their positions around him. The Duke frowned and entered his own carriage.

The procession wound through the streets of Elva again on its way back to the castle. But this time there was no father to follow, alive or dead. No brother riding ahead, urging him to keep up. There was only Ravelin and a few friends.

Several Guardsmen led the way. Two more rode almost as closely to him as Pate and his father did. Two rode behind with Wells.

Ravelin tried to focus on the people that lined the streets, their waves and well-wishes. He lifted his hand to wave back and noticed that his arm felt unusually heavy, like the lead weight of a cannonball. It moved oddly, stiffly in the air.

His heart began to race again. Faster.

The orange-red of the castle roof was visible over the

houses of the city. The street they were on slowly wound its way toward it. But the castle felt too far away.

Ahead of him, the road narrowed. The shops on either side closed in while the street rose and turned sharply. Two horsemen could barely go abreast. Ravelin wondered why this route had been chosen. *The Guardsmen must have chosen it.* His heart raced faster, demanding his attention.

Pate's horse was held up at the turn. His father's was just ahead. But before and behind Ravelin rode the inhuman metal beings. Each capable of murder in an instant.

This was it.

This was how his father died.

This was how he would die.

His heart ran wild and he could not breathe. If he did not lower his head instantly, he would black out. He crouched down, clinging to the horse, and fought to breathe. His knees tightened and the horse lurched forward, crowding the Guardsmen's horses ahead of him.

Blackness closed around his vision as a metal hand reached for him. "Get away!" he cried, but his heart was racing too fast for his body. He slid off his horse to the ground.

He was lying on the street, the sky above him framed by buildings. Wells gently lifted his head and begged him to drink wine. Pate's face came into view.

"Ah, there you are! Our good prince has come back to us! My father has gone for the Duke's carriage. It will be here soon. Praise to Drony the Guardsman who kept your horse from bolting and to Adam who stopped your fall!"

Ravelin listened dumbly, disbelieving, and sipped the wine that Wells pushed on him. The carriage arrived at the end of the narrow street. Wells and Pate helped him into it. He sank down into a corner. Aunt Olivia patted his arm and murmured something about a doctor. Petronia sat across from him and stared.

"You should have listened to me, Ravelin," said his uncle, "and come in the carriage at once. See what comes of your stubbornness?" There was a note of triumph in his voice.

Ravelin leaned his head against the carriage wall and closed his eyes.

23

Elusive Hope

Mama showed us how to balance the three large fish over the fire using the fire irons. After sharing pieces with Tike and the cat, we still had enough fish to satisfy. We were deeply grateful to the bear, and at the same time, unsure and confused about his presence. Our meal ended as it began—in a state of complete bewilderment.

"How on earth does a man get inside a bear?" asked Rosie, after swallowing her last bite.

"I don't know," I replied. "How does the belly of a great bird burn with a flame that does not kill it? How do roses from Mama's carry sack grow in the dirt outside the door?"

I shook my head in puzzlement. "I thought I knew

much about how the world works when we lived in Elva. I completed all my studies and read and observed as much as I could. But in these last few days I'm convinced that I understand less than I did before."

"Maybe the whole world changed when the king died," said Rosie.

"It did," said Mama quietly. "But I had heard tales of flaming birds years ago when I was a little girl. Griefs and wonders have always filled the world. It is only our experience of them that is new."

REDBIRD TOLD us that the bear was gone, so Mama sent Rosie and me to the stream to fill bowls we found in the cupboard with water. We stirred wood ash into some bowls for hair washing and let it settle.

Rosie found fragrant herbs growing in the forest and when evening fell, we gently washed Mama's hair. Her swollen eye reopened, and her sight appeared to be undamaged. We were so relieved.

After Mama's hair was rinsed, Rosie washed my hair and I washed hers. She fed the fire, and we all sat near it so our hair could dry. It felt so good to have clean hair.

Mama asked us to bring our skirts and underskirts to her, along with needle and thread. After assembling her materials, she sat in front of the fire stitching, her needle moving swiftly.

In spite of such unusual circumstances, it was a familiar scene. Mama sewing. A good fire going. Rosie and I chatting with our mother while our father was on duty. The only thing missing was the security and comfort of the sitting room in our Guardstown house. And the hope of Papa's return.

Sadness hit me in the stomach, taking my breath for a moment. Struggling against the swell of grief, I turned my eyes to watch Rosie. She was shoving the fire logs with determination, and I wondered what struggles were in her mind at the moment. When the fire was built to her satisfaction, she sat down on the floor next to me.

"What are you doing with my skirt, Mama?" Rosie asked. "It won't fit me anymore if you close it off like that."

"It will." Mama held up Rosie's skirt, looked critically at it, then continued sewing. "I'm turning your skirts into skirts with legs. If you have to run and climb and dig and work outside like country girls now, then you need a skirt that will move with you and keep you covered, even if you take to climbing trees."

She tied off the thread and added more to the needle before continuing. "I wore mine like this when I was a girl on the farm."

"Our cousins wear skirts like that," I said. "Sanna wore one when I helped her clean out the barn. She said it was good to be able to work and not worry about what your skirt was doing."

Mama snipped the thread and held out the garment. "Here, Rosie, try it on."

Rosie slid the pale blue skirt under her other one. Then she walked briskly across the room while bent at a funny angle, trying to see her skirt while walking.

"What do you think, Silvie?" she asked.

"You can't really see it. Kick up your feet."

Rosie grabbed her outer skirt and jumped a few times. Tike barked excitedly.

"It works perfectly," said Mama, the shadow of a smile on her face. "Give me yours now, Silvie."

Rosie and I both fell silent, watching her stitch. It was a time for thinking and for quiet talk.

"I can't stop thinking about the king's death," I began. "Was there another enemy in the forest? An enemy who attacked the king and the Guardsmen, and —and maybe Mago came and didn't understand what was really happening?"

Rosie leaned forward. "Like battle confusion?"

Mama looked up at us. The needle pierced the fabric of my skirt and waited to be drawn through.

"Mago said nothing about an enemy," she said slowly.

She took a deep breath, then moved the needle again.

"We need to find out somehow," I said.

"We could ask the bear," said Rosie. "Maybe he knows." She looked at me as if I had an answer and I shook my head.

"I hope to hear some news at the inn tomorrow," Mama said.

This comment drew my thoughts from the bear. "Do you really think you should go there so soon? The swelling is down, but the colors on your face are so dark, so purple and blue now."

"I can't put this off waiting for my face to look normal again," said Mama. "I have to try tomorrow. We need food. Dependable food. And soap. And a pillow or two. This is the king's land, and, yes, we are here without given permission. But I look at those two rosebushes planted so miraculously, and I agree with you, Silvie. I think the Sender means to plant us here too. At least for a little while."

"If that's true, then I won't feel guilty using the things from the king's cupboard," said Rosie. "I will take everything out of it in the morning and look it over. Then we can make ourselves properly at home."

"Yes," said Mama. "I suppose that's what we should do."

"But if there's no work at the inn, will we buy bread until our money runs out?" I asked.

"I really don't know, Silvie."

Mama's voice was so sad that I kept my remaining questions to myself.

THE NIGHT WAS DARK. No moonlight appeared in the shutter cracks. The fire burned low, and Mama and Rosie were both asleep.

I stroked Tike's back slowly, taking comfort from the warm dog lying next to me. In a wave of hope, Rosie and I had talked of planting gardens and making fish nets from dry grasses. But hope has a way of disappearing when the world goes dark, disappearing like smoke into the clouds. And it was hard to find again.

Tike lifted his head, alert. But he wasn't growling. The white squirrel leapt from Rosie's bed onto the table, twitching its tail.

Rosie stirred and sat up. "What is it, Silvie?" she whispered.

"I think the bear is back." I crawled out of bed and tiptoed to the window. "Come here, Squirrel."

I opened the shutter just wide enough and the squirrel slid out. In two moments it was back with hushed, excited chirrups.

"The bear is curled up with his back to our door," I whispered to Rosie. "It looks as if it will sleep there all night."

Rosie, half asleep, took no alarm at this. "I suppose you don't fear the wolf at the door if there is a bear in front of it," she said, folding her sweater into a pillow again. "But I'd hate to have to climb out the side window just to go to the necessary in the morning."

SHE SETTLED down to sleep again, but I couldn't. After I was sure Rosie was sound asleep, I opened the front shutter partway and put my head out. There was the dark shape, enormous in the thin moonlight.

"Bear," I whispered.

The shape moved.

"Could I come out and talk to you, Bear?"

He stood up and shuffled away from the door. I wrapped my cloak around me and stepped out, wondering that I dared to do this. And at the same time wondering why I knew I didn't need to be afraid.

"Wait," the bear said in his deep, rumbly voice. Before I could say anything more, he darted away with surprising speed.

I thought he went toward the river. In a few moments, I heard rustling. He came across the clearing carrying something in one arm, and set down a large rock.

"To sit on," he said.

I stared at him in disbelief. "For me?"

"Yes." He lay down on his belly with his head up, waiting.

I sat down on the rock. "Thank you. That's so kind. It's just the right size to be comfortable."

The bear lowered his head to his paws and let out a deep breath.

I wished I could see the expression on his face, but the dark was too great for that. The bear's eyes glowed, reminding me of the angry bear by the stream our first night away from Elva. *But this is not that bear.* I fought down the fear that flickered inside me. I didn't want it to keep me from asking the questions that filled my mind.

Was this bear connected to the stories of the bears we had heard in Elva? And where did the human inside of it come from? *But how to ask?*

"Is there anyone missing you now, Bear?" I said, as gently as I could. "Anyone waiting for your return? Looking out the window, watching for you?"

The bear grunted. "I don't know."

I waited, but the bear said nothing more. It turned its head away from me so I could not see the glow in its eyes. Deep sorrow emanated from him. Tears wet my eyes. I could ask him nothing more.

"I'm sorry, Bear," I said. "Truly sorry."

A small grunt came in reply, followed by a snuffle

sound. Long moments of silence passed. I could think of nothing more to say, but how could I leave a creature filled with such sadness?

I settled myself on the ground and leaned against the rock he had brought for me. I sat there for a long time, watching the dark form of the huge animal, listening to the night sounds, until drowsiness took me.

When I awoke, it was still dark. Bear appeared to be sleeping deeply. I got up as quietly as I could and went inside.

24

Almost Midnight

fter the horrible funeral day of sorrow, fear, and collapse, Ravelin had finally fallen deep into sleep. An exhausted Wells sat in a chair at the prince's bedside. A Wells who, Pate was convinced, never slept. Yet, as Pate watched, Wells' eyes slowly closed.

Pate stayed on his stool for some time after, studying one sleeper's face and then the other. His eyes strayed to the other side of Ravelin's bed, to an empty part of the room away from the firelight, shrouded in gloom. But it wasn't empty to the eyes of memory.

A few months ago they had all been stationed thus. Ravelin in bed, winning his first battle with the winter fever. Wells hovering by the bedside table, offering a wealth of food and drink, anything to strengthen the young man. And on the far side of the bed, standing with an arm wrapped around the bedpost, Dallen telling story after story.

Ravelin from his sickbed had challenged his brother to tell five stories about Elva Castle that no one else knew. Dallen responded immediately. Humor, intrigue, puzzles, absurdity—Dallen wove them all into his tales with zest, waving his free arm in places for emphasis. Some of his tales Pate knew to be true. Others, totally impossible. But they had all cheered his younger brother, to Dallen's great delight.

That was Dallen. A combination of energy, confidence, and cheer. A force that could not be silenced. Couldn't be.

Pate pressed his hands against his face. Hard. And took a deep breath. He looked intently into the gloom, willing the memory back. But where Dallen had once stood, there were shadows. And an absence so palpable it could barely be endured.

Pate shook himself and got to his feet. Wells' eyes opened at once.

"I'm going now, Wells," Pate whispered.

Wells began to rise, but Pate pushed down on his shoulder, begging the attendant to stay seated, and let himself out. It was time for Pate to check another source of concern, and one just as dear to him.

The castle corridors echoed with the sound of his footsteps as Pate hurried toward the newly reconstructed east wing. Usually all sorts of gatherings and entertainments would be underway in the castle at this time of night, as actors and poets, orators and musicians enlivened the evenings of those who had worked hard all day and those who had not.

But not tonight. This was a castle in mourning, and any attempts at mirth remained behind closed doors, in private apartments, in hushed voices with small groups of friends.

Lanterns lined the darkened halls as he passed, leaving arcs of shadow between their pools of light. He nodded to the bored and sleepy footmen, positioned at corners and important doorways, ready in case they would be needed, and turned aside any attempts to draw him into conversation.

At the end of a wide hall, he quickly descended a long staircase and turned to the east. A footman stood outside a set of tall, double doors.

"Are they working late tonight, Jack?" Pate asked.

"They are always working, sir. One of them is in there now."

"I plan to put a stop to that. Time to clear the halls."

"As you say, sir," the footman replied, reaching for the door handle.

Pate passed through and paused. Most of the new grand hall was in lonely darkness. At a distance down on the left, a cluster of lanterns illuminated a solo artist crouched on scaffolding, brush in hand, intently working on one portion of a large mural that swept the length of the hall.

Pate approached, letting his footsteps be heard so as not to startle the concentration of the artist. "Avelyn," he called gently.

She stood up and looked out into the darkness. "Pate, is that you?" Relief was in her voice. "I was afraid you were Master Taynor come to complain about the line of the heel."

Pate stood at the bottom of the scaffolding and looked up at her. "Does he complain about the heel line?"

Avelyn set down her brush and rubbed her arms. "He complains about everything." Her voice sounded so tired. "But I can understand. His reputation rests on this mural."

"Does he make you work late, too?"

"No, not usually."

"Then, *why,* my dearest?"

"Because—because I can't make anything right." She sounded close to tears.

"Is Taynor criticizing *all* your work? The man's blind! You're the best he has."

"No, Pate. It's not Taynor. It's the king."

Pate climbed the scaffolding and stepped out onto the platform next to Avelyn. He wanted to see her face. Her rich brown eyes. The red-brown hair half covered by a gray artist's kerchief. The expression on her lips. "Tell me, Avelyn," he said gently.

She lifted one lantern from its hook on the scaffolding and raised it higher so he could see the whole figure and not just the boot in the stirrup.

"It's King Adare," she said.

And it was. Towering above them. The expression on his face looked almost alive.

"Ravelin will *love* this," he said.

"What I meant was, I wish I could defend the king with shield or sword. I wish I could hunt the forest and find his murderer. But I can't do anything except sculpt and paint. This," she said, motioning toward the wall, "this is all I can do, Pate. And I feel that somehow, if I can get the strokes just right, he'll come back to life again."

"Avelyn, Avelyn—"

"I know. It's just a dream. But paint and brush is all I have. It's all I can do. It's such a small thing."

"Come, love. It's late. King Adare did not work his people so mercilessly. Rest was allowed. Take your rest now."

He took one of the lanterns and climbed down the ladder, waiting while she put things in order and extinguished the other lanterns, before climbing down after him.

He put an arm around her shoulders as they walked down the hall. "You're worn out," he said.

"And you're not?" she replied.

He grinned. "I don't know how either of us is still walking."

Her arm went around his back and he felt it pull tight.

Just before they reached the doors, Avelyn stopped abruptly. "Pate," the word came in a whisper. "The Duke came to see the mural today after the funeral. He doesn't like it. Not any of it. He took Taynor away with him for a talk and Taynor never came back."

Pate put the last lantern on a hook by the door frame. "Is the Duke himself on the walls yet?"

"He's not meant to be. The picture is of the king riding out with the Hosts of the North."

"Ah, yes." Pate wondered if any of the Guardsmen were on the wall and which faces would have been chosen. Perchance the face of a murderer was somehow immortalized on the wall. Those were heavy thoughts, and Pate was beyond weary. He had no energy for such a discussion, so he did not ask.

They meandered through the dark halls slowly on their way to the dormitory rooms where Avelyn stayed with other female artists. They spoke softly of whatever came into their minds, and Pate's heart was renewed.

"I mixed the perfect green for your father's painting, Pate. For his cape."

"Is it the same color as the mural's green?"

"No, Taynor mixes those. My green is just a bit brighter."

"When can I see this painting?" Pate asked.

"Only when it's finished."

"It's hard to wait."

"I love how it's turning out. I hope he likes it."

"I can tell you one thing for sure. My mother will love it and fall at your feet."

"If I could only sculpt it. The position and angle of your father's head, the shape of his cheekbones, would make an extraordinary sculpture."

"I'll have to tell him that. How would he react to that news, I wonder? Father, I can see you in stone."

He heard a gentle laugh and pulled Avelyn close to his side. They were walking down a corridor that overlooked one of the castle's grand halls, several floors below, when Pate heard the sound of a large door opening. The rest of the grand hall was in shadows, but light came from the open doorway. The doors to the Duke's reception rooms.

Something about the sound and the door opening made Pate crouch down behind the railing and peer through the balusters. Avelyn immediately did the same.

An eerie procession poured from the open doors. A row of men in single file, barely making a sound with their boots on the floor. Five, then ten. Several dozen came out and walked for a distance before turning down another corridor out of sight.

"Palace guard," Avelyn spoke quietly into his ear.

"Are you sure?" The men far below appeared to be shrouded in gray shadow.

She nodded. "Just before they turn, watch. The lantern picks up a glimmer of blue on their shoulders. *Their* blue."

He thought he could make it out, but he wouldn't have seen it without Avelyn and her keen eye for color. The last of the guard disappeared from view. The doors below closed and darkness reigned in the hall below. Pate stood up, almost too tired to think of what the procession meant. But he could not shake an uneasy feeling.

At the dormitory entrance, he hugged Avelyn tightly and whispered, "Make sure you bolt the door." She met his gaze soberly for a few moments and nodded.

On the way to his own small room, Pate took a detour by Ravelin's hallway. The Guardsmen were gone.

In their place stood silent rows of palace guard. Fewer than he had seen emerge from the Duke's rooms, but plenty all the same.

As he climbed the final stairs to his own room, Pate wondered why the thought of those silent watchers did not comfort him.

25

Tara's Decision

Tara woke early. She was tired enough to go back to sleep, but the hardness of the bench pressed into her back, pulling her from a drowsy state to full alertness.

Birds chirped exuberantly outside, the birdsong that comes with dawn. Silvie and Rosie were still asleep. Tike, on the floor next to Silvie, twitched and she wondered if he were dreaming.

Which brought to mind her own dream.

She had dreamt of Bevan's hair. His long, pale, white-blond hair. She loved his hair. It was the first thing that had caught her eye all those years ago. The second was the expression on his face. Those blue eyes that seemed so far-seeing, coupled with a smile full of kind interest. How her heart had leapt when she realized that smile was directed towards her.

The day they moved to Guardstown at the request of the king was the day he asked her to cut off his hair. It grieved her, but she did it.

"You can't give an enemy a place to grab you or hang on to you," Bevan explained as she snipped and the pale locks fell to the floor.

This possible enemy shaped Bevan's thoughts and his training. Then, his every waking moment. And, as he often told her, his dreams.

Bevan had lived in a constant state of readiness. Readiness to shield. Readiness to strike.

This constant awareness of a potential enemy was the hardest thing about the life of a Guardsman. At first Tara hated that emphasis and how it permeated their daily thoughts and actions. Then she had come to accept it. Talking with Zilla and the other wives had helped too.

But she didn't want to think of her old friends now.

She got up stiffly and went over to stir the fire, to see if any embers still glowed in the shallow depression on the floor of the fireplace. Only a very few.

She gently touched one of them with a piece of dry brush from the firebox. A tiny flame sprang up. She coaxed it with more dry brush and then added the dry twigs, watching to see if the fire would take hold.

Slowly it did. She built the wood around it and sat back watching the flames leap and glow.

What had become of Bevan's hair, the white gold that fell on the floor that day? She had woven some of it into the design of a brooch, along with dark green embroidery thread and a lock of her own hair. It had turned out beautifully. She kept the brooch wrapped in clean linen in her bedroom drawer and only took it out to wear on special occasions.

The brooch—like many things they loved—had been left behind in the scramble of packing. It now belonged to whomever had taken over their house. Would the new tenants think it beautiful? Would they realize how important it was?

She wiped her face with her hand and winced. The bruised side was still so tender. Maybe in another week it would heal.

But she couldn't wait another week to go to the inn, to ask for work, and to buy some food. She was so tired of the ache of an empty stomach. And she couldn't stand to think of her daughters being hungry.

There was another reason to go to the inn—one almost equal in importance to the other two. She was desperate to hear news from Elva. Stories of the king's death and the Guardsmen's actions must have penetrated into the countryside by now.

In East Rilken where she had grown up, travelers brought news to the inns, and folks who gathered at the inns spread the news to everyone else. It would be the same in the western forests of Rilken. And someone was sure to have a story of the northwest road.

THE BEAR WAS NOWHERE in sight when they opened up the windows and made their trips to the necessary, though Tara kept a watch for it. But before Silvie and Rosie could gather eggs for breakfast, the bear returned. Tara made the girls come inside and close the shutters.

The bear wandered around the clearing, sat under the trees across from them, and seemed to be watching them as carefully as they were watching it, their eyes peering through the thin cracks at the shutter's edge.

"We'll just have to wait for it to go away," said Tara. "We can do the day's dusting and sweeping now."

It didn't take the three of them long to wipe and sweep all the surfaces inside the hunting station. But when they had finished, the bear was still there. *How long would it do this?* They couldn't stay trapped inside the hunting station. They were hungry. They needed to collect eggs, and Tara needed to get to the inn.

"I suppose Silvie could ask him to bring more fish," said Rosie as she surveyed the clearing again through the crack in the window opening. Silvie didn't respond to this and it seemed to Tara that her eldest daughter was exceptionally quiet and thoughtful.

Tara removed the shutters from one window to see what the bear would do, how much freedom it was allowing them to have. The bear poked a stick into a fallen log and ate the disturbed and angry termites that ran out of it.

She asked Rosie to open the other window. The bear scratched its back against a tree and looked up at the sky.

"How can it act so very *bear* and yet speak like a

man?" Tara asked no one in particular. "Who *is* this creature?"

Could it be one of the Guardians of Rilken? She believed the old stories, even though Zilla didn't. But would a Guardian act so very *ordinary*?

"Maybe this is his territory," said Rosie, "and we're the new ones invading."

"I think he wants us to know that we can trust him," said Silvie.

Tara glanced at her. Silvie did not appear worried in the least. Her blue eyes revealed only calm.

Mid-morning, Rosie opened the door. "Come on, Squirrel. I have to work in my garden." And before Tara could say anything, Rosie was out the door with her fire iron, her bodyguard at her heels. The bear gazed at her with mild interest, then put its head on its paws for a nap in the sunshine.

"I really don't think he will hurt us, Mama," said Silvie. "A bear who took such great care to fish for us would hardly attack us now."

But would it? Tara couldn't begin to answer that, because if she answered wrong, she couldn't live with the consequences.

For another hour, Tara remained watching at the window. In that hour the bear roamed around, changing its position, but never once appeared threatening. Rosie worked in her garden, exclaiming over the plants, while the white squirrel yattered away. Rosie tossed it the acorns she found while digging.

Tike and the cat had been outside as well, and Tike came to tell Silvie that he had found more eggs. Silvie looked at Tara with pleading eyes. "I'm so hungry, Mama. I have to get those eggs."

Tara gave one more look out the window at the bear. If only the beast weren't so *huge.* "All right, but I'll come too."

They stepped out of the doorway together, Tara with a carry sack, Silvie eager to follow Tike to his latest find. The bear raised its head and looked curiously at them.

"We're going to gather eggs for our meal," Tara said in a firm voice.

"We won't be gone long," Silvie added.

Tara glanced at her, wondering why she said that. The bear lowered its head again, but there was something in its eyes that made her pause. She could not tell what it was and hoped Silvie knew.

"Do you want to come too?" Silvie asked. "We're not going far, but if you'd like some company for a while?"

It was an odd thing to say to such a powerful animal. But the bear got up on all four paws and moved in their direction. Silvie smiled at it, looking strangely happy. Rosie abruptly stopped digging and shifted the fire iron in her hand.

"It's all right, Rosie," Tara called, in a voice more confident than she felt. "The bear is going to keep us company while we look for eggs."

And it did. In fact, it could smell out eggs faster than Tike could. Tara had the curious feeling that the bear could easily have found all the eggs quickly, but was pausing on purpose to take turns with the dog. She mentioned this to Silvie.

"He *is* taking turns with Tike," Silvie said. "At least Tike thinks so."

Tara studied the bear. What kind of animal would show such graciousness to a small lame dog? Was it indeed one of the Guardians? She had always imagined them differently. She counted the eggs in her carry sack.

"We have enough now, Silvie," she said. "Tomorrow we can look again for fresh ones, and I don't want to get too far away from the hunting station."

Immediately, the bear turned and began to lead the way back to the clearing. Tara exchanged glances with Silvie and followed it back through the trees.

EGGS COOKED on the spoon over the fire made a good lunch. When they were cleaning up, Tara made her decision. She trusted the bear. She trusted his kindness toward a three-legged dog. Toward three hungry women that had greeted him with suspicion. If he meant them harm, he had already had plenty of opportunity to do it. Instead, he had brought them fish and helped them find eggs.

It was time to go to the inn.

"Girls," she said, "I'll need you to help me look as well-dressed and well-groomed as possible." Ignoring their concerned looks, she briskly set out the scarves and the hairbrush.

No matter how they tried, how Silvie parted her hair, how Rosie draped the scarves over her head and around her neck and chin, they couldn't cover the worst of the bruises. Half of her face looked almost normal, but the other half, the side that sustained Mago's blow, had turned purple and blue. And the beginnings of green. An instinctive turning of her head at the last moment had probably saved her eye from blindness and her nose from being irretrievably bent.

Tara stared into the small mirror. At least she could see out of both eyes again. "I don't want to *look* like I am trying to hide something, even though I am."

Rosie studied her. "It might be best, Mama, since we can't cover the bruising, if we make your scarves and hair look the most attractive for you and just ignore the bruises."

So that's what they did. Silvie brushed Tara's long curly russet hair, pulled half of it back and let the other half drape loosely over the worst bruises.

Tara gave one last look in the mirror. An injured woman looked back. "That will just have to do," she said, getting to her feet.

26

The Grumpy Rabbit

The girls accompanied her down the hillside path until they could see the inn. Tara stepped off the path and looked through the trees at the building. The activity around the yard and outbuildings encouraged her. Many tasks would need doing in a place like that. Surely there would be something she could do.

"Wait here until I return, and watch out for each other." Even as she spoke, she knew the last words were unnecessary.

Silvie answered anyway. "We will, Mama."

"You look nice, Mama," Rosie said, with an encouraging smile.

Concern and hope were on their faces. She could see

the same concern on Tike's face and the squirrel's too. Redbird and the cat watched silently. A fox appeared from behind a tree trunk. And there was the bear, ambling down the path toward them. The bear who let the dog find the eggs first. The animals showed no alarm at his presence now. Neither would she. She gave them all a confident smile, turned, and went on her way.

She stepped out from the bottom of the path onto the packed-earth road and followed its gentle curve back toward the inn. This road was not as large as the main roads that issued straight out of Elva, but it was broad enough to walk the edge while traffic moved by. A wagon approached her now, a man and woman seated on the driving bench behind the horses. As they passed, the woman waved at her and Tara waved back.

She walked near the road edge wearing the sturdy boots that Rosie had vigorously rubbed clean. The rose carry sack hung from her shoulder, concealed under her cloak. Even if she could not find work, she was likely to find bread, and the sack would be filled with loaves when she hiked back up the hill.

People would, of course, stare at her bruises. How could they not? But if she had a capable manner, they could look past her face to her abilities.

The inn looked larger than it had appeared from the hillside. Not the size of the West Road Inn to be sure. But, the stable yard had room to turn carriages easily, and a long row of stall doors for horses. A boy was shoveling scattered bits of manure from the yard into a bucket. He raised his head to give her a look as she went by, but did not stop his shoveling.

The main building of the inn sprawled to the left of the stable yard. Next to the entrance, a red sign with gold lettering bore the inn's name. The Grumpy Rabbit.

Draped over the sign were evergreen boughs, the custom for mourning in Elva. Boughs proclaimed the hope that those who died might remain somehow evergreen. These boughs would have been freshly placed for King Adare. The pine fragrance greeted her nose with the smell of sadness and longing. She took a breath, reached for the door handle, and stepped inside.

THE MAIN GATHERING room of the inn ran from the front of the building to the back, a fireplace surrounded by windows on either end. The fires, piled high with burning logs, cut the chill that was ever-present in Rilken in the spring, and Tara welcomed their warmth.

In the middle of the room, four men gathered around one of the tables, talking intently among themselves. Heads bent together, as if ears didn't want to miss a word.

There were no other customers except for an old man at a small table along the far wall. He looked up from his bowl of soup, gave her a nod, then lifted the spoon to his mouth.

She took all this in as her gaze swept the room. But what stood out to her the most were the smells of pork, potatoes, and bread. Her stomach gurgled in response, and she could have wept thinking of the girls' hunger. *Soon, Tara, soon.*

A polished wood bar stretched down a long side

wall. Barrels of ale, cider, and beer sat behind it, waiting to be tapped for refreshment. A man stood behind the bar wiping his hands on a rag. Thick brown hair covered his head and his upper lip. On the wall above him hung an odd picture of a rabbit with a frustrated expression on its face. It was cleverly done, and the frame was swathed in evergreens.

Tara took a few steps forward, and the barman dropped his rag behind the bar.

"What can I get for you?"

She pointed at the rabbit. "That's an interesting picture. Does it have a story?"

The man glanced at the rabbit over his shoulder. "It was done by a friend of my grandfather's when he first opened this inn. My grandfather took to the picture and named the inn after it. It's hung there for going on fifty years."

He had a welcoming voice, the kind ready to talk, ready to invite customers in and put them at ease. Tara was heartened at the tone.

"How proud you must be!" she replied. "To answer your question, I'm looking for work. I can do a great many things well. Cleaning, cooking, sewing, mending—"

The man turned away from her and called to the old man with the soup.

"Where's Alta?"

"Upstairs," said the man, between loud slurps.

The barman held up a finger to Tara. "Wait a minute." He went to the far end of the bar and disappeared through a doorway.

The four men at a center table still spoke energetically to each other. Elbows on the table. Heads nodded, coaxing the teller to continue. She could hear their words clearly.

"So, Daniel's the first at the window. He'd been waiting there since before daybreak or he wouldn't have been able to set foot anywhere on the grounds. He's tall. Sharp-eyed too, so he could see the speakers well enough. The first one spoke so elegant, he said. What the true nobility *should* do. What you expect them to do. But the next? He sobbed through his words 'til you couldn't understand a one!"

"Grieving the king," said a man, somberly.

"As we all are," said another, almost indignantly.

"He must have known him personal though."

They would be talking of the king's funeral. Tara took a step closer to where they sat, still facing the doorway the barman had gone through. The men didn't notice her. She dared another quick glance.

The speaker waved his hand in front of him. "But when Prince Ravelin spoke, what do you think? Daniel says he started off well, and then he just stops. Right in the middle. Staring. Saying nothing for a long time. Like he had lost his way."

"Silence by a bier isn't that unusual, Heth."

"Not for some moments, yes. But that's a planned silence. This was not. The people inside shifted nervous-like. Daniel kept his eyes on the prince. The look on his face was like the boy was far away somewheres. Not standing in the room at all."

Tara's heart wrenched for Ravelin.

"Poor lad! Poor lad!" cried one of the men. "When you think—"

A tall, thin woman came through the doorway, followed by the barman. She had a quick step and a purposeful eye. She wore her hair back in a kerchief, from which wisps had escaped and clung now to her damp forehead. A woman with authority who worked very hard herself.

"Gareth said you were looking for work." The words were sharp and to the point, spoken while the woman took in Tara's appearance from head to foot. The barman slipped back behind the counter.

"Yes, ma'am. I can do anything that you might need around the inn. Wash, cook, clean, mend. I have a skill at sewing—"

"I have plenty of girls for that. Don't need any more. Go on now." The woman waved her hand as if brushing Tara away. Then she turned abruptly and left through the same doorway. The rest of Tara's words remained unspoken on her tongue.

The barman busied himself, wrestling something unseen underneath the counter. But the old man with the soup was looking at Tara.

"Should have come to the back door," he said in a scratchy voice. "Alta don't like workers to use the front door."

Tara tried to swallow her disappointment and gave him a quick smile. "Thank you. I'll remember that."

There was nothing more to do, so Tara pulled the door open and stepped out into the inn yard. The spring wind blew chill and she pulled her cloak tightly around her.

Would the woman have hired her if she had gone to the back door? Was her rejection due to that simple mistake? She doubted it. The woman's gaze had been on Tara's face most of the time. On the hideous bruises. Bruises that would have resulted from a hideous story. And no one wants to be part of a hideous story.

But there was still bread to be bought. She had smelled it. The old man had said to go to the kitchen door, so she made her way past a flowering quince tree, through the chicken yard, around a tethered dog who barked at her suspiciously, to knock at a sturdy wooden door.

She waited, but no answer came.

She glanced across the back of the inn. A few people could be seen down the way, but they were busy with their work and seemed to take no notice of her. She gazed up the hill. Her daughters waited somewhere in those trees, and she would not leave without getting some bread.

She knocked again, using both hands this time. If no one answered, she would have to brave the front door again.

A creak and a groan and the door opened. A sober-looking dwarf woman stood there, wiping floury hands on a spattered apron.

"I came to buy bread," Tara said quickly. "Three loaves if you have them."

This woman stared at her face too, just like Alta had.

"How much would it be for three loaves?" Tara

named the price the bakers in Elva charged. "Would that be enough?"

The woman was still staring at her. "Were you the one who came looking for work just now?"

"Yes," Tara answered. "But I heard you don't need anyone, so I'll just buy bread if I may."

The woman named a price that sounded too cheap, but Tara didn't argue. She reached into her carry bag for the money pouch and fingered through the coins, then held out the amount the woman asked for.

"Here!" the dwarf woman said sharply. "Where did you get that?"

Tara felt confused. Her hand hovered awkwardly in the air. "The coins are from the last of my husband's pay—"

"No, no. The bag. The big one and that one. With all that rich embroidery. Where did you get them?" A hint of accusation was in her tone.

"I made them," Tara replied. "I made the carry bag this winter and the small one two years ago with leftover fabric and thread from a skirt. See?" She held them out and the dwarf woman peered at them.

"I've made many like these," Tara continued.

The woman looked from the embroidery to Tara's face, but not to the bruises. This time she met Tara eye to eye. "Could you embroider sheets and pillowcases?" She spoke now in an eager tone. "Drapery ties? Things like that?"

Tara smiled. "That would be so easy to do. And such a delight."

The woman opened the door all the way. "Keep your money. Come in and sit there. I'll talk to Alta."

Tara sat on the stool the woman indicated. A pan of buns sat cooling on the deep brick windowsill. The woman grabbed one and set it down on a table next to Tara.

"I'll need to take one of those bags to show her. You can eat this while you wait." The woman was smiling now. Friendly. And it warmed Tara's heart.

She slid off her cloak and handed the empty rose bag to the cook, for Tara realized that must be who she was. She had authority in this kitchen like Alta had over the whole inn.

The cook wiped her hands even more carefully before taking the strap of the bag. "I'll be careful with it," she said. "I know it's valuable."

With a quick step she left the kitchen.

ETTIE KNEW that she would command Alta's full attention. For she rarely climbed the stairs to the upper rooms unless it were a matter of importance. Which this was.

She found the innkeeper with one of the maids in their largest guest room examining the drapes for signs of moth bite. Moth-eaten fabrics would not appeal to noble customers. Ettie walked confidently up to Alta.

"I think your dream might be coming true today." She held out the bag. "Look at this needlework. Imagine it stitched over the linens and pillowcases in this room. It'll be just what you need to draw those nobles in."

Alta reached for the bag and examined it. "Where did you get this, Ettie? Who did this?"

"That woman who came looking for work. She came around back to buy bread, and when it came to paying she takes the money out of this. Says she did it up last winter."

"She must have been lying to you, Ettie. Many men and women wish they had the gift of turning thread to beauty. But they don't." Alta shook her head. "No, it's more likely she stole it."

"It's easy enough to find out," said Ettie stubbornly. "Give her a needle and thread. If she can make the patterns on this bag, why, can't you see the same on the edge of those sheets there? You'd get three rills a night *every* night, and those that pay would think it worth it."

Alta held the bag up to her face and looked at it closely. Ettie saw the hopeful look in her eye and pushed her point.

"Because of the king's death, nobility from everywhere are going to be on these roads for months now, coming to pay honor in Elva. The West Road Inn can't house them all. I know my cooking's as good as theirs. All we ever needed was fancy rooms."

When Alta still did not answer, Ettie felt a surge of irritation. She held her tongue.

～

THE BUN TASTED DELICIOUS, and Tara felt sure the cook would allow her to buy bread for the girls. Perhaps she could buy butter as well. The cook had been gone some time, and Tara started to be concerned.

An older woman with a faded blue kerchief around her gray hair busily scrubbed dishes at a sink in the corner. A girl about Rosie's age sat at the butter churn, wide-eyed. Her hands slowed on the paddle.

Tara smiled at her. "I'm Tara," she said politely. "Who are you?"

"Nissa." The girl pointed at Tara's face. "Did your husband do that?" she asked.

The words felt like a knife. Like Mago's accusation. "No, he didn't," Tara answered firmly. "He'd never do a thing like that. If he had been there, no one would have been able to harm me."

Bevan. Her heart squeezed tight in her chest.

"Oh," Nissa said. "Where is your husband?"

The older woman paused in her scrubbing. "Nissa, hush! Don't be rude." But she too turned a curious look toward Tara. And Nissa's question hung in the air.

Tara glanced down at her lap. "He died fighting for the king." It was the first time she had said those words to strangers and they held a bitter taste on her tongue.

"A soldier then?" the older woman asked.

The answer was close enough. "Yes," Tara replied. "A soldier."

"That's hard. Mine died of fever in his bed."

"That's hard too." Tara held the woman's gaze for a moment, and sympathy flickered between them. The woman returned to her rag and rubbed something in the sink vigorously.

Nissa, however, stared a few moments longer until Tara wasn't sure what to do. Finally, the girl moved her arms again, and the thump of the paddle sounded in the churn.

Tara studied the whitewashed walls of the kitchen, the brick oven that divided the huge fireplace in two, the broad worktables, the cupboards, and the kettles that hung waiting on fire-hooks.

The cook still did not return. Tara took a deep breath and continued to wait.

27

Questions on the Path

I watched Mama go down around the bend, then Rosie and I stepped up onto the rise of ground that banked the path and peered through the trees to watch the next leg of her descent. When Mama's red hair disappeared from view below us, we studied the inn.

"I wonder what she'll find there," said Rosie.

A boy carrying a bucket passed from sight around the corner of a shed. "I have no idea," I replied.

"We can't see the road or the front of the inn from here," said Rosie. "We might as well find a comfortable place to sit and wait. This gum tree has fat roots. I don't think it would mind if we made a bench of them."

I pulled my cloak snugly around me and perched on

one of the large roots. Rosie picked out another, then looked straight up into the rows of branches. As she gazed, a look of awe came over her face.

"Can you see the top?" I asked.

"No," said Rosie, still looking upward. "But I can tell where it is. This is a tree filled with goodness, Silvie," she said solemnly. "A very *good* tree in the true sense of the word."

"Tike seems to have found one he likes." I pointed to where the dog was nosing around the base of another tree across the path. "Aren't all trees good?" I asked.

"It's good to have trees," said Rosie, "but not all trees are good."

I blinked at her. In all her life, I had never known her to talk about the unseen essence of things. My sister had always been one absorbed in the moment of life, in the tangible, the touchable, the practical. What was the gift of the Sender calling out in her?

Rosie glanced around the woods as if she had said nothing out of the ordinary. "Where are the fox and the cat?"

"They went hunting. They promised to stay away from the inn yard."

The white squirrel dug busily in the ground not far from where Rosie sat. Redbird flitted in the branches above us. The bear sat partway up the path, exactly where he had been when Mama said goodbye.

"Would you like to come over here and talk while we wait?" I asked.

The bear slowly got to his four feet and shuffled toward us. He was so powerful in the way he moved, so large. How very huge he would be if he stood up on his hind feet like a man!

"C'mon, Bear," Rosie called out, in a friendly voice. "I don't have the fire iron, so it's safe."

The absurdity of this made me smile. "The fire iron probably couldn't do a thing to this particular bear," I said. "Could it, Bear?"

He sat down in the middle of the path in front of us and slumped forward, leaning on folded paws. "Probably not," he said. His voice sounded like a sleepy bass singer. "But it would be best not to try it."

"Have we seen you somewhere else before, Bear?" Rosie asked. "Before you came to the clearing?"

The bear hesitated. "Where would that be?"

"On the riverbank," she said. "But much closer to Elva. It would have been about a week ago at night. There was a bear fishing late and it saw us."

The terror of that night came back to me—the frantic stones we threw with shaking hands trying to drive the bear away—and I shuddered. I knew in my heart this was not that bear, but Rosie had her own questions to ask.

The bear shook his head, so human-like, that I tried hard to glimpse the man inside him.

"I first saw you by the hunting station," he said. "Not before."

She nodded, accepting this. "You are very powerful, Bear. Have you ever killed anyone?"

I started, feeling alarmed. When Rosie was five years old, she had tried to ask every Guardsman that same question. Until Papa stopped her and told her that killing a man was nothing a Guardsman would be proud of. On her own, she had gone back to every one she had asked and apologized.

From the composed look on her face now, I felt that Rosie was not being morbidly curious, but was doing what Papa would have done, yet in her own way. She was measuring the character of someone that could be a possible ally or a possible enemy. Was this creature disposed to take a human life? Had he already done so?

The bear lifted his head, seeming to consider her question. "As a man, or as a bear?" he replied.

"Oh." Rosie looked thoughtful. "Let's say as a bear."

He lowered his muzzle. "Yes. A long time ago. A long place ago. And I cannot tell you of it."

I asked the other part of the question, half afraid of the answer. "And as a man?" I said quietly. I kept my eyes on him, although I wanted to look away.

The bear turned his gaze to me. "No," he said. His eyes said even more, but I could not understand the message in them. Puzzled, I pulled the dry leaves from the new grass at my feet.

"Well, that's good to know," Rosie said. "How old are you, Bear?"

"As a bear, or as man?"

I stopped poking in the grass and raised my head.

"Answer the same as before," said Rosie lightly. "Bear first."

The bear turned his shaggy head and looked down the path, as if he were seeing through the trees at the path's bend, and far, far beyond them. "As a bear," he said slowly, "ageless."

I wondered at this, but Rosie persisted. "What do you mean? You're really old? Or you don't know how old you are?"

"The turning of the earth only has meaning for those born on it," he replied. "Other creatures think nothing of it."

Rosie gaped at him, speechless. She turned to me and whispered, "How can an ageless bear eat termites?"

"Does it bother you that we ask you things, Bear?" I said.

"No, but if I cannot answer, I will not."

The truthfulness of his reply calmed me, and made me trust him more. "How old are you as a man then?"

"That is something I cannot—"

Sadness seemed to halt his voice. Rosie didn't notice. "Silvie's almost eighteen and I'm sixteen," she said.

I barely heard her. All my attention was on the bear.

"You are a man and an ageless bear at the same time." I spoke each word with care. "I don't understand what kind of creature you are. Have you always been this way?"

The bear shifted, lifted his nose to the air, and began to rise. I wondered if this question was the kind he would not answer. He got to his four feet and looked straight at me.

"Not very long. And forever."

With that he walked past us into the trees a little, and looked down the hillside toward the inn. "There's your mother."

Rosie and I got up immediately and went to his side. Mama seemed to be knocking at one of the inn's back doors. I could see just the top of the door and the top of her head. The door opened, but I could not see who answered it. After a few moments, the door opened wider and Mama disappeared inside. *May something good meet her there.*

I didn't understand what I did next. I only knew that since the Sender had given me the gift, I reached out to the animals, ready to touch the ones who wanted my touch. To stroke Tike's back or the cat's brindled coat.

So without thinking who or what I was standing next to as we watched, I rested my hand on the bear's shoulder. My fingertips curled into the matted fur, feeling the softness deep underneath. And I was grateful for his presence.

28

The Test

Ettie was beside herself with impatience. The bread loaves had to go into the oven soon in order to be ready by dinner time. She had the stew to spice and the fruit to heat, and Alta was taking the longest time examining that woman's embroidered bag.

At last she could wait no longer. "I must return to the kitchen or dinner will be late and you'll have some angry woodsmen on your hands."

Alta looked up at her at last. "You can go, Ettie. I'm going to show this to Gareth."

Ettie shook her head. "I can't return to the kitchen without the bag. It's valuable and I believe it's her work. If I come back without it, she'll think we're trying to steal from her. She's seen enough trouble already. You can tell that by looking at her."

Alta's face tightened. "That's exactly it, Ettie. A woman in trouble couldn't have done this kind of stitching. It's *not* hers."

Ettie put her hands on her hips. "My brother's face looked just like that when he went flyin' off his sled into a rock wall. And he's still bookkeeper for his whole town. As for the stitching, all you have to do is spend a few moments watching her sew and you'll know the truth of it."

They went downstairs—Alta first, Ettie following— and laid the bag on the bar for Gareth to see. Ettie climbed onto a stool and gazed at the handsome work.

"Ettie thinks that woman could do this embroidery for us," Alta began. "For the rooms for the nobility. I already purchased the quality linens, remember?" But even as she said the words, Alta sounded doubtful.

"This is what you've been wanting, isn't it, Alta?" Gareth asked. "So, what's the trouble? If the woman can do this work, why not let her? It could be the making of The Grumpy Rabbit."

"I don't want to be fooled, Gareth."

He looked at his wife closely. Ettie saw understanding in his eyes and felt relief. No one understood Alta like Gareth.

"Alta, that was years ago," he said, gently. "And my mama was too hard on you. She made her own mistakes many a time. But look." Gareth's voice became more businesslike. "Crim's here. He's waiting a few more days before taking his goods into Elva—waiting until the stores open again after the king's funeral. Crim knows the value of everything. He's the one who kept you from paying too much for the linens you were talking about just now. Crim will know."

Alta's face relaxed. "Yes, let's talk to Crim."

They all went upstairs together to Crim's room. Ettie refused to leave the bag with anyone else, but mourned her dinner preparations all the way.

The door to the kitchen finally creaked open, and Tara looked up. The cook walked in holding the rose carry sack in front of her. She handed it to Tara with a smile on her face.

"Could you show them what you can do? Stitch something while they watch?"

The request filled Tara with hope. "Certainly," she replied.

The cook led her through the doorway and down a hall back into the inn's main room. The afternoon was moving on, and it was quiet in the inn. The four men who discussed the king's funeral had left. So had the older man with the soup. The cook motioned toward a table in the back, positioned by a sunlit window. Three people sat there.

Tara recognized Alta and the barman, but not the third. He wore the clothing of a merchant, a long rich brown tunic with flowing sleeves, trimmed at the neck with velvet. His brown hair and beard matched his clothing, except where gray marked his temples. His face was thin, but pleasant and intelligent-looking. He looked to be a capable man, and he had a certain watchfulness about him.

The barman spoke first. "I'm Gareth. You've met Alta. This is Crim. He's a smart man, a well-traveled merchant, and he knows the value of everything. He's also familiar with the embroidery that the nobility prize."

Tara understood. This was more than a demonstration. This was a test to prove that she was the needlewoman she claimed to be. Laid out on the table were several needles, and embroidery thread in pale pink, yellow, and green. A green just a shade too dark to be her favorite. Strips of sun-bleached linen lay nearby and a pair of small scissors.

Gareth had the congenial face that was always ready to welcome a stranger and offer a drink. Alta's eyes were suspicious. Crim did not look hostile. Just ready to assess the value of something. She smiled at them all.

"My name is Tara, and I would be happy to show you how I work. But first, I'll need a basin of water and some soap."

"Why?" Alta said sharply. "Everything you need is right here."

Tara held out her hands. "A needlewoman never touches thread or fabric without carefully washing her hands first."

Alta frowned and glanced at Crim. Crim nodded.

Gareth stood up. "I'll get it."

Tara stood where she was, eyeing the thread. It

looked to be of good quality. Something inside her began to glow.

Gareth set a basin of water and a round of soap on the next table. He also provided a towel.

"Thank you so much," Tara said.

She rolled up her sleeves and plunged her hands into the cool water. They watched her silently as she soaped her hands. Waves of distrust came from Alta. Even fear. Tara rinsed her hands again and again, just as carefully as she had washed them. The trio next to her took in every movement.

After she had dried her hands thoroughly, she sat down at the table and picked up one of the linen strips. She smoothed the material with her fingers and reached for the pale pink floss. "These are beautiful colors. What would you like me to make for you?"

No one answered until Crim said, with a slight nasal tone, "Anything you choose would be fine."

Tara nodded and threaded the needle with the pale pink. "I noticed your quince tree. What if I make some quince flowers for you? The color won't be exact, but the shape will tell you what they are."

Alta nodded.

Tara eyed the strip of linen in her hands and thought of quince blossoms. And all of a sudden it happened. As it always happened. Every time.

The needle and thread felt alive in her hand. She could see the flowers on the linen, could see the leaves she would put around them as if they were already there. The whole design, though still invisible, was living and fresh.

She poked her needle up through the fabric and began. And as she worked, she felt transformed.

It was something she could never explain to her friend Zilla, who idolized Tara's work to the point of embarrassment. Could never explain that the movement of the needle through the linen was so much more than practice or skill. Stitching could be taught, of course. Embroidery too. But what transcended these was the fact that the needle flew through the cloth because of love.

Tara had tried to reason it out. Was it love for embroidery that brought beauty to the stitches? Yes. Love for the materials themselves? Yes. Love for the sheer joy of doing it? Yes.

But there was more.

Love stitched itself into the things she made and into the lives of the people that used them. A love she did not create but that came from beyond her. An inexhaustible love that even now, in the middle of tragic sorrow, was stitching the stitcher to life.

She formed flowers along the linen strip, filling several petals with patterns. Switching to the green, she traced a few leaves, then began to fill them in. But this would take some time. She glanced up at her three silent watchers.

"How long would you like me to go on?" She laid the strip down on the table between them and spread it out so all could see her design.

"For the leaves I would also use different colors and stitches to give them some texture and to fill them in, until you see none of the material under them. I would do the same for the rest of the flowers. In the richest embroidery, you see nothing of the fabric beneath, but that is not always the best. It all depends on the purpose.

"All this stitching might not be comfortable to sleep on, so I would embroider only the edge of a pillow cover or a sheet. But for a piece to wear, like the front of a cape, or the rim of a hat, it would be filled with thread. Also for a wall hanging, or articles like that."

She laid her work on the table, and they stared at it.

Mutely. For some time.

She stared at it too, and thought it exquisitely beautiful. The petals radiated the glow that is springtime, and the positioning added to the enchantment. Another one of the Sender's gifts.

Finally, Gareth raised his head, his eyes wide. "The flowers, the leaves look real. I mean, that's not a sewn flower. I'd swear it's a real one."

Alta looked frightened, her lips pressed together.

Gareth asked, "What do you think, Crim?"

Everyone turned to him expectantly, even Tara.

Crim shook his head slowly and Tara felt a twinge of alarm. Yet, his eyes had a gleam in them.

"I never would have believed it," said the merchant, "if I hadn't seen it worked right before me." He looked up at Gareth and Alta. "You hear rumors of people who seem to have the Sender's own needle in their hands. Now I know there is truth in the rumors."

"But every needle is the Sender's own needle—" Tara began.

"What do you mean, Crim?" The words burst from Alta. "And what does that mean to Gareth and me?"

Crim turned his eyes to Tara. "Where did you come from?"

She met his steady gaze. "Most recently from Elva. I was born and raised in East Rilken and learned to stitch there. But I've lived in Elva for over twelve years."

"Who did you stitch for before?"

Tara knew Crim must be referring to actual employment, to high-paying clients. But she had never had any. Had never needed any. The Guardsmen and their families were taken care of so well by the king that she never thought of sewing for money. But what she could tell him honestly, she would.

"I made things for those who served the king. And their families." All her friends and neighbors in Guardstown.

Alta gasped and looked troubled.

Crim fingered the embroidered linen and nodded. "This is the quality of what you see around the palace. Even superior to it." He reached into a leather bag that sat by his side and pulled out a small wrapped package, which he laid on the table next to Tara's sample. He pulled back the surrounding cloth, and there in the middle lay an embroidered purse.

"Look here, Alta," he said. "This is the most expensive embroidered item that I buy and sell. It was worked by a fifty-year old woman who has been embroidering for forty years. She's a rich woman who lives just east of Elva, and does the best work I've ever seen. Until now."

He looked directly at Alta. "This small purse costs fifty rills and is going to a baroness in Leibent."

He picked up Tara's sample. "What this woman has done is already worth twice that."

A look of horror came over Alta's face. "But I—I can't afford anything like that! It would take us months, years, to recover the money in those rooms."

Tara was moved by the look on Alta's face. It was as if she had finally glimpsed a long-held dream, only to see it snatched away from her.

Gareth had been studying Tara while this was going on. "What made you leave Elva?" he asked.

She had expected the question and had already prepared her answer. "My husband died. After that my family was attacked. So we left."

He nodded in understanding. "Where is your family now?"

Again, she needed to tell the truth. But only as much truth as need be told. "My daughters and I are cleaning out the king's hunting station. I don't know where we'll go after that."

Again, the thoughtful nod.

Alta turned to her. "How did your husband die?"

Tara looked down at her hands. "I would rather not talk about it. I can barely accept it myself."

Silence fell. It seemed that none of the three at the table knew how to proceed. So Tara turned to Alta.

"I would like to stitch for you," she said, gently. "I would like to help you make your rooms beautiful." She looked towards Crim. "What would be a fair wage for me?"

Crim glanced out the window and fingered his brown beard. "I don't know how to make a just comparison. We could compare it to the other salaries at the inn. The owners excepted, Ettie's is the most important, followed by the head groom. The cost of what Ettie produces compared to what you produce each day, perhaps? A conservative guess would place your daily embroidery at thirty to fifty times the value of Ettie's cooking. And for a daily wage—"

He named a number that shocked Tara and made Alta groan.

"Alta," Crim said in a soothing tone. "Why do you think my clothes are only trimmed in velvet? Embroidery is very rare and quality embroidery like hers is as rare as a Galerine mirror. Of course it would be expensive."

"A needlewoman has to rest her eyes and fingers often," Tara said. "So my workday would be shorter than Ettie's, of necessity. Could we agree on a number at..." Tara thought quickly. "About five times your cook's pay? I would work with you until the rooms are exactly the way you want them. You would need to provide the supplies of course, and I would also ask for dinner for myself and my daughters, daily bread, and a few necessary items. Would that be fair?"

The merchant looked perturbed. "These are my friends and I would be happy for them, but I have to be honest. That is not a very good business deal for you, ma'am. I couldn't recommend it."

"But it's a good deal for *them*?"

"It's an excellent deal for them," said Crim. "One that they'll be talking about to their dying day."

Tara turned to Alta. "Could we do this? I can look at

your rooms today before I go, and we can decide what colors you'll need. And if Crim has them?"

Several men came in the main door. Gareth got to his feet. "These will be great days for The Grumpy Rabbit. Thank you, Tara." He turned his congenial smile on the newcomers and stepped behind the bar.

Alta looked anxiously at Crim one more time, then silently nodded.

After going over the rooms and listening to what Alta had imagined for them, Tara said, "I could work on the bedding for one room first, then you could raise the price some on that one, while I work on the other's sheets. Then I'll come back to the first and work on another part of it, while you raise the price on the second."

Alta's eyes widened, as if she hadn't realized the possibility of extra money coming in so soon. "Yes, let's do that," she said. "When can you start?"

"As soon as you can gather the list of supplies and have your seamstress prepare the panels. In a day or two?" Tara replied. "You may keep the sample I made as a promise."

An hour later, Tara left Ettie's kitchen with a crock filled with stew, several dozen rolls, butter, a round of soap, and three spoons. Crim met her in the hallway.

"Here," he said, holding out a small jar. "This is ointment for your face. It will heal it quickly."

"Oh," said Tara, slightly taken aback. "I—I thank you. How much do I—"

He waved his hand as if waving her question away.

"Nothing. Consider it part of the wages you deserve that you are not getting."

She smiled at him, heartened by the kindness in his eyes. "Thank you again."

She put the jar in the rose carry sack next to the soap and spoons, and walked down the road to where Tike waited at the base of the path.

Weariness settled on her shoulders, but she felt triumphant. She had food for her family and good work to do. Work that would earn money. And, at last, she would be in a position to hear the news from Elva.

29

—————

Wells Makes a Discovery

Ravelin dreamed often of the Guardsmen. Of swords and blood, images that wrenched him gasping from his sleep. He stared into the darkness, breathing heavily, and as he shook the dreams from his consciousness, he felt again the heavy weight in his heart. The weight that nothing could move. The loss of his father and brother.

After one nightmarish ordeal, he sat against his pillows, thinking. His mind continually imagined Dallen's body lying on the forest floor. Mangled by animals that must have torn Dallen's glove from his lifeless hand.

His uncle was right. It was time to stop hoping for

Dallen's return. Dallen must have met the same horrible fate as their father.

But this did not bring him peace.

Fear of the Guardsmen seemed to possess Ravelin. He tried to believe what Pate had said. That the Guardsmen had protected him when he slid from his horse after his father's funeral. But he wasn't quite convinced.

His fall stirred up more fears. The fear of collapsing again. And lately, the fear of his heart pounding out of control.

Sometimes it seemed that in the quiet of his rooms, all he could hear was the incessant pounding of his own heart. The loud pulsing in his head when he lay on the pillow. Once, the sound of it alone woke him in the middle of the night.

Fears made him unfit for company. He didn't want anyone around him except for Pate and Wells. So he had meals brought to his rooms and ate alone.

He thought that writing a short history of these days might help to calm him. But his whirling thoughts refused to confine themselves to definite sentences. His pen hovered uselessly in the air until the ink dried on its tip, making it impossible to write. So he had to clean it and begin again. Every new beginning seemed to lead nowhere.

At night, he read as long as he could, lighting candle after candle, choosing books from the stacks that filled his bedside table. The books Aunt Olivia had brought from Ophria. Books that were his father's. Books of history and of literature. Even some of his childhood favorites. But no book could completely soothe his agitated mind, or return his heart to its normal cadence.

During the day, he made a habit of regular steady walking, hoping that it would guide his heart's rhythm. He walked all over his apartments, from one end to the other and back again. Forty paces took him from the outer door, across his large sitting room, and into his bedchamber. He practiced walking at a consistent speed, keeping to a pace that was not too fast, not too slow.

He determined to use every inch of his apartments for this purpose, walking even into closets and alcoves for the extra steps they would give him. Today he walked into his dressing chamber, startling Wells, who was polishing his boots.

When he had progressed partway across his bedchamber again, an image from last night's dream flashed in his mind. Dallen sprawled in the mud. Ants crawling over his bloated face.

Ravelin's heart slammed hard into his chest, hard as the blow from a fist. He cried out and stumbled, grabbed for his desk, and knocked a pile of papers to the floor.

Wells emerged from the closet and ran to him. "I've got you, my prince. Lean on me. Let's get you to your bed."

Ravelin's face dripped with sweat. Shakily, he leaned on Wells.

"Allow me to take off your outer shirt, sir. You seem much too hot."

Ravelin sat against the bed as Wells did so. Wells also pulled off his day shoes and long stockings. When he had finished, Ravelin crawled in under the bedclothes.

"Some water would be beneficial, sir."

Ravelin obediently took a sip from the tumbler held out to him. He settled back into the pillows, but his heart was still taking its wild ride. He clutched Wells' sleeve.

"Wells!" he said, looking up at the attendant that had served him for years. "What is happening to me? My heart gallops like a charger at the sight of the enemy. I am afraid it won't stop. Then I am afraid it will. Am I dying?"

"No," said Wells firmly. "You are not dying. 'Tis only the lingering effects of the winter sickness come back to lash you in your grief. You have many, many troubles, my prince. But you will get through them."

Ravelin sank back into the pillows. He did not think he would make it through the troubles. "Perhaps," he said quietly, for Wells' sake. "Perhaps I will get through."

Wells wiped the sweat from Ravelin's face, opened the window to admit some fresh spring air, then came back to plump the pillows around him.

"Wells, I need to ask you a question. I don't want to ask Lord Kendall."

"I will answer if I can, my prince."

"I've been reading about Nordia and the Hosts of the North ever since my father received their Duke's invitation. In Nordian literature there are references to a group of people called 'The Fearless.' Have you heard of them?"

"Yes, sir. I have read stories in which The Fearless are mentioned from time to time."

"They seem to be an amazing group of people," said Ravelin. "Women and men are both in their ranks. As well as the young and the elderly. They defy the bounds of any category. And yet, in this one thing they are all alike. No fear common to man has the power to terrify them."

Ravelin stared up into the green velvet canopy above his bed. "I wonder what thoughts go through their minds if fears do not lurk there. I wonder how they spend their days." He hesitated a few moments, then finished quietly. "I wish I could be one of them."

"You may, sir. You may."

"But how, Wells? In all the histories of Nordia, I have not been able to discover how to become one of The Fearless. It can't be a test of strength. No child or old one could pass such a thing. And The Fearless have both among them."

"It's a marvel, sir. Could there be a different question to ask? Perhaps it's not about something one *does*."

Ravelin considered this. "Is it about knowledge? Something they *know* that the fearful do not? So I should ask what do The Fearless know?"

Wells pushed another pillow behind Ravelin's back. "I do not have the answer to that question either, sir. But should I uncover it, I will tell you immediately."

There was a knock at the outer door and Wells admitted Pate. Pate walked in with his cat draped over one of his shoulders and perched on the edge of Ravelin's bed as he had done for years. The cat leapt down and walked across the blanket to Ravelin. It stood there, looking closely at his face, waiting to be petted.

"I've no strength for this," Ravelin murmured. "I've just had another spell."

"So Wells told me," said Pate, compassion on his face. "I think somehow the cat knows this too. That is why she is insisting on it. The moment we think we absolutely cannot in any way imaginable pet a cat, is exactly the moment in which we should."

Pate leaned back against the bed post. "I noticed that the palace guard is on duty outside your door. Does your uncle's removal of the Guardsmen diminish your worries?"

"I asked him to remove them." Ravelin couldn't look at Pate's face when he said this.

"Do you feel safer now?"

Ravelin stroked the cat's head with his finger. "I don't think I will ever feel safe again. Perhaps a prince never can. You'll tell me that's why my father and many before him depended on their Guardsmen. And they were right. But they did not tell me what to do when I can't depend on the Guardsmen anymore."

He knew these words would be painful to Pate, since his own father had been the best of the elite corps, but Pate said nothing in response.

After a few moments Ravelin dared to look up. Pate gave him a friendly smile.

"I have come to keep you company while Wells returns to the daunting task of cleaning out your wardrobe after the long winter. Air, he says. All things need air! Even princes."

Ravelin caught the hint. "Not yet, Pate."

"Very well, my good prince. Until you are ready, this cat will tell you of the roof ledges she has walked across, the milk she's drunk, the mice she's eaten, and the dogs she has provoked. A daring cat, she is."

The cat curled up next to Ravelin on the bed and began to purr while he stroked her side. "Your cat is very useful, Pate," he said, attempting to smile.

"Oh, how fitting!" said Pate. "It is an honor to be useful! Do you remember how I got my nickname? Your father gave it to me."

"Tell me again," said Ravelin. "I am hungry for talk about my father and brother."

"I will be happy to give you some." Pate sat cross-legged at the foot of the bed. "I was not ten years old when my father was asked to come visit the king. He was asked regularly because King Adare never forgot a kindness.

"Such an unusual gift that," said Pate, interrupting himself. "Most men remember all their griefs and ignore all the kindnesses. As if the dark were held to be more true than the light."

"I would consider saving one's life as more than just a kindness," said Ravelin.

"There you are, Ravelin, as noble as your father! On this particular visit, my father decided to take me with him to see the king. I'm not sure why. Perhaps to spare my poor mother's nerves. Anyway, I came and was filled with awe at the sight of your father sitting on his throne in the audience room. I bowed so low, I fell over. My father grabbed me at the last moment before my head hit the marble and pulled me upright.

"I glanced sheepishly at the king and saw he was smiling at me. That merry kind of smile he had. Not a trace of ridicule, just enjoyment. And I was full to bursting with pride because I had made him smile.

"I vowed to myself then that I would do anything and everything all my life long to serve this king. And being only nine years old and not having much practice in holding my tongue, I blurted out, 'I long to be useful to you, Your Majesty!'

"He looked at me with a kind eye and said, 'I think you could be useful to me, young Pate, by being useful to my sons. From now on I will always think of you as Pate the Useful.'

"I don't think anyone else has ever had a title like mine. It is my life's ambition to have those words chiseled on my gravestone. *He was useful.*"

There was a pause in the flow of conversation, and they both watched Ravelin's hand stroke the cat for a while.

"What have you been thinking of lately, my prince?" Pate's tone was serious now.

Ravelin took a breath before speaking. "The forest road. That's all I can ever think of. My father. Dallen. Guardsmen. Swords. Arrows." After a pause he added, "Villains. And bloody gloves."

Pate nodded somberly. "The glove your uncle showed you?"

"I cannot keep from seeing it everywhere. I close my eyes to find it emblazoned on my lids. It haunts my every thought. At least my father could be honored with dignity, but if Dallen is truly gone—" He choked on the words and coughed.

Pate was on his feet in an instant, holding out the tumbler of drink to him, but Ravelin shook his head. Pate put the tumbler back on the table and resumed his place propped up against the bedpost.

"The searchers have not found anything at all, Ravelin. The best tracker I know of—Nally the Dwarf—was complaining of it to his friends at dinner last night. They have spent every daylight hour combing acres and acres of forest and have found nothing. No sign of Dallen. No sign of any human person. Only occasional bear tracks, which seem to go nowhere."

"No human sign except for that glove, you mean," said Ravelin.

"Except for that," said Pate. He looked off and away. "Now, I wonder…"

Ravelin had kept his eyes on the cat for much of Pate's report. At this he looked up at him. "You wonder what?"

"I wonder why I haven't heard anyone claim credit for the finding of the glove. One would think with all the frustrating searches, the finder would surely crow—"

"I know who found it," said Ravelin. "Mago did. My uncle told me later."

Pate nodded thoughtfully. "Mago, I wasn't aware he had joined the searchers. Ah, well. It is a big castle and I miss much."

Ravelin felt the fire of hope rise in him again. "Pate,

if by some miracle Dallen is still alive, what if this villain is holding him captive somewhere?"

"For what purpose?" asked Pate.

"I—I don't know. To protect his own life maybe?"

Pate looked doubtful, and Ravelin felt a surge of frustration.

"I haven't worked it all out yet, I know! But do villains always have reasons for what they do?"

"In their own minds I suppose they might, but of what good use is a villainous mind?" Pate shook his head. "This is hardly a helpful subject. Let us pursue a more enlivening topic."

Now Ravelin shook his head. "I have not had much luck coming up with enlivening topics, as you call them."

Pate rubbed his clean-shaven chin and looked thoughtful again, but did not speak. They fell silent for a long while. Ravelin's arm tired of petting the cat, and he rested it on one of the pillows that Wells had tucked around him.

"All right. You've heard enough about what I've been thinking, and I am weary of it myself. What are *you* thinking about, Pate?"

"A great many things, but this past week I have thought much on what type of woman would be the perfect wife for you."

This was so unexpected that Ravelin stared at him. "You're joking!"

"I am in earnest, I assure you. I ask myself, now what character traits should be found in the woman who would be the perfect match for my dear friend and highly esteemed Prince Ravelin?"

"You forget that my uncle says I am to marry my cousin."

"Yes, I do forget that, and will continue to forget it. Let's move Petronia aside." He moved his hand through the air as if brushing away a pesky fly. "Dear Petronia, over there. And remain over there. Thank you. Now, Ravelin, what have I uncovered so far about this woman in whose presence is happiness itself?" He cast a look full of intrigue at Ravelin.

"All right," said Ravelin, shifting the cat and propping himself up in the pillows against the headboard. "I'm listening."

"Ah, nothing like talk of a woman to make a man listen."

"Pate—" Ravelin began.

"Yes, yes, to the point, Pate. I often tell myself that. Well, here you are. My thoughts. You, Ravelin, are a very studious and thoughtful prince. In my imaginings, I see a woman who admires you for that, but who also can pull you from that when you need it most. A woman who believes in you and a woman you can believe in. She would need to come with an energy, a light of her own. Not like your beloved aunt, who often depends on the energy of others to move her. Isn't there a song about a woman's face like a light teaching the sun to shine?"

Ravelin didn't answer. In his mind he could see a woman's face, hazy in outline, its features hidden still, but strength emanating from it. A strength both healing and true. And with that strange vision, consolation seeped into his soul, and he felt the darkness loosen its grip.

Pate was watching him closely. "I take your silence as agreement, my prince?"

"Yes," said Ravelin.

Delight suffused Pate's face. He glanced up into the bed canopy as if seeing heaven's own joys there, before resuming his talk.

"This woman, wherever the Sender is keeping her, must have courage and boldness as well. Must be as true as steel just like you are, of course. And, and—here is Wells looking distressed. You object to the simile, Wells? Should I have said *as true as north?*"

Wells did look distressed. Surprisingly so. Ravelin sat up and leaned forward. "What is it, Wells?" The woman's face vanished from his mind as he spoke, and he was sorry for it.

"Sir, I have been going through your wardrobe very carefully and something appears to be missing." Wells held out a sheaf of papers marked in careful pencil lines. "I keep track of every single item belonging to you, sir, down to the last stocking."

"I know you do, Wells, so what's missing?"

"A pair of your hunting gloves, sir. The pair that Duchess Olivia gave to you and a like pair to Prince Dallen last year. Do you remember when you wore them last?"

Ravelin shook his head. "No, I can't remember."

"I can, sir." Wells consulted his papers. "You wore them on the second day of the third week of autumn's last month, on a hunting expedition at Lord Heves' estate."

Wells looked closely at a page, his finger following one particular line. "After which they were both returned and cleaned, and placed in their box awaiting their next wearing."

"Is the box missing, Wells," Pate asked, "or just the gloves?"

"Just the gloves, sir."

"Is the box in its usual position?" Pate took up the questioning, and Ravelin let him.

"Yes, sir. It is in the place it rests when the gloves are inside it. When they are not inside it, I move the box to the waiting shelf. The better to keep track of what is currently out of the wardrobe and should soon be coming back in."

"An excellent system, Wells. And as you say, the box was not on your waiting shelf."

"No, sir."

"So the removal of the gloves was certainly not your doing?"

"Absolutely not." Wells sounded indignant.

After his recent spell, Ravelin had little strength to follow along in this discourse. He was used to Pate rambling on about inconsequential details, but he couldn't remember seeing this look on Pate's face before.

"My good prince," Pate said solemnly. "What if the bloody glove you were shown the morning of your father's funeral was not Dallen's glove, but your own?"

Ravelin felt shocked. "But why?"

"I do not know. Perhaps someone wants everyone to

believe Dallen is dead. Someone who needs Dallen to be dead, but cannot prove it since no trace of him can be found."

"Who would need Dallen to be dead?" Ravelin asked, horrified.

"That is the question, isn't it? What does the sight of such a glove do but produce fear? Despair? You see the glove and can't see anything else.

"You are an astute prince, Your Highness. Your father often spoke of you in those terms. But fear blinds every man. If you can be kept from seeing—no, wait. Is that it?" Pate appeared to be speaking to himself.

"From seeing what?" Ravelin asked, in complete confusion.

"My father gave me good advice recently," said Pate. "For some reason, he is always concerned that I might get into trouble. He very pointedly told me to make sure that I never look where an enemy wants me to look.

"An enemy will always want to guide your eyes to a place beneficial to him, but not so beneficial to you. Now, I wonder if the reverse might be true also. If it could be a precept to make sure to look where an enemy *doesn't* want you to? It might be hasty to assume such logic, but I wonder."

Ravelin cut through Pate's rambling impatiently. "Are you saying that the horrible glove was really *mine?* Stolen and bloodied and made to look like Dallen's?"

"I do not even know what I say," Pate said slowly. "But I do say it."

What had Mago done? Or—or was it his uncle's doing?

Ravelin turned to his attendant. "Wells, what do you think?"

Before Wells could answer, a sharp knock at the outer door made Ravelin jump. Wells tucked his papers into the wardrobe and hurried to answer it.

In a moment, Wells' voice called from the outer room announcing the visitor. "His Royal Highness, the Duke of Elva."

30

The Duke's Concern

R avelin panicked. "Pate, what do I do?" he whispered.

"Don't give into fear, but for now, be ill." Pate hopped off the bed and straightened the bedclothes. "And take a deep breath."

Ravelin obeyed and leaned back against the pillows as the Duke of Elva strode into his bedchamber.

Pate bowed low. "Your Highness."

"Master Pate." The Duke said his name with condescension. "How is my nephew?"

He was wearing a hat and cape as if ready for an outing, and carried gloves in his hand. The sight of the gloves repulsed Ravelin, and he turned his gaze to the carvings on the bedpost.

"He is as you see, sir," said Pate, extending an arm toward Ravelin.

"Good day, Uncle," Ravelin said, in a voice just above a whisper.

The Duke gave Ravelin his full attention at this, and the smile on his face melted away. He stepped closer to the bed and scrutinized Ravelin's face—eyes widening with apparent alarm—until Ravelin felt like a pinned moth.

"I was not aware that you were as ill as this," said the Duke finally. "I was going to ask you to come with me to see the progress on the east wing. But clearly you are not well enough to leave your bed."

"I do not feel well enough, sir," Ravelin replied.

The Duke frowned and shook his head. "Is this a result of your collapse in the streets? Could it have such far-reaching effects? You must see my physician."

He looked over his shoulder at Pate. "And what is Pate doing here with this animal? Surely the cat is not yours, Ravelin." Wells brought a chair forward for the Duke, but he waved it away.

Ravelin glanced at Pate, hoping he would speak, and his friend picked up the cue.

"Yes, sir," said Pate. "The cat is mine. She came to assist me in cheer."

"I wouldn't think a court jester such as you required any assistance in mirth."

Pate brightened at this. "I am honored by that title, dear sir. Every royal court worthy of the name must have a jester. That you would consider me to be one, in the jewel that is Elva, means more than I can say. I do what I can to relieve the stresses of the Crown."

"Yes," said the Duke, nodding. "Every ruler has a fool nearby."

The Duke's tone sounded unfriendly to Ravelin's ears. He saw in Pate's eyes that his friend felt it also.

But Pate's expression did not change. Instead, he bowed again with an extravagant gesture. "I can only say, dear sir, what a pleasure it is to be *your* fool."

The Duke gave a short laugh and turned back to Ravelin. "The workmen have replaced all the weak stone on the east wing and have finished the outer walls beautifully. I think your father would have approved. They are laying the supports for the roof today and promise me that it will be complete by the end of summer."

"That is good news, Uncle," said Ravelin, politely.

"Yes, it is. Well, I will leave you to your cheer, such as it is. The physician will see you within the hour."

"Thank you, sir."

The Duke left the bedchamber. Ravelin held very quiet and still, straining his ears for the sound of the outer door's closing, waiting for the relief that sound would bring.

WELLS LED the way to the outer door of the prince's apartment and reached to open it, when the Duke held out his arm and stopped him.

"Wells," he said quietly. "You are one of the best

servants the royal family has ever known. I am concerned for my nephew. I want you to report to me daily as to his welfare."

"Certainly, sir. With my good prince's permission, I would be glad to report to you."

The Duke frowned slightly. "No, no. I don't think it needs to be as formal as that. Just keep your eyes and ears open and tell me whatever you see."

"My eyes and ears are Ravelin's own. If he wishes me to report to you, I will, sir. I assure you."

The Duke's expression hardened. He took a step back and stared at Wells' face. "Do you know who you are speaking to now? I am the ruler of Rilken, and I will remain so until Ravelin is old enough to assume the great responsibility of the throne. Do you *dare* deny me this request?"

Wells acted the part of the misunderstood courtier. His eyes widened and his hand smote his chest. "Oh, Your Highness, Your *Majesty*! How I beg your pardon!! How was I to know that you meant to hide your kind concern? I only thought you meant that I could serve you best by serving Ravelin first."

The Duke's face relaxed and he chuckled. "Oh, Wells. Would that I had a thousand of you."

Wells bowed low. "I am *deeply* gratified, sir." He opened the door as quickly as respect would allow, and the Duke finally took his leave.

. . .

THE ATTENDANT STOOD for a few moments, listening as the sound of footsteps faded down the hall. He was filled with doubt.

Had he handled that unexpected request wisely? What meaning was hidden behind the Duke's words? That he wanted Wells to spy for him was clear. But had the Duke truly accepted his response?

No. It was only a conversational side-step hidden by a compliment. The Duke would not forget that Wells had refused him.

No matter. That refusal would not be altered. For in heart and in word, Wells would remain true to the prince he had vowed to serve until death. He made his way back through the sitting room to report every word to that prince now.

Ravelin listened silently and stayed long silent afterwards. Neither Pate nor Wells rushed to interrupt his thoughts.

"It seems," said the prince at last, "that until I know the truth of the glove, I would be wise to consider my uncle an enemy. For who else would try to make my attendant his spy? And be angry that I would know it?"

31

Wheat Moving in the Wind

The gentle thrumming of morning rain woke me. As I blinked my eyes in the gloom, my first thought was for Bear. He left us when Mama returned from the inn yesterday, and I wondered where he had gone. Down what lonely forest paths?

I shivered suddenly and sat up, pulling my cloak tight around me. Mama's bed was empty. So was Rosie's. A good fire burned on the hearth. Mama was standing over by the table.

"Good morning, Silvie. I'm laying out our breakfast. Did you sleep well?"

"Well enough," I replied, getting to my feet. I folded up my bed things, then went to the front window and opened the shutter.

Gray, heavy clouds covered the forest and water dripped from the sky, the trees, the eaves, everywhere. Rosie was running towards the station. I reached to open the door for her and she darted in. "Everything is wet, wet, wet out there," she exclaimed, shaking out the shawl that had covered her head.

"It looks like we have a long, quiet indoor day in front of us," said Mama. "Those clouds have settled in to stay."

From the front window, I looked carefully around the clearing and as far into the budding trees as I could. There was no sign of Bear.

I could have asked him so many more questions yesterday, but his pervading sadness held my tongue. Even Rosie had stopped her asking. And, in the long wait for Mama yesterday, Rosie ran up to the station to get our book of *Tales from Nordia*.

I read them out loud as we perched by the path. Bear listened along with Rosie to every single one. And he watched me even more intently. As I finished one story about a ring of fire in the icy north of Nordia, I glanced at him and saw a curious look in his eye, an eye that said he heard more in the tales than we did.

I thought about that curious look and about Bear far into the night. I could not sleep for wondering who was really speaking when the bear talked. Was it the man or the bear? How could they share the same voice? How did they come to be together at all? And which of them held the sorrow? My vain search for answers through the night was the reason I slept late this morning.

Rosie added more logs to the fire. She answered my

question before I spoke it. "We have enough dry firewood," she said confidently. "The king's men left enough here for a month. I also put bowls out for rainwater so we don't have to go to the stream in the rain."

After our breakfast of rolls and butter, we washed our faces and hands in rainwater and brushed each other's hair. We could brush our own, of course, but there was something friendly and comforting about doing it for each other. As I brushed Rosie's hair, her bright red locks curling around my fingers, Mama told us more about the inn and the people there. Rosie and I soaked up every detail, from Ettie's floury apron to the purple on Crim's pouch for the rich woman in Leibent.

Mama pulled the chair up near the fire as she talked, and took needle, thread, and scraps from the sewing bag. It seemed that the bruises on her face were not so dark as before. This quiet rainy day meant another day of healing for her. And sewing.

Mama was good at gently leading us to do the practical things that needed to be done every day. To push against the sadness that threatened to numb us into lifelessness.

We all carried so many tears, tears ready to flow at any turn in the conversation, at any chance memory. We accepted this in each other, giving hugs, rubbing backs, and patting shoulders whenever we saw watery eyes. Practical work and tears were both signs of strength.

Tike returned from his wanderings, and I dried him with a rag. Then I sat down near Mama and the fire. "What are you working on?" I asked.

"There's an unusual picture of a rabbit hanging over

the bar in the inn," Mama said. "I'm going to put its likeness and the inn's name somewhere on every piece of embroidery I do. That could keep people from trying to steal the pieces. Anyone who sees them would know immediately where they had come from."

Rosie took a long time rearranging some small logs over the fire, then reached for the bellows. When she finished and sat on the floor next to me, she had a sad look on her face.

Mama noticed it too. "What's wrong, Rosie?"

"Something beyond missing Papa?" I asked, patting her knee.

"I think I'm just—missing things," she replied.

"What kinds of things?" Mama's voice was gentle.

"My green dress. Our feather bed. The sound of horse hooves on cobbles."

"I miss my kitchen and my own fire," said Mama. "And cabinets filled with things to cook."

I stroked Tike's head thoughtfully. "The call of the baker in the morning."

"The sound of the castle bells," Rosie added.

I sighed. "I miss the safety of walls."

Mama looked up at this. "Do you know something, Silvie? When we first moved to Elva, I hated the walls. I felt so trapped in the city, I couldn't breathe. I missed the broad sweeps of meadows and fields, and seeing the way the wind pushed its way through the grain. In Elva everything was hard stone."

"I didn't know you felt that way."

Mama measured another length of thread for her

needle, snipped, and knotted it. "It took two years for Elva to feel like home."

"And the walls didn't really protect us after all," I said slowly.

A few quiet moments went by. The fire crackled while the rain drummed on the roof.

"I miss the girl gatherings," said Rosie. "Meeting in each others' homes to talk and laugh. I miss Sukey and Lily, especially."

"I felt more alone in those gatherings than I do now in the middle of the forest," I said. "But I am sorry for you, Rosie, because I know they were fun for you."

"Well, mostly fun," said Rosie. "Not always. Martie acted coldly to you when she came. I didn't like that."

"Martie admired Ross. She saw me as her rival, I suppose, even though I didn't want to be. She could have had him. I wouldn't have minded."

Rosie picked up the fire iron again and moved a chunk of wood. "Ross," she said disgustedly. "If I would have had another clod of mud, he would have got it right on his forehead for doing nothing."

"Some people are not as strong in spirit as others," said Mama graciously.

"But look at the way we've lived," said Rosie, waving her fire iron in the air. "For most of our lives we've been surrounded by Guardsmen. By people who *are* strong in spirit."

"Until we think that is what's normal," I added.

"Yes, and it *should* be normal," said Rosie.

Mama bent over her stitching, her fingers moving

with their usual swiftness. "It takes time for strength to grow."

"Papa would say that love supplies the strength," I replied. "But I still wouldn't want to marry Ross. I could have waited for years for a type of strength, a type of love, that would never have come from him."

"That would not have been wise. The strength and love for a marriage need to be there before it begins." Mama glanced up at me with an understanding look on her face. "I didn't want you to marry Ross," she said. "That was only Zilla's dream."

I felt relief at this. Mama had never spoken so clearly about it before. Of course, Martie could take Ross happily now. Because I would never return to Ross or to Guardstown.

A sudden thought came to mind, and I gasped at the horror of it. My eyes immediately flooded with tears.

Rosie sank down next to me and put her arm around me. Mama raised her head. "Oh, Silvie! What is it?"

I felt stricken. "Martie's father was one of the Guardsmen who died, wasn't he? She lost her father too. And—and she must think—just like all of Guardstown —that Papa killed him."

Mama left her chair and knelt on the floor at my side. Her arms reached around me.

"I hate that people think Papa was a traitor and a murderer," I cried.

"I hate that too," said Mama. "But we cannot know what people really think. We only know what they were *told* to think."

"I wish I could prove that he wasn't," said Rosie. "I would prove it to the whole world!"

My tears were cried out for the moment and the floor was uncomfortably hard. We got to our feet, and I wiped my face. Rosie pulled a bench over for us. Mama sat in her seat again and picked up her sewing.

"How could we do that?" I wondered aloud. "How could we show others what we know to be the truth about Papa?"

"Without knowing the actual details of the king's death, it would be hard to convince anyone," Mama replied.

"And all we know now is Mago's accusation," said Rosie.

"Which is why I long to hear whatever I can in the common room of the inn," Mama said.

"You'll tell us everything you hear, won't you?" I asked. "And we can talk it all through. Every night?"

Mama paused in her sewing, her embroidery piece draped across her knees. She gave me a look that had promise in it. "I will. Every night."

"It will be hard waiting," said Rosie. "My garden won't take that much time and there are so many hours in a day. I long to just *do* something!"

"And yet we can't," I put in, "until we know something. Waiting is the hardest—" I couldn't finish my thought. My eyes caught sight of something on Mama's lap.

She had turned to reach for more thread and I looked at the outline and features of the rabbit that she had sewn so far. As I studied it, the ear of the rabbit —*twitched*. Side to side. Like it was flicking away a fly.

I stared at it. "Mama, your rabbit just moved."

"What?" cried Rosie.

We left our bench to stand by Mama's chair, and peered at the piece.

"The nose wiggled!" Rosie exclaimed.

"And the eye blinked." I glanced at Mama to see the look on her face at this marvel. But I saw no surprise there, only thoughtfulness. "Mama, has your stitching moved before?"

She took a deep breath. "Sometimes."

"You've *known* that it does this?" I asked.

"Did you make it move somehow?" said Rosie.

"No," she answered immediately. "I don't know why it moves. I only know that it—it does. Sometimes."

Rosie and I glanced at each other, eyes wide with astonishment.

I touched the edge of the fabric with one finger. It felt like an ordinary piece of linen. "When did you first notice this?"

"A few months before I married your Papa."

We both stared at her, eagerly expectant. *How had we not known this?* "Tell us!" I begged.

She hesitated a few moments, then said, "I was sitting outside the farmhouse where I grew up, stitching on a sunny day. My sister Jalie was there too.

"I was finishing a piece for Gramma, for my future mother-in-law. Of the wheat fields in the sunshine. Blue sky and white clouds. One of my favorite sights in East Rilken. I remember just being happy that I could make this for Bevan's mother. I held it up to look it over, and—"

"What did you see?" Rosie asked.

"The wheat was moving with the wind. On the linen."

"Oh, Mama," I whispered. "What did you do?"

"I did what you are doing now. I just stared at it. Shocked. Wondering if I was dreaming something while awake. I looked toward Jalie, and she was gaping at it. 'Does it look like it's moving to you?' I asked her.

"She didn't answer me. Her eyes narrowed, and she closed her mouth tight for a few moments. Then she said, 'I never want to see anything you make ever again.' She went inside the house and barely spoke to me all the weeks before my wedding. And not much since either."

"She must have seen it move, Mama," I said.

"What happened to that linen piece?" asked Rosie.

"I gave it to Gramma. She often says how much she loves it, but she has never told me that she has seen it move."

"Did Papa know?" I asked.

Mama nodded. "I was making a flower pattern one night after you girls were in bed. You were three and four years old then. The flowers appeared to grow. Bevan noticed them before I did. After we gazed at them for a long time, I told him my embroidery had moved several times before and I didn't understand it.

"He advised me to not tell anyone, because they would expect me to make it happen when *they* wanted it to happen, and if it didn't, they would think I was lying. But now you know, and I'm glad you do."

"I wonder why," I said, fingering the outline of the rabbit. "I wonder why it comes to life sometimes."

"You wanted to keep people from stealing from The Grumpy Rabbit," said Rosie. "If I were even tempted to steal that piece and I saw the rabbit wiggle its nose at me, I would drop it and run!"

"Would you, Rosie?" Mama examined the rabbit.

"What if the embroidery is obeying you, Mama, just like the animals listen to me?" I asked. "You don't want anyone to steal from Alta, so you're putting rabbits on the pieces. This rabbit—well, I'm not sure how to say it —but what if it knows what you meant for it to do? Can you remember what you were thinking when you made the wheat field for Gramma?"

Mama gazed into the fire. "I wanted her to be happy whenever she saw it. I love the wind in the wheat, and I think she did too." She turned to me. "That's all I can remember."

"The roses on the carry bag? Did they ever move?" I caught the look on her face. "They did? You've seen them move!"

"I was so afraid that Zilla would see them."

"Has anything else become something real? Gone from your linen to come to life like the rose bushes outside the door."

"No. That was the first I have ever seen."

"But what if it's not the first time it's happened?" I went on. "What if the things you stitch and the hopes and prayers you put into them actually *become* things, Mama? But you just haven't been there to see them?"

We could have no answers to this, of course, but for a long time we sat by the fire, listening to the rain pelting the roof, and wondered at things far beyond our comprehension.

A STRONG WIND made the shutters rattle and creak during the night. Tike barked at the sound several times, waking all of us just when we had managed to fall asleep. Some time later, a gust of wind blew straight down the chimney. Ashes and smoke flew out into the room making us cough. There was no maintaining the fire after that.

"We'll have to use people and animal warmth tonight," Mama said.

We pulled the bench beds to the wall farthest away from the windows and the fireplace, and settled in with cloaks and soft sweater bags. Tike, the cat, the white squirrel, and a fox tucked themselves in with us.

Rosie sang the song of the storm, of clouds talking to the rain as it fell, sending it on its way, and wishing it well. A song that had comforted us as children. And as I began to sink into sleep, I thought that maybe somewhere, someone was stitching raindrops onto a field of linen.

32

———

From the Hilltop

The storm swept the sky through the night, and the day dawned clean and fresh. At Mama's request, I opened the shutters at both windows to let the light breeze blow through to remove the stale damp. Puddles filled the clearing.

A chorus of birdsong resounded among the trees, and my heart lifted at the miracle of understanding them. Songs of instruction, information, caution, connection, and joy. Redbird flitted around her nest tree, very happy that the rain had gone.

But again, there was no sign of the bear. I had such a longing ache to speak with it again. Such a desire to break through its isolation.

Rosie knelt by the hearth, laying the kindling for a

new fire. Mama sat on a chair tying the laces of her boots.

"I'll leave the last of the rolls for you two. I'm sure I'll be able to breakfast at the inn." Mama looked up, worry on her face. "This could be a long work day. I need to show Alta that she can trust me. I hope you won't be hungry while I'm gone. "

"We'll be all right until you return," I replied. "I don't think we'll be able to find eggs after the storm, but if we're really hungry, I'll just follow Rosie through the woods and eat everything she does."

"You'd love spruce tips, Silvie," Rosie said from the hearth. "They taste a little like lemon."

This made Mama smile. She put on her cloak, hugged us both and picked up the rose carry sack, which held the cleaned stew crock. The roses on its side caught my eye. The roses that sometimes moved. The roses that grew right outside the door. I would never see Mama's embroidery the same way again.

We stepped outside to see her off. "Cat will walk you down, Mama. I'll have the birds watch for your return so we can have someone meet you at the bottom of the path."

Mama waved and started down to the inn, picking her way around puddles and the softest mud. Cat followed close behind. Cat loved Mama especially. They both were soon lost to sight behind the trees and the drop of the hillside.

"I would love to have seen their faces in the inn as they watched her sew," said Rosie.

"Yes. She said the quince flowers didn't move, but

they definitely glowed." I sighed. "I hope she can hear more about what really happened with the Guardsmen and the king today. "

"If only *we* could," said Rosie.

"We can climb the hill behind the station at least, and learn more about where we are. That would be useful."

Rosie's eyes lit up at my suggestion. Her eyes always lit up whenever there was an opportunity for adventure.

We ate a third of the bread that remained, then started on our way. I left Tike by the fire napping, but the white squirrel insisted on riding inside Rosie's hood. The red fox, a perceptive and companionable friend, joined me on the path as we started, and I was grateful.

Rosie pointed out the new growth on trees and bushes as we went. Flowering trees were beginning to appear among the light new green, brightening the brownish forest with patches of white, light purple and dusky red. I listened to the birds' conversation as we climbed. Fox occasionally left to nose around for earthworms.

A few trees crowned the hill, large slabs of rock strewn among them. We chose a good dry rock to rest on, with a view unblocked by trees.

"It's beautiful," Rosie said. "Just glorious!"

Trees carpeted the hills around us with touches of new green and evergreen. And we could see far in almost every direction. The cold breeze blew across the hilltop with nothing to hinder it. We huddled close together, grateful for our mittens.

"I wonder if the king ever used this hill as a lookout," said Rosie. "Which way is Elva?"

We stood up and squinted in the general direction of the sun's rising until we thought we could make out the tips of manmade towers in the distance. "The northwest road is the one Papa would have been traveling on," I said.

We looked for a break in the trees, until we thought we saw a small but consistent difference in the flow of the treetops.

"That road fits." I pointed. "I think what we're seeing could be the northwest road."

"That's where it all happened," Rosie said quietly, almost as if she were afraid of being overheard.

"Somewhere along that road. It could have been closer to Elva or even closer to Tellhaven." I couldn't keep my eyes from that small break in the trees. Somewhere out there was a section of forest road that held all the secrets we needed to know.

"Silvie." Rosie spoke in that same hushed voice. "Do you think Papa's body is out there somewhere?"

My stomach tightened. This was the question that haunted me, haunted all of us, since Mago's hateful announcement. I desperately wanted to know, and yet was afraid to know what the forest could tell us if it could speak.

"Would the animals know?" Rosie persisted. "Would any bird have seen anything? Could they tell us exactly what happened?"

I thought before answering her. "I don't know. I don't

think animals think quite like that. But maybe there is something I could ask."

I took a step forward on the flat rock, and called to the sky. "Crow, if you can hear me, come! Eagle, if you can hear me, come!" I turned slowly, pivoting carefully on the rock, and scanned the sky, calling again and again.

"There's something!" Rosie cried, pointing to a distant speck.

The speck increased in size, until at last a crow swooped out of the sky and landed on the ground before the rock, folding its dark wings to its sides. I sat down and looked at it closely. It looked back inquisitively.

"Thank you so much for coming." I hoped the crow could hear how truly I meant it. "I have something very important to ask you. Are you familiar with the human road that goes northwest out of the city? It runs through your territory? All right." I tried to think of words that would ask what I couldn't bear to ask—yet which would still have meaning for the crow.

"Do you remember a fight on that road maybe ten days ago?" All of a sudden I was unsure. Our days in the woods had no real rhythm with the outside world, and I had lost track of time. But the crow might remember the event more than the time or day anyway. "Men killing men with arrows, swords, and spears?"

I listened closely as guttural sounds came from the crow's throat.

"He remembers, Rosie," I whispered.

Rosie stared at the crow while I thought of the next

questions to ask. "Were any bodies left in the woods or on the road?"

His answer was long and careful, and it surprised me. "You're sure? Was anything left after that? Yes, please, I would like to see them."

The crow lifted its wings and sprang into the air, turning and flying back the way it had come.

"What did it say?" Rosie asked.

"He saw the bodies fall to the ground, but bears came and kept scavengers away. After that, men returned and took the bodies. There were none left, either in the forest or on the road. He remembers because the carrion birds were waiting, but were—were disappointed."

"So, Papa's body wasn't left there?" Tears welled up in Rosie's eyes.

"No, it wasn't. The crow was certain none were left. Absolutely certain."

"But Mago said something about not bringing back the bodies of traitors."

"And yet, according to the crow, no one was left in the forest. Only shreds of clothing." I stared off into the direction the crow had gone. "He's going to bring some to show us."

As I said this, my stomach tightened again. I didn't really want to see any blood-soaked pieces of green-on-green uniform. Any signs of the fallen Guardsmen. The shreds Crow had found were evidence of the destruction of everything we had grown up believing.

I didn't think for one moment that Papa had failed his vow. But somehow the Guardsmen had failed.

Because the king was dead. And I couldn't endure the pain of this.

The thought of seeing anything left from the attack filled me now with revulsion. Why had I told the crow that I had wanted to see them? I wasn't thinking clearly. But the bird was traveling a great distance to fulfill my request and now I was bound to see what it would bring.

I shuddered. "It's cold up here."

We sat on the rock again, pulling our cloaks tight around us. Rosie covered her cold cheeks with mittened hands. Fox hunted through clumps of wild grass. White Squirrel rooted through the scraps of leaves at the foot of the trees behind us.

At last, I saw the shape of not one dark bird, but three, flying toward us from the direction the crow had gone. They flew fast, seemingly heedless of the wind, until they alighted by the stone amid a tumult of flapping, and dropped what they carried in their beaks at our feet.

Rosie and I immediately slid off our rock to examine them.

"That's a buckle," said Rosie, pointing to a brass clasp attached to a bit of torn leather.

The shininess of such a thing would quickly draw the attention of a keen-eyed crow. Too small for a belt, it must have secured something else the men had been traveling with.

The second crow had brought a short piece of rope, no longer than the width of my hand, but Rosie and I recognized it as the kind bound to every Guardsman's saddle.

The third was only a muddied piece of brown cloth, but I could tell it held importance to the crow who had carried it. I sensed that she had only brought it because the others had urged her to. It was a valuable part of her nest, and she watched me anxiously. I removed my mittens and picked it up carefully.

"Oh!"

I turned the scrap of fabric over in my hands. There was no mistaking this.

"It's Mama's stitching, Rosie! Look. Little cabbages."

I brushed away the dried bits of mud, and held it between us so she could see it too. Dirt obscured most of the stitching, but there was enough to make out the fragments of careful rows of embroidery. The frayed ends of thread at the fabric edge.

"That's from Papa's pouch!" Rosie cried. "The one he wore on his belt. He must have taken it to Tellhaven."

The pain and horror of Papa's death stared up at us from the pale green cabbage leaves. We both wept openly. I turned back to the watching crow. "Is this all you found of this material? Was there anything more?"

No, there wasn't. The crow had looked industriously because she thought it so beautiful, but was sad there was no more. I could sense she wanted to have it back.

"Do you remember where you found it?"

She did. "Caught in a tree root near the base of a trunk," I said to Rosie.

"This was our father's," I told the crow. "Our father died on that road, in that place. This means so much to us. Could I trade you something for it?"

The crow cocked her head, but looked doubtful. I

held out my mitten. It was knitted in greens and blues with dark red trim at the cuff and on the thumb tip. I hoped she would find it attractive.

"Would you like this instead? You can have the whole mitten." I laid it down on the ground in front of her. Rosie set down the buckle and the rope in front of the other waiting crows.

The crow pecked at the mitten and relief filled me.

"She likes it, Rosie."

I thanked the crows and they flew away, taking their treasures and my mitten with them. We stood watching them go, noting their direction, until their shapes disappeared into the sky. I clutched the piece of Papa's pouch tightly in my hand.

"The unexpected witnesses, Rosie. The animals know what happened, but they don't realize what they know."

"The trees know many things too," Rosie added, her voice thoughtful.

"Would they be able to tell you?"

"I don't know. I'm only beginning to understand them."

Our eyes couldn't help but be drawn to the break in the trees, but we knew more about it now. We knew where the path of the crows crossed that road.

"How far away do you think it is?" I asked.

"I can't guess."

"There are a number of hills. It would be hard going for anyone on foot. And down among the trees we're not going to be able to see as clearly as we do now."

Rosie grabbed my arm, her face lit with a sudden

thought. "The road that goes in front of the inn. What if it connects to the northwest road? Or at least takes us partway there?" We hurried to the other side of the hilltop to see.

"It could give us a start," I said, "but after a while it would take us too far out of our way."

I knew what was happening. Rosie and I were going to try to see the place where Papa and the king died. We were deciding this without even acknowledging that we were deciding. But I would not attempt to argue either one of us out of it. I held in my hand proof that Papa had been in that fatal place. The thought that we might find something the crows could not know the meaning of compelled me to go forward.

"Mama will be working late tonight," said Rosie.

"And we can plan carefully and leave a note for her."

I gazed at Rosie, seeing the same determination in her eyes. Then without saying another word, we went down the rocky path as fast as we could go.

I WROTE a note for Mama using the pen, ink, and a piece of the small sheaf of paper I had grabbed in our frantic packing. I pinned the note under the hairbrush and placed it in the center of the table. Papa's torn pouch piece I laid carefully in a bowl beside it. I packed the rest of the food in my carry bag, while Rosie put our tinderbox in hers, along with the water flask. Rosie also went to the riverbank and gathered rocks to put in her carry bag. I didn't have to ask her why.

Fox and the white squirrel wanted to go with us.

Tike and the cat would remain at the station. Redbird would tell Cat when to meet Mama on the path. All was as ready as we could make it.

We left the station, cutting across the hillside behind it, the one beyond the inn where we searched for eggs each morning. Angling downward, we came to the road. If the road was clear, we would walk on it. Otherwise, we would stay in the trees, moving northward, keeping the road in sight.

Rosie took the lead and we started off at a brisk pace.

33

A Halted Stitch

Nissa, the butter-churn girl, answered the back kitchen door at Tara's knock. Her eyes widened when she saw Tara. "Ettie! She's here!"

"She'll need breakfast," came the cook's voice from within. "Have her sit down and get her a bowl."

The kitchen's warmth drew Tara in. Ettie was standing on her broad stool at the worktable. A mountain of dough rested on the tabletop in front of her. The cook's hair was covered in a pale linen kerchief. Flour dusted her bare arms up to her elbows. And her hands energetically patted a chunk of dough into the shape of a loaf.

"Hang your cloak on that peg and leave your boots there by the door. Kipp will clean them for you."

Tara handed the stew crock to Nissa, and took off her boots, setting them by the door as Ettie instructed. Ettie nodded towards the stool next to her worktable. Tara came all the way into the kitchen in her stocking feet and sat down.

"I'd greet you proper," said Ettie, "but I bake these three times a day, and the woodsmen are counting on them. Bread won't wait for anyone. I hear at the castle all those courtiers are served only two meals a day." She raised an eyebrow. "Is that right?"

"That's right," said Tara. "An early midday meal and a late dinner."

"Well," said Ettie, a look of satisfaction on her face, "here at the Rabbit there's always food for anyone. This morning it's oats, a boiled egg, and a sugar roll. Will that be all right?" Ettie paused in forming her loaves, her voice suddenly doubtful.

"It will be heavenly," Tara said with sincerity. "We loved your stew and rolls."

Ettie looked pleased at this. Her hands tore off another large chunk from the mound of dough and patted it into an oval shape. "The taste of stew is all in knowing how to best use your salt, pepper, and onion."

"Ettie uses rosemary too," Nissa put in eagerly. She handed Tara a bowl. A peeled, boiled egg and a roll covered with sugar rested on the surface of the thick, dark oats.

Tara took a spoonful. The oats were warm on her tongue, and she could taste the sweetness of sugar, the depth of molasses, and the distant fiery glow of cinnamon. Unexpected tears pricked her eyes. If only the girls could be eating this with her!

Rosie had planned to toast the leftover rolls over the fire and had carefully reserved some of the precious butter for them. They would run out of rolls, most surely, but tonight Tara would be able to bring more food up the hill.

A glance told her that Ettie had been watching her expression as she ate, and the cook was gratified with what she saw. If Ettie only knew how they had been eating before this.

"It's wonderful," said Tara. "The Sender's own handiwork."

Ettie couldn't hide her smile at this praise. She motioned to Nissa. "She'll need something to drink. Those oats are thick." Nissa handed Tara a tumbler, and Tara tasted the crisp sweetness of apples.

"That cider's from our apples," said Ettie proudly. "We have a small grove across the road. Don't know if you've seen it yet. We take them over to Fawnspell at the end of autumn where they've got a press. They barrel it for us, and we store the barrels in our cellar."

Clearly, there was more to the workings of this inn than Tara could see from the hill path. Her respect for Gareth, Alta, and Ettie grew.

When she finished her breakfast, she set off with her carry bag to find Alta and the seamstress. As she was leaving the kitchen, Ettie called out, "When you need a break from your work, come back and sit on this stool awhile."

Simple words, but they contained so much. Ettie was making a place for Tara, making room for her. Against the dark backdrop of Tara's sorrow, Ettie's kindness stood out like starlight. Tara paused at the doorway. "Thank you, Ettie," she replied. "I will."

ALTA WAS NO LONGER UPSTAIRS. A maid said she had been called away to the smokehouse. But the seamstress was waiting in one of the empty rooms, carefully laying out her cut panels on a table. The dark-haired woman dropped a quick, nervous curtsey. She pointed to the prepared linen.

"Alta has measured and approved them, ma'am," she began, chopping out her words in a fearful, defensive tone.

"Then they are exactly right," said Tara, trying to soothe.

The seamstress did not smile. "Here are your colors, your needles, and scissors. And she said you was to have that bowl of water and the soap and towel there to wash and then I was to leave you alone to do your work."

The woman clearly meant that Tara was expected to stay in this quiet room all day, and this Tara would not do. She had not tried this hard only to be cut off from any news about the Guardsmen. People must be talking about the tragedy, and she had to be able to hear what was said.

"Thank you," she replied. "I'll take these down to the main room and do my work in a corner there."

The woman looked surprised. A frown deepened on

her face. "And work in front of everyone? I'm afraid that's not done here." She shook her head.

"However odd that may sound," Tara replied, "that is what I will need to do. I like people talking and moving around me while I sew. That's what I'm used to. That's where I work best, where I create best. So that's what would be best for this project."

The woman did not seem convinced. "I'll go tell Alta that you're in the great room then. She will have to be the one to tell you where you are to work."

The door shut behind her, and Tara took a deep breath. She washed her hands carefully, then gathered her thread, needles, and scissors, and the gently folded linen strips and took them down the stairs to the back corner of the great room, a corner that caught the morning sun.

She settled herself at a small table. Bright sun from the windswept sky poured in through the east window illuminating the tabletop, while the chair itself was in shadow. A perfect place for her to work and also be an invisible, yet listening, stranger.

She did not fear being recognized here. The Rabbit was an average inn along a lesser used road. All the attention of the country, including that of her friends and acquaintances, would be on Elva right now. Not on a group of buildings tucked into the woods.

She laid the threads carefully on the sunlit table and looked closely at the linen strip in her hands. A combination of trees and leaves, seeds and acorns, suns and moons, would create patterns on the sheet's edge, imitating those around the bedroom fireplace upstairs.

Her eyes studied the linen, and she thought of the needs of weary travelers. Their need for beauty, for harmony, for healing of both soul and body. For kindness and light on a lonely journey. For peace on a troublesome one.

Her heart swelled as her inner eye traced dark green arcs across the fabric. Fingers moved restlessly in their eagerness to begin. She threaded her needle with the darkest green and took the linen in her hands.

THE MAIN ROOM of the inn was quiet for the most part. The old man who had given Tara the advice about going to the back door, sat at the same small table along the wall where she had seen him before. His spoon worked busily at the bowl of oats in front of him.

On the wall opposite the old man, Gareth was lifting a new keg into its place behind the bar with the help of a boy who appeared to be several years younger than Rosie. Was this the Kipp that Ettie spoke of? A certain similarity of look and manner made her think that Kipp could be Gareth and Alta's son. She turned her attention back to the linen piece in her hands and continued stitching the long graceful curve of tiny leaves.

Someone was standing nearby, and she looked up to see the old man. He held his empty breakfast bowl in one hand and a knitted cap in the other. His eyes were on the linen piece. He must have been watching her work.

"Good morning," she said.

"Morning," he replied. "Glad you got the job. My

name's Jarlath. I do all sorts of things around here. Have to fix the roof on the smokehouse. Part of it blew off in last night's storm."

"That wind was vicious, wasn't it?"

"That it was. Ah, well. It's always good to mend things." He gave a nod, put the cap on his head, and walked away, turning down the hallway that led to the kitchen.

After a while a brisk step made her look up again. Alta's long thin face stared down at her. "You're working down here," she said flatly.

"Yes, Alta, and it's a good place to work. See?" Tara held up the linen piece with the arcs of dark green dancing almost to the middle of it.

A light of wonder appeared in the innkeeper's eyes. "Oh. All right then," she said more quietly.

Boards creaked sharply above their heads, followed by the sound of heavy footsteps. Alta glanced up and hurried away.

A man and woman entered the great room from a doorway off to her left. Gareth greeted them with delight and ushered them to a table closer to the fireplace near the bar. The two were clearly well-to-do. They dressed in a manner like Crim, quality cloth trimmed in velvet. The woman wore knots of silver at her ears.

"Breakfast will be here very soon," said Gareth. "What can I get you to drink?"

Gareth could move as quickly as Ettie or Alta. In a few moments he set full tumblers on their table. "Did you sleep well?" Gareth asked, all the kindness of a concerned father in his voice.

The woman shook her head. "How can anyone sleep after this fearful murder? You lie awake and see our poor king struck down on the road. Ay, it troubles your dreams. If the Guardsmen couldn't protect him, are any of us safe? I don't think we'll recover from this for many a long year."

They were the only guests in the large room, and the woman's voice sounded loud in the empty space. Gareth shook his head solemnly.

"How could the Guardsmen fail to protect the king, Gareth?" asked the man. "I can't begin to figure that out. The strongest, quickest, best-trained men in the kingdom, and yet somehow they are defeated by this one man? What was the good of all this training? It's just shameful!"

Tara's heart beat faster at this, but she kept her eyes on her linen, kept her hand moving, and listened.

"Did you hear they haven't found the man yet?" said the woman. "Can you imagine? The story in Elva is that they are hunting everywhere, but can't find him."

Tara raised her head abruptly. The needle froze in her hand. *Bevan alive?* She couldn't breathe.

The man shook his head. "There's also a story that says he was shot dead on the spot. He could not have gotten away from the palace guard, my dear. Vile man! I wish I had been there to put my hatchet through his head."

"I don't know if that's true. I heard—" the woman began.

Nissa entered with a tray and placed bowls of hot oats, eggs, and rolls in front of them. The couple turned to their breakfast, and Gareth stepped back behind the bar.

Tara's heart raced and her hands trembled. She slid the needle through a tuck in the fabric edge and clasped her hands tightly together trying to calm herself.

They are not talking about Bevan. The only man who is vile is the real murderer. But Mago told people it was Bevan. And urged them on in their hatred. Is that happening all over Elva right now? People hating Bevan?

Yet, the woman said he was still alive. Alive and hunted. But who is being hunted? The real murderer? Or Bevan? Is Bevan being hunted now? My Bevan? Mago said he was dead. Where is the truth in all this?

The couple murmured occasionally to each other. Gareth fussed over the newly placed keg. Tara looked down at her work. She took a deep breath and pulled out the needle.

But, deep inside muscle and bone, her hand shook still. She poked the needle into the fabric and immediately withdrew it. The needle missed the place she saw with her inner eye.

A chill ran through her. She tried again.

Against her will, the needle dove for the wrong spot.

34

The Mines of Galerine

Tara removed the needle, tucked it into the edge of the piece and folded it carefully. What should she do now? It wouldn't do to be seen sitting in the main room doing nothing. But she was too shaken to sew.

Which of the stories coming out of Elva was true? Or had she not heard the truth yet? One thing she did know. If she started thinking about Bevan too much right now, she would come completely apart and wouldn't be able to sew for the rest of the day. That would help no one. She must make her mind think of something else. After a moment, she packed up her things, and headed toward the kitchen.

The smell of baking bread greeted Tara when she

entered. Ettie was still at her worktable, but was now scooping flour from a bowl into a row of stone jars in front of her. Her hand paused in midair.

"Kipp has your boots ready, if you'd like to put them on again."

There they were, right where she had left them. Cleaned and dried. Tara carried the boots over to the familiar stool and slid her feet into them. As she laced them, she realized Ettie was studying her and might need a reason for her return.

"I need to rest my eyes for a bit," she said. "Could I show you what I've done so far?"

Ettie lit up at this. She set the flour scoop down by the next jar in line and wiped her hands on her apron expectantly. Tara took the linen from her carry bag, and unfolded it. Ettie leaned closer, peering at the design.

"The curving leaves are the foundation for the whole piece," Tara said. "When they are finished, I'll fill in the spaces the curves make with pictures of things like acorns and moons."

Ettie's smile got brighter until her face glowed like a hot oven. She let out a whoop that echoed off the whitewashed walls. "I knew it!" she cried. "I knew what you said was true! I told them. They forget that I can always tell."

A bell rang suddenly, startling Tara. But Ettie calmly picked up her scoop and ladled flour into the waiting jar.

"Nissa," she called. "The folks from the end room will be wanting four bowls. Everyone seems to want breakfast late today, and there's my midday stew bubbling in the kettle and the woodsmen on their way."

Tara put her work in her bag and watched Nissa spoon the hot oats into bowls. The serving girl assembled everything on a tray and left the room.

"Ettie, you just said you can always tell. What can you always tell?"

Ettie's hands kept moving, but her face took on a confident air. "I always know when someone's lying. Can tell the truth from a lie in moments."

"You can?"

"Yep."

"How do you know?"

The cook shrugged. "I've worked at it from early on. Practiced for years, watching, listening for truth. Hearing how it differs from a lie. Studied it, just like the famous Master Redmond would do at that big university in Bremen, but in my own way, of course."

If only Ettie had been listening to the stories in the main room just now. "Can you tell when people think they are telling the truth but are really not?" Tara asked. She clasped her hands discreetly on her lap, willing them to calm.

Ettie gave her a quick glance, then considered her jars again. "Sometimes."

"Tell me. I'm very interested."

"Well, first you need to know that I'm not from Rilken. I'm a Galerine dwarf and Galerine is a land crazy for mining. Crazy for digging everything from the earth. Gold. Silver. Diamonds. Emeralds. And minerals even more costly than those."

"What can be more costly than gold? Or an emerald?"

Ettie cocked an eyebrow. "If you were raised in Galerine, you'd know. Lerin."

"Lerin? I've never heard of it."

"That's because your art is in thread and fabric. Lerin is used with jewels or metals or crystal or glass. It's a pale, pearly-like—"

Nissa came in with an empty tray. "More people for breakfast, plus new ones at the door. We'll need at least ten bowls."

Ettie jumped down from her perch and went over to the hearth where the oat kettle stayed warm over the fire. "I'll fill the bowls. You take them in."

Ettie's hands moved twice as fast and twice as carefully as Nissa's. Soon, a whole row of wooden bowls waited for the server across the front of the hearth.

Tara felt uncomfortable being idle while others were working. She stood up. "Can I help?" she asked.

Ettie looked horrified. "You just sit down and rest. You are getting paid for stitching, not for serving. Nissa will get Dona to help. They know what to do."

Ettie climbed back onto her perch and surveyed her jars. "Now, where was I? I was telling you about Galerine." She picked up her scoop and began measuring again.

"Galerine dwarves, even some in my own family, are all proud miners. Mining pays very well in Galerine, because the whole country sits on a wealth of riches.

"But I feel badly for the dwarves that mine lerin. They get higher wages than the rest, but you can't be around lerin for long. Many dwarves try to pull out before it affects them, but—" Ettie broke off and shook her head.

"What does it do to them?"

Nissa entered, followed by the older, gray-haired woman Tara had seen washing dishes before. This must be the Dona that Ettie mentioned. Dona nodded at Tara, but said not a word, quickly filling the trays alongside Nissa.

Ettie came to the end of her line of stone jars. She jumped off her stool and moved it back to the beginning of the line, then climbed up again. A pitcher stood on the table near the jars. Ettie measured water from it into a small cup and poured the cup into the first jar. She picked up a thin wooden spoon and stirred briskly.

"Ettie," Tara said, "what does lerin do to the dwarves? How does it affect them?"

Ettie shook her head sadly. "You won't believe this, but..."

"But what?"

"It turns them into liars."

"*Liars*?"

Ettie nodded firmly. "Yep. After a few years in a lerin mine, they can't tell the truth about anything. How many carts they filled. What color the lerin is. Their own mother's name. Even the number of toes on their feet. They'll swear they have seven, even though they have ten like every other dwarf." She stirred the contents of the next jar vigorously, her wooden spoon making rhythmic thwacking noises against the stone sides of the jar.

"What a terrible thing to experience," Tara exclaimed. "What happens to them then?"

"Oh, they keep working in the mine."

"But how could they be of use to anyone, if what they say is always false?"

"Well, they still have all their mining skills, and there's a way to tell a lerin dwarf, as we call them. Their voice gets a certain pitch to it. Almost like they swallowed a bee. There's sort of a buzz when they speak. You have to listen close, but it's there. I've had a lot of practice listening."

"Do the lerin dwarves *know* they are lying? Or do they think they're telling the truth all the time?"

Ettie moved down to the next jar. "I can't really say. I've only known one lerin dwarf personally. My second cousin. He lived in a grand house bought with all his earnings, but no one wanted to visit him.

"We younger cousins got our courage up and asked him once if he could hear the buzz he made whenever he talked. He got very red in the face and swore we were making fun of him."

"This must affect so many of your people," Tara said. "How heartwrenching!"

Ettie nodded. "It is."

"And yet the mining still goes on? What does Galerine do with all the lerin?"

"Why, they make things with it and sell them all across AllHallen, to whoever has enough money to buy them. It surprises me that some people actually do have money enough, because the cost of lerin is dearer than life."

"Is anything really dearer than life?" The words were out before Tara realized others would hear them.

"Well, now," said Ettie, stirring briskly, "when you make me stop and consider, nothing really is, is it?"

"The life of someone you love is dearer than your own."

Ettie put down her spoon and gazed at Tara with a serious expression. "Is that why your face is bruised?" she asked quietly.

Before Tara could think of a reply, the kitchen door opened and Alta strode in. "You're in here now?" There was a sharpness in her tone.

"Show her," Ettie said. "Show her what you've done!"

Tara unfolded the embroidery and held out the curving, lacy leaves for Alta's examination. Alta's expression brightened.

"I'd also like you to see this." Tara reached into her bag and pulled out the rabbit that had surprised Silvie and Rosie. "I thought we might put a likeness of the grumpy rabbit somewhere on each panel of embroidery, an image that could be the inn's signature. I worked up this practice piece yesterday. What do you think? Would you like that?"

Ettie stopped working completely at this and peered over Alta's arm. Tara watched their faces.

"I tried to make it like the picture over the bar," she said. "I think I got close to it. Translating the work of an artist's pencil into thread always alters the image a bit."

Ettie's mouth dropped open. Alta's eyes widened. Tara gave the rabbit a quick glance. One of the whiskers quivered.

"Is it all right?" she asked in a calm voice, as if she had seen nothing unusual.

"Yes," said Alta quietly. "It's—it's almost alive."

The cook, for once, was speechless, but her eyes gleamed.

"Everyone will know the linens are yours with the rabbit's face on them," Tara said. "They might not dare to steal them. Do you want me to put the rabbit on each one?"

After a few moments, Alta nodded, a look on her face that Tara had never seen before. "Gareth's grandfather would be proud." Ettie continued to stare at the design.

Something had passed between Alta, Ettie, and the rabbit. And whatever it was, it was the Sender's doing.

Tara had made the rabbit while feeling concern for Alta. Wanting to relieve her fear of being cheated. Now, as Alta gazed at the rabbit, her face softened. Her shoulders lifted a little, as if someone had taken a burden from her.

The trembling deep inside Tara ceased. The Sender was working. If he was working, then Tara could work too. Her hand felt steady again. She was ready to return to the main room. Ready to stitch—and listen.

35

Lord Kendall's Report

"Your Highness, it is my reluctant opinion that the boy is declining." Kendall said this with a sigh, as he lowered himself onto the satin couch the Duke had indicated.

"Ravelin has no strength in his hands. I make a point of taking his hand whenever I greet him, in order that I may have something more to test and report to you. And day by day, almost hour by hour, I detect a marked lessening of strength, of the grip, which is everything to a man."

Kendall took a deep breath and continued. "And that irritating Pate spends a great deal of time with the prince." The words felt distasteful on his tongue.

Anything about Pate was distasteful to him. "I cannot think Pate is a good influence."

"The silly lad appears harmless. And he has no political power. The prince could have worse companions."

Kendall thought it best not to disagree with the Duke on this. Best instead to come to his main point without digression. "We have not been able to continue Ravelin's lessons, for he seems unable to concentrate on anything. He used to be so brilliant at geometry. Now he can barely distinguish the qualities of a sphere from those of a cube."

Duke Allard, seated at his desk at one end of his grand receiving room, leaned forward. "Master Kendall, this news about my nephew's decline is serious indeed, and not what I was expecting."

Kendall's eyes widened. "But it is the truth, Your Highness, I swear it!"

The Duke raised his hand as if to calm him. "I know you speak truly."

Kendall felt a wave of relief. "I had to make the reluctant decision to delay his studies for several more weeks yet. Does that meet with your approval?"

"Whatever you as his instructor think best."

"Thank you, sir. I cannot tell you what your confidence means to me."

The Duke did not reply to this. Kendall perched awkwardly on the edge of the expensive couch.

"I hope that the gleam of light that is Prince Ravelin will shine brightly again someday. I must say that it is only because of you, our great Prince and Duke, that

Rilken's throne is secure. I am grateful beyond words for that. And, I believe the whole country agrees with me."

He dared a look directly at the Duke and was disappointed to see that the great man had not responded to his obsequious compliment. Instead, the Duke was studying some paper on his desk.

Kendall blinked several times, lest the Duke catch him in so direct a gaze, and then allowed his eyes to take in the beautiful room surrounding him. Kendall loved elegance. His heart swelled at opulent splendor, and he counted himself fortunate to live among those who so indulged.

He cleared his throat gently. "May I compliment you on your excellent taste in furnishings, good sir?"

The Duke inclined his head.

Kendall took the courage from that nod to continue. "The colors you have selected, the cream and gold, with such tasteful touches of green, why, the whole affect is—is regal."

He was having trouble choosing from all the words he wished to say. "And, that lovely, enormous mirror! Positioned behind your desk, it brings such light to the room. Yet, it is so cleverly situated that a guest may engage in conversation with you without being distracted by their own reflection. Marvelously done, sir!"

"How clever of you to notice such details, Kendall. I hope all my other guests will be as appreciative when I hold my reception for the court in this room." The Duke gave a quick glance over his shoulder. "I have to say, that of all the mirrors in my collection, I love this Galerine mirror the best."

Kendall got to his feet. "One can see why," he said with enthusiasm. He took a few steps closer to where the Duke sat, hoping to be able to see more of the mirror. "Its beauty! The light, the essence of it. I hope I am not presumptuous in my admiration."

"No, no," said the Duke affably. "You may look into it all you wish."

Kendall dared two more steps forward and looked deep into the sea of glowing pearl for as long as he dared. He felt ennobled by such beauty, but alas, the news he had heard made the beauty bittersweet. He sighed more loudly than he meant to.

"Another sigh, Kendall? This is no praise to my mirror."

"It was not for the mirror that I sighed, but that there can be no more like it."

"Of course there can be no more like it. Surely you know that every Galerine mirror has no equal. Each is unique."

"Oh, yes. Assuredly. I only grieve that no more can be made."

"That is a strange thing to say. I'm having another mirror made this very month."

Kendall felt confused. "Oh. They have not—not *told* you? I suppose I could be mistaken, but the man was very sure."

"Kendall." There was sudden anger in the tone, which Kendall could not miss. "*What* do I need to be told?"

"Your Highness, the artisans in Galerine City, those

that hold the secrets of these mirrors, the very ones that produce these exquisite creations, why—why their workshop has been completely destroyed! Have you received no word?"

The Duke of Elva got slowly, ominously, to his feet. Kendall found himself doing what he always did when fear called his name. He talked.

"I heard it from the Galerine messenger in the mayor's office just this morning, as the mayor and I were talking over some business which would be boring to you, sir, but the news was that the solutions and the potions that the chemists used in making the mirrors, not to say the very recipes, were all destroyed. There is nothing left! But, perhaps the man was mistaken. Yet he seemed so clear in his detail and—"

"*Who* destroyed them? Who did this? Answer me, Kendall!"

The Duke's shout unnerved him for a moment, then he found his tongue again.

"It—it is so strange. And you won't believe me. But I can get the man. There were witnesses, of course. Something like this could not be done in secret. It was a bear. A big bear. Unearthly. Powerful. No one could stop it. The arrows they fired bounced right off the monster. Nothing could slow him. Everything broken. Smashed. And then the fire. A fire so intense that even the rocks themselves were burning. As a result, everything is gone. Utterly, utterly gone."

At last, Kendall's words ran out. He stole a glance at the Duke.

The face of Prince Allard of Rilken, Duke of Elva,

was a mottled picture of gray and purple. To Kendall's nervous eyes, the Duke looked like a man half dead. Ghastly.

"If you have nothing else for me, sir–" Kendall began.

"Leave me at once." The words came in a hoarse whisper.

Kendall moved faster than he had for a long time, and did not risk a backward glance.

36

Deep in the Woods

Mud, mud, and more mud. The hillsides were full of it, sending us slipping and sliding down to the road. But on the road, mud from horse hooves and wagon wheels splattered us as we struggled.

Nor was the side of the road any better. A small stream ran along the edge of it, creating its own muddy banks, and our boots could not get a decent foothold.

"We have to go higher into the hills," I said, "and just keep the road in sight. We'll never get far in this."

Rosie turned directly for the slope and began the laborious climb with undiminished energy. But that was like Rosie. She was happiest when she was moving. Fox darted easily up the hillside on his light feet. How different it was for me!

After a while I noticed that in spite of the mud, Rosie seemed to find the best footholds on root and rock, so I began to imitate her every step. A thought crossed my mind.

"Rosie, are the trees telling you where to put your feet? Showing you places that won't give way?"

"Oh?" She sounded distracted. "I don't know. I'm watching for where their roots are just under the soil and I'm putting my boot there."

I waited for her to explain, but she didn't. I had to concentrate on watching her steps carefully in order to copy her, while working to keep up with her. The going was hard, yet when I glanced at my sister again, I saw wonder on her face. She caught my eye and smiled.

"What is it?" I asked.

"I can hear the trees *drinking*, Silvie! The forest is filled with wild happiness because of the rain. And the sap is rising in all the trees! I wish you could hear that pine tree."

She pointed to a tall giant that stood out from the other leafless trees on the slope. I tried to imagine what Rosie must be experiencing, what she must be hearing, but I couldn't. She seemed to be sharing in the forest's wild happiness.

A few steps farther she paused to look back at me. "Do you know what the trees are? What they do?" She reached out to touch a low branch studded with leaf buds. I was grateful, for her pause meant momentary rest.

"The trees keep the light, Silvie. They reach up into the sunlight and pull it down into the dark of the world. They are the lightkeepers."

I was breathing too hard as a result of our climb to answer her. But I had the sudden sense of walking between stately beings that connected earth and sky in a way I could not comprehend. We continued on until, at last, we came out at the top of the hill.

We could see the road we had just left down below us. But the gash in the trees that we had seen so clearly from the hill behind the hunting station was not visible now. It was blocked by another hill. Where should we go from here?

From the knees down, our skirts were all mud. Rosie's face was spattered with dirt that wagon wheels had flung at us on the road. Her fiery hair clumped and straggly. White Squirrel, riding as she did in Rosie's green hood, was almost lost behind the tangle of red hair.

The sun stood high in the sky and appeared to be moving faster than we were. Spring days were not long enough for what we needed to do, and we could not afford to get lost. We needed our guide sooner than I had thought.

I called the crow.

AMAZEMENT. Because he came. *And,* because he seemed to think it the most natural thing in the world to do so.

We had rested long enough to catch our breath and feel our strength return when I spied his dark wings through the lacy green treetops. Down he came to perch on the limb of a beech.

I asked him to lead us as directly as possible to the place he told me about before, but, because we could not fly, by gentler paths than straight up and down every hill. He understood right away and set off, flying from tree to tree, waiting for us to come near before leaping into the air again.

The going was still tricky in places. I began to slip once. Rosie grabbed my hand and held on tight, until I could find my footing again.

Crow led us to a narrow animal track that ran through the hills. The mud on it had hardened, making the going easier. Rosie stepped back and followed me, following the crow. Step by step we went, under a bright blue sky, through a forest slowly renewing itself. Because of Crow's graciousness, we were able to keep a steady pace.

Animals watched our passage. Spotted deer. Two martens. A weasel's face poked from a burrow. A hedgehog lodged on a tree branch. And enough ground and tree squirrels to fill a forest all by themselves.

I had never paid much attention to animals in my old life. I was grateful to the Guardstown cats for keeping the mice away, and I listened to Grampy and Gramma's excitement about their cows and pigs. And, of course, we needed horses for transportation.

Beyond that, I did not give them much thought. Animals were just there. Like bricks and stones and trees. Except animals moved and required human care.

Now, my former attitude seemed like blindness.

Animals thronged the world, yet each one had its own presence and hopes and purpose.

One of the spotted deer came along with us for a time, and when we stopped to rest and eat our bread, she approached. I held out some of the bread to her, but she didn't want it. I lowered my hand and gazed into her brown eyes.

She was hungry, but not for food. She wanted—I couldn't believe what I heard—*to talk*. To say things to me, and for me to hear them and answer back. She wanted to be known. And surrounding all this, she wanted the long silence between animals and mankind to be broken.

I touched the side of her neck as I listened, reading the message in her eyes. "I don't know when the silence will end," I said. "It has only just ended for me."

When it was time to go on again, I looked back through the trees to where she stood watching us, and saw the longing still in her eyes. *Why, in our great grief, were we surrounded with so many wonders?*

The crow did his best to pick out a good path for us. We left the first animal track and fought through the underbrush for a time before stepping onto another animal track. Crow said we were turning more to the east now in order to meet the section of road he had told us about.

I told Rosie this and we both walked faster, half-running where the way was clear, for the afternoon was spending itself quickly. The hills flattened out, and I felt we were descending one side of a broad, tree-filled valley.

Ahead of us, a well-kept road appeared through the trees. This was no mere mud track. This was a royal road out of Elva, carefully constructed with stonework, just as the west road had been before we took to the forest.

My feet slowed as we approached it. "This is it, Rosie," I said solemnly. "We're here."

Rosie moved past me and stepped out onto the paving stones.

I had expected the road to be busy with the same kind of traffic we had seen on the west road, but in the broad curve of the road before us, no one was in sight. I opened my mouth to ask Crow where the bodies had been laid, but before I could, Rosie spoke.

"Here. It was here." She walked over to an area off the road underneath some tall trees.

I came up to her and studied the ground. "How can you tell? What do you see?"

"Nothing," she said. "I know this is the place because the trees are still weeping."

Rosie stepped off the road and touched the rough bark of one tree. After a moment, tears ran down her cheeks.

I turned slowly, looking up into the trees and then at the ground beneath them. A penetrating sorrow hung over the place.

I thanked the good crow for all his help and bid him farewell. We would depend on Fox's nose to take us back home. Fox had been a silent companion all day. Now he trotted around us, going into and out of trees as he always did. Here, too, was another gracious animal, for I knew he preferred to be out in the nighttime instead of in the day.

"What do you smell?" I asked him, afraid to know.

The boots of many feet. The gloves of many hands. Older scents. Fresh scents.

"Could he smell Papa?" Rosie asked.

I shook my head. "He could, but he wouldn't know that it was Papa."

Rosie nodded sadly, the palm of her hand still on the weeping tree.

Fox gave a yip.

"He smells bears," I told her. "Many of them have been here."

I went farther from the road into the forest, turning slowly, studying the trees, the ground, breathing in the scents of the air as I turned. No matter what lie Mago told, Papa had at least been here. The last time he had been seen alive, it was here.

This was a hallowed place.

Fox skirted the area in wider circles as he went, nose to the ground, and I followed him. He often disappeared from view, emerging a while later in a different direction. I waited then, watching him, sensing the questions he asked as he went. So intent was I, that I didn't realize how far I had wandered. White Squirrel shrieked a sudden warning. I hurried back through the trees.

"What are you doing here?" a gruff voice called out.

A dwarf sat astride a muscular, gray pony. A tall man sat on a sorrel horse. The tall man had an arrow ready in his bow and the tip of it was aimed at Rosie.

37

A Note on the Table

It was almost dusk when Tara found the cat waiting for her at the base of the path. The cat gave a short meow in greeting and trotted a little way ahead of her as she made her way up the hillside trail.

Tara could not go quickly, for she was weighed down. With good food from Ettie, but with a heart full of anguish and confusion. Now that she was alone, rumors from the inn crowded her mind.

Was Bevan dead? Or was he alive? Was he being hunted even now? Running and hiding with no one to befriend him? With every arrowhead hoping to find him, and every man cheering its flight?

She stopped still on the path and choked back a

violent sob. She pressed one hand hard to her forehead and tried to breathe calmly, but she couldn't. After a few moments, she lowered Ettie's pail to the ground and covered her face with her hands.

When she opened her eyes, the cat was sitting on the path just ahead of her watching her closely. It cocked its head and gave an urgent yowl, then turned and ran up the path, its tail held straight up behind. The light of day was fading.

Time to move, Tara, she told herself. She wiped her eyes with the heel of her hand, picked up Ettie's pail again, and began to climb.

The clearing seemed empty when she emerged from the hill path. She heard no sound of the girls, but there was Tike at the half-open door, tail wagging to greet her. It struck her that he seemed lonely, but why would that be?

"Girls?" she called, hastening toward the hunting station.

She pushed open the door. The fire had gone out, and the room was filled with empty shadows. In the gloom, she felt her way to the table and lowered her heavy bags and the pail with the crock.

She went to the fireplace and reached for the king's tinderbox. Rosie's wasn't there. Tara turned all her attention to the fire, working for the sparks, feeding them until they grew into flames, deliberately ignoring the fears that sparked and grew along with them. When the fire was at last bright enough to cast its light, she looked around more closely. The girls' cloaks were not hanging on their pegs. Several carry bags were missing.

She stepped out the door and called. "Silvie! Rosie!" Again and again.

From the tree across the clearing, Redbird chirped excitedly at her, but she could not determine if it was meant to comfort or alarm.

She went back inside and lit all the candles against the rapidly approaching twilight. As she set candlesticks on the table, a small piece of paper, tucked halfway under a hairbrush, caught her eye and she snatched at it.

Dear Mama,

The crows brought us part of Papa's pouch this morning. It is in this bowl. I wonder if it wanted to be found. I will ask the crows to show us where they found it. Rosie and I hope that we will find more news about Papa there. We may not be back until late.

Fox and White Squirrel are with us. I thought the way would be too hard for Tike. We have taken Ettie's rolls, and Rosie thinks we will have tree food to eat on the way. I hope we will be back before you, but if we are not, please don't be alarmed. No animal will hurt us now. If we are late, it may be because Rosie has stopped to talk to every tree.

Always love,

Silvie

Tara felt in the bowl, lifted out the scrap of Bevan's pouch, and held it gently in the candlelight. The fabric was grimy and soiled, but the tiny rows of cabbages and roses could still be seen in places. As she touched them, her fingers twitched, remembering these particular stitches. Remembering them like whispers from a once-known song.

Oh, Bevan!

When Bevan had first come to her home to tell her parents that he was serious about their daughter, he had brought cabbages and roses. Cabbages for her parents as the courting gift. Roses for her as the gift of love. She had sewn them since on kitchen towels, on hairbands, on curtains, and most recently on this pouch for Bevan.

She sank down onto the bench by the table and reread the letter, shaking her head the whole while. She knew where the girls must have gone. The only place Bevan's pouch could be found. The place of the king's death.

Unless Bevan were running in the woods as some rumors declared. Then, the pouch could have been found almost anywhere.

Yet, in all the time she had known him, Bevan had never once lost a single piece of his gear. Not once. And for the pouch to be torn from him, as this piece must have been...

Her heart squeezed tight in her chest, and she closed her eyes against hot tears. For some moments she sat still, clutching the soiled bit of cloth.

But what of the girls?

Alarm stirred her. She examined Silvie's note again. Could they have meant to go to the northwest road? That would take them across rough forestland. And what if the attack on the king had been made miles away from Elva?

Silvie and Rosie were city girls, unexperienced in what it would take to traverse this type of country. And animals were not the only danger in the woods. Hunters were out there.

Tara tried to shake her fears away. She dished some of the stew into small bowls for Tike and the cat, then tucked the crock into a corner of the fireplace. She added more wood to the fire and built it high. The room must be warm when the girls returned.

She took a lantern from the king's cupboard, one they had not used before, and lit it, then placed a chair on the doorstep. She wrapped herself in her cloak, closed the door behind her and sat on her chair with her back to the door.

Behind the door, inside the station, all was peaceful and warm. Tike and the cat lay by the fire. A supper simmered.

Outside, Tara waited with the lantern at her feet. The lantern's small light did not reach far in the dark, but Tara felt better sitting where she could watch and listen for any sign of her daughters.

Time passed. No wind rustled the tree branches. Night birds called to each other. An owl hooted, answered by another. Still Tara waited. She would not move from this place until the girls returned.

Something soft pushed its way into her hand as it rested on her lap. Tara was used to the cat doing that, so she paid the nudge no mind—until she remembered that the cat was inside and the shutters were closed. The thing in her hand gave off a fresh, sweet aroma.

It was a bloom from one of the rosebushes that flanked the doorway.

Tara lifted the lantern. The bushes seemed to have

grown taller and wider. Their stems were heavy with blooms. One white and one red had laid themselves in her lap.

Was this hope or a warning?

"I don't understand you!" she cried out. "How can I know what you are trying to tell me? Can you speak?"

Another bird called in the distance. More stars emerged in the darkening sky. Tara put the lantern at her feet again and tucked her cold hands into the pockets of her cloak. She studied the blooms in her lap and tried not to think, not to fear.

Silence reigned in the clearing. A silence so complete that she could hear the distant sound of the river flowing through rocks and stones beyond the first band of trees. In the midst of the burbling, came the sound of quiet footfalls.

Tara raised her head, and found herself looking into the eyes of the great bear.

38

Hunters in the Woods

"What are you doing here?" the tall man shouted. "Who are you? Why are you here? It is forbidden!"

I opened my mouth to answer, but the dwarf said, "Are you poachers?"

Rosie held up empty hands. "Not hardly."

The dwarf slid off the pony. He and his companion were dressed in palace colors, blue with the green trim. "But you may have been looking for something," he said. "May have found something."

He ran toward us and jerked the bag from my shoulder, dumping its contents on the ground. "Humph. Bread crumbs and tree shoots." He ground them both into the dirt with his boot.

Rosie held out her bag. The dwarf eyed her with suspicion, but grabbed it anyway. Out came the water flask, Rosie's bread, and a cascade of evergreen shoots, tiny green leaves, pine cones, and rocks.

The dwarf took the flask and our bags and stuffed them into a pouch that hung from his pony's saddle. We didn't dare move or protest because the tall man's arrow was notched and ready to fly.

I hoped they would leave now, since they had seen we posed no threat. And they had taken everything we had. But the dwarf stepped closer to us. His bold eyes narrowed.

"What have you seen in the forest? What are you looking for? You must be hunting or you wouldn't be here. The Duke has closed this road to everyone."

He was a good deal shorter than Rosie, but he was thickset and looked strong. A knife flashed in his hand as he looked from Rosie to me. Before I could think of an answer, he made an impatient gesture, stabbing at the air with his knife.

"Tell me! Why are you in this part of the forest?"

We took a step away from his knife. Rosie sent me a furtive glance, but I couldn't think of the right words to say. If I protested that we found nothing, he would not believe me. Would he accuse us then of *looking*? My hesitation increased the dwarf's suspicion.

"You've found something! What is it? What is it?"

His insistence turned my fear to anger.

"Mud," I stated bluntly. "We have found mud everywhere. If you're looking for some, we've found it for you."

His eyes narrowed into a squint, and he mumbled something in a language I could not understand. He raised the tip of his knife and pointed at Rosie.

"Give me that squirrel."

Rosie paled and shot me another glance.

"The squirrel does not belong to us," I told him. "So I will have to ask her." I turned to where the bushy white tail flashed over Rosie's red hair.

"Squirrel," I said, "the dwarf wants us to give you to him. What do you say?"

A high-pitched screech split the air. A screech that ended in a violence of chittering and scolding. The dwarf covered his ears for a moment, then tried to look as if he hadn't.

"I think you understand her answer," I said.

The dwarf scowled. "It doesn't matter what she says. I can take her head from her body before she can blink." He took a step closer to Rosie. Rosie stepped back. The squirrel chattered fiercely. Out of the corner of my eye, I saw the point of the arrow follow Rosie.

"The white squirrels know all about that," I said, more boldly than I felt. "They have a saying. *Two blinks for a squirrel. One blink for a hand.*"

"What does that mean?" he growled.

"It means that the squirrels have devised a trick of their own. They know the motions that men use to wring a squirrel's neck. But the squirrels know how to remove the thumb from a man's hand and even his fingers, before he can grip a squirrel body. They practice these moves in the branches of the tough oaks. So now, a man will lose half his hand if he even tries."

White Squirrel let out a sharp shriek. It sounded very much like *Ha!*

"I don't believe you," the dwarf said.

"You don't have to," I replied. "But you will lose all ability with your knife or any other weapon you pride yourself on."

I looked at the tall man. "Lower that arrow," I demanded.

He gave a grunt. "No."

"The only reason you keep it raised like that is because you are afraid of us. And neither of you would want to return to Elva, to the palace, with a story that the other could tell of how you were afraid of two girls."

He gave me a look filled with contempt, but he lowered his arms.

"You say we are not supposed to be here. Fine. We will leave. There were no signs on the hills telling us to turn back, so we are innocent of all your accusations. You have taken everything of value we have, so we ask you to let us go now."

The dwarf was clearly the leader of the two men, so it was to him that I spoke. He did not reply, but his face took on a different and even more dangerous look. I did not want to consider what he might be thinking.

"We are not as alone as you think we are," I said, meeting the dwarf's eye.

My boldness gave him pause. He gave a quick glance around.

"There is no one with you!" he cried out. "I would have smelled them. I would have seen their tracks. Their boot prints would have been next to yours."

"We are not alone," I repeated. The Sender had given gifts and showed his promise. Now it was for me to believe.

I looked at the tall man's sorrel. "Dewfall," I said. "Take your rider away from here. Away from us. At once. Thank you."

The horse started to move. A walk turned swiftly into a gallop.

"Wait!" The dwarf cried out angrily. "Come back!" But Dewfall did not return, though his rider yelled wildly and pulled at the reins.

"You had better mount," I told the dwarf. "Or you will lose this great pony. And it will be a long walk back to the palace."

I didn't wait for his response. "Firefoot, get ready for your rider." The gray pony sidestepped closer to the dwarf.

The dwarf glared at me and laid his hand on the pony's reins. But he made no move to mount.

"Firefoot, you must be wiser than your rider. Take him far away from us. I thank you, good pony."

The pony began to move forward, stubbornly resisting the dwarf's hold on her reins. He swore at her, but had to trot next to her to keep his grip. She paused and waited, then moved forward a few steps again. At last he mounted, swearing at me all the while.

Rosie saw something before I did. She grabbed a handful of the rocks at her feet and let them fly swiftly, one after the other, stinging the dwarf's hand, wrist, and nose.

He cried out and dropped the knife that he would

have flung at us. Before he could do anything more, that good pony whisked him down the road.

As soon as he was out of sight, relief filled me. I grabbed Rosie's arm. "Good work," I whispered. "Very good work." I reached up to touch the rider in her hood. "Squirrel, you were marvelous."

"But what now, Silvie?" Rosie looked past me. "Wait. Where's Fox?"

"Behind that tree. If he would have shown himself, that arrow would have found him immediately. Here, Fox." Our friend bounded into the open.

"We better not stay here," I said. "You know what fighting men and hunters are like. They won't give up. They will return and maybe track us, though I hope they feel it's not worth it. If only they won't make those poor horses suffer for their obedience to me."

"Did you find anything?" Rosie asked, bringing me back to the reason we had come to this spot in the first place. "Did Fox find anything? Anything to do with Papa and the Guardsmen?"

I asked Fox. "Anything made by men?"

The answer was no, and I felt that his answer was true. Rosie and I wandered around the trees, looking for a few hurried minutes because our hearts needed to. But the sun had already dropped behind the tops of the western trees.

"We must go, Rosie," I said, after she had run her hands through the scrub between the weeping trees and come up with nothing. "It's dangerous to stay here and we have a long way to go."

She stood up, nodding somberly, and followed me back the way we came, across the road and up the broad flat hill. At the top of the hill, we turned for one more look.

"He's not here," Rosie said quietly. "We'll never find him here."

"No." We never would.

We turned our backs to the road valley and picked our way through the trees. I walked as quickly as I could for fear of more hunters. After going a short distance I realized I could not pick the direction we had come from. I had been too busy watching the crow to pay any attention to what the land was like around me.

Fox wove back and forth in broad lines until he found the scent of our boots. With a confident yip he set off at a trot, nose to the ground, and we followed close behind.

The energy that determination had given us soon evaporated. We were exhausted, and without food or drink. I began to feel slightly dizzy. Light dwindled to gray and after a time it was hard to see Fox in the dusk. Rosie stumbled in the gloom now, just like I did. Soon, the light disappeared completely and our progress slowed to one tentative step after another while we grasped hands.

"We have to stop," I said at last. "I can't see Fox anymore and I'm so tired." It wouldn't help to mention the hunger that gnawed my stomach and the dryness in my throat. Rosie would feel the same. "We'll have to stay the night here, wherever it is that we are."

Rosie still held tightly to my hand, but she took a few steps one way and then another. "Here. We'll rest under this tree. This is a good tree."

I peered up into the dark branches overhead. Rosie's declaration of good was reassuring.

We sat at the base of the tree, pulled our legs into our cloaks to cover and warm them as much as we could, then leaned against the tree trunk and each other. Squirrel settled herself on Rosie's lap and Fox curled up by my side.

"It's not the first night we've spent in the forest," Rosie said.

"No," I agreed. "We're forest dwellers now." I said the words without conviction.

"Should we make a fire?" she asked.

"I don't think so. It might tell more hunters where we are. And one of us will have to stay awake and tend it. Are you warm enough?"

"For now. Are there any animals about?"

"Fox says not very near."

I tried to imagine I was more comfortable than I was. Less sad than I was. I also tried not to think about how terrified Mama must be that it was so dark and we were not home. Though I had tried with my small note, in truth, it could not have reassured her much. How I wished we were back in the hunting station and that we had not attempted such a long journey without her!

Rosie took a deep breath and rested her head on my shoulder. In turn, I rested my head on her thick curly hair, which was almost like a pillow, closed my eyes, and willed myself to sleep.

SILVIE! Silvie!

I raised my head, blinking. I could see nothing in the blackness, and I was shivering with cold. Had I been dreaming?

Fox was on his feet at my side. He had heard the voice too, and more importantly, he was not afraid.

"Silvie." The voice came deep and rumbly.

Hope leapt in my heart. "*Bear?* Is it you, Bear?"

Rosie sat up. "What is it?" she whispered.

Bear answered. "Your mother sent me to find you. Come on now. I'll take you home."

"I don't think we can walk any farther, Bear," I replied. "We're so tired."

"You can ride on me, Silvie. It's as you said. I'm not like other bears."

Bear crouched down low so I could climb on his broad back. I leaned down and clutched the roll of fur on his shoulders, on either side of his neck. Rosie crawled up behind me and wrapped one arm around my waist. Squirrel gave a squeak from inside Rosie's hood. Fox crawled to a safe place under my arm. Once we were ready, the bear began to run.

So fast.

He moved swiftly in and out of trees that I could not see in the blackness. Leaping over the underbrush as if it were nothing. I lowered my head and pressed it against the bristly softness of the fur between his shoulders and held on tight.

After the bewilderment of the first moments, I knew I could trust to the bear's sight and speed. Something like comfort began to flow into my weariness. Rosie must have felt it too, for she began to sing.

> *Oh, sing me high*
> *And sing me low,*
> *And sing me where*
> *The wind blows.*
> *I'll listen high,*
> *I'll listen low,*
> *And find you where*
> *The wind blows.*

It was a song about seeking and finding the one you love. In spite of what we had been told about our father's death, we had been seeking him, or something of him, but had found neither.

Yet, before grief could overwhelm me, wonder filled me. The wonder of running through the night on the back of that tireless bear.

Above the bare treetops, stars moved through the sky and wispy clouds veiled the moon. The forest slept and the chill air stung our faces, while Rosie sang on.

> *I'll listen near*
> *And listen far,*
> *And find you at*
> *The bright star.*

THEY BURST into the clearing with a tumult, both girls calling to her before the bear stopped in front of her chair. Tara leapt up and held the lantern high. She could have collapsed with relief when Silvie and Rosie slid off the bear's back and threw their arms around her.

Tara studied their faces gratefully as they ate Ettie's warm stew in front of the fire—Fox with a bowl of his own. Between spoonfuls, they told her their story.

A story of crows who declared that no bodies had been left in the forest. Of Bevan's pouch piece that had been used in a nest. Of animal guides and animal sorrow. Of trees that gave them food, trees that sheltered them, and trees that wept. Of news that the northwest road was closed to everyone. And of a horse and pony that obeyed Silvie instead of their own masters. Tara listened wide-eyed to all of it.

Once the girls' story was told, they made their beds and settled in to sleep. They fell asleep immediately, but Tara lay awake, listening to their even breathing and to the rhythmic rumbling of the wondrous sleeping bear curled up outside their door.

She recognized the description of Nally the Dwarf. She had seen Nally proudly strutting across the palace lawn with his fellows. Bevan had considered him the greatest tracker in Rilken.

What was curious was that Nally, through his actions, admitted to her two daughters what pride would have kept him from admitting to anyone else. That he was still looking for something, and he was afraid someone would find it before he did. Afraid enough to make him uncivilized and ruthless. To treat his fellow countrywomen abominably.

It must have something to do with the Guardsmen and the king, or Nally wouldn't have been on that stretch of road. The fact that he was searching showed that the palace still had questions of its own.

39

The Entrance of Master Redmond

It was mid-morning the next day when Tara took her place at the table by the window in The Grumpy Rabbit. Her mind was full of the events of last night, but she settled herself with her tools, her hands ready to work. She was more eager than ever to listen to the news people might share as they came and went.

She unfolded her linen pieces and set out gold-colored threads on the table in front of her, studying their shades of color and brightness. A medium gold would work for the small suns that would be scattered through her design. Tara threaded her needle.

Gareth filled tumblers from the kegs at the bar and

handed them to customers, continuing his cheerful, welcoming banter. A few of the inn guests approached Tara's table respectfully while she stitched. When she looked up to smile at them, she saw faces alight with awe as they gazed at her work.

Jarlath—his worn cap perched on his head—came from the kitchen carrying a bowl for his meal. Instead of sitting at his usual table, he chose one next to hers, between her corner and the rest of the room. He gave her a friendly nod, then without a word, bent over his bowl, stirred it once, and began to eat.

The great room was getting noisier. More people came in. Travelers called for extra help with their horses. Jarlath leapt up and hurried toward the door. One man at a table with friends, recognized someone in a group that had just arrived and called out to them. Greetings echoed over the whole room.

Dona, Nissa, and Alta carried trays of hot food among the diners. Nissa gave her patrons friendly smiles. Dona patted their arms like a grandmother. Alta asked if everything were all right, a look of grave concern on her face, a look which switched to one of mild disbelief when they assured her that everything was fine and the food delicious.

The whole scene reminded Tara of the inns of East Rilken and her own childhood. For the people who occupied them were the same. Neighboring families looking for a change of scene. Travelers, of course. Workers. In the east they would have been farmhands, millers, and carters. Here in the west, the workers were mostly woodsmen and lumber haulers. A grouping of friends and strangers. Some wanted to eat their meal alone enclosed in their own thoughts. Others came for the people, whether they knew them or not, and to hear the news. Just like she was doing now.

The overall bustle made it hard to hear any particular conversation, but Tara caught phrases that told her many were thinking of the king's death. Sometimes one table would drop their conversation and lean toward another to listen with interest. That's how it always was at an inn. Some came to listen. Others came to be heard.

A group of six woodsmen sat at a table near the center of the room. The table next to them turned their chairs to share in the woodsmen's discussion. Voices from surrounding tables began to drop away as the argument in the center claimed the attention of all.

"It doesn't matter how you try to tell the story. You can't make it come out right." One of the woodsmen was speaking.

"I can! I can see in my mind just the way it happened." The voice was insistent. A younger woodsman.

"All right, then." The first woodsman's voice was thick with skepticism. "How do *you* make it out?"

"The king and all his attendants, which we know includes at least six Guardsmen, and horses, and grooms, and the wagons with supplies—what, at least forty people on the road? Then at the curve this one man, the murderer, moves quick behind a tree and—"

"Stop!" An authoritative voice from another table

broke in. "The king was not traveling with his full retinue. This we know. He left most of it at the town of Coyer where they had spent the night. The king was in haste to reach Elva, so he took his Guardsmen—"

"And Prince Dallen," someone added.

"And the prince," the authoritative voice continued, "and went at good speed for the capital."

The young woodsman frowned, but only for a moment. "Then the way I see it *must* have happened! The man had fewer people to deal with! He could have gone ahead with his arrows, waited by a tree—"

"Now, young Harry, was it an oak or a chestnut?" The tone of this voice carried a hidden joke.

"A *tree*," said Harry, with emphasis. "And waited for the rest of them to come while he raises his bow—"

"No, Harry," said an older voice with kindness. "One Guardsman cannot just go do what he wants to without anyone knowin' about it—"

"Have you ever seen them?" asked one of the travelers with a quick Elva city accent. "They move like a wall around the king. Even as they give plenty of room for the horses. They can gallop like the wind and still have their shields protecting the king from every possible angle. Now, do you think no one is going to notice anything odd about one of them saying, 'excuse me, fellers. I just have to go up the road apiece and relieve myself. I'll just wait for you boys up there.'"

A few chuckles greeted the absurdity of this.

The Elvan man continued, "Son, a gnat can't approach the king without a Guardsman knowing. They've got eyes and ears like the Sender's own."

"Well, since it couldn't have happened my way," cried Harry indignantly, "how *did* it happen?" His voice rang out with a challenge and the room fell silent for a few moments.

Tara finished another sun and threaded her needle for the next, pretending to take little notice of the general conversation. Jarlath came in from the back hallway, returned to his table, and began to drink his soup again. One of the woodsmen saw him slip in.

"Here's an old soldier. Let's ask Jarlath!" Heads turned to their corner of the room. Tara bent over her work, hoping that her hair would shield most of her face from public view. She watched Jarlath out of the corner of her eye.

The old man lowered his spoon and turned his face towards the woodsmen. "You got a question more important than my soup?"

Some people chuckled. One insistent voice cried out, "Yes!"

The older woodsman asked for all of them. "Jarlath, we're trying to get at the truth of the forest road, of the fight that took the king's life. You were a soldier for years. What can you tell us?"

"You want the truth?"

"Yes, please."

Jarlath shook his head. "You're not going to get it. In any battle, large or small, truth is the first one to die." Jarlath stirred his soup, but his eyes seemed to be seeing more than a crockery bowl on a wooden table. "Some say that truth dies before a battle even begins. And from what I've seen, I think they're right."

He put his spoon to work again as the room digested this. A few people got up from their tables, paid Gareth, and left through the main door, letting in a sudden burst of wind until the door was firmly shut again. Most of those left seemed to want to linger and puzzle it out.

"What do we have? Who's all on the road?"

"The king and his Guardsmen."

"The Crown Prince."

"The palace guard—"

"Now, wait. Didn't they come when it was all over?"

"Why did they come at all? They're not supposed to leave the palace grounds."

"I heard they had already met up with the king, and that the Guardsman ambushed them all."

"What? One man against all of them? While hiding behind Harry's tree?"

Much of the room laughed at this.

A serious voice broke through. "What of the bears? Does anyone know how many there were, and what they actually did?"

"Before we answer that," put in another, "I'd like to know this. Are the bears real or just a made-up story?"

"I think someone made them up. Look—the palace guard got there too late to do anything, right? So to save their pride, they had to blame someone. So they made up these bears."

"The palace guard arrived too late? Are you sure?"

"Is the king alive? I'd call that late."

"I heard the same story in Elva."

"That don't count for much. You can hear a lot of bilge in Elva too."

"But Elva news is all we've got to work with," said the oldest woodsman. "Let's talk about the palace guard. I heard from someone that they don't get along with the King's Guardsmen. They're rivals like."

"Wait! Are any of them here?" The speaker looked over his shoulder nervously.

"Naw," said another woodsman. "They go to the West Road Inn and we prefer to come to the Rabbit where a man can talk more freely. Right, Gareth?"

Gareth grinned and waved at them from the bar.

The nervous speaker relaxed at this and the oldest woodsman resumed. "I think we need to know what the palace guard was doing—"

The main door to the inn opened with unexpected energy fueled by a gust of wind. Some turned to look at the newcomer openly. Others bent over their bowls and gave him furtive glances.

The man who entered wore the dark blue breeches, cloak, and cap of a university scholar. His hat and cloak were trimmed in velvet, which announced high standing in the academic world.

"It's Master Redmond," said Jarlath, leaning over to speak quietly to Tara. "He's a famous professor, a doctor even, but he says that the title Master is more comfortable to his ears. He's a great favorite."

One glance at Gareth proved the old soldier's words. The innkeeper had a broad smile on his face, and his hand reached out eagerly to clasp that of the professor.

Gareth turned towards the room, one arm outstretched to draw attention, and cried, "Friends and company of The Grumpy Rabbit, I present to you our good Master Redmond!"

Scattered applause broke out and Redmond bowed his head.

"How long will you be with us, good sir?" asked Gareth.

"Weeks! Bremen is too noisy, so I determined to escape Tellhaven altogether and plunge myself deep into the rich, quiet green of the Rilken forests in order to get some writing done."

Gareth looked more than pleased at this. "Have you eaten yet? Can we bring you something?"

"I am starved," said Redmond.

Gareth pulled a rope that hung on the wall by the kegs. Tara realized that it must ring the bell in the kitchen.

Redmond turned to address the room. "And what were you all discussing before I arrived and rudely interrupted you?" He had an easy, pleasing manner, and the confidence that must have come from years of addressing rooms full of listeners.

"I see the look of interruption on your faces. Of bits of conversation stopped mid-chew. Be good to me and tell me what it is. I've only had my poor horse to talk to these past traveling days, and though the good girl has decided opinions, she has trouble finding the right words to express herself. As a result, I am as starved for conversation as I am for soup and bread. Come, what were you speaking of?"

One of the older woodsmen answered him. "We were trying to discover the truth of what happened to

King Adare on the forest road. Jarlath there said that we'll never find the truth."

"You are too kind!" Redmond exclaimed. "A philosophical discussion underway and offered to me? I must have some of this feast!"

He grabbed a chair and pulled it up to the woodsmen's table. Tara was surprised to see him do that, surprised also that the men readily moved their chairs to make room for him.

"So, what have *you* heard about it in Tellhaven?" someone asked him.

"Just that your dear king was murdered in the forest and one of his Guardsmen is said to have done it," answered Master Redmond.

"'*Is said?*' You don't believe the story then?" asked the oldest woodsman.

"I make it a habit to take at least three years of thinking before I believe anything."

"You're joking!" said Harry.

"I assure you, I am not," Redmond replied. "The nature of man makes truth elusive. We all believe what we want to and crush what we don't, whether we are philosophers or scientists. You cannot take that tendency out of man."

He looked around at all those gathered nearby. "Now, tell me what *you* have heard."

The oldest woodsman related everything the room had been saying about the forest road. Redmond listened with an attention so intent that the look on the speaker's face showed he felt the honor of it. The professor didn't even notice when Gareth set a tumbler of ale, a roll, and butter down in front of him.

When the woodsman had finished, Redmond nodded and said, "I think you may have already uncovered what truth there is to be had."

"What do you mean?" cried the man from Elva. "What do you see that we can't?"

"Why, how fast does it take one man to load an arrow into his bow? Even if he used a dagger, spear, and bow, he could not have enough speed to match those who are his equals in speed. Plainly, he *could not* in one moment destroy six other men, five of which have skills to match his own. Therefore, I think that he *did not*."

This statement was greeted with a variety of expressions from the listeners. Many with smiles of agreeing satisfaction. Others with doubt. For Tara's part, she felt that in that moment, she loved Master Redmond with her whole heart.

But the professor was not finished. "One of your Rilken sayings makes the rounds in Tellhaven. *You cannot surprise a Guardsman.* Right? That is not true for general guardsmen across the continent, for any one of them can be surprised and often are.

"But the Guardsmen of *your* king, Rilken's famous Guardsmen, have a drill that they repeat again and again to make sure that they are never surprised. Am I correct? They play hunter and hunted in every possible situation. Tunnels. Forests. Grassland. City streets. Yes?"

Tara found herself nodding, then froze, fearful lest she was seen.

Redmond's words swept on. "At the university, we

have discussed this drill many times over our coffee and ale. Rilken's Guardsmen have made themselves virtually immune to surprise. Go back to your sad forest road. What is the possibility that one Guardsman could ambush another?"

Redmond shook his head. "The whole incident raises so many questions—about the role of the bears, the Guardsmen, the palace guard, the missing prince, and your hardworking Duke, who is protected by this same palace guard."

He paused for a sip of ale, but no one spoke. All waited as one for Redmond to continue.

"Questions themselves take courage to ask," he said, returning his tumbler to the tabletop. "You would be surprised at how many are never asked or studied by either scientists or philosophers, simply from lack of courage. When questions arise at university, energetic men say 'but that is not proven, Redmond! Not proven! So it cannot be true.'"

"Surely, proof is required for anything to be true," put in a man from the next table, one of the original listeners.

"Scientific truth and philosophical truth each have their own unique tests," Redmond replied. "But what my eager colleagues *don't* say in their glee, is that the reason the matter at hand has not been *proven*, was that it has never been *questioned*. Hence, never been tested. And without questioning or testing, proof is impossible!

"So, my eager colleague should rather say, 'this has not been questioned!' Then, he would have spoken more truly. Of course, then he would have to admit the lack of courage to question."

"I admit, I don't have courage to question the palace guard," said a woodsman. "I prefer to swing my axe at things that don't swing back."

"I understand you, my friend," said Redmond, placing a hand on the man's shoulder. "I would not like to question them either."

The room seemed disappointed at this apparent conclusion to their discussion. Several stood up, held out money to Gareth, and left the inn.

The oldest woodsman stood up also and stretched his arms out in front of him. "I think I would rather be a logger than a philosopher. My job is not as confusing. You study a tree, then make it fall where you want it to."

Redmond looked up at him. "Is there no disagreement about which direction it will fall or what it will do?"

"Only with a new crew," put in another, "and young apprentices."

"And there's something about a falling tree," said the oldest, "that marks the line between truth and folly. You can't argue with a falling tree."

"Or should we say," added Redmond, "that you can only argue with a falling tree *once*."

The woodsmen erupted into wry laughter at this and took their leave. Most of the midday customers left with them. Jarlath had slipped out some time ago to continue his work.

Tara looked down at her linen piece. She had not made one stitch in the past quarter hour—couldn't—

because of all she had heard. This Master Redmond, a learned man, had just stated that Bevan could not have done what Mago accused him of doing. A man of arms like the captain of the palace guard would have known that it couldn't have happened.

No one had questioned Mago that day, but herself. No fellow Guardsman had spoken up. Which meant that even while Drony had escorted them out of the city, he must have known that Mago lied.

Tara had been looking for arguments of heart and character. For people to understand that nothing inside Bevan would have made him capable of killing his king. Or his fellows. She had not considered that it was physically impossible for Bevan to have done it as well. *If only everyone in Rilken thought like this Master Redmond!*

Redmond was strolling around the room, stretching his legs while waiting for the something special that Gareth said Ettie was preparing for him. Tara couldn't help but look up when he came near the back fireplace.

"Master Redmond," she said, "I was listening closely to what you were saying just now—"

He smiled at her. "If only my students would do the same."

She had been ready to ask more questions, but now she realized this was foolish and closed her mouth. Redmond hadn't been on the forest road and could know nothing more than what he had heard. But the great man must sense that she had more to say, for he was waiting near her table.

She gave him a quick smile. "Thank you for the reasonable way you sorted through the news."

A puzzled look came into his eyes. Had he been expecting something more? Did he sense the depth of her concern? The reason for it?

The puzzlement vanished. Redmond gave a small courtly bow in its place and simply said, "You're welcome."

40

An Odd Mercy

He opened his eyes and for several moments, the forest blurred around him. He turned his head slowly and blinked until the trees became straight again. Until the tiny green leaves that waved above him became reassuringly distinct. And he could breathe.

The dream had come again.

He was lying on the ground. Just like he was every night in the dream. The spears flew, the swords flashed, and everything spun in every direction.

The dream would not go away, because he was not listening to it.

It had spoken to him first in waking hours.

Then, because of his anger, it began to come only at night.

Every night.

Telling him what it had seen.

What *he* had seen.

What he didn't want to see anymore.

But the dream came nightly.

Insistent.

Forcing him to notice the details that were clouded by anguish. Details that pointed to a terrible and hopeless truth.

In the dream he could not close his eyes and turn away.

Yet somehow he sensed that the dream was being merciful to him.

The dream would not let him forget.

But the dream understood.

41

———

The Court Jester

Pate studied his reflection in a wood-framed mirror fastened to the wall by the door of his room. He frowned at the image, then picked up his candle and held it closer to the glass.

This scrutiny was not vanity, he reminded himself. This was protection. He knew very well that his breeches, hose, shirt, vest, and coat were messengers with meanings that would be interpreted by every person attending the Duke's reception. A single glance at his attire could grant Pate goodwill or hostility.

Pate had not worried this much about his dress when King Adare was alive. Adare had a certain stability, a reasonableness about him, that made factions at court unnecessary. Ludicrous even. The king had not been perfect, by any means, but he had never tried to manipulate people, or play them off each other. And had never approved of or elevated anyone who did.

But his brother the Duke was a different kind of man. A man who kept his thoughts and intentions hidden. A man concerned mostly with his own power and prestige. And a man who used the insecurity of others to mask his own.

After the king's death, the attention and aspirations of the court had naturally been drawn towards Ravelin. But as Ravelin fell ill and the Duke's authority as regent became more pronounced, the court pivoted toward the one whose power was predominant.

Tonight, no one in the kingdom could stand above the Duke. No one except for Dallen, who would have been of age to be king.

Dallen remained unfound. The ghost of a king that hunters searched for in vain. And every day, fewer and fewer hopeless hunters went out into the woods.

Dallen, my friend! My king! How can you be gone?

Pate took a deep breath to calm himself and looked in the mirror again. Green breeches the color of pine needles topped gold legs. A dark blue vest covered the pale linen shirt. One of his "curious coats" completed the costume.

One side of this coat had a shoulder and sleeve of blue and a skirt of green. On the other side, the coat skirt was blue and the shoulder and sleeve were green.

The coat, vest, and breeches were well-made, but unadorned. His fingers displayed no rings. No gold chains hung around his neck. Thus, he gave no signs to the noble guests that he had aspirations to rival their standing. In truth, they had nothing to fear from him.

In one adornment only, he took risk. Without a qualm.

Instead of gold around his neck, there lay an embroidered cord, crafted in the brilliant colors that made the nobility drool. It came to a stylish knot in the center of his vest, while its ends hung loosely and tastefully below.

He wore it to remind himself that whatever the Duke thought about him now, King Adare had trusted him completely. For this cord was the gift to Pate from the king, on the ten-year anniversary of having been in his sons' service.

"I thank you again, gracious Sire," Pate whispered as he fingered the cord. "And miss you and your noble character more than you could know."

A meow of protest broke through his reverie. His cat rubbed herself against his leg, then leapt up onto the bed, eyeing him with reproach.

"I would hug you properly, dear cat of mine, but you would repay me by leaving hair all over my coat. And the Duke would not approve."

Pate turned around and held up the candle to get the view from behind. In the middle of his back the green pieces formed a diagonal, while the blues did the same.

A rap sounded at the door. Avelyn stood there, a tired smile on her face. The colors of his outfit immediately caught her attention. She peered at him.

"You look like a jester, but a subdued one."

"It's best to avoid the bright colors, anything that

would draw attention away from the royal family."

"Is there a reason you chose your jester coat tonight?" Avelyn sat on the edge of his bed and studied him.

"Yes," he answered, setting the candlestick on the table. "I am sending a message to the Duke of Elva that I, Pate, am only the court fool. Worth only the notice of laughter, and worth no other attention at all."

"That's not true," she said indignantly.

"Ah. Thank you. No. But as long as the Duke believes that, then the coat will have served its purpose."

It was time to leave for the reception. His feet took him instead to the window, a place he often went to get his bearings. Avelyn joined him and they gazed out over a slice of Elva, illuminated by a pale moon and bright stars.

"It looks beautiful from up here," Avelyn said. "Our windows give no view at all."

"I could spend half the night just staring at the view," he replied. Atop a high tower, the flags of the reigning family whipped in the wind. Dallen. Ravelin. The Duke.

"Now, how long will those three be allowed to fly together?" he asked himself out loud.

Avelyn stared wordlessly at him. He put an arm around her and held her close for a few moments.

The sight of Ravelin's flag so lashed about, aroused his compassion and filled him with new energy. He kissed Avelyn's cheek, turned from the window, and called to his cat.

"I must go now, my faithful pet. Behave yourself. Remember what an honor you are given this night. For the rest of your life you can brag to all your feline friends that the greatest artist in Rilken condescended to spend an evening with you in order to sketch your humble likeness. And to protect my furnishings from the claws of your lonely fury."

Avelyn laughed and drew out a pencil from the artist apron she still wore.

"Thank you, my love," he said to her. "I hope I can be the attendant that Ravelin needs tonight. It will be difficult for him."

Understanding softened her expression. For one moment, all he wanted to do was stay by her side. Then he was out the door and hurrying down the stairs to Ravelin's apartments.

A WORRIED-LOOKING WELLS ADMITTED HIM. The prince's outer room was dimly lit. Wells closed the door to the hallway, but they took only a few steps inside before the attendant spoke in a low voice.

"He's asleep, Pate, and I am grateful for that."

"What? Asleep? He's not going to the reception?"

Wells shook his head. "He had a bad spell just a half hour ago. Collapsed by his desk before I could reach him."

Wells paused for a moment, and Pate saw the pain of the memory on his face. "I have already sent word to the Duke that the prince will not be in attendance. But Ravelin still wishes for you to go, Master Pate. He wanted me to tell you that he looks forward to your account of the evening."

"May I see the prince? I promise I'll do nothing to wake him. It's just that he looked so much better this afternoon. I don't understand it."

"Follow me."

Pate walked on tip-toe to Ravelin's bedroom. Wells held a covered candle above the prince's bed, enough for Pate to catch a glimpse of the damp, grayish face on the pillow.

No optimism could counter what Pate saw there. Ravelin was sleeping, but it was not a peaceful one. Suffering strained the prince's features. Pate turned and quietly left the bedchamber. Wells followed.

"Wells—" Pate paused by the outer door. He had trouble speaking. "What is happening? We can't lose him too, Wells."

"We won't, Master Pate," the attendant said firmly. "But I share your concern."

Pate stood still, trying to shake off the fear that threatened to turn his limbs to lead.

"Sir," Wells continued. "Ravelin appreciates all you do for him, and I know it set his mind at ease that you would be attending the Duke's reception. 'Pate will know what to do. He will be better eyes and ears than I could be right now.' Those were his exact words."

Somehow the attendant had sensed his struggle. "Thank you, Wells," Pate replied. "For Ravelin's sake, I would take on the entire palace guard."

"I believe it, sir."

Wells opened the door, and with a nod of farewell, Pate was on his way.

42

The Duke's Reception

Pate gave his card to the footman and stepped into the Duke's newly redone audience hall. The spacious room was full, but not overly so. Three cittern players sat in one corner, plucking and strumming the strings of their instruments, creating an atmosphere of sober geniality befitting a castle in mourning.

Yet, the gathering seemed oddly timed. Why hold a reception now just because the Duke had repainted his walls? Why not wait until the traditional month of mourning was over? *Questions look for answers as a man seeks a wife.*

Pate took his place in the receiving line. The Duke must have a particular reason for the time he chose, and that reason was what Pate must discover. What was it that couldn't wait?

The line moved steadily. Pate bowed a greeting to those in front and behind him. They barely moved their heads in response. All their attention was directed toward the man who stood by the head of the line, toward the moment in which the most powerful in the land would recognize them, and by that recognition, further their ambitions.

Duchess Olivia, Lady Petronia, and Duke Allard, all wore the proud regal green-on-green. The right to wear the green-on-green was the only thing that superseded the nobility's lust for embroidery. And the sash that draped across one shoulder of Olivia's gown was heavily embroidered. Jewels sparkled among the threads. Petronia dressed like her mother, but her sash was thinner.

The Duke's vest and breeches were green-on-green, but his cape was completely embroidered, and studded overwhelmingly with jewels. His every movement made him sparkle with light.

Pate remembered the clothes that Ravelin had requested Wells to prepare for this night. They were not this ostentatious. If Ravelin had been able to come, the Duke would clearly have won the clothing war.

Duchess Olivia held out her hand, and Pate bowed low over it.

"I am grieved to hear that Ravelin is so ill again," she said. "I heard he was doing well this afternoon. The Duke is so disappointed."

"I thought the prince looked well this afternoon too, Your Highness."

"Please, give him our best wishes."

"Most assuredly, ma'am."

Petronia held out her hand too, but only because her mother had. He bowed over it quickly and opened his mouth. But since she did not speak, he closed it again. She was already looking toward the next person in line. Pate moved on.

"Good evening, Pate," said the Duke.

"Your Highness," Pate replied, in his most respectful voice, with his deepest bow.

"Did you see my nephew before you came? What did he look like?"

"He was asleep when I called, sir."

The Duke nodded, then turned to someone else, and Pate stepped away.

The receiving line deposited him in front of a wall covered with a heavy green drape. Not odd in itself, except for the fact that it was flanked by two members of the palace guard, each looking more rigid than stone. One of them was none other than the infamous Captain Mago. Pate blinked, turned, and found himself immediately accosted by Lord Vallenro.

The man's haggard face betrayed deep suffering. His once proud height was bent forward, and the skin that stretched across cheekbones indicated he had not eaten well for weeks. He had a glass of wine in his hand. A tense smile appeared.

"Good evening, Master Pate."

Pate bowed willingly.

"I saw you noticing the curtain just now," Vallenro said. "The Duke has a surprise for us all tonight. Something I've been graciously allowed to see before, but not in this magnificence."

"Something from his collection, I suppose," Pate answered. He gave another glance at the curtain. "Something taller than a clock and shorter than a spire."

"The Duke is so good to share it with us. But, the Duke is always very, very good." Vallenro gulped. "His brother the king was killed on my land, you know. Struck down right on my land, in my woods, and the Duke has been nothing but gracious to me." Vallenro's eyes were immediately wet, and his face took on a mournful cast.

"You are a true nobleman, and I have no doubt the graciousness is deserved," Pate said.

Vallenro looked confused. "Is it? No. No—I don't think so." The mournful expression returned. "The fault is mine. Mine alone. I'm sorry, Pate. I must apologize to you, to everyone, for the loss of our king."

"The murderer, whoever he is, would be glad to put all his guilt on you, I'm sure. But do not be cast down, your lordship. The murderer at this moment must feel all the weight of what he has done. So great is that weight, that he really can't spare any for your shoulders."

The puzzled look returned to Vallenro's face. Pate could see a struggle behind the man's watery eyes and pitied him.

"Lord Vallenro," said a deep voice. A man decorated in embroidery approached.

Pate bowed and quickly turned away. He took up an unobtrusive position on one side of the fireplace in order to study those whom the Duke had invited.

Lord Locke was immediately evident, Lady Locke at his side. The king's secretary conversed in his usual serious way surrounded by a small group of attentive listeners.

The castle chamberlain, Lord Farnworth, walked slowly through the room, his hands clasped and hovering just below his chin, as if he were praying. Lady Farnworth was one of the cittern players. Very skilled from what Pate could see and hear.

Tibbett, the castle steward, stood at the opposite end of the fireplace from Pate. He was speaking to Harmon, the caretaker of the Duke's public rooms.

Beyond a group that included the Mayor of Elva, Pate distinguished a cluster of unfamiliar, but highly ornamented, nobility. The tallest of them had dark thick hair and a beard, and looked continually to either side of him with a swinging gaze. Hm. *Distrustful?*

Tables filled with food and drink waited beyond the groups of talkers. Pate thought he smelled almond cakes and moved toward that part of the room. Kendall was stretching his hand out to take a goblet of wine when Pate walked up behind him.

> *"Oh, what a devious thing is wine*
> *It has such might and power.*
> *O'er all who drink without a care*
> *It rules within the hour."*

Kendall spluttered and turned on him. "Pate! What are *you* doing here?"

Pate bowed. "Invited by His Augustusness, just like you."

Kendall put his goblet down and grabbed Pate's arm. "Listen, Pate!" he said in a rough whisper. "This is not the place or the time to behave in your usual idiotic manner. The highest worth of the country is here, and you must do nothing to diminish the respect of the ruling family in front of them. Do you hear me?"

"Might I demand the same of you, Master Tutor?" Pate replied playfully.

"Hush," said Kendall. He tugged on Pate's arm and pointed discreetly to the tall man with the swinging gaze. "That is the Earl of Sormin. He is the most powerful man in all of West Rilken. He rarely ever comes to the castle."

"People will do anything for almond cakes."

"This is an important night for both the earl and the Duke!"

"Who is the young man by the earl's side? The one who is doing an imitation of someone who has just emerged from a hole?"

"What? Why, that's the earl's son!"

"And if he can't see the sun, he will crawl back into his hole and sleep for seven more weeks. My, it would be hard to see the sun through a father like that—"

Kendall tugged at him to make him stop. "Look over there, Pate," he said.

And as Pate looked and listened to everything Kendall said about Lord Gretnow from East Rilken and

Lord Heves from the south, he realized that Kendall was scared.

The master tutor, though at a high station in the castle, was currently besieged by strange nobility on all sides. No one from Elva Castle had talked to him or been near him since Pate arrived at the reception. For all his bluster and criticism, Kendall needed Pate in this moment.

Well, needs must be useful, thought Pate. He listened to everything Kendall had to say until the tutor's flow of speech evaporated, and he found it necessary to engage the attention of someone new.

Lord Farnworth had stopped his coursing through the room in order to speak to Lady Locke. The main reason Farnworth talked to anyone was to tell them about his passion for carpentry and maple wood. His hobby consumed him, and his work was excellent. But he loved to tell people about it as much as he liked to do it. Pate knew Lady Locke well, and he could see the fatigue behind the patient look in her eye. He inched forward.

"With a cut like the one I have described, I can get an unseamed board for use as a large night table," Farnworth was saying. "And you must know the difficulty of finding a night table the right size for all the things one needs by one's bedside. Books—"

Lady Locke nodded politely.

"—a good-sized candelabra, one that must hold at least five candles. And then there is the drinking tumbler, the candle-snuffer—"

"Oh, yes," said Lady Locke graciously. "Nightstands

are never large enough for all the things you want near you when you sleep."

Pate leaned in. "My dear Lady Locke, was it difficult to find a nightstand that would accommodate his lordship?"

Farnworth looked surprised at this, wondering what to make of the interruption. Lady Locke burst into laughter and smacked Pate's shoulder with her hand. "Dear Pate. You *are* Pate the Useful. The king was right in naming you so!" The warmth in her eyes told him that she appreciated his interference, and that it had brought the relief he had planned.

With this approbation, Farnworth laughed politely. Pate bowed and strolled on, receiving a grateful wink from Lady Locke.

He studied the massive green drape at the far end of the room again, and the immovable figure of Mago next to it. Whatever hid behind that curtain necessitated placing the strongest man in the kingdom at guard. *Oh, what a curious night this is.*

Kendall's insistent descriptions of the guests stayed in Pate's mind. For they all circled around one thing. Power. The powerful men of the kingdom. The Earl of Sormin from the west. Lord Gretnow from the east. Heves from the south. Vallenro, weak though he appeared now, controlled most of the land to the north of Elva, beyond the royal domains.

The Duke had collected the four powerful winds and brought them to his hall tonight. As gentle as the mood was in this room, it covered something else. No one would gather the power of the land just to show them a new toy, a new clock, or a new mirror, no matter how tall and broad it was. *Would they?*

A hand grabbed his shoulder, startling him. Lord Locke pulled him into a small group of unfamiliar guests.

"It's tedious to wait, young Pate. Give us a joke. Give us a laugh."

He barely remembered the one about the weaver, the skein, and the near-sighted rat. Fortunately, those with Lord Locke had not heard it. He was relieved when they laughed and he could move along.

On the wall above the fireplace, and on the other walls, hung specimens from the Duke's famed mirror collection. All increased the light from fire and candle until the whole room glowed. The effect was one of great beauty. Pate stepped close to one wall to admire a particular mirror.

A poem from long ago came to mind.

> *We are drawn to windows*
> *To look at the light.*
> *In the night our eyes*
> *Seek out planets,*
> *Moon and stars.*

> *We gaze into firelight,*
> *Candlelight,*
> *Into the faces of others,*
> *Hungry for the light.*

> *A mirror's glass*

We search again
For all the light
We'd see within—

Pate gazed at the mirror, and his mouth dropped open. He blinked and looked closely at it again. *And what of a mirror with light, but no reflection? In which you see no faces?*

Something disturbed him, and he felt the need to see—absurdly enough—faces. He stepped back, and with a chill, he realized that the Duke was standing nearby, watching him.

"You don't think much of my collection, Pate?" he said.

"I think it magnificent, sir."

"Then why the frown?"

"The craftsmen have made this one undeniably beautiful, but—"

"But, what?" A hint of tightness appeared on the Duke's face.

"But, they haven't made it do what mirrors do. Reflect. As long as you look, you will surely never see yourself."

Surprisingly, the Duke raised his chin and laughed out loud. The gentlemen at his side laughed as well.

"Just wait, young Pate," said the Duke. "In a little while you will see something beyond magnificent."

"I am very gratified, sir." He bowed low, and the Duke moved away.

Farnworth, the Lord Chamberlain, roamed the room as he had before, hands clasped under his chin, head slightly bent, with that determined gait of his. Pate clasped his hands under his chin and followed him, imitating the chamberlain's walk. Scattered chuckles followed his progress through the room. Those deep in talk didn't notice. Neither did the chamberlain.

Lord Gretnow was speaking to Duchess Olivia.

"Yes, we have seen the bears, your highness. Impressive creatures! But I swear to you, they have not harmed anything in East Rilken. Lately we have been troubled with packs of wolves coming over our northeast border. Three of my squires have seen a bear frightening the wolves away. The people cheer for the bears."

Pate circled the group again, at a normal walk this time, so he could listen.

A man asked, "How many bears are there?"

Gretnow looked apologetic. "I have been talking of bears, haven't I? In truth, in all the reports, no one has seen more than one at each incident."

The Duchess had a look of disbelief on her face. "And you are sure this bear has not been violent? Not destructive in any way?"

Gretnow shook his head. "Not at all, ma'am. The presence of the bear actually reassures the farmers. Some even say that the Guardians of Rilken have returned."

Duchess Olivia's eyes showed confusion. Her brow puckered. And Pate knew why. The Duke claimed the bears he encountered in the forest were maliciously evil, nothing at all like those Gretnow was telling of now. But the duchess excelled at diplomacy. When she spoke, she simply said, "My husband will be glad to hear it."

Pate took a tour of the room again, helping himself to a fig cake as he went. Kendall was expounding on the appropriate time one should wake up in the morning, making emphasis by waving his handcloth. In all his conversations there was room for only one. Politeness froze on his listeners' faces.

"Seven o'clock is a civilized hour for arising," said Kendall in a lecturing tone. "Six is industriousness, to be sure. Five o'clock, however, is only for the anxious—"

"Or the bakers," put in a listener.

Pate inserted himself. "Why, five o'clock is the exact time our good Duke awakes!"

Kendall startled at this. "What? Are you sure? I—I didn't know. Our Duke is not an *anxious* man. Certainly not..."

While the listeners laughed at this discomfiture, Pate wiped his sticky fingers on Kendall's handcloth and darted away.

"Pate!" Lady Farnworth laid her cittern on her lap and beckoned to him. "Why don't you dance a little for us, Pate? We can play a light air."

If the musicians were already bored with the evening, what hope was there for anyone else? And his own heart was so heavy.

"Come, Pate," she begged. "Dance."

Pate shook his head to decline when the Duke turned toward them.

"You may entertain us with a dance, Pate. I give you leave." This drew the attention of more nearby.

Pate bowed low. "I thank you for your leave, good sir,

but I cannot dance while my heart still weeps for your brother, my king."

When Pate lifted his head, he saw a cold look in the Duke's eyes. Silence fell on the room.

"For the month of mourning, sir," Pate added quickly.

The Duke's eyes studied the cord that hung from Pate's neck. They did not approve of what they saw. But when the Duke spoke, it was not about the cord.

"We are all mourning, Pate, and you refuse to dance to ease the heaviness of our grief. What kind of a jester are you?"

"It seems a very poor one, sir," Pate replied.

He bowed again to avoid those penetrating eyes. Mercifully, the cittern players chose that moment to begin their light air without him.

43

The Duke's Purpose

After this, Pate found the night intolerable. Not even almond cake and wine could cheer him. But he had promised that he would be eyes and ears for Ravelin, so he continued on—spouting doggerel, inserting quips, flattering here and there, and as he went, he watched.

The Earl of Sormin's son cast mole-like looks of appreciation at Petronia.

Petronia, with a fierce glance at her father, accepted them.

Vallenro apologized to Sormin for the death of the king.

Captain Mago did not blink once.

Heves and Gretnow spoke together, each with caution in their eyes.

The musicians looked tired.

Tibbett was almost asleep on his feet.

Kendall and Harmon expounded on the beauty of the Duke's new walls, talking at exactly the same time. Each as proud of it as if they had invented the color of ivory themselves.

Vallenro apologized to Lady Heves for the death of the king.

The reception seemed interminable.

At last, the Duke stepped in front of the green drape and raised his hand. The musicians stopped their playing. Harmon and Tibbett ushered people to the Duke's side of the room, gently and expertly rearranging the guests until all could clearly see the Duke standing in front of the tremendous curtain.

Pate, being shorter than most, his height a gift from his mother, had been placed in the front row at the edge of the semicircle. Lady Locke leaned over and whispered to him.

"So, we finally come to what the evening is all about."

Pate gave her a knowing wink in reply. She stifled a laugh, because the room had fallen silent and the Duke was beginning to speak.

"My good people," he began, using his brother's style of addressing the court. "Thank you for your indulgence in coming to my little reception tonight.

"In gratitude, I will show you something that most of you have never seen before and the like of which you will never see again. This great mirror, covered behind me, is one of only three of its kind ever made in Galerine. This is the largest of the three. In its depths hides the most beautiful luminescence, the rare pearl fire. The longer you look, the brighter it glows. I will not keep this treat from you any longer." He nodded at Mago.

Pate was beyond curious. Mago pulled on a thick rope and the drape began to slide away. As it did so, Pate heard his father's words in his head. *Never look where the enemy wants you to look.*

Pate dropped his gaze to think. He had long felt the Duke was his enemy. There was no safety in avoiding that unpleasant thought. Therefore, he dared not look at what lay behind the curtain.

Pate unobtrusively shifted his stance. He held the position of one who was looking, but his eyes were on the watchers.

A gasp went up from the group.

Eyes widened, even those of the Sormin mole.

Faces showed astonishment. Awe.

Lady Locke's mouth dropped open—something a well-bred mouth never did in court. Everyone looked captivated, as completely entranced as if they had been allowed a window into the Sender's Hall.

The Duke seemed pleased by this response. After a few moments, he spoke again.

"Please, continue looking while I talk, dear friends. I have only a few more things to say, and I want each of you to see the elusive pearl fire. Who will be the first?

"As young Pate pointed out, this *is* a sad time for our country. We *are* still in mourning. Yet our country, our lands, our people, our resources, all need us to be faithful.

"I know that *you* will faithfully do what I will have you do. You *know* what I desire, and I trust each of you will act accordingly."

The faces became more sober as they listened. But no one broke their gaze. The Duke's voice went quietly on.

"I know, my good people, that I will receive your utmost allegiance and loyalty in everything I ask or will."

There was no mention of Dallen or Ravelin. This was strictly the Duke's show. The Duke's hour.

A shift of some kind had taken place in the watching guests. Even in Lady Locke, by his side. Pate struggled to determine exactly what it was that had changed.

"Pate."

The voice startled him. He had drawn the Duke's attention to himself. He quickly lifted a hand and rubbed his eyes hard.

"Don't you like my mirror, Pate?" The Duke spoke calmly, with the ease of one who has complete control.

Pate responded eagerly. "Of course, sir! Very much, sir! Only a fool would not. Forgive me, sir. My eyes are burning. Lady Locke wears much perfume."

Before the Duke could reply, a shout rang out. "There it is! *I see it!*" The Earl of Sormin, more animated than he had been all evening, cried out, "I see the pearl fire!"

The group pressed forward anxiously, crowding each other.

"I see it too," cried a lady.

More voices repeated the phrase, and Pate felt unease deep in his soul. Words played in his mind. *Sight. Un-sight.*

He didn't understand what was happening, but he knew that the Duke's whole reception had been planned for this moment.

This one moment.

Even now the great man was looking closely, hawk-like, at each of the watching faces, an odd smile on his own.

Before the Duke could notice him again, Pate began to clap. Enthusiastically. The watchers eagerly applauded with him. Pate hoped that the show would be over and Mago would cover the mirror.

But it was not to be.

The Duke waved his arm. "Let's have cake and wine and music. Go enjoy yourselves!"

The guests immediately did as he wished, with an exuberance that surprised Pate. Harmon passed out cakes while Tibbett filled goblets and thrust them into empty hands. Lady Farnworth and her musicians struck up a livelier tune, and some on the far end of the group began to dance of their own accord.

Lady Locke walked over to join them. As she passed by Pate, her face turned toward him for just a moment. Her icy glance startled him like a slap. A hostile stranger looked out through her eyes. All friendship, all goodwill entirely gone. He stared at the back of her head as she went on.

A chill shook him. With determination, he moved

through the throng, intent on avoiding the Duke, and yet needing to discover exactly what it was that had changed.

The Mayor of Elva took a bite of peppercake and lifted his eyes to heaven in delight. Pate blinked and looked twice. The mayor's eyes were still brown, still topped with thick black eyebrows, but in the brown and the white of the eyeball, there lingered a strange pearlescence, as if the pearl fire had left an imprint.

The same pearly glow came from Lord Heves' eyes. There it was in Lord Gretnow. And on Lord and, yes, also Lady Locke.

Kendall's eyes looked the same. Pate came closer. Kendall's eyes looked the same because they had been pearl already. They must have been pearl for some time.

Pate's heart sank.

Windows of the soul. According to his mother, that's what eyes were. What she saw in his father's eyes had made her want to marry him. *What had just happened to the souls of these people?*

Pate glanced around the room. Petronia was holding onto her father's arm and laughing with him. Vallenro stood by himself, staring off into the unknown, his face as pale as death.

All of a sudden, Pate felt the need for flight. He had to think. And, he had to get out of there so the Duke would not see his eyes. He couldn't use Lady Locke's perfume as an excuse for long.

He went to Duchess Olivia and bowed. "I must take my leave, dear lady, and beg your pardon. The almond cake does not sit well with me, no matter how much I love it."

"Why, of course, Pate." The calm voice was hers, but her eyes were pearly, and the gentle, friendly manner she had always shown him was absent. "May you be well by morning," she added civilly, then turned away.

Pate slipped past the musicians. A footman opened the outer door to him. Pate stepped through gratefully, then paused.

"Excuse me, my good man, but can you see the time on the corridor clock from here?"

The man stepped closer to the candlelight in order to be at the right angle to see the clock. "Half-past midnight." Candles caught the glow of pearl in his eyes.

"Thank you."

Pate walked down the corridor as sedate as a gentleman, his mind swimming with fearsome possibilities. After the unveiling of the pearl fire, the Duke had told everyone to eat and drink and dance. And no one had hesitated for a moment. The Earl of Sormin had been the first to move his feet to the music. Something he would surely never have done before the pearl fire.

What had the Duke been saying while the people gazed into the mirror? It had struck Pate as insincere regal babble, and less well put than Ravelin's speech had been.

He thought hard as he ascended the first staircase. A phrase came to mind and Pate almost tripped.

You will faithfully do what I will have you do.

Those were the words, surely. And the people had done the Duke's very next innocuous command without hesitation. Even Duchess Olivia's attitude at his departure had been more like the Duke's than her own sweet kindness. Pate shuddered and gripped the stair rail to steady himself and his thoughts.

If the Duke had been using this horrific Galerine tool to gain power, then tonight marked one of his greatest victories. Which meant, he would feel no need to delay in exerting his control over the rest of the kingdom, any way he wished.

He had gathered the strength of the four winds to himself tonight—Sormin, Gretnow, Heves, and Vallenro—and made them bend to his will. The most powerful in the land would agree with everything he did now. Would obey his every wish.

If what Pate had seen was true, the Duke had gone beyond demanding the allegiance that might be his due. He had reached out to grasp the very souls of the people. Had taken without their realizing, what could ever and only belong to the Sender.

Nothing could hinder the Duke now. What would he care about the rumors of bears? About a missing prince? The life of an ill nephew would mean nothing to him.

Pate leapt up the remaining stairs, ducked into a connecting hallway, and ran like a hare chased by the hounds all the way to Ravelin's room.

44

At the Doorstep

I must have been dreaming about my father, because when I awoke, he was already in my mind. Not as I had seen him so often—heroic in his flashing armor, riding at King Adare's side while my heart burst with pride—but when he would hold his hand out to ten-year-old me and say, "Come, Silvie, let's walk into the city."

It only took a quarter hour's walk to get from Guardstown to the heart of the city. Papa held my hand all the way. I used to be surprised to see how many people knew my father. How many waved. How many cried, "Hallo!" But I was not surprised at the respect and high regard people had for him.

I learned young that the people of Elva loved and trusted the Guardsmen, that their presence gave everyone a sense of security. And, as Papa said, when people feel secure, they prosper.

Women on the cobblewalk would often stop to smile, pluck at my chin with their rough fingers, and say, "I can tell she is your daughter. Look at that hair! Look at her eyes! She looks just like you!" Papa smiled and thanked them, and squeezed my hand, while I grew two inches in that moment.

Before we visited the shops and market stalls for Mama, we rested on a bench together. Not that Papa needed rest, but he thought I might need it. I eagerly took a seat because it meant we were going to play what we called The Guardsman Game.

Rosie always wanted to do what Papa did. Throw things with great accuracy. Climb high. Run fast.

I wanted to see what Papa saw. Think what he was thinking. So, he invented this game for me. I would sit up tall and study the market square or street length where we were, and he would say, "Ready, my Rose White? Tell me what you see."

"Window. Door. Potted flowers. Tile roof. Horse. Man. Boy."

But Papa would see the crack in the window. The boot mark where a toe had kicked at a stubborn door. Flowers that needed water. A bird nest on the roof ridge. A nervous chestnut. A retired soldier. A lost boy.

"How did you know he was lost, Papa?" I asked after we had found his home for him.

"His eyes told me."

I practiced our game every trip we took into the city. Once I imagined all sorts of stories for the things I saw. Papa laughed and loved the stories. But they couldn't really stay in our Guardsman Game. Pretending is very important work. But it is not Guardsman's work. A Guardsman can't see what he wants to see. He has to see what's really there.

So I kept practicing. And I got better at it. Soon, he told me that I was able to see most of what he saw. But I knew I could never see it as quickly.

One particular day we were playing the game on a bench at the northwest corner of the flower market. I had already identified a white cat with one green eye, a carpenter, a broken-down nag, and the stall with the freshest flowers, when a line of mounted men entered the square and rode past us down its north side.

I whispered what I saw tied to their saddles or slung on their backs. A two-handed sword. The hilt of a rapier. A longbow. A war hammer. The telling point of a halberd.

A true Guardsman's daughter.

"All correct, Silvie," my father answered quietly. "There are not many in Guardstown as quick-eyed as you."

"But there's something else you want to tell me, Papa, isn't there?"

He nodded, glanced in the direction the men had gone, then turned his cool blue eyes to me. "When you meet an enemy, Silvie, don't look at their weapons.

Watch their eyes. The sword will tell you nothing. The eyes will tell you everything."

"Yes, Papa."

I wondered what he had seen in the eyes of those men, because we did not go to the shops that day. We went right home, and after a few words with Mama, Papa left for the castle.

I THOUGHT about this as I stirred the fire and set out things for our breakfast that morning in the hunting station. Lovely rolls and cheese from Ettie graced the table. I moved quietly, so as not to wake Mama and Rosie.

It had been a number of days since Crow had led Rosie and I to that dreadful place on the northwest road. Days we spent close to the hunting station while Mama embroidered at the inn. We had vowed never to leave, never to worry her again.

This morning, all my dreams and thoughts about my father surrounded me. I stepped outside in the chill damp of sunrise and stood alone in the clearing. As the birds sang and the world stirred to life, I took a deep breath, covered my face with my hands, and cried.

Crow had said no bodies had been left in the woods, but Mago could have done something else with my father that I could not bear to think or imagine. If only Papa could have seen something that had saved him!

I had seen Mago's eyes when he struck my mother down. The anger in them. He would not have let my father live. He had been glad to accuse Papa and proclaim his death. Too glad.

I wiped my face with my hands. Mago *had* been too glad, and what if there was something behind that? Violent emotion is a force of its own. But it can also be used to cover something else.

My father had explained it like this. One person's anger forces an emotional defense of some sort in others. If the others are busy getting angry in turn, the opportunity to see what lies behind the original anger is lost. That's why a Guardsman always stays calm in the presence of an enemy.

Redbird flitted busily from tree to tree. I asked her if Bear was nearby, wishing I could talk about this with him. Redbird hadn't seen him in a while. Neither had any of her relatives.

I went back inside to set out buckets and soap and the clothes that needed washing. This would be the morning task for Rosie and me. Jarlath told Mama yesterday that the weather would be changing soon. The birds in the trees were saying the same thing. If we could at least get the clothes washed in the stream, we could hang them inside to dry.

It was a quiet morning for all of us. We ate our rolls and cheese without speaking. I wondered what Mama and Rosie were thinking about, and if their thoughts were as heavy as mine.

As Mama gathered her things and put on her cloak, ready to go to the inn, Rosie let out a deep sigh. "*When* can we come with you, Mama? I miss seeing people *so* much!"

"Soon, Rosie. Let me think how that visit would best be handled."

We accepted this and Mama went towards the hill path, stopping to wave once before the path took her out of sight.

THE LITTLE RIVER, flowing from the western hills, chilled us as we prepared to do the washing. In Guardstown, we took our laundry to a laundress. When we were younger, Rosie and I had stayed to watch her paddle swirl the clothes in big tubs, amazed at her skill. We were not as adept in a rocky stream with water that made our toes numb.

I soaped each piece vigorously in the bucket, then handed it to Rosie to rinse in the stream. Afterwards, we carried the damp clothes back to the station and spread them across benches outside to dry. Today, judging from the way gray clouds were filling the sky, we would hang our clothes indoors.

Rosie was not in a talkative mood. She crouched on low rocks, letting a stream of water flow through one of Mama's skirts. Often Rosie sang. Not today. We both worked quickly, and as the wind began to blow, we hurried to put on our shoes so we could get back to the station.

Suddenly, White Squirrel was in the middle of our laundry, trying to make herself heard in a fury of squeaks and chatters.

"Men on horseback," I told Rosie. "Half a dozen.

Coming up the hill. We'd better get inside before they come."

Rosie grabbed the bucket and soap and clambered up the bank. "Do you think they've come to turn us out?"

"I wonder if they've tracked us. Mama said that Nally could track anything. They must know we're here."

"But Bear didn't bring us up the hill," she protested as we plunged through the trees. "They can't be tracking us."

The clearing was empty when we started across it, but before we gained the door, men on horseback emerged from the inn path. The first called out to us in a voice of sharp command.

I ignored him. "Here, Rosie, take the laundry inside." She took the rolled up clothes from my arms and darted through the station doorway while I turned to face the men.

There were six of them. All men-at-arms, and heavily armed at that. They did not have the disciplined movements of the Guardsmen, or the colors of the palace guard, but their shirts and vests had the blue and green of the castle. Rosie reappeared at my side, the squirrel riding on her shoulder.

The men did not stop until the heads of their horses were barely six feet away from us. I did not fear the horses. But their riders looked down at us intimidatingly, as we stood on the doorstep, our backs to the door.

I couldn't breathe. Rosie's vibrant beauty had drawn their attention. Papa would unsheathe his sword at the sight of those men's eyes.

"Who are you and what are you doing here?" one of them demanded.

I steadied myself and answered firmly. "We are all caretakers of this corner of the king's domain." I wanted him to think there were more of us. Which, if you counted Mama and the animals, there were.

The man frowned. "Caretakers? Of a hunting station? I don't know anything about this."

"We are servants of the king," I cried out boldly.

He didn't believe me.

Just then the rain started. Not lightly. Not a gentle sprinkle. A torrent. Straight down.

Several of the men swore.

"Let's get in there," one called out. "We'll be dry at least."

Rosie's grip tightened on my arm. White Squirrel shrieked.

"No!" I yelled over the roar of the rain. "We are servants of the king under his protection!"

The leader did not answer, but narrowed his eyes.

"Good horses—" I began.

The men snorted, but the horses watched me closely. Several of them licked their lips and shifted their feet. Directly in front of me, dark, serious eyes gazed out from under a brown forelock.

"Enough of this," a rider said, beginning to dismount. "We'll drown out here."

"Keep him on!" I shouted. His horse moved unexpectedly and the man scrambled to cling to its back.

I spoke to the horses without looking at the men.

"Return to Elva at once and *never* bring anyone here again. Go now!"

The horses turned as one toward the inn path.

The men exploded in curses, jerking on the reins and kicking at flanks. But the horses were in control of their own bits. They were intent on returning to Elva, with the Sender's fire in their bellies. Nothing could stop them. They galloped toward the head of the inn path and only slowed their speed to navigate the downward turn.

I watched them go, as my father would have watched them. Oblivious to the rain, like a Guardsman. When they disappeared from view, we scurried inside. Rosie immediately stirred the fire. I barred the door and closed the shutters with trembling hands.

We crouched near the fire to warm and dry ourselves. The rain had wet us completely through. I couldn't seem to stop shaking and not just because I was cold and wet.

It was scary enough to meet armed men when we had entered a forbidden place unknowingly. But these men had come to the very door of our refuge. They could quickly find a way to outsmart their horses' obedience to me.

If they came again and left their horses at the foot of the hill, I would have no defense against them but what a lame dog, a fox, and a squirrel would do. Bear was not in the area or he would have been here.

And if these men spoke to Nally the Dwarf at all, they would soon know that Rosie and I were the same ones who had intruded on the forbidden area. The colors of our hair made us unmistakable. I explained all this to Rosie as she stirred the fire for the tenth time.

She sank down on the floor next to me. "Oh, Silvie!" she whispered. "What should we do now?"

"We do what Mama would want us to do if she knew what had just happened. What Papa would make us do."

Rosie jumped to her feet. "I'll start packing."

45

———

The Opinions of Master Redmond

Tara didn't notice when the rain started. She was sitting on the stool in the kitchen, resting her eyes and talking to Ettie, when Jarlath stepped in.

"There's Galerine dwarves in the main room wanting food, Ettie. Gareth wants you to come take a listen."

Ettie laid down the knife she had been using to cut up pieces of hare, and wiped her hands on her apron. She nodded towards Tara.

"Come watch from the hallway and you'll see what I mean, if they are lerin dwarves."

Tara followed Ettie and Jarlath down the passage. Jarlath returned to his work of sealing the cracks around the front window in the main room. Tara lingered at the edge of the hallway, her back to the wall.

Two dwarf men sat at one of the tables in front of the bar. They looked tough and muscular and wore scowls on their faces. These vanished as Ettie strode right up to them. A broad smile crossed her face.

"How now, countrymen? Are you really from old Galerine? I'm from Nardon. What are your birth towns?"

The dwarves spoke in low gravelly voices, and Tara couldn't make out what they were saying. Ettie, however, raised one eyebrow as she listened.

"Well, you've come to the inn with the best food in Rilken. You'll get a bowl of hash, a tumbler of ale, and one of my honey rolls, all for the coin of one ken."

The dwarves fished in their pouches and each handed Ettie a coin. She held them up in front of her, side by side, one in each hand.

"Thank you. Gareth will bring you your ale and I will go get your food."

She laid the coins on the bar as Gareth immediately began to fill tumblers from one of the casks along the wall. He set both tumblers in front of the dwarves at exactly the same time.

Ettie bustled to the kitchen, and Tara followed her.

"Well?" asked Tara.

The cook ladled hash from the kettle into a bowl. "They are definitely lerin dwarves, poor shovels! Did you hear the low buzz in their voices that I was telling you about?"

"I couldn't understand what they were saying."

"That's part of it. The buzz blurs their words. They

also said they were born along our northern river, and yet they spoke with southern accents you couldn't miss if you were a weasel in a room full of eggs."

"Why did you hold the coins up?"

"A precaution. One angry dwarf could tear this place apart. So you never want to get into an argument with them. They'll lie about how much they paid you or what food you promised them, and get upset real fast."

Ettie set the bowls on a tray and examined them. "However, we've noticed that lerin dwarves never lie in the same way. They won't agree in their lies. One will say 'you promised sausage and oats!' The other will say, 'no—eggs and bread.' If we're careful to treat them exactly the same, they'll turn their lying arguments on each other instead of us."

"Do they ever get over it? The effect of working in the lerin mine, I mean?"

The cook shook her head. "I don't know, but I've never known one that did."

Ettie placed the honey rolls at exactly the same place in each bowl, perched on the side of the hash. She tucked in a spoon opposite the roll. As Nissa approached to take the trays, Ettie waved her away.

"I best take these in, girl. You can clean up once they've left."

Tara held the door for her, and Ettie went down the passage toward the main room.

Tara hesitated before following her. Would these dwarves be dangerous? Gareth was in the main room. So was Jarlath. Kipp was nearby too. She heard Redmond's voice coming from the main hall, exclaiming about the rain. She hoped Silvie and Rosie hadn't got caught in the rain with their laundry.

She washed her hands in the kitchen with the basin and soap that Ettie always set aside for her, grabbed her embroidery bag, returned to her usual place, and set to work. Half a dozen tables were occupied in addition to the dwarves' table. Gareth at the bar was doing what he often did, wiping down everything within reach. Several travelers, in cloaks, hats, and boots, stared out at the weather.

"This rain will turn the roads into a sea of mud."

"Ay, it will be tough going until we pass Grinspring."

Redmond settled himself at a table next to hers. One ink-stained hand gripped a tumbler, but his eyes gazed thoughtfully at the dwarves.

"How is your writing going this morning, Master Redmond?" she asked.

He pulled his attention from the dwarves and turned to her. "I am steadily filling pages with ink. However, I'm an expert at arguing with myself, so I may finish a hundred pages only to find I've written nothing of value to anyone."

He waved his tumbler toward her. "The work that you do creates beauty instantly. It calms a mind. Eases a heart. I could sit here for hours just watching the pictures grow on your linen, stitch by stitch."

Tara smiled at the compliment. Many of the projects in the first guest room had been completed, and Alta already charged more for it. Tara was working on a canopy piece for the second room. At the moment, she was stitching a dark brown bear to look up at the moon she had already made.

"What do you think of when you sew?" Redmond asked. "That is, when wandering professors aren't interrupting you?"

Silvie had asked her the same question when they were trying to connect her thoughts with the embroidery's unusual qualities. How funny that Redmond would ask too. Tara glanced up at the professor. There was something very trustworthy about him.

"In truth, when I began this piece," she said, "I was concerned for our younger prince, for Ravelin. I've been thinking how alone he must feel without his father and brother. I wished for something to guide him in his grief. Some light, somehow."

Redmond gazed at her quietly for a few moments after she finished speaking.

"It's just a hope. A hope and a prayer," she added.

"You could be stitching good into his life right now."

"If I knew that, I would never stop stitching," Tara answered lightly. "And you? The words you wrote on those pages upstairs could be whispering good in someone's ear right now."

Redmond chuckled. "Then I would never stop writing, I suppose." He ran his fingers through his hair roughly, leaving some of it sticking up in odd places.

"The work of a philosophy professor, one that concentrates on ideas and beliefs behind governing, is very similar to that of a court jester. You tell the truth as well as you know it, but at any moment a king could take offense. Some days I would rather be a court fool." He gave her a surprised look. "Maybe I already am."

Tara smiled at this, and her response seemed to please him. Nissa came to their corner and set a bowl down in front of Redmond. He began to eat.

The rain fell heavily, pummeling the roof of the inn and all the outbuildings. The thread moon on the dark linen began to glow of its own accord. The head of the bear already gazed at it. Its eye seemed to blink. Tara glanced at Redmond. Had he seen? But the professor's eyes were on his meal. She poked the needle into the fabric and began to outline the rest of the bear's body.

Travelers consulted Jarlath on what tomorrow's weather might bring. Gareth refilled tumblers and kept an eye on the dwarves. Footsteps sounded overhead.

A spoon scraped a bowl nearby. Master Redmond leaned back in his chair again and sighed. He seemed in no hurry to return to his desk upstairs.

"I think I best stay awhile and air my mind. I drove it too hard on the ethical boundaries of governance this morning and it has not forgiven me yet. And—" This with a glance out the window. "My limbs resent the loss of their midday walk."

He sighed. "But my real frustration is that I must write carefully, concealing what I would rather write openly."

Tara changed the color of thread in her needle, from the bear's dark brown to a forest green. She would outline the trees before filling in the rest of the bear. "What do you wish to say openly?"

"I would tell the people of the continent what their

rulers are truly like. It might not help them to know, but it would get a weight off my chest."

"If it would help you to speak of it," she said sincerely, "I would be glad to hear your thoughts."

"And thus with a listening ear save this professor from death by exasperation?" He was grinning at her.

She gave him a serious look in return. "I *am* very interested. Our work at the hunting station will not last forever. I often wonder what other lands are like. Where there are good places to live."

"You have given me reason enough," he replied, his eyes lively. "In the interest of helping a fellow human being, I begin. At your request, a tour of the continent, with recommendations by one S. Redmond." He dropped his voice. "All the things I dare not say in print."

"The lovely duchy of Ardemount to our southwest," he began, speaking in a lower, but light-hearted voice, "is ruled by a man who is a fanatic about making cannons. He stores them by the hundreds in his artillery warehouses, where the weight of them sinks the foundations of the buildings deep into the earth."

"Really?" Tara couldn't imagine.

"Yes," he replied solemnly. "South of Ardemount is the small country of Prellum. Its ruler, in my opinion, is a complete fool. A man who glories in his incompetence. His family has ruled Prellum for a hundred years and will continue on for many more, because his subjects are as foolish as he."

Tara must have shown her disbelief at this, for Redmond paused and shook his head.

"Make no mistake. Only the wise look for wisdom in

a ruler. Everyone else is happy with—" Redmond made a flourish in the air with his hand. "—just a certain *panache.*

"Next to that small country is a tinier one—Crenel. Tucked into the underside of Ardemount like a pebble in a shoe. Crenel is a complete mystery."

"A mystery?" Tara asked. "Is it a dark, secret place?"

"Oh, no," he replied. "Their geography is open, sunlit, and welcoming. I was referring to the Crenelian mind." He tapped his forehead.

"One night in an alehouse in Plume—that's their capital—I had a discussion with three Crenelians about a tax on eggs. And do you know that among the three of them they had *four* differing opinions. It's true! I swear it," he said, in answer to her look. "The Crenelian mind is indefinable, even to those who have them. Lucky for Crenel that they have Ardemount's sturdy cannons to defend them."

His flow of words stopped for a moment, and the sound of other voices broke in. Gareth was at the dwarves' table. She listened a few moments. Was the talk friendly? It was hard to tell. Jarlath had found something else to fix in the main hall. A weak chair leg. Was he purposely staying nearby until the dwarves had finished?

Tara turned back to the professor. "Please continue, Master Redmond. What other rulers stand out among the countries of AllHallen?"

"I warn you, I could answer for days. But—because you ask—a few more. Are you familiar with Meratame, far to the west, along the coast?"

Tara nodded. Bevan had traveled there with King Adare.

"Their king boasts: *My people can say whatever they like, and I will do whatever I like.* And what he likes to do most is hate Falland, which lies across his northern border. Hate coming from jealousy, of course. How Meratame holds together, I do not know. At least their king is not arrogant enough to try to control the minds of his people."

"Are there any good countries that you would recommend, if—if someone would wish to start anew?" Tara kept her voice steady and her eyes on her stitching.

"My own Tellhaven and Ardemount are stable. But if you are looking for the best, the countries I admire beyond my own beloved Tellhaven? I would say Falland in the northwest and your own Rilken."

She looked up at him. "But those countries are so large and Rilken is so small. What do you admire here?"

He took a swallow from his tumbler. "Many things. Do you know what people across the continent called your king? Adare the Good. Because of his character, your court in Elva had very little chance to work up the layers of intrigue that exist, for example, in Prellum, for the simple reason that Adare listened to everyone.

"Court intrigue is a great manipulator of kings, but Adare could not be manipulated. He honored his family and his country and loved them both. He might not have been a superb administrator, but he was good enough, and for the rest he had Lord Locke. I'm sure his brother the Duke was of value. Although they did have philosophical differences on the nature and use of power."

"Did you know the king?" Tara asked.

"Only through correspondence."

Tears wet Tara's eyes. "Adare *was* a good king," she said quietly. "I believe his sons are just like him." She stared at the moon and the bear in her hands and sent up a prayer for Ravelin.

Raised voices drew their attention again. Gareth still stood at the Galerine dwarves' table. His face wore a strained look. "This is The Grumpy Rabbit," he said. "Not the West Road Inn or the Grinspring Trotter. You're in *The Grumpy Rabbit*. I'm the rabbit." This last bit of levity sounded desperate.

Tara could not make out what the dwarves were saying. But she heard Gareth clearly.

"Of course I'm not lying. You're both intelligent dwarves. Go outside and look at the sign."

Chairs scraped the hard floor. The two Galerine men shoved hats on their heads and walked straight out into the pouring rain. Gareth shut the door behind them and watched from the window.

"They don't feel the rain," said Redmond, almost to himself. He glanced at her. "Rather, they feel it, but they don't mind it. Rain, sun, mud, rock, tree, night, day—it's all the same to them. Dwarves are amazing people."

Gareth turned from the window and let out a heavy sigh. "They've gone," he said, directing his words towards Jarlath.

Tara shook her head slowly and began to move her needle again. "It must be horrible to have your mind lie to you all the time," she said to Redmond. "From the lerin, I mean. Not to be able to distinguish what is true from what is false."

"My dear madam, you have stated the predicament of all mankind."

She stared at him for a moment.

He shrugged. "The lerin makes it obvious, that's all."

46

What the Rain Brought

There was one thing Tara didn't dare ask Ettie about Galerine for fear of offending her, but she could ask Redmond. The professor clearly delighted in conversation and seemed disinclined to move from his chair.

"I grew up in East Rilken, Master Redmond," she began, "in rolling meadows filled with farms. We could see the huge rounded hills of Galerine in the distance, standing out starkly in the sky. Everyone spoke of the mines hidden deep in those hills."

She poked her needle into the linen and pulled it through. "Some people envied the riches underneath Galerine. Other people warned of the poison in those same riches, a poison left over from the Great Horror that took place there thousands of years ago." She looked up at him. "Do those warnings tell the truth?"

He nodded gravely. "I would have to say yes. Galerine has a hard time restraining the picks and shovels of its desire. I believe they have forgotten the injunction against delving anywhere near the Horror. A people could forget anything important after several thousand years. But where else would they have uncovered something as strange as Ierin? Pray they haven't uncovered something worse."

A gust of wind threw the rain hard against the window and made her jump. She peered out. The stables could barely be seen through the downpour, even though they were just across the yard. But she saw several figures running and wagons behind them. Someone must have just arrived.

The main door of the inn opened and shut quickly, and Crim stood there dripping. Gareth ran to help him off with his cloak.

"Grab a seat by the fire, old friend! I'll have Ettie bring you something warm."

Gareth's arm indicated the front fireplace, but after a quick look around the hall, Crim came over to where Tara was sitting. She was glad to see him. He had come to the inn several times since the day of her testing and was always friendly. Always concerned with how she was getting on.

"Have you just come from Elva?" she asked. "You've had a wet ride."

Crim eyed Redmond before he answered. Redmond took a long drink from his tumbler.

"I have," Crim said, sitting down at last, and giving her a smile. "And a miserable road it was too. My wagons were almost run into the ditch by a group of crazed horsemen galloping hellbent for the city. Then we ran into a wall of rain. Stopped for a beggar lad on the road. Hate to see anyone out in this mess. Leastways someone the age of our Kipp."

Tara thought of the figures in the rain. "Poor thing. Where is he now?"

"I sent him round to the kitchen. Alta prefers it that way. Ettie will feed him well."

Nissa ran into the main hall and looked around. "Jarlath? Ettie needs you!" The urgency in her voice stirred Tara. She glanced out the window at the relentless rain. Her daughters would be by the fire in the hunting station, safe and warm.

Crim leaned over her work with open admiration on his face. "She could be the richest woman in Rilken if she'd let me sell things like this for her." This he said to Redmond.

"Maybe someday I'll hold you to that," she said with a smile. "Once you've had a chance to rest, Crim, maybe you could tell us the latest news from Elva."

Tara had sat in her corner, patiently stitching and listening, day after day. Very few days had brought information of substance, and she found it harder to wait and listen patiently.

Redmond had just given her an understanding of Rilken's place among the other countries of AllHallen. Crim usually brought news of court and business in Elva. News of Prince Ravelin's prolonged illness. Of the fears and distrust in the city. But no word had come of the missing Guardsman. Or the missing prince.

Gareth brought Crim a tumbler, a bowl of hash, and one of Ettie's small loaves. Redmond asked for his tumbler to be refilled and appeared ready to stay for any forthcoming conversation.

Another gust of rain blew hard against the window panes. Loud. Insistent. Again she thought of the girls. They would stay safe in the station. Surely. They had promised and promised never to leave the station again without her knowledge.

Crim took several spoonfuls, swallowed, drank from his tumbler, and sighed. "Always good. Ettie is the queen of cooks." He shifted in his chair to see Tara better. Redmond waited, keen-eyed, looking for something of interest.

"There's a host of unusual things happening in Elva," Crim began. "The city feels different. Nervous. Afraid. Regarding the news, it seems an accepted belief now that Prince Dallen died in the woods with his father. There will be a memorial gathering for him soon."

Tara's heart sank. Another death. Another hope shattered.

She slid her needle into the side of her linen piece and rolled up the moon and the bear. "Do they have proof of his death?"

Crim looked awkward, as if he would prefer to avoid saying what he knew. "The hunters found a glove that belongs to Dallen. It was—not in good shape."

She could not help looking at Redmond. "Do you think that is proof enough?"

Before he could answer, the main door to the inn flew open. Two sodden travelers entered, weighed down with bags. And Tara forgot about Crim, Redmond, embroidery, and Elva.

Gareth stepped out behind the bar with a friendly welcome. But Tara got there first. She knew her daughters at once, before they pushed the hoods back from their wet faces and plastered hair.

Silvie spoke into her ear. "Mama, we all need to stay here tonight. The hunters found the station. But we're fine. Not harmed."

"Silvie sent their horses away," Rosie whispered. "Then we packed everything." White Squirrel poked its head out of her hood.

Tara nodded. For a moment she couldn't think. Questions flooded her mind. But first, they needed a room, a place to stay.

She turned to the innkeeper. "Is there a room available, Gareth? One the three of us can share tonight? These are my daughters."

"We're pretty full," he replied. "Most of the travelers are staying over because of the storm. I gave the last good rooms to Crim and his company. There's one simple room available, and its window is blocked by the quince tree. It's the one on the end upstairs. You deserve better." He looked apologetic.

"The simple room will be just fine," she assured him.

Gareth seemed to glance around for Jarlath, but Jarlath wasn't there, so he reached for the girls' bags himself. "Kipp, come help me with these," he called. "We'll need to get the fire started."

"Thank you, Gareth. I'll get the girls warm in the kitchen, then we'll go upstairs."

But the kitchen was in commotion when they entered. Ettie wasn't at her usual worktable. She and Jarlath were kneeling on the floor by a thoroughly drenched boy. The lad must have collapsed. Ettie was mopping the water off his face with rags, and Jarlath was at his side, rubbing his arms. The lad wore only shirt sleeves and breeches. His stockings were torn and a pair of mud-covered shoes sat by the kitchen door.

Tara motioned a dripping Silvie and Rosie over to the wide hearth and the broad, ever-burning kitchen fire. But they were distracted by the boy's more urgent need, and Rosie, never one to hide her curiosity, edged closer to the group on the floor.

"There, son. There, son. You'll be all right now." Jarlath spoke gently over the boy like a concerned father.

"A hot drink!" cried Ettie.

Nissa, who had been watching with wide eyes, ran to get one.

"Jarlath, can we help him sit up?" said Ettie.

Ettie tossed the wet rags to the side and put a strong arm under the boy's shoulders. With Jarlath on the other side, the two of them lifted the stranger up and half-carried him over to a place in front of the kitchen fire.

"Settle him on the floor again where it's nice and

warm," Jarlath said. "He'll go pitching off a stool. Floor will be safer."

They lowered him gently, leaning him against a side wall near the hearth. The lad appeared to be conscious, just weak and dizzy. Rosie bent down and looked into the boy's face.

"Darrit!" she cried out.

Tara gasped. She stepped forward and peered at the pale, damp face. It was true.

Bevan's armor boy was on the kitchen floor of The Grumpy Rabbit.

A Soldier's Widow

Darrit blinked. "Rosie?" he whispered. He stared up at them. "Tara, ma'am? Silvie?" His face contorted, struggling for composure.

Tara knelt down next to him. "It's all right. We'll talk later. First, drink what Ettie gives you." The cook held a cup to Darrit's lips with a firm hand, and the boy took slow swallows.

Jarlath got to his feet and looked at Tara and the girls with surprise. "You know him?" he asked.

"Yes," said Tara. "He's a friend from Elva. A good lad. One of the best. I can do that for you, Ettie. I know you're busy." Tara took the cup from her hand. "Here, Darrit. Take some more."

Ettie stood up and rubbed her hands on her apron

front. "I heard a loud thump at the back door," said Ettie. "Opened it and he fell in."

Tara felt a flash of anger at Crim for not taking better care of him. But Darrit would have worked hard to keep his need from showing to anyone. And Crim would have been distracted, worried about his wagons in the rain.

Silvie and Rosie took off their dripping cloaks and hung them on pegs at Nissa's direction. The girls joined her on the floor next to Darrit, silently watching until he finished drinking everything in the cup.

"Jarlath, he needs to rest and be comfortable and Gareth just gave us the last room," Tara said. "Can we take him there for now? The room by the quince tree?"

The old soldier nodded. "I'll go see if the fire's ready."

"I'll return to my stew then," Ettie said.

Ettie went back to stirring one of the bubbling big pots. Nissa brought a small blanket she had warmed at the fire and draped it around his shoulders. Tara thanked her with a full heart.

"Tara, ma'am..." Darrit's words came with effort. His eyes stared at her, a hollow grief in them. Then his face crumpled and he looked away.

She exchanged silent glances with her girls. Darrit had gone with Bevan and the king to Tellhaven. What had happened to him? Whatever it was, they could not speak of it in front of the inn people.

Nissa handed her a bowl of warm hash.

"Here, Darrit," Tara said. "Can you manage this? If not, I'll feed you."

Ettie vigorously chopped her vegetables at the long

wooden table. "Get that warm stuff down him as fast as you can. There's no better way to warm up when you're cold through."

After a few mouthfuls, Darrit took the bowl and spoon into his own trembling hands. Tara could not take her eyes off him.

The boy had started with the Guardsmen when he was eleven. His mother and sister lived just outside Guardstown. Bevan and his good friend Lunn had been training Darrit for two years. How often had he been at their house sharing meals when Bevan was not with the king, or when Darrit had not been working with Lunn.

Jarlath returned. "Dona made a bed on the floor in front of the fire," he said. "I can help him get up there."

Darrit had recovered enough to walk slowly up the back stairs, one arm over Jarlath's shoulder, while the old man's arm gripped his waist. Tara followed them. Silvie and Rosie came silently after.

The room was small, but warm and inviting. A plain plank floor. A shuttered window. A bed for two against the wall, a table by its side. And a wood chair by the fire's raised hearth. After the threat of the hunters, the simple room felt like a haven. Gareth had set their bags neatly in a row underneath the window.

"You all wait out here," said Jarlath, "and I'll get him tucked in. He could do with another drink and a plate of Ettie's rolls by his bed."

Tara went downstairs to get them, while the girls waited in the hallway. When she returned, Darrit was tucked in on the floor mattress, head on the pillow, swathed in blankets. His wet clothes spread on the hearth to dry. He looked half asleep.

Tara placed the tumbler and rolls on the hearth near him. Rosie sat on the bed, her white squirrel perched on her shoulder. Silvie took the chair by the fire. Both watched Darrit, their eyes troubled and filled with questions.

Tara followed Jarlath out into the passageway, shutting the door softly behind them. She wanted to thank him again and again, but Jarlath stopped her. He rubbed his forehead with a scarred, rough hand.

"Nissa said you were a soldier's widow. If I were gone and had left my heart behind, I'd like to think that someone would watch out for her too."

Tara's eyes filled and overflowed. She pointed to the closed door.

"He was one of my husband's armor boys. He's like family to us." She tried to say more, but no words would come.

Jarlath's eyes showed he understood all the things she meant to say.

48

The Temptation of Color

Pate heard the news in the great hall and at once took himself to the long connecting corridor where the artists worked on the huge mural. On either side of the broad hallway, painters stood, perched, and knelt in the scaffolding, brushes in their hands, paint pots at their sides, peering closely at each brush stroke. Assistants held lanterns to counteract the inevitable shadows in the hall.

Pate scanned the corridor as he went and found Avelyn at its far end, stirring paint and examining the color on her wooden spoon by the light of an open door. She was alone, and he was grateful.

Her face lit up at his approach, and she waved the

spoon at him. "Look, Pate, a red for the jewels in the king's stirrup."

He barely heard her. "Avelyn, is it true that the Duke is holding a reception for all the artists?"

She looked at him warily, responding to the anxiety he had not attempted to conceal. "Yes. He has offered us a lovely evening as thanks for all the hard work."

"Where?"

She frowned at his abruptness. "In his audience hall where all his receptions are held. He's going to choose one of us to paint Duchess Olivia's portrait. Taynor thinks I may be chosen."

Her eyes glowed and Pate's heart squeezed tight in his chest. Impulsively he reached for her hand and held it tightly.

She wriggled her fingers. "Pate," she protested. "The paint—"

"It doesn't matter. Avelyn, last night the architects were invited. Two nights ago, the librarians and scribes—"

"He's inviting everyone in the castle. Is that what you're trying to tell me?"

"Yes, he's inviting everyone in the castle, but—" He dropped his voice to a whisper. "Everyone who goes to those receptions comes back changed, and the prince is very concerned."

He told her what he had seen at the Duke's first reception as quickly as he could. About the pearl fire. About the strange luster of the eyes afterwards. Lady Locke's changed face. As Pate talked, Avelyn watched him closely.

"From the corner of my eye I saw the glow, Avelyn, even as I saw the watchers' faces. They stared at the mirror wide-eyed, and as they did, something was taken from them without their knowing. Do you remember the night that you and I looked over the railing and saw the palace guard? The Duke brought the guard in one group at a time, and they too were changed."

"But *you* went, Pate, and it didn't affect you."

"I had to use all my wits not to look. To hide that fact from the Duke, I left as soon as I could afterwards. If I had stayed, you wouldn't know me now."

"Then I will make sure I don't look. I will do the same as you."

"And have the Duke suspect you too?" He shook his head. "Oh, Avelyn, don't take the risk. I've seen your face when color calls you. The praise of color lives in your fingertips. You search every sunrise and sunset for new colors. How could you resist when the mirror fires gold across the face of its watchers?"

He pulled her gently closer to him. "Please, Avelyn, I am not the jester now." He put his forehead against hers and looked deeply into her eyes. "Please, don't go tonight. Don't make this the last time I see the true Avelyn."

49

____

What the Duke Wishes

I t felt best for Ravelin to stay in his bed. He didn't
fear his heart spells, or collapsing, as much if he
were already lying down, though it was still
unnerving to hear his heart thump and race.

Some books in his library, including one on his bed,
spoke of people dying of grief. A mother for a child, a
warrior for his lost general, a man for his beloved. Is this
what had happened to them? Did their hearts weaken
from sadness until they no longer supported their
bodies? Did they ache, just as he did, to see the faces of
their family again?

Ravelin gazed up at the canopy above his bed. Dark
green velvet and brocade draped across an oak frame. A
craftsman at the castle had made the bed for him when

he was seven. The man had carved symbols of Rilken on all four bedposts. Oak and acorn. Cone and needle. Wheat and flax. And on every post a bear with a different expression.

When his bed was new, he had been sick with winter fever too. His mother had kept him company during his illness, sitting on a chair by his bed, her embroidery in her lap, talking of the carvings on each post.

"The bears are the strength of Rilken," she said, while she stitched. "The watchers and protectors of our country."

She believed what she said, for she was stitching all the symbols of Rilken into one beautiful picture. In addition to bears, there were going to be forests and wheat fields; the outline of the castle roof; and then the symbols for each person in their family. An oak tree for his father the king. A wren for herself. An acorn, the traditional symbol for the Prince of the Crown, for Dallen. And for Ravelin, a rabbit. *Because you are strong, quick, and inquisitive,* she said.

He watched the picture grow under her needle. When he tired of that, he imagined what the carved bears on his bedposts might be thinking. The one by his head had been carved with its mouth open. What was it saying? Or singing even?

Ravelin had been scared in the night after his mother left him. But Wells sat in a chair nearby, getting up to replace his candle or add more wood to the fire. Wells asked about all the names Ravelin had thought of for the bears, and listened as Ravelin explained each one. In the end Ravelin could decide on none of them.

He put his head back on his feverish pillow and imagined that the bear was saying, "You need fear nothing in the night, young Ravelin. We are the watchers of Rilken. We will watch all night."

It had comforted him. Then.

After his mother's death, he had asked for the large embroidery picture, still unfinished, to be framed and hung in his room. And there it hung still, to his left, on the wall facing the windows that flanked his bed. He could see part of it easily from where he lay.

Wells entered the bedchamber and placed a filled pitcher and goblet on the table by his bed. Ravelin forced a smile.

"What is the news from the world outside, Wells?"

"Dark clouds are slowly approaching from the west. It is too soon to know if they will come to Elva or move north of us. We could have heavy rain in the night. But at this moment, Duchess Olivia and Lady Petronia are in the outer chamber and wish to see you.

This was surprising. "What do they want?"

"They seem ready to settle in for a long visit. The Duchess has her embroidery bag and her ladyship is carrying several books."

They weren't the company Ravelin would choose, but now he could see for himself what Pate had seen at the Duke's reception. The imprint of the pearl fire in the eyes of his aunt and cousin.

Aunt Olivia greeted him and inquired about his health, then withdrew to set out her embroidery on his writing table. Clearly, she saw herself as a mere chaperone. Petronia took the chair that Wells brought to the bedside and patted the books in her lap.

"My father says I should read to you since you are not well. *And* since we're going to be married. You must be bored all day long. Are you bored, Ravelin?"

Her reference to marriage surprised him. It took a few moments to gather his thoughts and reply. "Not much," he said, honestly. "I am grateful to Wells and Pate for that."

She held up one of her books. "I can read to you from a cultural history of Ophria or from a book on Ophrian folklore." She looked at him questioningly.

"Which do you like best?" he asked.

The first book fell back in her lap. "I don't know. I don't read much. I only have these because they were important to the duke's son. So I had to have them. But I've never read them."

"Well," he shifted on his pillow, "pick either and let's hear a few pages and see what they're like." He gazed at the canopy above his head and waited while she turned the pages.

She took a deep breath and began.

"'Ophria, located in the center south of the AllHallen continent, is a fertile land famous for its vineyards, fruits, and greens. The Ophrian people are as vibrant as their land, and their music and song are famous the world over.'"

Her voice sounded flat, each word coming in its turn without the rhythm or pacing of normal speech. It was disconcerting, and he felt relieved when she suddenly closed the book.

"I know I don't read well. Can I tell you what I like about Ophria instead?"

"Certainly," he replied. "We can make it a game. Tell me five things you like about Ophria." As he said those words, memory stabbed him with sorrow.

When they were young, his brother Dallen had made so many things into a game for him. *Five arrows or five stones. How many can we make hit the hollow of that old tree?*

For some reason, Dallen had always chosen the number five. *Five books. Five laps around the courtyard. Five sentences in a different language. Five handsprings, Ravelin. Now five vaults.* And he would leap around after Dallen as Dallen called them out.

As they both got older, Ravelin would suggest his own five, and Dallen, like the excellent brother he was, willingly took part and followed. In his mind he could see Dallen chasing him around the castle's exercise room on his hands, both of them trying to complete five laps, until they collapsed in laughter.

But a voice was speaking. A nervous, high-pitched voice. He took a deep breath and forced himself to listen to what Petronia was saying in the present. He had started the five-things game with her. He needed to attend to it. It would be unkind otherwise.

"The ducal palace. Oh, Ravelin, you have got to see it! It's twice the size of this one and sits on the edge of a vast lake. The city circles the lake and when the sun sets, the buildings across the lake and the lake itself glow like fire! The first time I saw a sunset there I felt that if I could just see that spectacle every day of my life,

I would be happy." She sounded wistful and he felt sorry for her.

"Surely you'll see it again when you marry the duke's son."

"No! I'll see it only if you and I visit there after *we* are married. If my father wishes it, of course," she added hastily.

This was a different Petronia. Cowed. Meek. And with a sadness behind her usual energy. She had never been so amenable to her father's wishes before. How unlike that family dinner when she had demonstrated Ophria's way of eating with the balancing fork despite her father's scowl.

Ravelin never wanted someone to be sad to marry him. He hoped for bold, true, and open love. And someone more like the woman Pate had imagined for him. *Why was Pate taking so long at the library?* Ravelin wished he were here to help him with these guests.

Ravelin tried to listen as Petronia told him about the way Ophrian cooks prepared peacock, using the tail feathers to decorate the roasted bird. Of a court dance that seemed more like a parade. Of the way everyone in the Ophrian court had treated her with such attention and respect.

She spoke rapidly and his weariness made it hard to follow every word. He was afraid he would insult her by falling asleep. A thought struck him. Something that he wanted to find out. Something he had almost forgotten.

"Petronia," he said, when she had drawn breath. "Are your eyes the same color as your father's, or are yours darker?"

She frowned. "Mine are darker."

"Could I see? Do you mind coming closer? Stand near the candle."

She came and held her face over his bedside candle. His heart skipped a beat. The orb of her eye glowed with an unnatural pearl.

"Aunt Olivia, I can't make it out. I think Petronia has the darker eye. Can you come look?"

His aunt obligingly set down her needle and thread and came over to the bedside to gaze into her daughter's eyes. "I always thought Allard's were darker, but things may change as a child grows. Mine are the lightest, to be sure."

"Are your eyes green or blue, would you say?" asked Ravelin.

"Sometimes they change depending on what color I am wearing. You can see the color of this deep blue gown in them."

"Yes, I can. Your eyes look very blue today," said Ravelin. *Blue pearl.*

Olivia politely waited while he examined her eyes. Waited with the air of a civil stranger. Where was the aunt who had rushed to him in his grief? Who had brought him books from her travels? What had he lost when his aunt looked into her husband's mirror?

"Thank you, Aunt Olivia," he managed to say.

"I am sure my eyes are the darkest in the family," said Petronia.

PATE WAS, at this moment, making his way to Ravelin's room with a heavy heart. The disturbing news he had just heard made him run up the stairs to his own room first, in order to retrieve his cat. He scooped her up, tucked her in one arm, and stroked the silky fur on her head and neck with the other hand.

"Ravelin needs me, oh cat-of-mine," he said in a gentle tone. "And I need *you*, so come."

He walked back down the stairs and corridors, deep in thought. Distressed by what Lord Locke had just told him, and by what he had so clearly *not* wanted to tell him.

King Adare's secretary had been sitting at his desk in the library an hour's half ago when Pate had entered to search out a book Ravelin wanted.

"Oh, it's you, young Pate," the secretary said brusquely, as if he did not want to be interrupted.

"Only me, your lordship. The prince requests a book. *Travels Across the Kartan Sea.* Do you know it? He said Lord Vallenro gave it to his father the king last year on Gifting Day."

Locke laid down his quill and sighed.

"You've read it then, sir?" Pate asked. "Not a good book for our prince? Too wet, perhaps?"

"This is not a time for foolery, Pate," the secretary answered. "Vallenro is dead."

The news staggered Pate. "Dead?" he echoed.

"The man took his own life. He left no heirs. Now I have the daunting business of getting all his land and properties transferred to the Crown. If you knew how tedious this all is!"

Pate opened his mouth, then quickly closed it. The Crown meaning not Ravelin, but the Duke. The disgruntled secretary was still speaking.

"I have to have inventories done. The Duke is most insistent on that..."

No grief darkened Locke's face. Only complaint at the work he had to do because of the man's death. Hadn't Vallenro been a friend of Locke's? Even a particular friend at one time? *What hardness this?*

Then Pate knew.

Locke was expressing the feelings of the man whose wishes he would faithfully do. Locke had seen the pearl fire. But so had Vallenro. Had he by taking his own life also done the will of the man who controlled the mirror?

Pate shuddered.

"And then," Locke continued, "I must see to the reassigning of Guardstown, because the Duke trusts no one else with this matter."

Pate's heart began to pound. *Guardstown?* He hadn't seen his parents in some time. What had he missed?

"What is your business in Guardstown?" Pate asked, as innocently as he could.

Locke flinched. A small movement of the head and hand.

Pate waited.

Locke composed himself. "It is my business and the Duke's," he said stonily. "Most assuredly not yours, Pate. Now go."

Pate left without the book.

· · ·

Wells opened the door to him. "The prince has guests," he said quietly. "But he has been anxious for your return."

The sound of Petronia's chatter came from the bedchamber. Pate raised his eyebrows. "This is a first, isn't it?" he whispered.

Wells nodded in reply.

"And unfortunate, because I have news that the prince must hear."

Pate entered Ravelin's bedchamber as unobtrusively as he could and took a chair on the opposite side of the bed from Petronia. Both Duchess Olivia and Petronia barely noticed his arrival, and their glances in his direction carried a new coldness. Not even noticing the cat who leapt onto the bed and lay down at once.

A quick look at Ravelin's grayish face showed that this visit was exhausting the prince. But Pate could not help him. Only the prince could send such high-ranking visitors away.

Petronia was speaking of the way the Ophrian ladies wore their hair—in detail—when Ravelin interrupted her. "Petronia," he said weakly, "Do you know what The Fearless know?"

Petronia frowned. "I don't know what you're talking about."

"The Fearless in *Tales from Nordia*. They must know something the rest of us don't."

"No one in Ophria reads the Nordian tales, Ravelin."

"Are you sure?"

"Why would they be interested in something so very far north of them? Oh!" Petronia exclaimed. "There's something I want to tell you! Father is going to give us a beautiful gray stone manor north of the city as a wedding present. It doesn't sit on a lake, but it's near a river, and we could turn it into a palace if we wish. At least, I think he said we could."

Her voice trailed away, and Pate's stomach turned cold. Vallenro's home was made of gray stone and was situated on a river. It was a large, beautifully designed place. Pate had accompanied the princes there some years ago. Would Ravelin recognize the description?

The prince seemed half asleep. "I must rest now, Aunt and Petronia. Wells, will you see the ladies out?"

Wells did so in his usual gracious and respectful manner. But as they left, Pate saw that Ravelin had no strength left to hear his tragic news and ponder its meaning.

Pate came around the bed. "May I get anything for you, Your Highness?"

"Do you remember," Ravelin's voice came weakly, "the girl that you imagined for me?"

"Yes, my friend."

"How will I recognize her?" Ravelin's eyes were almost completely closed, and his words came in a whisper. "Will she ride into Elva on a white horse?"

The reference was to a common nursery rhyme and not the way Ravelin usually spoke at all. Pate looked closely at him. Ravelin's weakness made him seem a little boy again, waiting for a cheering word before going off to the dark land of sleep.

If he needed cheer, then Pate would cheer.

"No, my prince," he said gently. "Horses are the glory

of Ardemount. *We* are the proud of Rilken. She will come riding in on *our* glory. She will come on a bear."

Ravelin's eyes were shut, but his hand made a motion toward the bedpost by his head, where a carved bear never tired of watching.

"Just like that one," Pate said reassuringly.

Ravelin was silent for a time. Pate watched closely to make sure he was still breathing, not daring to move until he saw a slight, regular movement of the bed linen. *And you must live to see her, my prince.* With a sigh, he picked up his cat from where she had curled up on the foot of the bed.

A whisper came from the pillow. "My uncle is afraid of bears." Pate waited, but Ravelin said nothing more.

In the outer room, Pate had a short consultation with Wells in which he told him the awful news. But there was no time to talk it through now.

"I will be back later with the prince's dinner tray," Pate promised.

PATE wished he could curl up somewhere like a hibernating bear and think. Even though it would be more pleasant not to think.

Vallenro's death. Petronia's babble about marriage to Ravelin. The new coldness he, Pate, sensed in formerly friendly eyes. Ravelin's weakness. The odd mention of Guardstown. And everywhere the presence of the pearl fire.

It was deeply unsettling.

Pate climbed the last of the stairs with his cat tucked

under one arm and pushed open the door to his small room. He shut it firmly behind him and dropped the small bar over the door edge that served as a type of lock. Would that he could as easily shut out evil and sadness, sickness and pain!

He hugged his cat, walked over to the window, and pulled back the drape. Twilight. Dark clouds pressed in from the west, darkening the day before its time. The wind was strengthening.

From habit, Pate turned his gaze towards the rooftop flags. The colors of the Duke of Elva and Prince Ravelin snapped in the stiff wind, but Dallen's flag was gone.

Dallen dead?

A chill filled him. Dallen had disappeared on Vallenro's land. *What if he had indeed met his end there?* Now that the Duke had taken Vallenro's land, no one else could search there for the prince again. Could this have been what the Duke intended all along?

Pate stared straight west at the dark gray clouds roiling toward him, and tightened his grip on the cat.

50

———

Dream and Memory

The bear sat on a hilltop west of Elva as evening came. The hill was not as tall as the one by the hunting station, but he could pick out the heights of Elva Castle easily from the roofs of the town.

The stout walls and turrets of brown brick. The red tile roofs looking like whimsical hats on top of each tower. The massive western wall of the castle. And at the tallest tower, a series of flagpoles.

Three flags topped the poles. Three different colors. As he watched, one of the flags began to move.

Downward.

Until it disappeared from sight.

The bear rose onto his hind legs to see better.

Another flag began to move downward until it, too, disappeared.

The bear stayed motionless. A monstrous statue in the darkening forest.

The second flag reappeared on a different pole. Unseen hands pulled at ropes that raised it higher and higher, far above the only remaining flag.

The bear waited.

The first flag did not reappear.

The bear still waited as the wind increased in strength and rain began to beat on his back

Two flags flew from the castle tower. One higher. One lower. That was all.

Something stirred deep in the bear.

Memory.

Understanding.

Insight.

But with them, deep sorrow. And—anger.

He moved to tear down the trees beside him with the power of his fury.

The bear stopped the man inside who willed this.

He started down the hill toward Elva, determined to enter the city and tear down the castle gates.

The bear would not let him go past the creek that ran across the bottom of the hill.

Back up the hill he went to look again.

Two flags. One higher. One lower.

Very much lower.

Lower and alone. Vulnerable.

He threw himself to the ground in frustration as the rain came even harder. At last he turned away from the city, moving through the forest slowly at first. Then faster, until he was running alongside the northwest road.

No. Not northwest.

Run west.

He could run through the forest in a dark rain as no other animal could.

Because he was no animal.

As he ran, his nightly dream came back to him, unafraid now to speak to him with day's awareness.

And for the first time, he accepted it. Examined it.

He saw the lift of the hand.

Heard the point of the spear split the air as it passed.

Felt his shoulder hit the hard ground.

Saw the shield over him.

Protecting him.

Run!

And he had.

He had run as he was running now.

Run!

51

News from Elva

As Tara and her girls watched Darrit sleep, her mind whirled with questions that she could barely wait to ask.

What brought you here, Darrit? And in such a beggar state?

Talk at the inn said only the Guardsmen themselves were with the king, so you couldn't have been with Bevan on the northwest road. There should be no accusation against you. But how came you here?

As she studied his face, her mind wandered to Guardstown, and she allowed herself to think of the life they had left behind. Of Bevan, Silvia, Rosabel, and herself living in one of the tall, gray stone houses that bounded Guardstown Square.

A Guardsman led a life of hard work and rigorous discipline and by it earned generous reward from his king. Bevan's constant willingness to give, to sacrifice, brought his whole family respect and honor from all who knew what her husband did. And with the wives and families of Guardstown they had formed a strong bond, the kind that came only with such shared values and shared sacrifices. A bond that was irreparably broken the day of Mago's accusation.

In the end, Bevan *had* given everything for his king, Tara was sure of that. But in the wake of his sacrifice came punishment, hostility, and exile. The promise of the Guardstown life shattered for her family.

Something must have destroyed it too for young Darrit. For his presence here had something to do with the king's death and the mystery of the Guardsmen's failure. There could be no other explanation for it.

The boy stirred, rolled onto his side, and blinked.

"Darrit?" she said softly.

He saw her in the chair and sat up abruptly. He glanced quickly around the small room, his eyes resting for a moment on Rosie and Silvie, where they sat on the bed with the squirrel between them. Then his eyes came back to her, as a boy searching for his mother.

"Tara, ma'am!" It was a cry of alarm. Of desperate warning. "The palace guard took over Guardstown!"

She stared at him, not comprehending. "What do you mean?"

He shook his head from side to side, over and over. "The castle said that everyone had to leave Guardstown. Everyone. By the end of the day."

Which day? Tara wanted to ask. But Darrit was so distraught, she didn't interrupt him.

"I was at Lunn's house. We packed as fast as we could. But there were no wagons allowed in the square, and we couldn't send for them. We could only carry things. Dolly and the kids were brave. But Lunn, he knew there would be more coming. He pulled me aside and told me to take his family to my mother's house. I promised him.

"There was a trumpet blast, a sign we were all to go. Everyone came out of their doors. I saw the palace guard standing in the shadows between houses, trying not to be seen. Lunn caught my eye. He had seen them too. He just nodded and whispered, '*Aware.*'

"I looked up as we passed the old captain's house. He was standing there in the window just like always. But his arms were raised. Face against the glass. Like—like he couldn't believe what he was seeing. And right at that moment, an arrow struck Lunn in the throat and he fell —" Darrit's voice broke.

Tara gasped. "*Lunn?*"

Rosie gave a small shriek. Silvie sat deathly still.

"Then Tam went down," Darrit said. "I—I couldn't tell where the arrows were coming from. Behind us the palace guard formed a line, swords out, and pushed us down the street. We had to leave Lunn lying—lying there." His voice broke.

"People were chanting. *Enemies of the king. Enemies of the king.* I took Dolly's arm, and we each grabbed one of the kids and held on and pushed with the crowd until we could break away and go to my mama's door."

Darrit's words stopped suddenly, and he looked down at the blankets he was twisting in his hands. His own face twisted in torture at the remembrance.

Tara knew these people as well as she knew Darrit. Lunn's deep laugh, so recognizable at parties and gatherings. Dolly's admiring eyes. How deeply she loved him. And now...

Silvie and Rosie silently moved closer until they were sitting on the floor near Darrit's bed. Tara left her chair and knelt by his bedside. "What happened then?" she asked softly, feeling a weight like lead in her stomach.

Darrit sobbed openly, and the words came between gasps for air. "I don't know what happened—to anybody else." He shuddered and took a deep breath. "I just had to save Dolly for Lunn.

"We got to Mama's house and she took us in. But her neighbor said the palace guard was searching through Elva for any of the Guardsmen that had gotten away. So I hid behind boards up in the attic. And was there when they came looking for me. They didn't find me, and my sister told me to come out.

"I didn't, because Bevan taught me about second searching. I stayed where I was and the guard came again. All of a sudden. After they left, I came out and went over the roofs to the city wall. A friend of mine was on patrol. He looked away while I climbed down the wall and ran for the trees."

Darrit seemed to be describing another world. An alien, horrific place. "Where did you go then?" asked Tara.

"I slept in the woods. Did chores for someone in a cottage in return for a meal. But I couldn't feel safe. I kept seeing Lunn lying on the cobbles." He turned his head and looked at her with wide eyes. "Why did they do it, Tara?"

"I don't know, Darrit," she said softly. "I don't know. But truth will come out. You're safe now. You don't have to run tonight. You can stay here and rest."

He lay back on his pillow and closed his eyes as if he believed her. She studied the brown of his eyelashes where they lay against the grayish pallor of his skin.

"Then—Guardstown is gone," Rosie whispered. "The people are..." Her voice trailed away.

Silvie gazed past Darrit into the fire. "Everything that the Guardsmen stood for is being destroyed. Their identity. Their honor. Their very selves." She turned to look at her mother, and Tara saw something she couldn't name in her daughter's eyes. Something so very like Bevan. "Is this some sort of punishment for—for the northwest road?"

"Yes," said Tara, barely above a whisper. "I believe so."

Darrit's eyes moved, but he kept them tightly closed. Moisture seeped out from under the lids.

Tara took a deep breath and patted his shoulder. "You need a good supper, Darrit. Ettie makes the best stew in West Rilken. And you already have some of her bread over there on the table. What if I go get you a bowl while the girls keep you company?"

. . .

SHE MADE her decision on the stairs, what she would tell and to whom. Darrit needed help, more than she could give him. She would have to ask advice from others.

When she stepped into the kitchen, only Jarlath and Ettie were there. Nissa and Dona hurried in and out with trays of food as fast as Ettie could fill them. Which was fast, because Ettie had quick hands.

Jarlath was stirring one of the kettles over the fire. Something she had never seen him do, but she had never stayed so late at the inn before.

The sun set behind the black clouds of rain. All was dark outside the window, but the kitchen fires and the lanterns against the whitewashed walls gave the room a heartening glow.

Jarlath looked up at her expectantly. "How is the lad?"

"Not good." Tara sat down on her usual stool by the side of Ettie's table, well out of the way of the kitchen bustle. The cook was scooping dried currants from a crock into a bowl, but Tara could tell Ettie was ready to listen. Busy though she was, she was ready. *How to begin?*

"Jarlath," Tara said, "have you heard any travelers speak of a—a disturbance in Guardstown?"

"You mean like the palace guard and the Guardsmen fighting?"

Tara felt startled. *How had she missed this?* "Something like that."

"A few people from Elva spoke of it. Made them uneasy. When armed men go after each other, nobody's safe. I wouldn't want to be in Elva right now."

"Is that what you heard?" she asked incredulously. "That armed men went after each other?"

Nissa and Dona came in for more food trays. Tara and Jarlath stopped speaking and didn't continue until after they had gone.

"I take it you just heard more?" Jarlath asked, pausing in his stirring to let Ettie spoon her bowl of dried fruit and spices into his kettle.

"There, now stir that," said Ettie. "And go on with your story, Tara. I just have to lay out these cakes."

"Darrit was in the middle of it. He was at the house of one of the Guardsmen when the orders came that everyone had to leave their homes. They had to pack quickly to leave. But out in the street, arrows started picking out the Guardsmen, and they fell right in front of their families. Right in front of Darrit."

She could barely speak and barely believe the words she was trying to say. Lunn stood tall in her mind's eye. Burly, keen-eyed, and good-hearted. He had been one of Bevan's special friends. Along with Drony. She had just lost another part of Bevan.

"It wasn't a fight," she said quietly. "It was murder."

Ettie's hands froze, gripping one of the cake trays. She stared at Tara.

Nissa and Dona came through the kitchen door. "The room's full tonight," Dona said. "No one wants to go out in this rain."

Ettie's hands moved again. "Is Harper here?" she asked.

"Yes," said Nissa, picking up a bowl from those waiting on the hearth, "and he wants some more stew."

The serving girls left again, and Jarlath, Ettie, and Tara all looked at each other.

"So," said Jarlath soberly, "it was an attack."

She nodded slowly, and as she did so a sick feeling rose in her. She had just said enough to make Ettie and Jarlath know of her connection to the Guardsmen. Jarlath would know that her husband had been a Guardsman now. And perhaps even *which* Guardsman, owing to when she had showed up at the inn. Had she just put them all in danger with her words? Silvie, Rosie, and Darrit? She was afraid to look Jarlath or Ettie in the eye. Afraid of what she might see there.

Ettie set out wooden trays filled with cakes until her long worktable could hold no more. She took a knife and deftly cut them into squares. Tara watched silently for a few moments, then roused herself and stood up.

"Could I have some stew for Darrit?"

"I can take it up to him," Jarlath said, laying his spoon down on Ettie's table. "I know what the boy's been through. I've sat with many a lad working through battle stun. You and your girls go have your dinner now, and give a listen in the main room. On such a full night, you could hear more news. Or ask Crim what he knows."

Tara stood still, unsure, until she realized they were both looking at her.

"Go, Tara," said Ettie. "This is a hard day, and you could use some music and cheer. And don't worry about us. We're no friends of the palace guard. Didn't realize they ever left the palace until a few months ago. After the king was well on his way to Tellhaven.

"Some of them came here back then, and sat all high and mighty in the main room, scaring everyone to death with their boasts and taunts. Waving their daggers around as if they were feathers."

"Palace guard is supposed to guard the palace," said Jarlath. "What they came to the middle of the woods for I don't know."

Tara looked from one to the other. "What did you do?"

"Gareth killed them with politeness and soured their ale," Ettie said. "I over-salted their pigeon and made sure each one was a little burnt. It hurt to damage my reputation like that, but—" She shrugged. "They have their weapons, and I have mine."

She went on. "Harper tuned his strings off pitch that night and sang badly. Everyone pretended not to notice. The palace guard hasn't come back since."

Jarlath held a bowl of hot stew in his hands. "Ettie, cut a big wedge of that Grinspring cheese."

The cook went over to a cupboard on the far wall and brought back a creamy chunk of it.

"Now," Jarlath said with a reassuring smile, "I'll feed this hungry boy."

52

———

A Stormy Night at The Grumpy Rabbit

Darrit sank back onto his pillow after Mama left. He stared up at the ceiling, his face pale and distant. Rosie's eyes looked as hollow as I felt. Then my sister did what she always did. Stirred the fire to make the room more cheerful.

I stayed sitting on the floor by Darrit's bed, wondering about the question that I wanted to ask him. It was a hard, heavy question, but we had just been talking about hard and heavy things. I would be gentle, but I had to ask.

"Darrit, do the people of Guardstown really think our papa killed the king?"

Rosie took her place next to me again. "Do they think he killed the other Guardsmen too?"

Darrit took his eyes off the ceiling and looked at us. "I don't know. Every few days someone came to Guardstown Square to denounce him. Again and again. Forbidding people to speak of him."

Something inside me tightened into a hard knot at this.

"So people didn't talk about him," said Darrit. "But after one of the speakers had finished and Lunn and I went back inside, Lunn said, 'You're too smart to believe everything you hear, aren't you?' Then I knew he didn't believe the man."

"But Lunn didn't say anything more?" Rosie asked.

"No. Because of the spies all over Guardstown."

"*Spies?*" I cried out.

Darrit nodded. "Yes, Silvie. All over Guardstown. They were mostly outsiders and easy to spot, but some of the wives whose husbands died with the king joined them. And people were afraid to say anything anywhere then."

"It would be awful to live in a Guardstown like that," I said.

"Guardstown is gone," said Rosie. "All gone."

Darrit went back to staring at the ceiling. I wished I could close my eyes and pretend that we were back in Guardstown, gathered around the sitting room fire with our friend Darrit, and that everything was all right, just how it used to be.

But Papa said that Guardsmen never pretend. And he had not taught his daughters for nothing.

With a soft rap, the door opened quietly and Mama

and Jarlath came in. Jarlath held a tray of welcoming food.

"Time to go downstairs for dinner, girls," Mama said. "Jarlath brought a meal for Darrit."

The small room felt suddenly crowded. But going to the main room meant we could be with those who heard the hunters' stories. Hunters who may have spoken of our distinctive hair.

And Darrit talked of spies.

I pulled some scarves from our bags and handed one to Rosie. Even though the scarf was a little damp, I tied it over and around my hair. Rosie did the same. Mama took a look at us and nodded approval. We left the room as Jarlath settled himself in the chair.

THE MAIN ROOM of the inn was filled with a sea of strangers, shadowy in the flickering light. At each end of the room, fireplaces were heaped with logs, which cracked and snapped in the flames. Small lanterns sat at the center of many tables. Others held fat candles with several wicks each. The murmur of conversation flowed from table to table, broken by a sharp word here or a short laugh there. We stood in the hallway, trying to glimpse an open table.

I looked around for the other inn people that Mama had told us about. She had described them so well that I recognized them already.

Gareth appeared to work tirelessly at the bar, a smile on his friendly face. Alta, with her tight and worried expression, worked at his side. Nissa and Dona darted past us carrying trays of food.

Crim the merchant was sitting by himself at a table against the wall. He stood up with delight on his face and beckoned to Mama. With relief, we followed her over to him. He held out the chair next to him for Mama. Rosie and I sat on the opposite side. I was across from Crim; we both had shoulders to the wall. Rosie sat across from Mama on the open side of the table.

My position suited me. With a glance I could take in everyone at our table as well as see many of the people at the other tables.

"I wrapped up your embroidery and gave it to Gareth to take to your room," Crim said to Mama. "You'd left it behind."

Mama thanked him and introduced us. Crim shook Rosie's hand and then mine, as courteously as if we had been members of the Elva court. I saw admiration in his eyes when he looked at Mama. But Mama responded to him as she would to any friend.

Nissa brought a tray over to our table and placed a bowl of stew in front of each one of us and a large loaf of bread in the center of the table for us to share. Mama tore off portions for each of us and held the plate out to Crim. "I was looking forward to hearing more news from Elva. We've heard such disturbing reports lately. What can you tell us?"

"About the fight in Guardstown, you mean?" He took the plate from her and put the hunk of bread on top of his stew.

"Yes," Mama said softly.

"People can't remember something so violent breaking out from the castle. They are afraid. It's very bad." He spoke in a low, cautious voice and seemed ready to abandon the topic.

He glanced at each of us then, and must have seen on our faces how ready we were to listen to him. After another look at Mama, he set down his spoon and picked up the topic again.

"Michael is a friend of mine," Crim said, in the same low voice. "He's a dealer in fine cloth and a supplier for the palace. He took me to the rear of his shop and shut the door so we could talk, the two of us alone. And even then he kept getting up to check the door to make sure we weren't overheard.

"He said the palace guard had taken over Guardstown, destroying the Guardsmen and sending their families into the streets." He paused for a moment and looked regretful. "I hate to speak of such things to you," he said apologetically to Mama.

"It's not good to hide from hard things just because they are hard," she replied. "Please, tell us all you know."

Crim nodded. "Michael says the Guardsmen were either killed or imprisoned. Their women and children knock at his door now, begging, and he gives to each one of them. He can't stand to see them in this state. He said that Elva has always loved their Guardsmen and, in spite of the king's death, the city couldn't accept any of this."

The three of us held idle spoons in our hands, so intent were we on everything Crim was saying. He dipped a chunk of his bread in the stew broth and chewed it.

Elva has always loved their Guardsmen. I knew that. I had seen it so many times. Why did that statement give me sudden hope?

Crim went on. "I was never more glad to leave Elva than I was this morning."

"It's so sad," said Mama, her whole heart in her words. "So very sad."

"Horrible," said Rosie. I glanced at her, concerned what else she might say in the passion of her feeling, but she said nothing more.

Crim went on to tell of bands of soldier-hunters that had been sent out from the capital city. His voice was not as low nor as cautious when he told of seeing the bands leave from the west gate and the north gate too. Mama's eyes were on me for a moment, but I took a bite of my stew as if the hunters did not concern me.

A man at the table next to us caught the last of Crim's words. He pushed his chair back from his table and turned toward ours, one hand holding his pint. "You're talking of the hunter bands?"

His voice had a natural loudness to it which pulled the attention of those nearby. "I saw them riding east out of Elva on my way in. I got off the road at a byway. Didn't want to be on the same road as those fearsome chaps." He shivered and took a large swallow from his tumbler.

"How many in the band? Did ya see?" The question came from the table beyond.

People nearby began to shift their chairs and turn to take part in a general discussion about something that concerned them all. Both Crim and Mama accepted this as natural. Indeed, with our thirst for news, this is what we had hoped for.

"Maybe six or eight," the first man replied. "And armed to the teeth."

"I heard these bands are going out all over the country." I couldn't see who said this, but heads nodded in response.

"What are they hunting?"

"It can't still be that Guardsman, can it? Don't tell me they haven't found him yet?"

Hope leapt in me. I couldn't keep it down. I lifted my spoon to my lips, determined to act as if the words had nothing to do with us.

A voice of money, of authority, spoke from the middle of the room. "I heard they're looking for *all* Guardsmen. Prince Ravelin lost confidence in the Guardsmen after his father's death, so the Duke's getting rid of all of them."

"What? All of our Guardsmen? I'm shocked to hear that!"

"How terrible!"

Rosie whispered fiercely in my ear. "Ravelin wouldn't do that."

I stared at her, for I sensed something more behind her words, but she tore her bread as if she had said nothing.

"They're *not* looking for Guardsmen," a strong voice asserted. "They're looking for *bears*."

I gasped, then hoped the sound I made was lost in the sounds of surprise that moved through the company. Crim's eyes were on me for a moment, until a man at the table behind us cried out, "*Bears?* Rilken's bears?"

The man stood, pulled a coin from his pocket, and held it up. "Look at this, everyone. One rill."

"Treat me to an ale, Tom!" someone cried out.

"Hush! Just look. On one side is a bear. On the other, our last, dear king. What I'm saying is this. We're proud of our bears. Why are we hunting them?" Having made his point, he sat down.

"They're not hunting normal bears," the strong voice said. "They're hunting those monstrous bears, the ones that have been seen in Rilken for some months now."

"I've never seen no monstrous bears."

"Nor I!"

"I'm from Ardemount," a throaty, accented voice said. "We've heard nothing about strange bears. We just have the usual kind. The kind that like to steal your honey."

"We have that kind too," he was answered. "And they do more than steal honey!"

A man by the fire stood up to make himself heard across the room. Thick white hair stuck out from beneath his cap, and his gaze had depths in it, the depths of one who has seen much of life. "Has *anyone* here laid eyes on any of these bear monsters?" He searched out the room. "No one?"

The room fell silent as each considered their neighbors. The three of us sat motionless. I kept my face as blank as possible and hoped Crim's eyes were not on me. I was afraid he saw too much.

"Well then—has anyone *heard* of these kinds of bears before? Before recent months, I mean."

"Maybe in some story from years past."

"There are strange and wondrous things all over this world." A man's melodious voice came from the middle of a lively group along the far wall.

"Master Redmond is among us tonight," Crim said, as if explaining something to Rosie and me. "He's a famous writer and professor from Tellhaven." I nodded in reply, as if this were the first I had heard of him.

"In Falland, there are large birds of falcon shape that burn with fire as they fly," Redmond said. "They're called the Sender's Own."

Rosie squeezed my arm under the table and I thought of our desperation that first night in the woods, until the flaming bird had come.

"Own? Own *what*?" someone called out.

"Messengers," Redmond replied.

"You think these *bears* could be messengers?"

"Stop, please!" a woman cried out. "Please! I don't like talking of things that aren't—aren't natural. *Especially* on nights like this."

"My dear madam," said Redmond, "then you will have to restrict your speech severely, for much in this world is not *natural* as you put it, no matter how fervently one might wish it."

He said it in such a cheerful, compassionate voice that the woman could not feel insulted or corrected in any way. I marveled at the gift of such a voice.

"Well, Master Redmond," she replied with good

humor. "I choose to restrict my attention to Ettie's currant cake in front of me."

"One should pay close attention to the joys of the world," he replied, "and one of them is Ettie's cake."

It was clear that part of the company yearned to be lighthearted on such a stormy night. Another part wanted the comfort of talking through matters of grave concern with others.

"Are these bears something that the Hosts of the North let through?"

"I thought these bears would be *helping* the Hosts of the North!"

"Wait!" cried a voice. "What do the Hosts do?"

"Haven't you learned anything at your mama's knee, Charley?"

There was an attempt at laughter, which quickly died.

The authoritative voice spoke again. "The Sender's Hall protects us, keeping the worst of the darkness away from our world. What the Hosts of the North fight and protect us from is the lesser darkness."

"The *lesser*?" A thin man near the bar leapt to his feet and stared at the owner of the authoritative voice. "*Lesser?*" he repeated. "Have you *read* the tales of the Hosts of the North—of which our dear king was going to be one? The stories tell of gruesome evils, of terrible, hideous monsters that they fight for us, for everyone in AllHallen. Monsters beyond imagination."

"These are grim thoughts for a dark night," Crim said. He glanced at both Rosie and me, and I felt he was concerned for us.

The woman in Redmond's party spoke up again. "The idea that there are worse things than I can imagine does not comfort me."

Crim leaned on the table and whispered, "Women have the courage to say things that men wouldn't dare admit."

I tried to smile at him. But I felt the change in the atmosphere. The room chilled. The thin man sat down. The darkness out of the window seemed full of new terrors. Rain lashed against the doors and windows, and pounded on the roof. How easy it was to imagine that it was not rain, but an unearthly hand thumping the door! People fell silent and shifted nervously, pulling their shawls and cloaks tighter around them.

I yearned for something, some thought, some truth, that would fling fear aside. The Guardsmen were meant to protect. The Hosts of the North were meant to protect. Above all, the Sender's Hall protected. And protection had everything to do with love.

Love was still a great force in the world. This realization calmed me some, but fear gripped the room.

Alta stood still at the bar. Her hand clasped a tumbler, and she stared wordlessly at her husband. Gareth stepped out from behind the bar. "Kipp, put some more logs on the fire," he called in a hearty voice, even though everyone could see that both fires were already blazing away. "Harper, play us a song!"

A man from Redmond's group stood up and went to the corner by the front fireplace, where a stool and several instruments leaned against the wall, waiting for him. He had long, blond hair and an energetic manner.

Grabbing a cittern, he perched on the stool and tested the strings while he faced us all.

"Do you know why the Sender made birds?" he called out in a cheerful voice.

No one answered. It seemed an absurd question to ask while we struggled with thoughts of darkness.

"So that at any time," said Harper, answering his own question, "all over the world, there would be some creature singing.

"There are no birds here tonight. I hope they've all found a dry place to roost. So we're the ones to fill this room with song."

He was working hard to calm us. His tone meant to soothe like oil. But glancing around I could tell that fear bit deep.

My eyes were drawn instinctively to Rosie's face. When we visited Grampy and Gramma in East Rilken, our habit was to go with them to the local inn to gather with friends. Rosie was invited to sing every time.

Now, her lips moved silently to the words as Harper sang his song. When he finished, people clapped, but it was clear that fear slowed their hands, and I saw with a glance that Rosie felt for him. Without explanation, and as if it were the most natural thing to do, she pushed her chair back, got up, and threaded her way through the room to Harper's side.

Crim stared in surprise. Mama caught my eye. There was concern, but no alarm in her look. "That's Rosie," I said lightly, shrugging my shoulders.

Rosie bent to whisper into Harper's ear. From his smile and the way she positioned herself next to him, I guessed she asked to sing with him. This drew the attention of the company in a favorable way. Eyes lit up and faces expressed the hope of something good.

Harper and Rosie began to sing together, and their voices blended beautifully. The song they had chosen couldn't have been more perfect.

> *On the heights a blazing fire glows*
> *Held in the Hosts' right hand.*
> *Their horses bold race to the foe,*
> *Who quaking make their stand.*
> *Love and strength race on before them,*
> *Melting monsters as they sing.*
> *Swift they ride, Light their weapon,*
> *And make the Northlands ring.*

The song was "For Love of AllHallen." The anthem of the Hosts of the North. I had heard it triumphantly sung in Elva last, with horns, strings, drums, and a whole choir in the city square. Now, even though only one stringed instrument accompanied the two singers, the song had lost none of its power.

With each word, the atmosphere in the room changed yet again. Spirits lifted. Fear fled. Hearts gained courage.

Rosie waved her arms, urging all who knew the words to join in the chorus with them. Mama and I sang, and after a few lines, Crim did too.

> *O AllHallen land,*
> *See to the good.*

Bring not the evil in.
Live in beauty strong,
And sing the song
Of Love that will not end.

The next verse told of Strength shattering darkness, of Truth that can't be turned. And of Joy that gives songs to the Night. Then the whole room sang the triumphant chorus again.

No more did the wind beat like an unearthly fist on the door. It was only wind after all.

Applause and cheers begged Rosie to sing another. She and Harper agreed on a livelier tune this time. And after that, it seemed only natural that Rosie would sing her favorite old song.

Oh, sing me high
And sing me low,
And sing me where
The wind blows.

The wind thumped the door at this. Rosie burst into laughter, and I admired her for it. Again she waved her arms, inviting everyone to join in. The whole room rang with the song, voices young and old, smooth and scratchy, on key and off—all of them hallowed the moment and sang to the very end.

...And find you at
The bright star.

The applause was loud and long and several people leapt up to shake Rosie's hand as she made her way through the tables and back to us.

We stayed and ate Ettie's cake while Harper sang three more songs to hearty applause. Then we got up, thanked Crim for his company, and followed Mama to the bar to pay for our meal.

Gareth shook his head firmly when she held out the coins to him. "No."

Mama looked bewildered. "No?"

Gareth pointed at Rosie. "The songs were worth every bit of the food you ate tonight. And more." Alta, with her ever-worried face, gave a short nod.

53

Heavy Thoughts and a Strange Moon

Back upstairs in our room, Darrit looked more like himself. He was dressed in dry clothes and sitting cross-legged on the floor. In his hands was a plate holding a piece of Ettie's currant cake, a portion that was at least twice the size of those being served in the main room.

"We're doing fine here, Tara, ma'am," said Jarlath. "Swapping stories like the old soldiers we are."

"We've been talking of other things too," said Darrit solemnly.

"Yep," said Jarlath. "For some time now, I've been telling Alta that Kipp and I could use more help. The stable boys are already worked off their feet, and there's more inn to repair than I can see to in a whole season.

That won't do if Alta's out to attract rich folks. So, I figured I can tell everyone that my great-nephew has come to help me."

"Your great-nephew?" Mama said, puzzled.

"He's from the same town as my grandpa," said Darrit.

"So we figure we've got to be related," said Jarlath.

JARLATH TOOK Darrit to a room above the stable, after assuring us that he would watch out for him and make sure he had everything he needed. The bed in our own simple room was not big enough for three people, so we planned to sleep crossways. Our feet would hang out over the floor, but we didn't mind.

"It just feels so good to be in a bed again!" Rosie said as she pulled back the covers and crawled in. White Squirrel curled up in one of her shoes on the floor.

Mama had other things on her mind. She sat in the bed between us, her back against the wall. "Tell me about the hunters now."

So we did. I told her what they had said and described the trace of castle blue on their clothing and on their saddles. Rosie told of the startled looks on their faces when, because of the Sender's gift, their horses left without hesitation.

"But we knew then, it was time to leave the station behind."

"You did right," Mama said. She wrapped her arms around us and hugged us tightly.

"Mama," I said. "The way the talk went in the inn

tonight, it sounded as if some people thought Papa was still alive."

Mama looked across the room to where the fire danced on the hearth. "I know."

"What do *you* think?" asked Rosie. Her eyes searched Mama's face. "*Is* he alive?"

Mama gave a sad smile. "I don't know any more than you do."

The events of the day and the news from Elva were heavy weights on our hearts. The courage from the Nordian song faded away. Rosie built the fire to warm the room for several hours; after that it would just burn low. We made ourselves as comfortable as we could and settled our heads on our pillows.

Harper's music came up the stairway from the main room. He was singing a familiar tune, and Rosie began to sing quietly with him. The rain and wind seemed to be less ferocious after a time, content to just steadily come down.

In spite of all the sorrow, or maybe because of it, I was glad we were here. Around people again. Hearing brisk footsteps in the hallway and sleepy voices beyond the door.

After the song ended, Rosie said what I had been thinking. "It's good to be with people. And so good to hear music again."

"You were marvelous tonight, Rosie," I said. "And that Nordian song. What a perfect song to sing."

"Lovely beyond words, Rosie," Mama added.

"I wonder if the Hosts ride into battle singing," Rosie said.

"If they do, they probably sing that song," I replied.

"Does Harper play every night?" Rosie asked Mama.

"I don't know," Mama said quietly. But it seemed that her thoughts had gone somewhere else and I thought I knew where.

I turned on my side, facing them both and pulled my sock-covered feet up into the warmth of the covers. "I hope someone helps Zilla like she helped us," I said.

"Yes," Mama replied in a sad voice. "Sender, help all those poor people." The way she said it made me realize that she had enough tears inside to flood all of Elva. I rested my hand on her shoulder.

"I'm glad Darrit found us," said Rosie. She had turned on her pillow to face both of us too. "Lily's family would go east, I'm sure, to her great-uncle's town. I—I hope her father is still alive. But Guardstown is gone for all of us. There's no going back now."

"It seems that everything to do with the Guardsmen has been destroyed," said Mama. "Just like you said, Silvie. Everything true and right and noble and good. That's what the Guardsmen were. That's what they've always been! And this—this clearing of Guardstown! What lies, what accusations were brought against the rest of them? Lunn wasn't even on the forest road!" This last came in a fierce whisper.

"It's all fear, Mama," I said. "Didn't someone say that the prince was afraid of the Guardsmen now? Fear doesn't care about the innocent."

"Ravelin wouldn't do this!" Rosie insisted.

"I agree with you. But the orders came from somewhere in the castle."

"Ravelin is too young to rule right now," said Mama. "Such things would have to come from the Duke."

We fell silent. The rain still drummed on the roof and slapped at the window from time to time. Behind the wall at our head, loud rumbling snores sounded from the sleeper in the next room. The firelight showed the stain of tears on Mama's face.

I lay there thinking of Redmond and what he said about the Sender's glowing falcons. Of Tike and the cat alone at the hunting station, hoping they were all right. I determined to check on them in the morning, no matter how muddy the hill was.

But after the brightness of Rosie and Harper's music, my thoughts kept returning to the destruction of Guardstown and the fear in Elva. I remembered the ruthless faces of the hunters at the station. They would have no mercy on the hunted. On Papa, if he might be alive. Or on the bear. Our Bear.

Fear for them threatened to drown me, and my heart ached for missing them. Finally, I slept, but only by clinging to the words of that bold chorus in my head.

And sing the song
Of Love that will not end.

THE STORM CRASHED into Elva with a fury, sending howling winds and punishing rain through the streets of the city. It woke Ravelin, and he moved restlessly in his bed while the tumult pounded on his window pane.

Sleepless, he stared at the moving shadows the firelight created on the canopy above his bed. After a time, he rolled onto his side, his back towards the fire, and was surprised to see a small light in the shadowy side of the room.

He sat up and looked more intently. A gentle, comforting light was shining on his mother's unfinished embroidery. It would be the moon, of course, its beams coming through the window. But then, no moonbeam could make its way through this storm.

Ravelin slowly got out of bed and, with slippered feet, walked across the wood floor toward the place where the frame hung on the wall. Above the dark forest in the picture, a small, ivory-thread moon glowed in the unfinished sky.

A moon that hadn't been there before.

He reached out a hesitant hand and touched it. The softness of thread underneath his fingertips revealed that it was truly embroidery. Nothing more. Yet—it *glowed*. And Ravelin was not the only one looking at it.

In the corner of the picture, a new figure had appeared. A dark brown bear gazed at the moon, its light reflected in his eyes. *How had this come here?* His mother had been resting in the Sender's Hall for years. Who could have stitched this?

In the picture, all was serene. As he gazed at the moon with the bear, peace filled him. He forgot the storm and his bewilderment. And after a time, he crawled back into bed and slept.

54

Invitation for the Artists

Avelyn stared in the mirror at her reflection as Callie arranged the braids on her head with dexterous fingers. "Just a little higher on that side, Callie."

Her fellow artist adjusted the coiled braid she had been working on and pinned it securely to the side of Avelyn's head. "There. What do you think now?"

Avelyn scrutinized her appearance in the mirror. "I think it looks very well. Only you could have done such good work with my thick hair." She tilted her head forward and tucked an errant strand into the back of the larger braid. "Yes, it looks very well."

She glanced up at Callie's reflection. Callie had the darkest eyes she had ever seen and beautiful glossy black hair to go with them. "We both look very well," Avelyn said.

"Well enough to eat and drink with royalty?" Callie sounded anxious. "Suppose we look horribly out of place. Suppose royalty doesn't like braids. Suppose I don't hold my glass in a proper way. I usually drink from a tumbler in my paint box. How am I going to know what to do? I couldn't even get all the paint stains off my fingers."

"You know what Master Taynor said. When we are not sure what to do, it's best to do nothing. In everything else, follow his lead."

Avelyn gazed into the mirror one more time, trying not to think about mirrors and Pate's warning. "Besides, Callie, I'm sure the Duke knows what artists are like. He often sees us at work in the corridor. I'm sure he's not expecting too much."

"He's going to be looking at us closely, if one of us will be painting the Duchess." Callie bit her bottom lip, then blurted out, "I'm sure he's going to pick you."

"He's just as likely to pick you, Callie. Your brush strokes are sublime."

"That's very kind of you, I'm sure," said Callie politely. "I better go check on Moira now." She walked stiffly away.

Avelyn was ready for the reception. There was nothing more to do but wait until Master Taynor would call them. She sighed and sank down onto her bed, spreading her olive green gown as she sat so she would not crease it. *Oh, Pate! I'll be all right. Don't worry about me.*

But Pate was terribly worried, and she knew it was because he loved her. And because he saw danger in the manner the Duke's power was growing.

Pate had more wisdom and understood things more clearly than anyone she knew. Though he could be silly to distraction, she had never heard him speak falsely. Not once. If he said there was serious menace in the Duke's mirror, there was.

So—it wasn't a question of not believing Pate. She believed him.

Then why was she dressed so finely tonight, ready to go to the very place he had warned her against?

Around the corner came the sounds of nervous laughter. Callie and Moira giggling about something. She had no desire to find out what it was.

She picked up the leather pouch that laid on the bed next to her and checked to make sure she had put several clean folded linen cloths inside. She had.

Did she trust Pate? Yes. Beyond a doubt.

Did she love him? She must ask herself this. Because —knowing Pate's heart and his character, and all the grief he carried along with his concern for the princes— knowing all this as she did, then going to the reception tonight, while ignoring his warning, would be the most unloving thing she could do.

He called her his dearest. Openly and freely. No jest had ever been in those words. Was he her dearest in turn?

Please, Avelyn, he had said. While she drank in all the vibrant color of his rich blue eyes.

But the reception was such an opportunity!

She had been ordered to go by Master Taynor. Well, not ordered. The Duke's invitation was command enough. And Taynor had said that she had a good chance of being chosen to paint the Duchess, which Callie had unfortunately overheard. Presumably, the Duke would announce his choice tonight.

The mirror, too, would be part of the program. Because Pate never told a lie.

Did she love Pate? Yes. Absolutely.

What she needed now was courage. Courage to do what Pate asked because he was right about the danger. Courage to stand firm like Pate, even though she wished she didn't have any evil to stand firm against. But mostly, she needed courage to place her ambition at the service of wisdom.

A sharp knock sounded on the outer door. "Ladies!" Taynor's imperious voice rang out. "It's time!"

Moira and Callie came around the corner, followed by the others, and hurried to the door. Their gowns flowed around them in blues and golds and greens. Avelyn did not move.

Please, Avelyn. She could still feel his warm breath on her face. *Please.*

The door flew open and Master Taynor entered, dressed in burgundy velvet. Avelyn placed her hand on her stomach and took a slow, deep breath.

"What's this? What's this?" Taynor cried. "Avelyn, get up now! We'll be late!"

She rounded her shoulders and hunched down. "I— I can't, Master. The pain is so bad!"

He strode over to her. "Pain? What pain?"

"It's been coming slowly. I tried to ignore it—"

"Did you drink from your paint water again? The yellow ochre?"

"I don't think so." She flopped sideways onto the bed and moaned.

"You can't go like this, girl, what would the Duke say?" Taynor looked around at the crowd of worried faces. "She can't be alone when she's so ill. Someone will have to stay with her." A dozen horrified gasps filled the room.

Could she save others besides herself? Avelyn opened her eyes and looked hopefully at her companions. Would any stay with her? Ambition was strong in all of them, just as it was in her. Too strong. They ignored Taynor's request and moved toward the door.

"Well then." Concern left the master's voice. The real business was at hand. He had spent enough time on this setback. "We must go now. Everyone? Ready?"

Avelyn lay still on her bed with her eyes closed, listening to the rustle of skirts and the soft tread of slippered feet.

"So sorry, Avelyn," came Callie's whisper. But her voice carried tones of triumphant pride, not sympathy.

Avelyn nodded without opening her eyes. The door closed behind the last rustling skirt, and the dormitory fell silent except for the rain drumming on the roof. Avelyn still did not move. She pulled her feet up onto the bed and with one arm reached for the blanket to cover herself. The dormitory was always chilly.

One coiled braid pressed into her head uncomfortably. She would take it out soon. What had she done?

What kind of choice had she made? She thought again of all the concern and love in Pate's eyes.

Please, Avelyn, he had said.

Avelyn sat up on the bed and leaned against the wall, spreading the warmth of the blanket over her gown. She had done it. She had listened to Pate. Time would show what this meant to her future work with the castle artists. If anything. She sighed and reached up to pull the pins out of her hair.

SOMEWHERE DEEP IN the middle of the night, Avelyn was awakened by the opening of a door, the swishing of gowns, and a series of tired but happy sighs, all indications of a satisfying experience. She felt a pang in her chest, a pang of being separated and apart from all the others.

A candle hovered near her bed. "Avelyn?" It was Callie. "How are you now?"

Avelyn stirred and opened her eyes. "Better, I think. All I did was sleep." She raised herself onto one elbow. "But what of you? Was the reception grand and glorious?"

Callie sat down on a stool by her bed and talked of almond cakes and spiced wine, musicians and dancing. She barely mentioned that Master Taynor would be painting the Duchess, in her haste to talk about the beauty of a mirror and the pearl fire.

Avelyn barely heard any of it. All she saw was the unusual glow the candlelight bought forth from Callie's eyes.

55

The Forest Road

*S*ilvie.

The voice came low in the dark. A dream voice, acting the part of a drama in my sleep.

Silvie!

The whisper rumbled into a growl.

I sat up straight and looked around. I was in our simple room in the inn. The fire had gone out, and Mama and Rosie still slept on the bed next to me. Light was coming around the shutter's edge, and I no longer heard the sound of rain.

I got up, unlatched the shutter, and opened it a little. Light gray clouds were breaking up in the face of a blue sky. Puddles the size of small ponds filled the inn yard.

And outside our window, in the branches of the quince tree, perched Redbird.

I opened the window at once. "Is Tike all right?"

Yes, she replied. *He is still asleep in the station. But Bear has returned and is looking for you. I told him you were here.*

Bear was back! "Are there hunters in the woods now, Red?"

She flew away to see. I turned from the window to find Mama and Rosie awake and watching me. I told them what the bird had said.

"Will you go talk to him, Silvie?" Mama asked.

I hesitated and glanced at Rosie. We had caused Mama unneeded anxiety because of our rashness before. More fear was in the air, more danger now.

Yet, Bear was waiting and the station wasn't far. "I think I must. But only after we make sure there are no men in the woods."

"There wouldn't be if Bear is at the station," Rosie said practically. "He can smell for miles."

A pitcher of water had been placed outside our door during the night. I poured it into the basin and washed my face and hands, then dressed quickly. Redbird returned before I had finished lacing my boots.

The woods were clear, she said. And Bear was waiting for me at the base of the path.

"I'll be safe, Mama. I'll be with Bear." After the fears of last night, I half-expected her to forbid my leaving.

Instead, she nodded and hugged me tightly. "You'll be in the Sender's care then, Silvie," she said softly. "There's no safer place to be."

I picked my way carefully around the puddles in the

inn yard. The stable boys were up and active. Though it was early yet, the stable doors were open, and one carriage was being pulled out. Jarlath was crossing to the main house.

"What are you out so early for?" he called.

"I need to check on my dog," I replied. "Do you think he could come to the inn? He's lame and won't be much bother. There's a cat too."

"I think that will be all right. The inn will welcome cats. But the dog best stay in Darrit's room."

"How is Darrit?"

Jarlath took off his cap and rubbed his frizzy gray hair before putting it back on his head. "You can never forget seeing a man killed like that. The memories are hard. Darrit's trying."

"Thank you, Jarlath. You're doing what we can't do."

He shook his head, uncomfortable with my gratitude, and pointed up toward the hunting station. "You watch out for the mud on that hill. You slip once and you'll be sliding clear to Grinspring on your backside."

"I'll be careful," I said.

Bear was waiting for me behind a thicket at the base of the path, just as Redbird had said. He, too, had an eye on the mud.

"The mud is too thick for you. Get on my back, and I'll take you to a place where we can talk."

His fur was damp and a bit slippery, but I was able to climb up the way he had taught us.

"There were hunters at the station yesterday, weren't there?" Bear asked.

"How did you know? I thought the heavy rain would have washed every scent away."

"The smell of some things does not so easily disappear." A certain note in his voice told me that he meant more than the scent of men and horses. "Are you holding on?"

"Yes," I said, tightening my grip on his roll of fur.

Bear moved swiftly through the trees, as if mud were a thing that didn't exist for him. After we passed through the clearing, he took the path that led up the hill behind the station. I lowered my head and held tight to the fur at his shoulders as he ran.

In moments, we were at the top of the hill. He stopped before a broad, flat-topped rock next to a stand of trees, and I slid off. The rock was mostly dry, but rainwater pooled in its crevices. I found a place to sit and pulled my cloak tight around my shoulders. Bear crouched down on the slab of rock beside me.

The sun had yet to warm the morning, but columns of gray rose from the inn far below us, filling the air with the smell of woodsmoke. I slid my arms underneath my cloak to warm them. Bear watched me intently.

"I have something to tell you, Silvie. Many things, actually."

"I am listening, Bear."

"Do you remember the day your mother first went to the inn? When I sat with you and your sister on the hillside waiting?"

"Yes."

"Rosie asked me if you had seen me somewhere before."

"Our first night out of Elva we ran into an unfriendly bear. She wanted to make sure it wasn't you."

"Do you remember what I answered?"

I studied him, sensing more in his words. He answered his own question.

"I told you that I first saw you by the hunting station. Not before."

"I remember."

"The bear told the truth. The man inside stayed silent."

This sounded odd. "What do you mean?"

"I mean that I have seen you before. A number of times."

How could I not be curious! "Where?"

"In parades along the streets of Elva. At celebrations in the castle grounds. During the ceremonies when new Guardsmen would take their oaths. You were there with your father, Captain Bevan of the Guardsmen."

I stared at him, not knowing if I should be pleased or afraid. He knew who we were. He must have always known who we were.

"I used to watch for you at each parade," he went on. "Hoping to see you standing along the store fronts somewhere. When I found you, I would wave. But I never knew if you realized I was waving at you."

"I don't understand this," I cried. "Who *are* you?"

"I am the missing. The presumed dead."

He was studying my face, and I was studying his in turn, trying to read the answers in his eyes.

"My father admired your father," he said. "He once told me that Bevan was exceptional, even among such an exceptional company as the Guardsmen. And he knew all of his Guardsmen well."

Understanding hit me like a bolt. "*Dallen?* Prince Dallen? Is it *you?*"

"Yes," he replied, and I heard relief in his voice. "I am here. And the bear is here."

"Then this—this is how the Sender tucked you away! How he kept you safe! How he kept Nally the Dwarf and the others from finding you! But that must mean it wouldn't be safe for them to find you..." My voice trailed away. I was speaking of things I hadn't completely understood until now.

The talk at the inn last night made me fear for him. "They are still searching for you," I said. "I mean, now they are searching for the bear. I think they want to destroy the bear."

"I know," he said. "That's not important. I need to talk to you about my father's death."

My heart began to pound, and I shuddered. But I determined to control myself. "You know exactly what happened on the forest road," I said quietly.

He shook his massive head. "Only some of what happened. But I did see my father die. I saw the blow that killed him. Over and over, I see it still in my mind. I will never stop seeing it."

He looked far out over the treetops as if he were seeing it again, right at the very place the king fell. Perhaps he was. Because for a spell, he did not speak.

I summoned all the bravery I could. "Your Highness,

Captain Mago told all of Guardstown that my father killed your father."

The bear's head swung back to me. A roar came from his throat. "What?!"

The sudden fierceness startled me, and I slid away from him, back along the rocky seat. But the bear demanded an answer.

"What did Mago say?"

I told him. Everything. Everything I had seen and heard that awful day in Guardstown. From the time Rosie first heard the noise in the street, to our passing through Elva's west gate.

The bear looked at me gravely. "And you have lived in the woods, all of you, struggling to survive, with this horrible tale hanging over you."

"Yes," I whispered. I bowed my head because I could not look at him.

"Silvie. Dear one. Your father did not kill his king."

At his words, something broke inside of me. My sobs came in torrents, and I covered my face with my hands.

I had built a stout defense around my heart to protect me from Mago's lie. The defense crumbled at Dallen's words, because I no longer needed it. A bear arm encircled me, and I found my head resting on a strong bear shoulder.

"It's all right, Silvie." A rumble came from deep inside the bear. These weren't Dallen's words anymore. This was the bear. Or—someone talking *through* the bear. Someone stilling my heart.

After a time, I wiped my face on my hands, and we

looked out over the woods of West Rilken from our rocky perch, side by side.

The sun rose higher. Finches and sparrows flew from tree to ground and tree to tree, busily gathering food for their young. Nurturing life while we struggled with memories of death.

"Will you tell me your story now?" I asked him. "My ears are yours, for what comfort they can give."

The bear's head drooped toward the rock-covered ground. Then he raised it and turned to me.

"The only ones of our company on that road were my father and I, two of his attendants, and his six Guardsmen." The bear's words came slowly.

"A messenger brought word early that morning that my brother Ravelin had taken dangerously ill. So we left the rest of our company behind with the slower-moving wagons, in order to make better speed. We hoped not to be too late. We hoped to see him again.

"On the road ahead, my uncle approached with some of the palace guard. Which surprised me. The guard's presence meant that something of serious importance had happened in Elva.

"I think my father felt the same as I did. That my uncle was coming to tell us some dread news. That Ravelin had died before we could reach him."

"Prince Ravelin's flag still flies," I said.

"I know."

Bear rubbed his nose on the back of his paw.

"My father urged his horse forward to meet his brother. Before I could do the same, a spear flew from close behind me. I saw it pierce the center of my father's back. Saw him reel with the blow.

"Another spear flew. I heard the sound of it. I did not see it strike him, because at that instant I was dragged from my horse and into the fringe of the woods.

"A Guardsman had his sword out, but held a shield over me. *Down!* he said. *They'll come for you next.*

"He pulled me to my feet and made a quick motion toward the woods. *Run! They will not get past me.*

"So I ran. Weeping. Angry. Because I wanted to stand with my father. In my dreams since, I realized that the Guardsman knew what I didn't want to know. My father was dead already, and this Guardsman was defending the next king of Rilken."

His muzzle was turned toward me, but I could not see him clearly through my tears.

"I looked back once," Dallen said, "and saw him blocking the route I was taking. Standing between me and my father's murderers. An arrow struck his shield while he stood there.

"Silvie, his helmet was off. He was not an old man, but his hair was almost the color of snow. Just like yours."

"No other Guardsman has that hair, but my father," I said hoarsely. I knew that, for we had lived in Guardstown with them all.

"Yes, Silvie. It was your father who *saved* my life."

My heart swelled, and I rested my hand on the back of his paw.

"When I turned and saw him like that," Dallen went on, "I also saw something else. The palace guard unleashed arrows at the Guardsmen still on their horses, yet not one of them raised a shield in their own defense except your father. They were killed where they sat. Only your father was left at the last."

He moved his head from side to side in disbelief. Then he looked at me. "I turned to run again, so I did not see your father's final stand. I am very sorry. I owe him so much."

I felt numb. But I had to repeat the truth he held out to me.

"My father did not kill King Adare."

"He couldn't have," said Dallen. "The spear came from the other side of me."

"My father did not kill the other Guardsmen."

"No. The palace guard did that."

I had been weeping throughout his story, and tears covered my face again. My precious father was dead. But he had stayed faithful to the last.

Dallen watched me for a long moment, then continued his story.

"A moment afterwards, the forest was filled with growls, and bears burst through the trees."

"The Guardians of Rilken," I said.

"Yes, but I didn't realize that at the time. I was so full of fright that I ran to get away from them, and found myself running faster than I had ever run before. But I was turning in an arc that led me to cross the road again. In my confusion, I thought that if I could catch the palace guard, they would take me safely back to the castle.

"I came out of the trees just as they galloped by. I ran

right out onto the road and chased them. But they did not turn back.

"I dropped on all fours to catch my breath, and the most tormented cry I have ever heard resounded around me. It was like the cry of my soul.

"It was then that I realized I had been running like a bear. Like *this* bear. One of the Guardians of Rilken had swallowed me up somehow, and I was *inside* it, moving with it. I don't understand how it happened. Yet, when I should have panicked, I felt solace.

"We returned to the site where it all happened. Other bears were there, keeping watch over my father's body. Five spears had pierced him. Working together, we pulled them out and laid out his body, as best as bear paws can do. I dropped to my knees beside my father and kissed him. And the bear kissed him with me.

"I spoke to him as the bear wept. *Father, I will bring you justice.* But it was the bear who formed the words in my throat.

"I stayed by my father's side while the other bears attended to the fallen. The horses returned to stand by their dead masters. Even my own came back. The horses had no fear of me, no fear of any of the Guardians. Then the Guardians spread out through the woods, watching.

"And after a long time, the Duke and his men came back.

"They could smell me and see our tracks. I could smell their fear, but beyond that I smelled nothing else. Nothing. No sorrow. No grief. Silvie, they were *not* grieving. They showed no distress at what had happened. My uncle never even looked at his brother.

"The palace guard—those who had served my father for years— behaved like people who had successfully completed their work. I was furious and confused at the same time.

"I lived in the forest after that, as you see me now. Roaming alone with this one bear as my only companion, until I found relief in the company of your family.

"At night, in my dreams, I saw the forest road again and again. And small details arose from my confusion. Details, like the color of your father's hair, so like yours. And with other details, I realized that I had seen the signal given to kill my own father.

"When my father spurred his horse forward, my uncle raised his arm and called out. It looked like a greeting, but immediately the spears flew. As he had surely commanded them to.

"I went to my uncle's manor and marked his trees and columns. I wanted him to know that I had seen. That I was watching him.

"Yesterday, he had my flag lowered, pronouncing me dead." The words came in a growl.

"I'm a prince not twenty years old. My realm and my younger brother are in the control of the man who murdered my father." He turned his head toward Elva.

"The Duke cannot know that *you* are in this bear," I said, "but he must suspect that the bears know what he has done. He has sent out hunters to kill the very Guardians of Rilken!"

"Of course he would," Dallen said. "They are his greatest enemy now."

"But I don't understand how the Guardsmen could

have killed their king. I have lived among them most of my life. None of them could have done what you saw them do! And yet, they did..." My speech trailed away in agony.

The bear looked at me closely. "What do you remember about the Guardsmen before they left, Silvie? Anything at all?"

I struggled to think, to remember as he asked, back to the lifetime of several months ago. "Nothing unusual. Guardsmen coming and going on assignments are part of the life of Guardstown. Even Guardsmen replacing one another on duty is fairly common.

"My father was not originally assigned to go to Tellhaven. But Captain Hurd became desperately ill the night before you all were to leave.

"Rosie and I had already gone to bed when the message came for Papa to prepare to leave the next morning. I was so sleepy when he left that I barely remember saying goodbye to him." My words caught in my throat at this last.

"I don't remember my last words to my father," Dallen said. "We didn't talk much on the road because we were trying to go with all speed. Then in one brief moment, my father was gone." His voice fell away and he lowered his head to his paws.

I gently put my hand on his shoulder, numb with all the grief we shared. We sat thus for a long time as the sun rose higher above the sea of treetops and the tiny noise of men and animals filtered up from the inn far below us.

"What now?" I asked quietly. "What do we do now?"

"I don't know. This bear has had much to do these past weeks. Comfort my grief. Instruct my anger. Keep me alive. And teach me wisdom—such that I thought I had, but had not. I know that he is waiting for a word, for a command. Then he will act. He will tell me then what I must do.

"But I do know this, Silvie. The battle of the Hosts of the North has come to us."

"What do you mean?" I asked. My thoughts went at once to the special armor that only Tellhaven knew how to make. We had none of that in Rilken.

Dallen answered soberly. "The evil that my father meant to fight in the north was already at work in his own kingdom. I wish I could tell you more, but that is all I know."

Sobering as it was, this thought did not surprise me. I had felt the evil since the moment Mago had ridden into Guardstown Square.

But the presence of evil raises fear. A fear that cripples. Hadn't I seen it do that last night in the inn room?

"If the evil has come to us," I replied, "then so must the song."

The bear raised his head slightly to look at me.

I sang part of the Song of the Hosts as the bear and I sat together in the morning breeze. Even though I sang quietly, each word came out into the sunlight, ready for battle.

> *Sing of Strength that shatters darkness,*
> *Of Truth that can't be turned.*
> *Sing of Love that strikes the prowling ones,*

Of Fear it will not learn.
Love that searches, with compassion,
Finds and rescues, triumphs long.
Binds the darkness with great Joy,
And gives to Night this song...

56

Gift of a Painting

Avelyn spent a troubled night. Her dreams disturbed her, and she woke with relief. It was early, and the rest of the women artists still slept. As she tiptoed to the washroom, she gazed at the sleepers wrapped in their blankets in the row of beds. *Did they all have the pearl eyes?*

She washed and dressed as quietly as she could, then let herself out the door. The castle was waking up. Servants flitted down the hallways, carrying ash buckets, pitchers of water, and trays of food.

Down the stairs she went, to the long room with high windows that served as the studio for the castle's many artists. Here, they painted and drew and learned together, practicing techniques and color choices for the all-important mural. After a late night, Avelyn didn't expect anyone else to be in the studio this early, and she was right.

She had come to be alone. She wanted to paint and she wanted to think. And the two activities always went together for her. But her heart and hands longed to work on the portrait of Pate's father. The old captain was the most famous of the older Guardsmen. And one who stood out in her mind as something just and dependable, solid and true.

She had almost finished his portrait. The green of the Guardsman cape had turned out beautifully. Today she would paint his hands. Sketching the injured one had been the hardest part of the piece, but at last she was satisfied with the shape. The injured hand was a powerful symbol of the man's dedication and sacrifice. It was so important to get it just right.

She pulled back the huge curtain, and morning light streamed in. Her work station was just as she left it. Except—her easel stood empty. No wood panel waited there. The painting of Pate's father was gone.

She looked around her workplace frantically, then opened the curtain even wider and looked again. Paint pots with their carefully mixed colors sat in a row. Her palette hung on a hook. Brushes lay in their box, clean and awaiting work. Only the painting was gone.

Perhaps someone from the castle cleaning staff had moved and then misplaced it. That was a slim hope. They rarely came in the studio except to wipe the windows. The artists cleaned everything else.

She walked slowly up and down the rows of easels,

hoping to catch sight of the misplaced painting. She dug through storage chests and fingered through the row of finished pieces waiting for Master Taynor's approval. The painting of the old Guardsman was not anywhere.

In desperation she opened the scrap bin and scanned the pile of worn brushes, torn papers, dirt and dust from the sweeping up. She lifted a fragment of wood out of the pile and stared at it in disbelief. The edges of the piece were splintered, as if someone had struck the wood then ripped it apart. On that scrap of wood was the sword of Pate's father.

After a moment, she dropped it into her deep apron pocket and scrabbled through the pile of debris. There was the piece with his neck and chin. A portion of the precious cape with the perfect color of green she had sought for so long. *Who would dare do such a thing to an artist's work?*

The sound of voices approached. Avelyn dropped the lid to the dustbin and stepped away from it, struggling with her anger.

Henry and Elwin walked in. They had both been trained at the art school in Elva and worked closely with Master Taynor. Elwin moved sleepily and yawned when he saw her. Henry had a hunk of bread in his hand and was chewing.

"You're here early," he said around a full mouth of bread. "Why weren't you at the reception last night?"

She stepped closer, an indignant question about her painting on her lips, when she caught sight of Henry's eyes.

"What is it?" he said. "Why are you staring at me?"

"Oh." She caught herself with great effort. "Nothing." Bravely she smiled. "I—I was just wondering if you left any breakfast for me. I'm starving."

IN THE CORRIDOR PASSAGEWAY, as all the artists began their day's work, Avelyn found Callie on her own scaffolding, painting over the figure of King Adare.

"We have to make some changes," Master Taynor said, his eye on Callie's active brush. "Prince Allard's figure will be there instead. And the palace guard are a more appropriate choice than the old Guardsmen. The result will be much more satisfying." He clapped his hands, a look of great admiration on his face.

But Avelyn watched in horror as the figure of her beloved king—all those months of painstaking brush strokes—disappeared beneath the onslaught of the indifferent beige.

57

A Roofing Accident

As soon as Olivia saw the shoes her maid set out for her, she knew they would not do. "Menta, take these back, and bring my dancing slippers."

"Your dancing slippers? They'll be ruined walking where the building is being done. And you'll need to keep your feet warm. You've been ill all night and all morning. Are you sure you're well enough to go out? Shouldn't you stay in your bed longer, ma'am? Your head was nigh to killing you just an hour ago!"

"Let the slippers be ruined, then," Olivia answered calmly, ignoring Menta's other concerns. "They are the only shoes I have without heels."

"That is true," said Menta, "but your boots would be

so much better on a chilly spring day. You shouldn't even be out of bed, ma'am," she added stubbornly. "You haven't been well."

"I have decided never to wear heels again," said Olivia, just as firm in her stubbornness. "So, until the shoemaker can finish all the new shoes I have requested from him, I will wear dancing slippers."

"Is it all for the Duke's sake, ma'am?"

"Menta—"

"I'm saying nothing about his height, ma'am. Nothing at all! It's just that you have been very concerned about him these last days—"

"Menta!" Olivia said. "I will permit *no* criticism of the Duke. None at all!"

"Yes, ma'am," the maid said humbly. "None meant, ma'am. *Of course*, none meant. Would you wear double stockings then, to protect your feet from the damp? It's going to be muddy where the workmen are."

"Yes, Menta." Olivia turned in her chair and held out a leg toward her maid.

It took too much energy to argue with Menta. Because, in truth, Olivia's head hurt terribly, and at times she felt too weak to stand.

She had lain on her bed for hours, weak and feeling so unlike herself. And then that ever-present headache threatened to crush her. It hurt to think. It hurt to question. Especially to question.

Her mind had turned into a tangle of thorns, and she dared not challenge them. But wasn't a mind made to think? And didn't a sick person naturally try to reason out the cause of their sickness?

Yet, even one question, one gentle thought floating like a soft butterfly into the sea of thorns made the thorns lash like a snake. Her head throbbed as if it had been struck by the points of many knives.

She would question nothing. And keep Menta from questioning too.

THE CLOCK STRUCK three of the afternoon when Olivia walked cautiously into her husband's reception hall. Allard had made his study at one end of it, so he could work at his desk with his back to the large and beautiful mirror he loved. Olivia was happy for him.

He was seated at his desk now, piles of papers in front of him, but he raised his head as she approached. "Ah, Olivia, how delightful that you come on time so regularly now."

"Of course, Allard," she said quietly.

He rose from his seat. Harmon hurried over, draped a cloak around Allard's shoulders, and handed him his hat.

"I hear the day is fine," her husband said. "Let's walk through the gardens on the way to our new east wing."

She did not have the strength, but she readily agreed.

The gravel walks led them through shaped greenery, amidst yellow and purple spring blooms, and trees just beginning to flower. It should be beautiful, but she was too distracted to enjoy it. Sharp edges of gravel poked into the soft dancing slippers as she walked. She tried very hard to pretend they were nothing and walked on, keeping her stride as even and graceful as she could.

Allard took her arm and tucked it in his. "My dear," he began. "An incident has been on my mind for some time. A memory. I must speak of it, because I am so weary of this month of mourning for Adare."

"It will be over very soon," she said.

"It has lasted too long already, and I can barely contain myself. That's why I felt I must have this moment to talk with you."

He slowed his step, and she was grateful. "What memory is distressing you, Allard?"

"I am not *distressed*, Olivia. I am *never* distressed."

"Forgive me!"

"It happened almost twenty years ago, yet I cannot get it out of my mind. The King of Falland honored the royal family of Rilken by inviting us to be his special guests at Falland's famous autumn dances.

"On the third day of the dances before the nightly ball began, young King Theodore asked my brother to see his collection of jeweled treasure chests. We all rose from our chairs at this. Theodore's attendants were ready to accompany their king. But Adare never turned to me, never bade me to come with him. They walked away and left me alone, standing humiliated by my chair." His face darkened at the remembrance. His features took on the harsh lines of anger.

"And this—this is the king everyone prattles on about," he said. "This is the one selected to become *legend* with the Hosts of the North? Legend! This man who thought only of himself and saw no other mortal?

Adare pursued his own glory, as if the planet turned for him alone. How it *pains* me to hear people talk of love for the man. It is more than I can endure!"

Allard waved his free arm to emphasize his angry words, but the movement jerked at her. It was no longer comfortable to have her arm tucked into her husband's. Olivia gently slid her own arm free.

"All these fools going on and on about Adare," he said. "If you had seen me standing there!"

"But I *did*, Allard," she said. "I *was* there. I was sitting next to you when Adare left with Theodore."

He stared at her, incredulous. She would have to supply him with the particulars of proof.

"It was two months before our wedding and Falland's invitation came to me along with the rest of the royal family. Our queen was not feeling well, so she stayed resting in her room. You and I attended Theodore's private dinner with Adare. So, when the kings went off to see the collection together, I was left also."

His mouth set in a firm line, and he began jerking the gloves he held in one hand through the curved fingers of the other. He did not believe her. She struggled to pick words out of her memory, while the thorns threatened her mind.

"At the ball, the men were supposed to choose a lady they were especially fond of for the first dance of the night. You chose a Falland countess, while I, your betrothed, stood aside and watched."

He frowned at her, and her head winced at the prick of an internal thorn. "Olivia, you must know that the whole reason for visiting another court is to engage in every possible way with the royalty and nobility of that particular country. I was serving Rilken. *Obviously,* I would have to dance with the countess."

"Yes, Allard," she answered meekly. "Of course I understand now."

That night had stayed long in her mind. Because the pain of her humiliation had been overshadowed by an act of grace that her heart could never forget.

She had seen Adare—

The thorns suddenly tightened in her head. She bit her tongue to keep from crying out.

No, not Adare. The memory had nothing to do with him because he would have done nothing good.

She said this to herself over and over. Until the pain in her head eased. And she could think clearly again.

They were close to the east wing now. Allard abruptly quickened his steps to speak with the workmen, leaving her behind. She took the opportunity to take a long, slow, deep breath. She would let all such memory go, shove it aside, and turn her attention to the east wing. That was why she had come out on the gravel with bad shoes anyway.

Allard was with the master architect and master mason when she caught up to him, so she stood to one side and watched the activity before her.

Work on the roof was in full earnest. Men crawled along its surface like ants in a garden. Ropes and pulleys worked away, groaning as they lifted slate in buckets from the ground to the workmen far above. From the first rows of slate, one could see how beautiful the finished roof would be.

She marveled at the agile and sure-footed roofing men. Felt dizzy just thinking of working at that height with such heavy materials.

Sudden shouts broke out. A workman tumbled down the broad slant of the roof, limbs flailing in desperation, and plummeted over the edge.

Olivia screamed.

The architect and mason ran towards the place where the man fell. Allard stayed where he was, watching.

Silence hushed them all. Then—unbelievably—a tumult of cheers arose.

"What is it, Allard?" she said, stepping over to him. "What happened?"

"The man's alive," he replied. "He fell into the safety net that the mason strung around the building. The rope was strong enough to catch him."

A strange look of pleasure spread across her husband's face. A look that seemed to have nothing to do with the saved workman. He spoke to himself as if she weren't there.

"A rope strong enough to catch him. Strong enough to break the force of his fall. A rope that nothing can penetrate."

He fell silent and strode forward towards the crowd of men by the net. She lost sight of him as he moved among them. When he returned to her, he laughed exultantly.

"Allard, what is it?" she asked, confused.

"The answer, Olivia. The solution. So very, very simple. Those monstrous bears can't be harmed by arrow or spear, can they? Well, that's no matter now! Forget the arrows. I will trap those beasts instead!

"Nets like these will bring them to my dungeons. Men can take the same ropes that brought my mirror from the hills of Galerine, and work those ropes into nets. Then, finally, all Rilken will see the bears answer to me!"

Olivia smiled at him. Then she shivered with the cold, just as Menta said she would.

58

———

A House in Elva

T he street narrowed as Pate hurried downhill. Houses leaned toward each other as if sharing secrets. When he was younger he used to imagine what they were saying, making up mysterious stories. Now, their closeness reminded him that it was in another cramped street such as this that Ravelin had panicked on his horse and misunderstood the actions of the Guardsmen who had saved him.

The Guardsmen.

Pate could barely believe what had happened to them since.

He knocked on a blue door flanked by large clay flower pots. These pots were usually eager to hold the new colors of spring. Today they cradled boughs of fir and pine. Spring had to wait for mourning.

The door opened. An old woman stood there, short in stature like himself. Wispy white hair poked out from under her kerchief. Her face wrinkled with fine lines. Deeper lines showed that she had once been in the habit of laughing.

She held out her hand to him and he took it. Her fingers felt cool and thin.

"Nana," he said.

"Dearest Pate."

He stepped in. The interior of the house was dim. His grandmother pointed down the hallway that ran from front to back of the small abode.

"He's in the back room," she said quietly. "We couldn't get him upstairs."

Pate kissed her cheek and tiptoed down the passage. At the end of it, on one side, a door stood open. The room had been a small storeroom as long as Pate could remember. Cabinets and chests had held cloth and thread—clothing waiting to be mended and finished pieces waiting for customers to pick them up.

Another chest had been filled with yarn. Nana knit sweaters, caps, socks, scarves, and gloves, selling what she made. People would watch her little front window daily, and as soon as a new cap or pair of socks appeared in it, someone would be knocking on her door asking to buy it.

Once, when he was a boy, Pate had removed the yarn from the chest and climbed in himself. The work of a moment had taken him hours to repair, hours to untangle and wind the yarn again, and then to replace it in the chest in orderly rows.

Today, the chest was still in Nana's old storeroom. But it was holding up one end of a pallet. And on that pallet lay his father. His face gray. Eyes closed and still.

His mother rose silently from a stool next to this makeshift bed, and wrapped her arms around Pate. He hugged her tightly in return, then raised one eyebrow and looked toward the bed.

"His heart." She mouthed the words in reply. "He couldn't bear this, Pate. He collapsed just after we got here."

"Guardstown?" he mouthed back.

Tears spilled from her eyes, and she nodded. She stepped out of the way and pointed to the stool. Pate sat down and studied his father's face.

He knew his father was over seventy years of age, but he had never once thought of him as old. At King Adare's funeral, in his half armor and cape, he had looked as much of a Guardsman as those around him.

Not two years ago his father had still beat him in an arm strength contest, even with just half a hand. The other half had been taken long ago by an assassin, who found his attempt on the king thwarted by a faithful Guardsman.

But now, lying there so still, his revered father looked closer to death than life. Pate wanted to take his father's hand, but it was tucked under the blanket that covered him.

"Poppy?" he said quietly. It was the name Pate had first called his father, in the days when his father would perch his tiny son on his shoulders. Pate would grab onto his father's forehead, and as they walked the streets of Elva, his small heels bouncing on his father's collarbone, Pate had felt all the world was his. All his optimism had come from his father's great height.

He laid his hand gently on his father's shoulder. "Poppy?" he said again.

The eyelids lifted. "Pate?"

Pate tried not to hear the weakness in that voice.

"Poppy, I should have warned you not to crawl into Nana's yarn chest. You'd never fit."

The light words had no effect. His father stared up at the ceiling, unhearing.

"I should have known." His voice creaked like a door askew. "I should have known when I saw what happened to Tara, to that poor woman...when I saw them taking her things, her house...I should have known it would happen to us too."

Pate squeezed his father's shoulder and listened.

"The Guardsmen are all gone, Pate. Dead. Or in prison. They are no more. No more."

The last words came in barely a whisper. His father's eyes closed with a painful grimace. And Pate's heart squeezed tight in his chest.

"Such a horror is unheard of in Kilken," he replied. "There's no talk of it in the castle. Only silence."

He could have said more, but this was not a time for the stirring of angry discussion. Not when any sentence could be his father's last. And it did not appear that his father had heard him anyway.

Pate leaned closer, watching for a sign that his father

still breathed. A slight movement of the blanket rewarded him. Then he leaned back on the stool and clasped his hands around one knee.

He had come hoping to ask his father's advice—to tell him of a daring act that had yielded unexpected knowledge. *What should I do now* was the question he wanted to ask.

But his father was clearly beyond giving advice, and Pate felt the loss acutely. Even his mother and Nana— their hearts so full of sorrow over his father's collapse— could have no energy, no thoughts left to spare for him. His thoughts ran as if he could say them.

Father, the noose is tightening. The same evil that took Guardstown moves through the castle halls.

A Guardsman never runs, you said. And I never will, because the prince needs me. But how I wish there were five more comrades and not just me.

Pate cleared his throat and spoke aloud. "You were right, Poppy. Everything you did for the Guardsmen and for the king was right. I want you to know that. I have always been so proud of who my father is."

No movement came from the bed. Only the slightest indication that breath was still flowing in and out.

Pate watched the breath. Studied his father's face for another quarter of an hour. At last he stood up, bent over, and kissed his father's forehead.

A rustle came from the doorway. His mother was watching him. He went to her and held her more tightly than before.

.   .   .

Pate made his way through the huge castle kitchens, dodging busy workers, until he reached a smaller room where only a dozen aided the castle's master cook in preparing food for the highest nobility and the royal family. An aproned man looked up at his approach. "Ho there, Pate! Are you here for the prince's tray?"

"Not yet," he replied. "The prince is asleep. But Lord Locke is busy in the library and asked me to bring his dinner to him."

"Lord Locke?" the castle cook himself came forward. "Not the prince?"

Pate shook his head. "Prince Ravelin is asleep and will not need his tray for another hour's half at least. Lord Locke, however, is already past hungry and is becoming quite irascible. I dare not return to him without food in my hands."

Cook nodded and turned, calling out instructions to those behind him.

In a few moments, Pate was carrying the heavy tray up the back stairs. He passed the library floor and took the tray all the way up to Ravelin's room. Wells let him in, and Pate carried it right to Ravelin's bed. Ravelin stirred and sat up in surprise.

"Come, good prince," Pate said, with as much cheer as he could manage. "See what I have done. Come, Wells, you look too. This is a tray meant for Lord Locke, but I have brought it to you."

Ravelin was fully awake now, consternation pushing his sleepiness aside. Wells placed pillows behind his back to help him sit comfortably.

"Why is this, Pate?" Ravelin asked.

"Just an experiment of mine, Your Highness. Yesterday, when I so playfully invited Petronia and the Duchess to share your luncheon tray? It was to ask a question I had. Today I got my answer. Both of those royal women fell ill afterwards, and Petronia is still keeping to her bed.

"So, tonight I'm asking another question. Tonight, I brought Lord Locke's tray to you, and I will take your tray to him. I wonder how he will feel in the morning."

Ravelin was staring at him, comprehension growing in his eyes.

Pate lifted the lids off the plates with a theatrical swoop of the arm. "Pigeon stew, Your Highness." He silently watched the prince take a mouthful.

Ravelin chewed and swallowed it. "Not bad." He scooped another spoonful and looked at Pate. "I expected you to make a joke about what message this poor pigeon failed to deliver before becoming part of my stew."

"I cannot help but think she is delivering it now, sir."

Ravelin raised his eyebrows. "This is about something more than suspicion, isn't it? What else do I need to know?"

"Cook's eyes had an unusual look to them tonight."

Ravelin lowered his spoon. "A look of pearl?"

Pate nodded. "I don't know how long they have been that way, but I suspect sometime before the Duke's reception. Perhaps about the time of your first spell. There must be some innocent-looking herb that can make the heart race."

Ravelin and Wells both stared at him.

"I never thought..." said Ravelin, his voice trailing away. "I mean, I thought it was a return of the winter sickness. Made worse by grief. I—I..." His gaze dropped to his plate as if he had never seen it before.

"We'll know more once we hear how Lord Locke spends his night," said Pate.

A HALF HOUR LATER, Pate returned to the kitchen and took Ravelin's tray to Lord Locke in the library. That noble lord was irritated to hear that the pigeon stew was not available because the pigeons were off. But Pate assured him of the cook's apologies and presented him with some of the favorite dishes of the royal family. He waited until the mollified lord began to use his spoon and knife.

Pate returned to Ravelin's room and spent the evening with him until the prince prepared to sleep. Pate wished him good rest and wearily climbed the stairs to his own abode. He was relieved to be alone at last, alone to think about his own sorrow.

On the landing, before the last flight of stairs to his room, stood four members of the palace guard. Two had swords in hand. Two others raised their bows, arrows notched and ready. All were aimed at him.

Pate took a deep breath. "Ah, gentlemen, welcome. I see the dance you have planned for me, but where are the ladies?"

MINUTES LATER, Pate was shoved into a dungeon cell in the castle's depths. The heavy door with its tiny window was locked and barred behind him. The sound of the bar falling into place echoed around the small stone room.

"It wasn't instant death, at least," he said to himself. "And this accommodation may be larger than my own father's current bedroom. I have a plank bed, no doubt made from the finest imported mahogany, and judging from the smell, a waste hole in that corner. Oh, but the sound of rustling in the dimness makes me wish for my cat!"

He lay down on the bench on his back and put one arm behind his head. A small barred window was cut in the stone wall far above him, but no light came through it now. The only light that penetrated this gloom came from the lantern hung on a hook outside his door.

He lay there for a long time, looking up into the darkness. Feeling the weight of the castle stone pressing into the earth. Feeling the silence and lostness of the dungeon depth. Until it was almost too much for him.

"Well, Pate, my lad," he said. The words echoed slightly off the dismal stone that surrounded him. "At least you were useful."

IN THE MORNING, the news was spoken of among the dungeon guards, for everyone in the castle freely shared any gossip they had heard from any other part of the castle. Pate heard it along with his morning gruel, received from the hand of the grimiest and lowliest of dungeon servants. The old man's one delight at that moment was to have someone lower than himself that he could announce the news to, as if he were an esteemed town crier.

The man chose his words poorly and spoke them with such a slurred northern accent through the few remaining teeth he had, that it took some time for Pate to understand them. But at last he realized this much.

Lord Locke had died during the night of a heart attack.

59

An Unnerving Command

The three of us sat close together, shut away in our small room in the inn, while I told them Dallen's story. That he was indeed in the bear, and the Guardian of Rilken was keeping him safe.

We spoke in hushed voices. Rosie sat on the hearth, her back to the fire. Mama was in the room's one chair, her sewing in her lap. I placed myself on the small rug between them. So close together that with a tilt of my head I could have rested it on Mama's knee.

When I repeated Papa's last words—*Run! They will not get past me*—we cried openly together.

"That is just what your papa would say. And just what he would do." Mama spoke quietly.

"Papa saved the Prince of the Crown," Rosie whispered. "*Saved* him! Mago was lying all the time, and the Duke must have told him to do it!"

"But what would make the Guardsmen do the unthinkable?" Mama said.

"I can't begin to know," I said. "Every possibility comes up wanting. We know these men. Nothing makes sense!"

Mama shook her head and began to move her needle again. She had come to the end of the linen strip she was working on and had begun to outline the picture of the rabbit she put on each piece.

"Ravelin doesn't know that Dallen is alive, does he?" Rosie asked. She stared down at her hands. "He must think his brother's dead."

"According to Crim, the people of Elva *do* believe Dallen is dead," Mama said. "The proof that they had came from the castle."

"Then Ravelin is all alone," said Rosie. "I can't stand that. Ever since I met him at his tenth birthday— remember that tradition? On the castle lawn? When all the nine- and ten-year-olds in Elva came to the castle grounds to celebrate with the prince?" She glanced at us.

"Silvie would have gone to Dallen's celebration," Mama said, "but they didn't hold the event when he was ten because the queen was so ill."

"But I remember you going to Ravelin's party, Rosie," I said. "I remember helping you get dressed for it."

Rosie nodded. "I've thought about it so much since then. Especially when Prince Ravelin walked among us all, taking everyone's hand. Thanking us. Wishing us good birthdays of our own.

"He was so careful, so attentive to each of us. He seemed so sincere, and—and good. He had just grasped the hand of the boy next to me, and I was going to put mine out when the music began, calling everyone to refreshments.

"But Ravelin didn't turn away. He made sure to take my hand and those next to me before inviting us to follow him to the cakes. He turned to lead the way and I followed, keeping him in sight for as long as I could. I've cared for him specially ever since." She blushed. "I know it must sound silly, but—"

I interrupted her. "You've never been silly, Rosie. Purposeful always. Never silly."

Rosie looked at me gratefully.

"Ravelin *meant* his good wishes," she said. "You could just see it. He cared about everyone."

"I've seen that in him too," Mama said.

"Ever since then, I've watched for him in Elva, prayed for him when he was sick, and thought about him so very much. Do you know how much I like the song 'Sing Me High'?"

"Yes," I replied. "Papa liked that song."

"It's also one of Ravelin's favorite songs. They sang it at his birthday party."

I had never guessed. I thought about all the times she had sung that song. Had she been thinking of Ravelin too, every time?

"Lucky Ravelin to have a staunch friend like you," I said sincerely.

"Yes," Mama agreed.

Rosie turned to poke at the fire. "He must be in danger. I wish I could help him now," she said quietly.

I watched her work at the fire, thinking about everything she had said.

"Where is our Bear?" Rosie asked, pushing at a log with the fire iron.

"I don't know. He said he'd be careful. He said we weren't to worry because he can smell the hunters at a distance eighty times farther than their arrows can fly."

Rosie's poker hovered in the air with astonishment. "Really?"

"Which means he will always know where they are, and they won't be able to reach him. He said they've shot arrows at him before, but the arrows just bounce off."

We sat thus for a long time, speaking quietly by the fireside, Mama's embroidery occasionally idle in her lap. So many things had to be talked through to be understood.

The Duke had killed his own brother, and—against everything that was possible—used the Guardsmen to do it. And then had turned on all of Guardstown.

Dallen was safe at the present moment, but Ravelin couldn't be. What must be happening in Elva Castle now? As we worked through these things, a knock came on the door, startling all of us.

"Tara?" a woman's voice called. "Alta wants you in the kitchen."

Mama opened the door. "I'll be right along, Dona. Thank you."

AFTER TAKING a few moments to wash her face and make herself more presentable, Tara descended the back stairs to the kitchen. The request struck her as odd. If Alta wanted to see her privately, she would have asked to see her in the small room with table and chairs that she used as an office. But no, Alta was indeed in the kitchen. Pacing back and forth in front of the huge kitchen hearth, and wringing her hands.

"Tell her," said Ettie, who was cracking a basket of eggs one at a time into a large bowl at her worktable. "Just tell her."

"Is it something about Darrit?" Tara asked. "Is Darrit all right?"

"Darrit's fine," said Ettie. She nodded toward Alta as if encouraging her to speak.

"An unexpected guest arrived today," Alta said. "The Earl of Sormin is staying in a room upstairs with his son. They left Elva early this morning, but their carriage broke down on the road nearby, so they and their whole retinue are here."

"That's good, isn't it?" Tara asked in a bright voice. "Did they like the room we've finished?"

"They came from the *palace*," Nissa put in, as if she hadn't heard Tara's question.

Alta didn't answer the question either, but instead looked to Ettie for support. Something had severely shaken the innkeeper.

"He *did* like the room, didn't he?" Tara asked again.

It was Ettie who answered. "He likes the room fine

enough, but he *loves* the embroidery. And that's under-stating it."

Tara looked at Alta, feeling waves of alarm. "He's not going to steal it, is he?" she whispered.

Alta finally spoke. "It's not the linens he wants. It's you."

"*Me?*" Tara gaped at her.

Alta and Ettie both nodded. Nissa sat motionless in front of the butter churn, hands on the paddle, staring at all of them.

"What do you mean he wants *me*?" said Tara.

"He wants to take you with him when he leaves tomorrow," Alta answered. "I'm supposed to send you up to him at once. He'll be leaving in the morning, as soon as his carriage is mended."

Alta was now looking at Tara with something like defensiveness. The thought struck Tara that the innkeeper thought she was going to abandon her, that Tara was going to leave with the project not yet complete. Alta's dream undone.

"But I can't—" Tara began.

"It would be quite a privilege to sew for an earl," said Ettie.

"I suppose it would be," said Tara, feeling bewildered. "But I'm not going to sew for this person no matter who he is."

Alta stared at her in disbelief. "You can't mean that?"

"Of course I do. I can't leave here now. I'm not ready to. And I don't just go off with strangers. I've got my daughters to think about."

Nissa stared at her, openmouthed. "You're going to tell him that?"

"Right now. You put him in the largest room, I suppose?" Tara looked at Alta.

"But he's an *earl!*" said Alta, with a low moan. Fear had returned. Perhaps now, fear of what the earl would do to the inn if they would not relinquish their embroiderer.

"I've seen earls before," said Tara. She pushed open the kitchen door and began to mount the back stairs. But before she reached the top, she stopped. Her courage had begun to slide away.

Who is this Sormin? Bevan had the names and places of the nobility memorized. But Tara could remember nothing about this earl. *What kind of man is he? Is he honestly offering me a good position, willing to be patron for an artist? What would he do if I refused? Would he just take me, kidnap me? Does he have the power to do that? What of Silvie and Rosie?*

With a pang, Tara remembered that she was not the wife of a Guardsman any longer, and that legacy brought protection no more. No, she was just a woman with a needle, working at the local inn. And that's all she was. A woman watching out for her daughters while trying to manage her way through a cloud of griefs and wonders.

Yet, could she possibly learn anything about what was happening in the castle from this nobleman who had just come from the there? She stood on the back staircase, frozen in thought. On impulse, she turned, went back down the stairs, and jerked open the kitchen door.

"Ettie," she cried. "Please come with me!"

Ettie stared at her. An egg yolk fell from the shell in her hands and plopped into the bowl.

"Please, Ettie!" Tara pleaded. "Because—because you can always tell."

The cook blinked, then abruptly wiped her hands. "Nissa, finish cracking these and make sure that not one bit of shell gets into this bowl." She whisked off her apron, washed her hands carefully in the sink, smoothed her hair, and came over to Tara.

"I'm ready. What do you want me to say?"

"Just watch and listen for whatever is true and whatever isn't."

"Right."

Ettie followed her up the stairs. "I don't look fitting to meet an earl," she whispered.

"Neither do I," Tara replied over her shoulder. "But that doesn't matter now."

They started down the long upstairs passage. Silvie and Rosie had the door cracked, and peered through the slim opening as they went by.

At the far end of the hall, the corridor turned to the left. A footman stood stiffly outside one of the larger guest rooms. Tara went up to him.

"I'm here to see the Earl of Sormin. He is expecting me."

The footman nodded. He gave Ettie a look. "And who is this? Is the earl expecting her?"

"She is my helper," Tara answered firmly. "The earl will want to see us together."

The footman nodded and rapped on the door.

"Come!" came a bellow from within.

The footman opened the door and stepped aside.

Tara heard Ettie suck in her breath, and they walked in together.

THE ROOM WAS familiar to Tara, of course. She had helped Alta and the seamstress set out the embroidered pieces in a pleasing way, in order to spread their beauty through the whole chamber. A large canopied bed stood on one wall, an oak desk and chair on another, and a fireplace on a third, with armchairs at either side. In one of these armchairs sat the Earl of Sormin.

He was a big, broad, heavily bearded man, but what Tara noticed first was that he held the embroidered mantel cover from above the fireplace in his lap. His thumb and fingers slid rapidly over the raised design of the cloth, as if he were counting money. She wondered if he had washed his hands before touching it.

As Tara and Ettie stepped forward, the earl glanced at Tara, then at Ettie, then back to Tara, suspicion in his eyes.

"Which one of you stitched the design on this cloth?"

"I did, Your Lordship," Tara replied.

He turned all his attention on her. "You are the one who made this moon glow as if it were real?"

"I cannot make a moon glow, sir. I only stitched the design."

He held up the mantel cover. "But everything on this piece looks *alive*. Every piece of embroidery in this whole room looks alive!" He stared at Tara, waiting for some explanation.

She opened her mouth and closed it again, unsure of what to say.

Ettie spoke up. "It always looks that way when she stitches, Your Lordship. The thread comes to life in her hands."

A gleam appeared in the earl's eyes. "Then you are exactly what I want. You will now become my master embroiderer, a position above all my other artisans. Pack your things. Gather whatever belongings you have. You will leave with me in the morning."

Tara bowed slowly. "I thank you for the compliment, my lord. It would be a high honor indeed to work for you. But I regret that I am not at liberty to take your offer."

The man rose from his chair and scowled at them. He was even taller than he first appeared.

"What is this babble about liberty?" he said, in a voice suddenly belligerent. "I've offered you a position, and you will come with me. Who dares to hold you back?"

Fear flashed in her, but anger rose to take its place. An anger that lent fire to her determination.

"It is true that I am an embroiderer, but I am also a servant of the king. I oversee some property that is valuable to him."

Sormin frowned at her. "King? What king?"

"I work for the one who rules all of Rilken. You know who I mean." She could not mention Dallen, so this was all she could say. The last best argument she had.

Sormin stepped back. He looked suddenly uncertain. "You are speaking of the Duke, of course?" he asked in a moderate, even humble, tone.

She hadn't been, but a mention of the Duke had brought about such a change in his demeanor that she held his gaze and waited.

The earl winced, carefully folded the mantel cloth, and laid it over the back of the chair. "I will never interfere with anything the Duke wishes," he said civilly. "You may go."

The footman opened the door for them, and they were once again out in the passage, turning down the long hallway.

After they were out of sight of the earl's rooms, Tara took a deep breath and shook the tension from her hands and wrists. She felt like a prisoner freed. Ettie did not seem to share her relief.

"What is it, Ettie? Did you notice something?"

Ettie nodded slowly. "But I can't figure it out."

"Come to my room and tell me."

"We've been to see the Earl of Sormin," Tara said to the girls when the door opened, and she and the cook hurried inside. "He's just come from the palace, and Ettie noticed something."

In only a moment, Ettie was in the chair by the fire, and all three of them were sitting on the floor eagerly waiting for her to speak.

"Was he telling the truth, Ettie?" Tara asked.

"That's the question I'm struggling to answer. He told you to come with him and you said no. That part seemed clear enough."

Silvie's eyes widened at this. Rosie gripped her sister's hand.

Ettie went on. "It was when you said *why* that I heard it."

"Heard what?"

"I swear he began to sound like a lerin dwarf."

"Did he? I think I was too frightened to notice anything."

"It was around when you said you were a servant of the king. When he spoke next, a kind of buzzing started. It was faint, but it was there. And when he said he would never interfere with the Duke, it got louder.

"I've never heard the like before. I mean, when a mining dwarf has been filled with lerin, it affects all of him. It's not here one time and gone another. But this earl—" She shook her head slowly, absorbed in the puzzle of it.

"And yet, his last words weren't a lie," Tara put in. "He *did* let us go."

Ettie stood up. "We can't be sure until he's gone. Be careful. Stay in this room. Lock the door. I'll bring your dinner to you myself." At the door she paused. "I'll put Gareth and the others on watch. Don't leave this room until Jarlath tells you that this man and all his company are truly gone."

After Ettie left, Tara stood with her back to the

closed door and told her girls the details of Sormin's request, including his abrupt change of mind.

"So the earl wouldn't go against anything the Duke said," Silvie repeated thoughtfully.

"But why would a mighty earl sound like a mining dwarf?" asked Rosie.

"And especially when he thought you were serving the Duke, Mama," Silvie said. "Is there some connection between the Duke and this lerin?"

"Redmond thought the Galerines might have discovered something *worse* than lerin," Tara said.

"But lerin makes a person lie," said Rosie, "and you said that he let you go, just as he said he would."

"What if—whatever it is—it makes a person lie to their own minds?" said Silvie. "A lie *inside* their own minds. And they wouldn't know they were lying, just like the lerin dwarfs don't know. What if the earl believes he wants to do whatever the Duke wishes?"

"He winced, Silvie," Tara said. "The earl winced as if he were in physical pain when he thought he was about to go against the Duke."

Rosie shuddered. "That's horrible!"

"It is," Silvie said gravely. "But horrible things have been happening. Bear said an evil of a kind the Hosts fight was working here already in our country. He could have meant this."

"And if the Duke has this kind of power over an earl," Rosie began.

"Could he have had this kind of power over the other Guardsmen?" said Silvie. "Making them do whatever he wished without them knowing it?"

Rosie's eyes shot fire. "And punishing all of Guard-stown for it afterwards!"

Tara sat down in the chair, her heart heavy with the weight of it all. "Those poor, poor men," she whispered. "What must have been done to their minds?"

Her head spun with the implications of everything they had learned that day. Rosie and Silvie stood nearby, eyes on her, waiting for her to say something more, perhaps give some direction to them, or suggest what they should do. Her mind staggered with fresh grief, and all she could think of was this.

"Jarlath said that truth died before the king ever went down the forest road."

Silvie rested a hand on her shoulder. "Jarlath was right."

60

———

Ravelin Alone

Wells sat on his stool in the middle of Prince Ravelin's wardrobe room. Ravelin was resting, and all was quiet in his chambers except for the scratching of a mouse somewhere behind the boards of the wardrobe.

Wells held an empty wooden box in his hands. A box that should have contained a pair of Ravelin's hunting gloves. They had been stolen, to be sure. And Wells believed that one of these gloves had been used to show faulty proof of Dallen's death. The whole castle believed that Dallen was dead now.

If the Duke knew the glove was a lie, why would he lie to Ravelin at just that precise moment? The worst time to show a young man something of his brother's blood would be before his own father's funeral. Had the Duke wanted his nephew so shaken as to give up hope?

Had he worked to frighten him into his collapse—a collapse that poison prolonged—so that the people would see the weakness of the prince? And, unthinking, give their allegiance to the Duke?

Yes and yes.

Wells could see it all so clearly. But what to do now?

The mouse scratched industriously in the depths behind the wardrobe walls, in the old unused servants' passage, from the days when monarchs did not want to see their servants in the castle hallways. Instead, the servants had to run their errands inside the walls of a dark labyrinth, until King Adare's father put an end to it.

Now servants hurried down the sides of the hallways while castle residents and guests used the broad middle. So much nicer than before. The old passages were rarely used. But that was not what Wells wanted to think about just now.

The mouse scratched again, and Wells determined to ignore it. As long as it stayed on the other side of the wall, that is. The last thing he wanted was a mouse in the prince's wardrobe.

A loud scratch was followed by the sound of a mewing cat. Wells stood up and put the empty box away. The cat he could not ignore. Pate's cat could have found its way into the labyrinth and if it didn't find its way out, it would die there.

Wells cleared the boxes from the front of the door to the old passage, turned the key that never left the lock, and opened the door to see the cat—in Miss Avelyn's arms. A look of deep distress was on her face.

"Miss Avelyn!"

"Please, Wells. I must speak to you. The palace guard has taken Pate, and I don't know where he is. I would have come to the prince's door, but the palace guard lines the hall, so I dared not approach that way."

Wells felt stricken. "They've taken Pate?"

Tears filled her eyes. "Please, tell the prince. Maybe he can free Pate."

Wells nodded thoughtfully, but could give no words of honest hope.

"Pate was right," Avelyn continued. "The artists—every one of them has the pearl eye. I'm not allowed to paint King Adare anymore. To do any painting unless I see the Duke personally. I'm scared, Wells. And I'm worried about Pate and about his cat. At least I could bring the cat to you."

She held it out and Wells took it in his arms at once.

"But, what will you do, Miss Avelyn?"

"I don't know, Wells. I don't know where to turn. Where to go. Except to tell the prince."

He looked into her face and knew what the prince would have him do.

"May I suggest something?" Holding the cat in one arm, Wells reached for a small box half hidden on the wardrobe shelves and lifted its lid. "I think it safest for you if you leave the castle at once. The old servants' tunnel could take you to a place where you could emerge into the castle grounds without much notice. If you are stopped, tell them you are on an errand for the prince."

He placed a good amount of coins into her hand, and her eyes widened. "This money is yours," he said firmly. "A gift from the prince. Use it to go somewhere you will be safe. Prince Ravelin would wish it, I know."

"Thank you, Wells. Please—please, thank him with all my heart."

"I will, miss."

As she turned to go into the dimness, he said, "Dear Miss Avelyn, take care!"

A rustle of skirts and she was gone.

RAVELIN HAD NOT BEEN RESTING. He had been reading. He sat in his bed, unusually alert. For the first time in weeks, his mind felt like itself and that brought relief.

He was grieving, he was deeply troubled, but he was not inherently weak. Through his uncle's machinations, he had been kept in a weakened state, doubting himself, walking dark paths in his mind, despairing of life. Pate and Wells had kept him from complete despair. And so had that curious piece of embroidery his mother had begun long ago, a piece some unseen hands seemed intent on finishing now.

He had not told Wells about the glowing moon that night of the storm, waiting instead for his attendant to discover it too. Since then, a golden sun had appeared in the linen sky. Roses grew under the forest trees. And another rabbit had appeared next to the one his mother had made. This new rabbit looked thoughtful, dignified, and very capable.

The picture was telling him a story, even though he didn't know what it was saying. But each time he stopped to gaze at it, his spirits lifted. His mind felt clearer.

Two books lay on the blanket next to him. One had belonged to his father. *The Thoughts of Kings*, by Professor Samuel Redmond, University of Tellhaven. The other, *Tales from Nordia*, came from Dallen's library. It had been a gift from the Duke of Nordia himself when Dallen turned ten. Looking through their books made it seem as if his father and brother were still with him.

He opened his father's and saw again the name on the flyleaf, written with his father's own hand. With his favorite oak-gall ink. A wave of sadness smote Ravelin, and he almost closed the book. He took a deep breath and turned the pages slowly.

This had been one of his father's favorites in recent years. Ravelin had seen it in his hands often. Whenever his father read it, he looked thoughtful. A marked passage caught Ravelin's eye.

"The hatreds of individuals affect families and destroy communities. The hatreds of monarchs affect whole peoples, kill thousands, and destroy countries. The greater one's responsibility, the greater the need to disrupt one's own hatreds."

Ravelin lowered the book and thought. *The need to disrupt one's own hatreds.* His father had practiced this. Always. And taught his sons to do the same, especially when they were at odds with each other.

One night when Dallen was fifteen and Ravelin only twelve, his father had sat in this very room as late as midnight with an angry Dallen and a sullen Ravelin, talking through the events of the day that had brought about such hostility. He remembered his father's determined patience as he listened to Ravelin's story and then Dallen's.

His father hadn't stopped there with some dismissive judgment of his own. Instead, he had stayed two hours, teaching his sons to ask questions of each other. Leading them to listen carefully to the answers. Back and forth. Giving them time to think their way through to friendship again. Giving them a different way to see.

To see that there was something greater than the issues surrounding the chestnut gelding, issues Ravelin had long since forgotten. And that greater thing was the treasure of a brother, a treasure meant to be kept for one's whole life.

Ravelin put the first volume down and picked up Dallen's book. After studying the familiar cover for a long time, he turned to one of his favorite stories about The Fearless, a story that captivated him. Every human can be fearless at certain times, with certain tasks. When need comes, boldness can wipe away any thought of fear. But, according to this story, The Fearless were never, ever afraid. Never. *Why was that?*

He leaned back against the pillows and concentrated on the story. More than ever, he needed to be fearless, not foolish, in the face of hatred. This would take more wisdom than he had.

The sound of a subdued cough caught his ear, and he turned to see Wells holding Pate's cat.

RAVELIN GRIPPED the book of Nordian tales in his hands. "Pate is in the dungeon? What on earth for?" Ravelin stared at his attendant. "And you tell me that he was *right*? Lord Locke *is* dead? Wells, that was meant to be *me*!" He felt his heart begin to race.

Wells seemed thoughtful. "The substance may have worked rather swiftly on him. Your aunt and cousin were ill but are recovering, I believe."

"Petronia, Olivia, and Locke only ate from my food once. I must have eaten it any number of times!"

"Your Highness is very strong and resilient," Wells said firmly.

"I'm sure this frustrates my uncle," Ravelin said wryly. "If the corridor outside my rooms are filled with palace guards, why don't they burst in here and finish me with their swords?"

Wells looked grieved at this. Ravelin motioned to him. "Here, give me that cat." The cat leapt into Ravelin's arms and immediately curled up on his lap. He stroked the soft warm fur.

"Your Highness, forgive such dark speculation, but it seems that your uncle needs the removal of your person to look as natural as possible." Pain tightened Wells' face as he spoke. "I believe it is because you have a great deal of power in your person. That is, you and your brother are more loved by the people of Elva and of Rilken than you realize.

"The Duke must suspect that this esteem is a greater force than his mirror. It is a love he cannot yet control. As far as I know, he would not be able to crowd every resident of the capital city into his reception room and have them look into his mirror."

Ravelin looked at him closely. The tone in his voice gave him hope. "Do you have a plan, Wells? Something in mind?"

"I would be reluctant to suggest anything that might increase the danger to Your Highness. But, while we think, I believe I may follow Miss Avelyn's example and use the old passageways to get food directly from the castle bakery and meat stores. You will need your strength, sir. That is of paramount importance."

"You will need yours as well," Ravelin replied.

"Thank you, sir. I will take that into account." While he spoke, Wells crossed the room, opened a chest that sat against the wall, lifted out a polished scabbard, and brought it to Ravelin.

"May I place your sword behind this bedside table, sir, so it will be nearby should you need it? Within reach?"

Ravelin nodded without speaking. The sword. Did he even now have strength to defend himself?

"And I will lock all the doors as well before I go."

Ravelin watched his attendant secure everything, then disappear into the wardrobe. A faint creak told him that Wells had entered the old passageway.

Ravelin sighed and stroked the cat on his lap. A wave of sorrow rose in him and crashed painfully into the corners of his heart.

"We have to save your master, Cat. But I can't begin to think of what to do."

The cat raised its head and blinked at him. He pretended he could understand the look in her eye.

"You ask me what I need?" he said. "Strength. Wisdom. Fearlessness. Opportunity. Food." He paused, barely able to go on. "My brother. Your master. My father. The Bears of Rilken."

The truth of it all threatened to crush him. He had been cut off from almost everyone he trusted. And the Duke even now sought to take his life. He felt himself sink into despondency. The cat put a paw on his arm and looked up at him.

"I can't outsmart him, Cat. He has closed every avenue." But even as he said this, Wells' voice came back to him. *You are more loved by the people of Elva and Rilken than you realize.*

"But they are out there, Wells," he said to his absent attendant. "And I am in here." He could no longer speak for the sorrow of it.

Avelyn emerged from the castle walls into a potting area by the kitchen garden. She brushed the dust from the unused corridors off of her skirts and sleeves quickly, then took a firm, purposeful step through the gardens and to the servants' entrance to the castle. The gate guards noticed her, but merely nodded, and then she was through and out onto the streets of Elva.

At first she could not think of where to go. Guardstown had been destroyed or she would have gone to see Pate's parents. Would she be able to find her way to his grandmother's house, even though she had only visited there once? At least she remembered which neighborhood it was in. Once there she could ask someone. The neighbors would know.

She set off at a brisk pace down the cobblewalk, intent on her purpose, when the sound of a horn startled her. She darted into the door of a shop just as a carriage went by. Its footmen wore the Duke's blue and black cloaks, but their heads boasted new hats of green on green. The Duke himself.

She gripped the door handle and took a slow breath. *Of course the Duke would not go in person to seek a runaway artist.* He would have some greater reason for taking out his carriage and livery.

"May I help you, miss?"

Avelyn turned to find that she had darted into a bakery. A gray-haired woman in a flour-covered apron stood behind a wood counter and baskets filled with breads.

"Oh—oh yes," Avelyn replied, closing the door to the street. Composing herself, she bent and pretended to examine the breads.

"A loaf of the almond bread, please," she said without thinking, and reached into her pouch for one of Wells' coins.

The woman slid the loaf into a small, woven sack and handed it to her. Avelyn took one look at Pate's favorite bread and burst into tears.

61

A Visitor at the Narrows

The old Guardsman captain lay on a bed in a converted storeroom in his mother-in-law's small home, listening.

For years—decades—he had trained groups of new Guardsmen in this practice of listening. And listen they did.

For hours.

Day after day, week after week, they listened, until they could distinguish the sound of an arrow from a spear in flight. Blindfolded.

Determine the number of horsemen and the direction they were riding from. Blindfolded.

Distinguish the gait of an individual horse and estimate its speed. Blindfolded.

Determine the number of men marching. Determine the number of men shouting. Without sight.

Determine the direction from which an arrow had been fired. And much more. By hearing alone.

The old captain knew that his heart was damaged. That it was weak. And though he did not speak of it, he knew he would not live long. But his ears, his ears still heard everything.

The light scraping sound of knitting needles.

The stirring of a pot over the cooking fire, even which spoon Nana was using. The dull scrape of the wooden spoon. The sharp scrape of the steel.

The creak of a door, each door unique in the sound it made.

The different dogs that spoke in the night.

And the sound of his dear wife's crying when she went upstairs to hide her tears.

He had been so tired since his collapse. The days and nights both brought sleep. Both brought wakefulness. And memories.

Some memories he had to refuse. They troubled his chest and hastened the day that would make his dear Mary cry without ceasing. With effort, he banished the murders at Guardstown from his mind, and led it to other remembrances instead.

Like the day he first saw Mary. She was helping her mother at their knitting stall in the city market. The injury to his hand had just made him retire from active guarding duty to become a recruiter and trainer.

At forty-five he was no longer a dashing young swain. But he was ready for marriage at last. And somehow—*somehow*—a delightful smile filled Mary's lovely eyes when she saw him. He needed gloves or mittens. Something that could work with the crippled shape of his hand.

Mary sat right down on a stool in the stall and knit one that would fit him. He watched fascinated as color and warmth grew under her fingertips. He stayed by her side and talked with her the whole time she worked. By the time the mitten was finished, he knew he wanted her and only her for the rest of his life.

He thought of their wedding in Guardstown Hall, which the king himself had attended. Of Pate's birth. A son, so very tiny. So clever at such a young age. Quick to see and understand. As quick as a Guardsman.

The captain took a deep breath. Slowly. Gently.

A knock sounded on the front door. A knock that had the sharpness of authority behind it. He heard Mary's quick step and the sound of the door opening.

Voices. Hers and...

His chest began to tighten.

Calm. Calm. A Guardsman knows how to be calm in the presence of an enemy.

He was watching for her when she entered the small room where he lay. She swiftly knelt by his bed. Her face close to his. Her eyes large and frightened.

"My love," she whispered. "The Duke of Elva is here. He said he will see you even though you are ill. I told him I must get you ready to receive visitors."

"Mary," he whispered back, drinking in the life from

her beautiful eyes. "You must do something for me. After you show him in, go immediately. Take Nana to the home of Gerald the Mason. Tell him that I say you have need of his cellar. He will hide you there."

Her eyes widened even more.

"I—I can't leave you," she said, clinging to his shoulder.

"It's the only way—the last way—I can protect you," he said.

"But—"

"Mary. Love. No one ever disobeys a Guardsman."

She closed her mouth and nodded once. Then kissed him firmly on his forehead. Got to her feet. Touched his lips with her fingers. And left the room.

Her tread went down the hallway. Her light voice spoke some words. Then, a heavier, slower tread approached. Someone stood in the doorway looking down at him. He didn't care. He stared at the ceiling of the little room, listening for a sound that meant more to him than anything. He could barely breathe until he heard it.

The front door creaked open again. A pause long enough for two women to exit through it. The creak of its closing.

He shifted his head slightly on the pillow and turned his gaze to the Duke of Elva.

"I AM unable to rise in order to bow to you."

The Duke walked into the middle of the small storeroom. His presence felt oppressive. "You wouldn't bow anyway." He tested Mary's stool, pushing on it with a firm hand, then sat on it with a swirl of his green cape.

"Why have you come?" The captain's voice was softer than he wished.

Hate was in the Duke's eyes. "To make some things perfectly clear to you," he said proudly.

The captain waited.

"You are looking at the reason you lost part of your hand all those years ago. You are looking at the incident on the Leibent road when the Guardsmen protected the king from 'robbers.' Yes," the Duke nodded slowly. "I can be as tenacious and patient as your famous Guardsmen. But I am infinitely more clever. Who else could make the Guardsmen kill their own king?"

The old captain had nothing to reply. Nothing to do but practice a Guardsman's calm. This seemed to displease the Duke.

"All your great care, all your excessive drilling of these men. And what was the result? They became tools in my hand. I thank you for that.

"And now, I no longer need them. I have had my revenge on you and on them for daring to oppose me."

The captain gathered his energy. "Adare tried to believe that you were better than you were—"

"Definitely better than he!"

The Duke's voice swept over his own and he could not continue. The effort was too great.

"The court of Rilken follows me with greater loyalty than they ever gave to my brother. *Complete* loyalty."

He stopped speaking for a few moments, and the old man felt malevolence in the eyes that studied him. "I do have something planned for the Guardsmen that linger in my dungeon. And for little Pate too—"

The Duke was building up to something—something unthinkable. A pain began to grow in the old Guardsman's chest.

"That foolish, pathetic jester is in my dungeon also. In the depths of the pit. Still alive at the moment, because I believe he might be useful to me. *Useful*, you see? The last joke, the last trick, the last hand dealt is mine after all."

The old captain fought through his cloudy memory of Pate's visit. He had a vague feeling that Pate had wanted to tell him something. Ask him something. But the memory blurred.

The Duke was babbling on about something. It didn't matter. The old captain saw Mary's face in his mind. Then Pate's face. Then Mary again.

"It will be the performance of a lifetime to see him laugh his way out of the arena—"

That much penetrated the old Guardsman's thoughts. He knew what it meant. And he was powerless to fight the knowledge.

Pate!

The boy had no capability with a sword. He had tried to teach him, and Pate had tried to learn. But they both knew his skills lay elsewhere. Skills that would do him no good in any arena.

Oh, Pate!

Sender, help him!

The pain in his chest increased. Rapidly. Crushing him. Crushing his very breath.

The Duke rose from his seat. Bent over him. Stared into his face with a look of pleasure. Until darkness blocked it out.

A moment later, the old Guardsman found himself looking at something much more glorious.

62

The Duke of Elva

The Duke of Elva returned to the castle in an unusually good mood. He entered the main doors and walked through the large hall, receiving the bows and curtseys that were his due with a satisfied heart. He knew himself to be a triumphant man, and he exulted in it, even smiling on the bent, servile heads. On the great landing, he paused momentarily, then climbed the stairs towards Ravelin's apartments.

Wells greeted him with a sober face. After several fitful days, the prince had just now fallen into a deep sleep. A tear was in the man's eye.

So what of that? A tear could lie just like a tongue could lie. But let the boy sleep or not, it made no difference now. The Duke readily turned from his nephew's door.

His feet took him down the stairs to his luxurious reception hall and to the large desk placed in front of the mirror of astounding beauty. He regarded the mirror with a loving eye before he sat down to his desk. Its gentle glow warmed his back, as if the mirror were approving of him, pleased as he looked over the deeds to Vallenro's land. As it should be.

An unexpected flicker of light raised a slight suspicion in him. He turned in his chair to study the mirror's placid shimmer. To try to account for his unease.

This was *his* mirror. He owned it surely. It had been born like a child to him. Had he not gone through the owner's ritual and with first sight claimed *its* sight for himself?

The ritual had taken place in a large workroom in the hills outside of Galerine City. The mirror—made of lerin, folkwhite, and a mineral whose name remained a secret even to him—had finally finished cooling after burning in a ground pit for four days.

The massive thing had been propped up by iron bars against a wall in the workroom, and, while it was still veiled, artisans climbed ladders and from the top poured sealing oil down its hidden face. That part of the process took careful hours.

At last, the workmen climbed down, removed the ladders and left the room. The master artisan came over to him.

"You remember what to do?"

He nodded and handed the man a purse filled with

more money than he had ever paid for anything in his life. The man thanked him and left.

No one was in that vast space except him. Allard of Rilken. And the weighty presence of the mirror.

He walked over to it, pulled back the curtains, and gasped in awe. For a few moments he struggled to breathe.

He composed himself, looked boldly into the mirror, and commanded, "Show me the pearl fire!"

The mirror began to glow.

Warmly.

Alluringly.

The fire that had burned it for days re-ignited deep within, sending flaming pearls across its face.

Instantly, he spoke in an authoritative voice. "I am Owner! Make all who see you do my will!"

The pearl fire blazed up, then rapidly receded into complete coolness.

With great effort and many men, he had brought the mirror from Galerine to his manor north of Elva, eager to learn what it could do.

A lazy gardener doubled his work hours.

An excellent cook with opinions of her own no longer disagreed with him.

And perfect harmony developed between himself and his steward Maynard.

That success had driven him to try a harder challenge. Could he bend someone's will to his own, even if it made them go against their own internal character?

The master mirror-maker had told him that the lerin in the mirror caused the viewer's mind to believe it was still guiding and commanding its own thoughts. The other two minerals in combination bent the viewer's mind to the will of the mirror's owner.

So, could he, the Duke, make a certain count in Rilken sell the champion horse of his bloodline, the foundation of his stables, for the price of a nag?

He invited the count to see the mirror and bought the horse that night for the handful of coins that were scattered in the drawer of his desk.

When his brother Adare received that hateful invitation from the Duke of Nordia to join the legendary Host of the North, the Duke brought the mirror to Elva Castle.

He used it first on Mago. The huge man became his lapdog from that very hour. Slowly, the Duke built a circle of men who followed him first before all others, before even the king.

Then came the mirror's ultimate test. Could it turn the minds of the king's own? He tried every trick he knew, and at last six of the Guardsmen gazed into it.

Yes, the mirror's power had never failed him. Even on the forest road.

A faint whisper sounded above him. He turned slowly in his chair and lifted his head. A streak of gold glowed at the top of the mirror. Without his direction.

For some reason, fear rose up inside him. Like smoke from a dampened fire. The presence of that fear annoyed, then angered him.

He was no sniveling Vallenro! He controlled this mirror, didn't he? He had been the first one to look and claim it. He was owner, wasn't he? No one else could have looked first. He had watched the whole final process to make sure.

Light whispered from one side of the mirror to the other. Another corner of the mirror gleamed anew. The Duke grabbed the goblet of wine Harmon had placed on his desk and drained it in one breath.

This fear was foolishness. And he would not stand for foolishness. He, Prince Allard of Rilken, no, *King* Allard of Rilken, First Prince and Duke of Elva, controlled this mirror of power. And *no one* controlled him. He was doing no one else's will, but his own.

He glared at the mirror defiantly. The mirror responded by humming with a soft golden radiance, soothing him.

"All right, then," he said aloud.

A rap at the door jolted him. "What is it?" he called out.

Mago stepped into the room with power and dignity. Yet he stopped and bowed at a deferential distance. The Duke's mood softened. The man's soul was completely his own.

"Mago, I have heard that you are concerned about these few bears that are proving an annoyance to our kingdom."

"You saw how they could not be killed in the forest," said Mago. "Every blade, every spear, every arrow was completely useless against them."

The Duke rose from his chair and went over to him, deigning to reach up and place a hand on the large shoulder. "Do not be discouraged about these lumbering piles of fur. I have something I want to show you that will cheer you tremendously."

The Duke paused for emphasis, while Mago watched him.

"You have your knife on your belt, don't you?" the Duke continued. "I want you to throw it with force, as if to kill a man, but aim it towards—" He waved his arm toward the wall where it hung. "That mirror."

Mago pulled his knife out hesitantly. "This knife has great weight, sire. The mirror will break. You can't want me to do that."

"But I do," he answered with a smile. "I'll step back over here and watch. Proceed."

He could feel waves of reluctance from the strong man, but Mago obeyed. The Duke watched carefully as Mago eyed the distance to the mirror, took a few steps toward it, and adjusted his stance. He raised his arm and with great force let the knife fly.

The point of the knife met the mirror's surface, but it did not penetrate. It did not fall to the ground. Instead, it flew back toward Mago, as if repelled by a greater force, and fell at his feet. Mago picked up the knife and turned it over in his hands.

"You see?" said the Duke with delight. "But let's try again. This time, use this figurine." He lifted a sculpted brass bear from the mantelpiece and handed it to Mago. "I think this weighs about seven pounds, the same as a small cannonball. Let's see what you can do with this."

Mago backed up, took a few running steps, and hurled the brass bear directly towards the center of the mirror. A loud crash rang throughout the room. The bear fell to the ground with a thud. But the mirror was unharmed. The Duke made Mago run his amazed fingers across the mirror's surface to see for himself.

"So, my friend," the Duke said with condescension, "let's have no more talk about how indestructible those bears are. You see before you a power that cannot be thwarted. A power that answers to me alone."

The Duke felt gratified. Courage had returned to his strong man. And the mirror had been duly disciplined for daring to cause him any unease.

A discreet rap sounded at the door. At the Duke's call, Harmon entered.

"Your Highness, a messenger has come from Nally the Dwarf. He brings news he says you have been longing to hear."

The Duke's heart leapt with joy. "Send him in at once," he cried.

63

A Game in the Woods

The enormous bear played with the hunters for days. Baiting them with distant growls. Running them in circles. Leading them by tortuous paths away from any thought of the hunting station or the inn at the bottom of the hill. Always moving them farther north, farther east.

At night, when the hunters lay exhausted in their camp, he crawled silently up to an overlook from which he could see them, while he lifted his incomparable nose. He studied the scent of everything. The metal of their weapons, the ash wood of their arrows, the dried meat and hard bread in their sacks, the wet wool of their socks and tired feet, and the stench of hemp and tar, an odor that permeated everything.

As each new day succeeded the old, the number of hunters increased. New groups of men and horses came with their own camps and their own stench of hemp and tar. Trying to place themselves around him.

He could have run from their game at any moment. But he didn't.

He moved more slowly. Letting them think he was tiring. Letting them think they were slowly confining him. Letting them think they were keeping him from the river and the fish he needed to live.

Occasionally they would unleash their arrows at him, then curse in fury as the impotent things fell to the ground.

He watched them drape their huge rope nets in the trees, blocking the paths where a bear might run. He smelled the horsemen picking their way through the woods around him, smelled the hope in their hearts that their plan would work. That they would encircle him and drive him into one of their enormous spiderweb nets.

He could destroy those nets with one swipe of his paw.

But he didn't.

One morning, he sensed the time had come. He turned down a forest path and walked straight into a rope net.

64

A Broken Shield

The Earl of Sormin did not leave the next day. It took several days for his carriage to be repaired to his satisfaction. Tara and her daughters stayed confined to their room the entire time.

True to her word, Ettie brought them their meals. Nissa, who always enjoyed the dramatic, eagerly brought them pitchers of water and attended to their other needs.

The girls didn't complain about the boredom of such restriction. Rosie tended the fire, took charge of making and airing their bed, and spent hours gazing out the window, while Tara sat in the chair and embroidered the remaining linens for the second noble room.

"Do you see a lot in those tree branches, Rosie?"

Tara asked, giving her daughter a glance as she rethreaded her needle.

"More than I can begin to explain, Mama," Rosie replied.

"That quince tree has grown fast since we've been here," Tara said.

"I've been speaking love to it," said Rosie.

Tara marveled at the change in her daughter's voice. Something deep in Rosie's heart had come to life with the Sender's gift, something that reached farther than the leaves and flowers of a quince tree.

White Squirrel went out the window each day, but never went far. They heard her scrambling across the roof above their heads and saw her leaping from branch to branch in the tree outside the window. When Rosie laughed, Tara had the feeling that the squirrel was doing her antics on purpose, just to hear that laugh.

In the evenings, when the sound of Harper's strings came up the stairway, Rosie quietly sang along with the songs she knew.

Silvie spent the days mending their clothes, reading the entire book of Nordian tales out loud, and watching over the comings and goings of her dearly loved animals. Cat was welcome to wander the hallways of the inn and became Ettie's favorite when she discovered a nest of mice near the flour bin. Redbird came often to the window—a crow came occasionally too—and Tara wondered what they thought of this in the inn yard. But Redbird said that Tike looked well and often kept Darril company.

Fox roamed his usual territory and kept an eye on

the hunting station. The roses still bloomed in the doorway, and Redbird once brought a petal from each in her beak for Silvie. But how Silvie had changed from the fearful girl who had been attacked by a bird on her first day in the forest.

As evenings came on, Tara put her work for the inn aside and resumed embroidering Bevan's shirt, the one she had started back in Guardstown. There were no pictures on this shirt, nothing that could come alive, only patterns of reds and golds and greens that traced circles around each other. The girls sat on the hearth as she stitched and told each other stories about their papa.

Rosie told of how he taught her to throw to a target, and how to build a fire. Silvie spoke of the Guardsman's Game. Tara shared a memory of Bevan in the kitchen.

"If I dropped something while I was cooking, he always caught it. If he was nearby, it never hit the floor. Remember the crock of butter?" Bevan had caught the crock in one hand and the butter that fell out of it in the other.

The girls laughed at the memory, and with their laughter Tara's secret hope grew. A hope that Bevan would somehow, by some miracle, wear this shirt after all. She threaded her needle with deep red and wove it through the fine linen. The thread became alive again, as it always did, rushing now with hope and purpose as it wove and looped in and out.

Silvie and Rosabel watched her, enthralled. Tara kept her eyes on her work as she talked.

"Do you know what your Gramma told me when I first met her?"

"Tell us, Mama," Silvie answered softly.

"She said that Bevan's hair was so light, almost white, even from a young boy. And Gramma said it was because she was already old when he was born. 'Ya,' she said. 'He was born when my hair was already white. That's why his was too.' Then Grampy said, 'Your hair was white when I married you, and you were seventeen at that!'"

"How old was Gramma when Papa was born?" asked Silvie.

"Grampy said they had to wait twenty years for him to be born. Gramma said he was a miracle baby."

"I like that story," said Rosie. "I like that Papa was a miracle baby."

Once, between stitches, Tara glanced up and saw concern on Silvie's face as she watched her. But Silvie said nothing out loud, and Tara was grateful for it.

ON A WARM SPRING MORNING, Ettie brought the glad news that the earl and all his company had left that very hour. Tara and the girls celebrated by going to the main room of the inn for their breakfast. Redmond was there already, eating a raisin bun in the back of the room. They sat down at a table near him. The morning sun came through the windowpanes and warmed the pine tabletop.

"So, you've escaped the noble clutches," he said with a smile.

"Yes, for now," Tara replied. "I hope for always."

While they were eating, Jarlath came by their table. He assured them that Darrit was doing all right. "He's cleaning up the inn yard right now. Tara, he says there's something he needs to tell you."

Tara grabbed her shawl at once, leaving her daughters to enjoy Redmond's banter, while she found Darrit. She went out the back and walked past the chicken coop, the smokehouse, the laundry house, and was almost at the stables when she saw him with a shovel and bucket, picking up manure at the far edge of the inn yard.

He looked much better than he had the day he first arrived. Jarlath was taking good care of him. But there was no real light in his eyes. How could there be, with such sorrow on every side?

The heaviness surrounding him seemed to increase as she approached. A furtive glance came her way, then obvious concentration on the shovel and the squashed horse droppings.

"You're looking well, Darrit," she said. "Has this been a good morning for you?"

"Good enough, Tara ma'am," came the polite reply.

Silence. He scooped another pile into the bucket while Tara watched. He had been more open to her the day he first came to the inn.

"Jarlath said there was something you wanted to tell me."

"Yes, ma'am." He put down his bucket and rested the tip of his shovel on the ground. He held onto the wood handle and faced her at last.

She recognized the look on his face. The look when he was going to do something brave that he really didn't want to do. But he would do it anyway, because he was Darrit.

"It's about Captain Bevan's sword and shield," he said. "When we got to Elva and learned that the king was dead, and—and the lies that everybody was saying, the palace guard said they were going to burn Bevan's shield and break his sword. They planned to do it in front of everybody."

Darrit stared at the ground. "I stole the shield and sword before they could, and I buried them at night behind my mother's house. I just wanted you to know what I had done for Captain Bevan. And if you thought it was all right."

He looked at her then, questioningly, while pain pierced her with a cruel spear. She could barely breathe.

Nothing could have told her more clearly that Bevan was truly dead. *His sword and shield.* They never left a living Guardsman's side. Were as close to him as his own skin.

"What did his shield look like?" Darrit would know what she was really asking.

"It was beat up real bad, ma'am, and had a big crack in it."

Darrit studied her, a frightened look on his face. She reached out to touch his shoulder with her hand.

"You—you did well. Very well. Thank you," she said.

From unthinking habit, she walked down that familiar short stretch of road and began climbing the path to the hunting station. Her bones felt heavy, leaden. Her gait slow like that of an old woman.

The sun had fallen out of the sky for her, and the air was as cold as winter.

CRIM HAD LINGERED at the inn well past what was necessary for his business purposes, just to make sure Tara was safe. He sent his younger partner south with wagons bound for the city of Dor on the Ardemount seacoast. He himself was supposed to go west, to the south of Tellhaven and beyond. He had delayed too long already.

He admired Tara. Admired her person, her incredible skill, her steady bravery as life struck her blow after blow. Admired the daughters she had raised. He would be happy to provide for all of them and had ample means to do so. But when should he speak to her?

He saw her with the lad in the inn yard. Saw the light die in her eyes, the shuffling step as she walked away. He didn't have the right to interfere, to help her with her business. Not yet.

Maybe on his next trip he would finally be able to speak to her.

SILVIE AND ROSIE found her sitting on a rock by the side of the hill path, and wondered at her anguish. Slowly, she told them what Darrit had said. They clung to her arms, and the three of them went back down the path again and, ignoring all watchers, crossed the inn yard, entered the back kitchen door, and went up the stairs to their room.

Rosie built the fire slowly, wiping tears. Silvie put her feelings into making her mother stretch out on their small bed the proper way, so she could truly rest.

Cat jumped onto the bed next to Tara, but she barely noticed. Instead, she gazed at the fire, staring past the leaping colors of red and gold to the vision of a face who once proudly carried his shield, a face who smiled at her with eyes full of love, then faded into the flames.

The song of the Mourner played in her mind, the sound of the sorrowing river that must surely have taken Bevan's blood to the Sender. In the Sender's Hall he would be treated with greater honor than he had been in Rilken.

Tara covered her face with her hands for a long time.

Darrit's burying of the shield was a funeral of sorts for my father. The only funeral and honor he would receive.

None of us felt like company. We stayed in our room again that day, and Rosie went to bring up our meals from the kitchen. She told the inn people that it was because Mama wasn't feeling well.

That afternoon, Redmond left some books at our door. Crim brought perfumed soaps. And Jarlath came by with one of the inn's tumblers stuffed full of spring wildflowers. We were grateful beyond words.

I sat in the chair and read aloud while Mama listened from the bed. Rosie sang gentle lullabies. And Sorrow kept us company.

I did not know that a person could hold so many tears inside for so long.

After dinner, I gazed out the window and watched the night come on. Above the tips of the tree branches, clouds stretched across the sky, and stars slowly appeared in their pockets.

A glossy, black shape swooped down and landed on a branch below the window. I was startled, but not frightened. I knew this bird.

"Crow, what is it? What brings you here?"

Hunters in the woods with rope traps. They caught a big bear this afternoon away to the north. The one that's been running in these woods this past moon. You asked me before about men in the woods. So I came to tell you about this.

I clung to the windowsill, stunned. "Did you see where they took the bear?"

They took the road to Elva. Had him tied down on a large wagon. I followed them for a while, then came to tell you.

Crow leapt out of the tree and up into the night air. He disappeared over the roof and out of my sight, leaving me grappling with the message he had brought.

Bear was strong. Ageless. *How could this happen?* How could he be taken by evil men? Anger rose in me.

Dallen, you promised! You boasted you could smell farther than their arrows could fly. You knew where they were. You knew! How could you let this happen to you! Dallen, what have you done?

I turned from the window. Mama and Rosie watched

me from the bed, waiting to hear what the crow had said. Waiting for the part they couldn't guess.

"The hunters have captured our bear and taken him to Elva," I said. I didn't dare speak Dallen's name aloud even in the quiet of our room. "The Duke has everything under his control now."

I saw on Rosie's face the same feelings that roiled inside of me. But Mama's gaze dropped to her lap where her hands lay limp.

After a few moments, Mama raised her head and watched the flames dance in the fire. I saw the expression on her face steady itself. As it always did when she set herself to do something hard.

65

A Message from Elva

The girls tossed and turned during much of the night, and Tara did not sleep at all. *Dallen taken by the Duke!* Surely, the Duke could not know that he had the prince in his grasp, could he?

But Dallen was still in the care of the great bears, as in fact, he had always been—before they had even met him. Tara's concern had to be for her daughters and their future. Through the sleepless hours of the night, she realized that Rilken would never be safe for them. Not while the Duke held power.

The best thing to do was move to a place where false stories about Bevan couldn't haunt them. Where Silvie could wear her hair uncovered. A place far beyond the Duke's reach.

What countries had Redmond recommended? Tell-haven, perhaps? Or Falland or Nordia? And that would take a good amount of money.

Crim had said that she could make a good income from her embroidery. Very well, she would do it. She would begin today.

The girls slept soundly at last by the time morning light came through the window. Tara stole from the bed and quietly washed and dressed. As she wrapped a shawl around her shoulders and picked up a packet of embroidery, Silvie stirred and raised her head.

"Mama?" she whispered.

"I'm just going down to talk to Gareth," Tara answered quietly. "I won't be long."

Gareth was already at the bar, filling tumblers for early risers with breakfast ale and beer.

"Is Crim around this morning?" Tara asked after they had exchanged greetings.

"In the stables, getting another wagon ready to travel."

She felt alarm. "Is he leaving too?"

He gave her a curious look. "I believe so."

She thanked him and turned away, but he called to her. "We need to put you and your girls in a larger room. There are a few you can choose from now."

She thought about this as she walked away. A larger room would cost more, but they did need more space to be comfortable. A wave of sadness swept over her. The inn had begun to feel like home, but it could not hide them forever. It would be a long time before the Duke forgot to hate anyone connected with the Guardsmen.

· · ·

CRIM'S loaded wagons had been pulled out of the stable and into the open yard. Horses were in harness, ready to travel. His men scurried around. Some climbed up to the drivers' seats and took the reins in their hands. Others mounted horses, shields hanging from the sides of their saddles. Crim and his merchandise traveled with their own guardsmen. Sudden panic rose in her when she didn't see him. *Had she missed him already?*

"Crim!" she called, hurrying forward. "Crim!"

He stepped out from the other side of a wagon. "Tara?" Surprise was in his voice.

He signaled to his men to wait, and strode toward her, a puzzled expression on his face. "You're feeling better, I hope."

As he approached, she unwrapped the paper and held out the piece she had chosen to make a beginning with. A sash designed to go at the waist of a woman's dress. She had started it in Elva and finished it just last night after the crow brought its message.

"You've offered to sell things for me before. Could you sell this?"

Crim removed his gloves and carefully unfolded the long linen strip. It was filled from end to end with leaves and berries. The leaves seemed to wave gently in a breeze, flickering in a sunlight of their own. He shook his head and whistled softly.

She studied the merchant. "The girls and I will need a home, someplace to live. If you can sell this for me, keeping a portion of it for yourself, of course, then we could plan to make a new start somewhere."

He had been examining the sash as she spoke. Now, he folded it carefully and turned his gaze on her. Such kindness in his eyes.

"Tara, I would do more for you and your daughters than this, if you would let me. I have a manor in Patlo, and I would gladly provide for you all. I know that Gareth—and Redmond—claim that I am a man who knows the value of things. But I know the value of people too. I know you are of great worth. I would joyfully make you my wife, if you wish it. Whether now, or months from now. All you have to do is say the word."

Her heart felt numb. Incapable of any emotion, any feeling for a man other than Bevan. And her mind had dwelt for hours on only one thing. Getting her daughters to safety. Yet she could not help but feel warmed by Crim's generosity.

"Thank you for your great kindness, Crim, but my daughters and I plan to leave Rilken."

"Are you going to Tellhaven?" he asked, an odd note in his voice.

"I am thinking of the Falland coast. But you see that at last I have taken your advice." She pointed to the embroidery in his hands. "I am taking the next step in becoming a woman of business."

"This will bring good money for you," he said. "I promise."

Behind him, Crim's company of men sat ready for departure, but he seemed in no hurry to leave. "If you would, please still consider my offer. I will wait, Tara, for whenever you can."

He was being gracious and reasonable. She gave him the best smile she could manage. "I will think of it. And thank you again."

He studied her for a moment, then gave a nod and turned to rejoin his men, carefully putting her precious package into the wagon before mounting his horse.

She stood and watched the whole company of men move out of the inn yard and down the road toward Tellhaven and Ardemount. Crim's words left a sense of great kindness, of unselfish provision. And yet, they made the grief in her heart ache even more. Someday, she would tell the girls about Crim's proposal. But not for a long while.

SHE WAS HEADING to the main door of the inn, when the sound of furiously galloping hooves and a loud "Ho, there!" stopped her. The rider, dressed in the green and yellow of the royal messengers, looked as exhausted as the horse he reined in.

"Do you work here?" he called, making no move to dismount.

"Yes," she said.

He reached in a pouch at his side, pulled out an envelope, and handed it down to her. "See that this is read out loud to everyone in the inn, by command of His Majesty, Prince Allard of Rilken. At once, do you hear?"

"Yes, sir," Tara replied. "At once." She pointed to the inn door. "Can you stop to take a drink or rest a little?"

The man gave her a rueful look. "Not for ten more miles." He turned his horse and spurred it out of the inn yard.

Jarlath had come up while the man was speaking. "That horse isn't going to last ten more miles."

Tara held out the missive in her hand.

"Best take it right to Gareth," he said. "I'll bring in the boys from the stables. See you in the main room in a few minutes. Then we'll hear what's going on in Elva."

Gareth looked bewildered when she handed the letter to him.

"What am I to do with this?" he said.

"The messenger said to read it to the whole inn. Every worker, every guest."

"Tara, I don't think I can do this. I—I don't read very well. And Alta's no good in front of an audience."

She glanced around the room and saw a familiar figure, his hair already sticking up from the habit he had of shoving his fingers through it when frustrated at his work.

"Redmond's here. Have Redmond read it."

IN A HALF HOUR everyone on the inn grounds had gathered into its main room. Guests sat at the tables, some very annoyed at being awakened earlier than they wished. Surrounding them were maids, launderers, stable boys, and more people than Tara had ever seen at the inn. Ettie and her helpers stood in the hallway to the kitchen. Alta and Kipp behind the bar with Gareth. Jarlath brought in Darrit and took a place by the wall. Tara and her daughters perched at a small table.

Redmond stood at one end of the room. He wore his university cap as befit the importance of the occasion. "Ladies and gentlemen, without any preamble, let me read what the letter contains, and we will all find out what is so important to hear."

The room hushed immediately. Annoyed looks were replaced with curiosity. Redmond cleared his throat and began.

To my people all across this great land of Rilken—

From His Majesty, Prince Allard of Rilken, Duke of Elva, Count of Noster, Lord of the Northwoods:

I bid you come to the arena of Elva Castle, at the third hour of the afternoon, on the day of the week's turning, to witness the defeat of our traitorous enemies and especially, the destruction of the monstrous bear that has spread terror among us from east to west and north to south. This will be a great day, a day you will tell your children and grandchildren about, for years to come.

REDMOND FELL silent and stared at the paper in his hand, a frown on his face. The crowd waited.

A woman's voice cried out, "Is that all?"

Redmond nodded slowly, turning the paper over in his hands. "That's all."

The assembled began to murmur.

"Doesn't leave much time for a body to get ready."

"Well, I'm already heading west. I can't turn around and go east. Do you think this is a command?"

"It can't be, can it? That arena won't hold all of Elva, much less all of Rilken."

"Won't be able to find a room for the night anywhere in the city anyway."

"What enemies is he talking about? Were we at war? Did I miss something?"

"We're heading that way. Can anyone guess what we're actually going to see? Some bear baiting? Didn't King Adare's father put a stop to that sort of thing?"

The suspicion of the woodlanders remained. The inn workers left, muttering. Tara glanced to where Darrit had stood, but he was already gone. Neither Silvie nor Rosie said a word, but they looked ready to explode.

"Let's go upstairs and talk," Tara said.

BACK IN THEIR ROOM, it was not Rosie, but Silvie, her gentle one, who had the fire in her eyes. "We have to go to Elva and save Bear!"

Rosie's fire was not far behind. "We're the only ones who know who he really is!"

"What we need to do is sit down and think this over clearly," Tara said. The girls immediately sat down on the hearth. Tara sat in the chair facing them.

"Will the Duke try to kill the bear in front of everyone?" Rosie asked.

"It sounds that way," Tara admitted. "He used the word *destruction*."

"He plans to do to the bear what he did to the Guardsmen," said Rosie.

"But Bear *can't* be killed!" Silvie cried. "It's impossible!"

"The Duke might not know that," said Tara.

"What if the Duke plans to do something awful to him instead?" Rosie replied. "Something like torture?"

"No!" Silvie cried again.

Tara shook her head. "I can't see the people of Elva sitting for that. He doesn't dare. And I can't believe he has that much power over the bear."

"The Duke's message spoke of other enemies," said Silvie. "Is this what he plans for the last of the Guardsmen? Some sort of bear fight? Bear won't *do* that!"

"I don't think the Duke knows what he's doing with this bear," said Rosie. "How can he?"

"I don't think *either* Bear or the Duke know what they are doing," said Silvie.

They fell silent for a time, each alone with their turbulent thoughts while the fire snapped and cracked.

When Silvie spoke again, her voice was quiet. Calmer. Measured. And Tara knew that a decision had been made.

"Mama, what if the Duke plans to *turn* this bear? To twist his mind like the earl's. We have to go free him. I don't know how, but we must. No one knows who he is but us. Papa didn't save Dallen's life for him to be trapped like this! I am Papa's daughter, a *Guardsman's* daughter. This is mine to do."

"*And* mine," said Rosie.

Their faces were set and determined and in their

eyes Bevan lived again. But these were not highly trained fighting men, they were her daughters! They had never experienced even one of the rigorous drills Bevan had practiced regularly.

"You must think, you must realize what you are saying! You would be going against strong men, men that have slaughtered Guardsmen. No one is stronger than that!"

"But we have the Sender's gifts," Silvie countered. "Animals will listen to me. They won't attack anyone if I am there."

Rosie nodded vehemently.

"I am grateful for that, Silvie," Tara said. "And yes, we have been given gifts. Our gifts were fine in the woods. They helped us survive, gave us a place to live, provided for us, comforted and yes, protected us. But they are not exactly gifts of war.

"In Elva, some dark, twisting evil is taking hold. Something that can hold even Guardsmen in its grasp. And what do we have? Birds. A cat. A squirrel. A needle and thread. Tree leaves."

"And Fox," Rosie added confidently.

Tara did not reply to this.

The look on Silvie's face showed that she was thinking fiercely. "I agree with you, Mama. It would be foolish to think that we can fight like the Sender can. Our gifts are no match for dark evil. But maybe they are not supposed to be. What if—just what if—we were given the gifts for something small? Then we must go do that small thing! Papa said that love was the greatest weapon on earth!"

Tara remembered when Bevan talked like that.

"The Sender will fight the great evil," said Rosie, "and we'll sneak into where the animals are kept under the arena and set the bear free. What if we just do that?" She turned to Silvie. "Remember when Papa took us down to see the animals after the acrobatic shows during Festival a few years ago?"

Tara gazed at them both, Silvia and Rosabel, her white and red roses, and thought of all the things she could say. Of danger and pain. Obstacles and opposition. Armed men—evil men—and barred gates. Of how easily a strong blow could strike them down and leave them on the cobbles. Her head throbbed at the memory.

Yes, she could speak using Fear's voice. She could dull their bright eyes and take all their courage away. But that would be an offense against the Sender. Wisdom, not Fear, is what she needed now.

"Mama," Silvie spoke gently. "Back in the clearing, the morning we saw the roses for the first time, we realized that the Sender meant to give us courage."

"We've seen a fiery bird in the night." Rosie counted wonders on her fingers. "Miraculous roses. We've ridden on the back of an ageless bear. The bear has a prince inside of him. All the animals obey Silvie. And I can find us food anywhere in the forest."

Tara listened. Soaking their words into her soul. Pleading silently for wisdom as they spoke.

After Rosie finished, she turned around on the hearth and energetically stirred the fire. Silvie moved out of her sister's way and went to sit on the bed. The cat immediately jumped into her lap and she began to stroke its fur.

"Remember when we heard about Guardstown, Mama?" Silvie asked. "When it seemed that everything to do with the Guardsmen was being destroyed? Everything true and right and noble and good."

Tara kept her eyes on Silvie.

"Such things can never be destroyed. Because they belong to the Sender. And as long as the Sender lives, truth and rightness and nobility and goodness will never pass away."

Rosie picked up the energy of Silvie's argument. "Darrit survived. Guardsmen are imprisoned, but still alive. So are two princes of the kingdom. There's us. And the Guardians of Rilken have got to be somewhere."

"Mama." Silvie came over and knelt by her chair. "We must go to Elva because of everything we've been taught all our lives about honor and loyalty and strength and love. We go to Elva because we love those we want to save."

Tara dropped her gaze to where her own hand rested on the arm of the chair. What had she told Ettie in the kitchen weeks ago?

The life of someone you love is dearer than your own.

Both Silvie and Rosie were kneeling by her chair, looking at her closely. Wide open eyes, sparkling with hope. Was it true that everything they believed in had come down to this one moment? This one decision?

Bevan had spoken of times when a person could turn back from where one was needed the most. How it was a temptation, even for Guardsmen. And how they practiced thinking around such temptation. A Guardsman placed himself where he was called. Where he was needed. Always.

Bear would most assuredly be held under the arena as the girls said if the Duke meant to use him there. Should they go and be ready, in case the Sender truly had something else he meant for them to do?

Ravelin could not know where Dallen was. Yet they knew. For a reason.

"*I am valor for my Valor, the King,*" Tara whispered. The words felt like living things in her mouth. So the words had felt to Bevan.

"Then we'll go, Mama?" Rosie asked, eagerly.

Tara closed her mind to fear. She got to her feet. "We'll go," she said, feeling strange relief as she said the words.

Silvie hugged her arm. Rosie looked suddenly distressed. "But Mago said he would kill you, Mama, if he saw you again!"

"And the huntsmen will recognize us, Rosie," Silvie added.

"I will hide my face and you girls will cover your hair," Tara said with unexpected calm as she took their hands. "We'll do what the Sender gives us to do."

"That will be enough," Silvie said.

66

A Princely Scheme

The idea had been Ravelin's. Wells would never have planned something that would involve such an overt challenge to the Duke and such risk to his master. Yet, risk had become part of their lives, hour by hour.

First had been the deception over the meals Ravelin ate. In addition to pilfering from the castle kitchens to feed the prince, Wells daily took the trays brought from those same kitchens and deposited them in the old castle garderobe.

Pate's cat was in full agreement with this practice. It came to the door each time a new meal tray arrived, sniffed discerningly, and let out a loud howl. It refused to eat from any of them.

However, it gladly ate the sausage, cheese, fruit, and bread that Wells brought for the prince.

"Pate's cat is better than a royal taster, Wells," Ravelin said.

Second, the prince continued to be very ill, buried in blankets whenever Lady Petronia and Duchess Olivia came to visit. Afterwards, Ravelin walked around his apartments, slowly at first, but with increasing speed each day.

New thread had appeared on the queen's picture, and Wells was just as astonished as his prince.

"It—it must be the Sender's own needle, Your Highness!" Wells exclaimed.

Red stitching, then green, and lastly gold encircled the bottom half of the picture, while outside of the circle the new rabbit watched. As he walked around his chambers, Ravelin pointed out that he and the thread were doing the same thing, going around and around.

"Do you think that could be what it wants me to do?" The prince spoke in a light-hearted manner, but Wells knew Ravelin thought seriously about even those things he said in jest.

Along with stamina, the prince would need strength, but there wasn't much time to gain any. Ravelin tried pushing himself up from the floor, using only his arms. At his first attempt, he had broken out in a sweat, and his arms had shaken so badly that Wells begged him to stop.

"I may be weak," Ravelin said, wiping his damp forehead where he lay on the oak planks. "But I will not die in the way he intends for me to die."

Several hours later, Ravelin tried again. And pushed himself up once. In the evening Ravelin pushed himself up one more time.

This morning the prince had completed three, steadily. Even though he did not have the strength he used to have, it was increasing and his heart beat more regularly.

They both agreed that the Duke was quickly tightening his control over the people of Rilken, and as he did the danger to Ravelin increased. Soon, the Duke would no longer need to poison the prince in secret. He could send the palace guard to kill him with swords in the middle of the afternoon. How Wells and the prince wished for the true Guardsmen now!

The tasks were clear. They needed to escape from the Duke's power. And they needed to rescue Pate. Somehow.

That was why Wells was on his way to speak with the Duke this very moment, choosing the time when the Duke was looking over his favorite building project, the new east wing of the castle. And one key element of their plan gave him courage and hope.

Though the Duke held the court tightly in his grasp, he did not so tightly grip the citizens of Elva. They were intelligent and industrious, and had dearly loved their king and both of his sons. And word had it, that in homes throughout the capital city, people still hoped and prayed for Dallen's return.

The city had also not understood the need to clear Guardstown. The Duke's plan to stir animosity toward the legendary company had not been as successful as he would have wished. When the Guardsmen had been destroyed, Elva did not approve. Indeed, they had been repulsed.

The mayor and his wife—those who had seen the mirror—were completely for the Duke. Others, however, though they respected the Duke and admired his kind Duchess, did not love him. Still others, even people of great means, thoroughly distrusted the man.

Concern over the opinion of Elva is what had induced the Duke to plan an exhibit in the arena. Lord Farnworth's attendant told Wells this. The attendant was a man without pearl eyes, one who had been Wells' friend for years. The attendant had also said, with a raised eyebrow, that the Duke planned to get rid of *all* his enemies in the arena. It was to be a great triumph, a demonstration of the Duke's power, after which a party was to be held in the Duke's reception hall.

In both Ravelin's and Wells' opinions, such an event would be contrary to what Rilken thought and valued. But those near the Duke would never tell him that. They would only do his will. Even so, Ravelin feared that Pate was destined for the arena and would not leave it alive. That was why—Ravelin had urged—they must be bold now.

Wells came down the stone walkway at the edge of the gardens to where the Duke and Mago stood gazing at the roof's progress. Other palace guards watched from a discreet distance.

Wells bowed low. "Your Highness? May I speak with you a moment?"

The Duke eyed him with surprised interest. "You may."

"Some weeks ago, you asked me to report directly to you on matters regarding His Highness." Wells paused.

"Yes, go on, man."

"There is something that I fear will cause you great alarm."

"Don't tell me he's dying, Wells!"

The concern failed to be convincing. Anger rose in Wells, but he replied equably.

"The people of Elva think so. And, worse, there are strong rumors throughout the city that he is being slowly poisoned, and that by your order."

The Duke's face darkened. "Who dares say these things?"

"It is all over Elva, sir. Many of the people who believe it will be coming to the arena at your invitation."

To Wells' surprise, Mago took a step nearer and said, "I have heard of these rumors as well, Your Majesty. The man is right. They are everywhere, spoken by more people than you could possibly imprison."

The Duke let out a long string of oaths and curses, culminating in a series of expressions which would not endear him to the people of Elva.

When he paused for breath, Wells continued.

"I have served the royal family for twenty-five years, and I care for its dignity and honor as much as any man can. Let me propose something, sire, if it please you."

The Duke glared at him, but gave a curt nod.

"If Ravelin were to attend the festivities, sit in the royal box, and be seen with Lady Petronia, then all Elva will know that the rumors are false and your good name would be restored." Those last words were especially hard for Wells to say, but doing a job well requires something from the depths of all men.

The Duke thumped his walking stick on the stone at his feet, once, twice. Again and again. He said nothing, his eyes averted.

Wells waited. This was the important moment. He must do nothing to interrupt it. At last, the thumping ceased.

"Do you think the boy is strong enough to attend?"

"To tell you the truth, sire, I do not know. But I will have him rest well in the short time we have. I can also practice walking in his room with him. If I stand beside him, I can support his elbow in a way hard to detect. Perhaps, Lady Petronia could do the same? And if he must lean on her, will not the crowd think they are much in love?

"As to increased health, Ravelin must have the best food and the best medicines immediately. The honor of the royal family depends on it."

"Yes, yes, I see that," the Duke said ungraciously. He took a deep breath, uttered another curse, and gazed at the east wing.

"All right, Wells. It must be. Tell your master his presence is required at the arena. I will take no refusal. Even if he feels the effort too great for him, he must be there. I will not change my mind."

Wells bowed deeply. "I will tell him, sire."

He would tell the prince that his idea had worked.

Ravelin would be in the arena, perhaps near enough to help Pate, if he could.

THAT EVENING, when Ravelin's dinner tray arrived from the kitchen, Pate's cat sniffed it eagerly, then began to nibble with enthusiasm at a piece of roast pork in raisin sauce.

67

———

The Gathering Threads

Once the three of them had made the decision to go, they all turned to the practical side of things. Silvie's first thought was the animals. Tike must stay, but she felt they should take the white squirrel, the fox, and the cat with them. Crow was already on watch and she could call for him, if needed, before they got to Elva. For other help, they would look to the animal friends they could meet in the city.

Tara went to speak to Jarlath. She found him twisting wire to add to the fence around the chicken coop.

"Jarlath," Tara began, "could I borrow that cart you fixed last week? A friend of ours in Elva is in trouble. We must go see him tomorrow."

Jarlath shook his head slowly. "You're picking the worst possible time, you know. There'll be no gettin' through those city streets with the Duke's show going on."

"Have you ever known trouble to pick a good time?" Tara asked.

"No," said the old soldier with a rueful smile. "It never does."

"Is there a horse we might borrow too? We might be gone for several days, but we'll bring them back. Could you ask Gareth for me?"

"With all the work you've done, the stable could belong to you by now. Sure, I'll ask. But I know Gareth won't mind. He's never liked that old cart anyway. And we've got a mare that could use the exercise. I'll make sure everything's ready for you in the morning."

THEY GOT up at sunrise after a night without much sleep, and dressed quickly. In spite of the early hour, Jarlath had the cart out in the stable yard waiting for them.

"I put a blanket in the bottom of it, to make it more comfortable," Jarlath said. "Even then, it's not going to feel like a fine carriage."

"As long as it gets us there," said Tara. "How long will it take to get to the city?"

"A good half day with this cart, I would guess. It'll take an hour to get to the west road, then more hours to get to the city. The road will be crammed, you know."

"Will the cart hold up if we drive fast?" Rosie asked.

"I believe so, miss. I like to fix things to stay fixed. And Ettie put a bucket of food in there for you. Enough for a week, I'm sure," said Jarlath. "Since you're ready, let me get the horse for you."

Silvie followed him into the stables. Darrit was with them when they brought the horse out and attached its lines to the cart. Silvie and Rosie handed in Fox, Cat, and White Squirrel, then climbed in with Tara. Jarlath handed the reins up to Silvie.

Tara reached a hand down to Darrit. "If I see your mother, I'll tell her about you. That you're safe."

Darrit squeezed her hand in a grip much stronger than his size. "Thank you, ma'am."

"It's time now," said Silvie. Without a motion of the reins or the traveling whip Jarlath had given them, the horse moved forward. In a few moments, they were trotting briskly down the road to Elva.

I KNEW that the horse was putting all her heart and strength into the journey, but the trip to Elva took much longer than we had hoped. As we neared the city, we found the west road clogged with carriages and wagons. Solo riders on horseback cut through the slower conveyances. Curses flew from carriage drivers to the riders, and curses flew right back again.

"How will we know when it begins?" Rosie asked. "We have no clock."

"Do you remember the trumpets?" Mama asked. "There's a certain sequence the trumpeters play an hour before any pageant starts, then another a half hour before—"

"That's right!" Rosie cried. "Then they play the quarter hour, then the final call to attention. I can't believe I forgot."

"We've had other things on our minds," I said.

We were four carriages from the city gate when the hour trumpets blew. Rosie groaned. "We're never going to get there in time."

"We will," I said, with determination. "We *have* to."

The streets leading to the castle were even more crowded, and I had begun to despair along with Rosie, when we reached a point where a group of guards blocked the way.

"No wagons, carts, or carriages allowed into the castle grounds!" One of them pointed to a road that led away from the castle. "They must go down there."

Mama reached for the reins. "I'll take the cart, Silvie. I'll find somewhere to put it. You and Rosie go. Stay together! And—and do what you can."

Rosie and I leapt out at once. "Fox, stay with Mama," I said, taking the cat into my arms. "Help her find the way to us."

Then Rosie and I plunged into the crowd. White Squirrel rode on Rosie's shoulder as always, but now she began to chatter and squawk and hiss. This alarmed the people immediately around us, and they naturally stepped back.

"I'm so sorry," I cried. "We work with the animals and we're going to be late. Please let us through."

Most people listened, in spite of their own urgency.

An angry squirrel can make quite a fierce noise. Still, the quarter hour trumpets were blowing by the time we reached the entrance to the arena.

"All seats taken! Standing room only! All seats taken! Standing room only!" A man's voice bawled as we approached.

"Where are the animals kept? They're expecting us!" I cried out.

The man pointed over his shoulder at a narrow flight of steps that led downward. Relieved, we darted towards them.

I put Cat down. "You go first. You know how to tell me what you discover."

The minute her feet touched the ground, Cat bounded ahead, and leapt down the shadowy stairs.

RAVELIN WAS IN HIS APARTMENTS, getting dressed before the arena show. He held out his arm, and Wells slid the sleeve of the embroidered jacket onto it, then followed with the other one. Ravelin's heart beat anxiously and he tried not to notice it. He took a deep breath.

"What gruesome spectacle are we going to see today, Wells? I hope the castle gossip you heard is wrong. My uncle cannot truly have a bear in the arena, can he?"

"The report is that the animal is indeed there, sir. Kept in a cage of the stoutest iron."

"What if this bear is one of the true Guardians of Rilken? Would my uncle try to show some sort of triumph over it? I can't understand why."

Wells had a discreet look on his face.

"What is it, Wells? No secrets now. Not between allies."

Wells gave a little cough, then held out Ravelin's gloves. "It is my belief, sir, that the Duke feels he has *already* triumphed over the Guardians of Rilken."

Ravelin knew what he meant. The thought sickened him. He took the gloves and stared down at them, then slowly pulled them onto his hands.

"You believe my uncle had my father killed, don't you? My mind has whispered that same thing, keeping me from sleep for many a night. Oh, Wells! A treacherous murder is evil enough. But the bond between brothers is sacred!"

Wells looked him over with a careful eye, then plucked a thread from his shoulder. "I honestly do not know if he did, sir. But I think his behavior does not deny it."

Ravelin stepped in front of the mirror and looked at his own reflection. Once the reflection had been energetic, eyes alive, skin the color of life. Now it was paler, thinner. The eyes wary.

"I wish Dallen were here." He turned to Wells. "If he were, he would have nothing to fear from me. Ever."

Wells looked back at him solemnly. "Nothing at all, sir. You would be his most trusted and valuable friend."

"I wish he knew that, Wells."

"I am sure he did, sir."

Ravelin met Wells' gaze for some long moments, then nodded slowly. He turned to the mirror again and tried not to be discouraged by his pathetic image. "Nevertheless, I'll do what he would have done. I'll do everything I can to save Pate."

Wells examined Ravelin's attire closely. "If you will allow me, sir, I will get the cloth and rub those boots one more time."

He left for the wardrobe, and Ravelin walked over to view the embroidery picture on the wall, hoping for some comfort, some guidance. He studied the miraculous stitches again, the sun and moon, the watching bear, the forest, the roses, and the wide circles of red, gold, and green.

The circles fascinated him. Today they seemed to be moving, racing one after the other, blending their colors in a glorious blur. His eyes went to the dignified rabbit, to see what he thought of this joyous race.

But the rabbit wasn't there.

Wasn't watching as it had been for days.

Instead, the rabbit had found its way into the middle of the circling thread.

Ravelin stared in amazement. *How did the rabbit get there? It's made of thread!* How do rabbits get anywhere? It must have jumped. He shook his head in disbelief.

Wells returned and bent to rub Ravelin's boots while he studied the picture. After a few moments, Wells got to his feet and drew Ravelin's attention to the clock.

A chair with wheels waited for him in his sitting room. The chair was to save his strength until he must leave it behind and walk on his own feet into the public eye. He sat down and Wells draped his cape over him.

Ravelin turned and put a hand on Wells' arm. "If I sit in the stands with the Duke, won't everyone think that I approve of what is going on in the arena? That I am a part of whatever horror he has planned?"

"I have been concerned that it would look that way, Your Highness. You must watch for an opportunity to show that you do not agree."

PATE sat on a bench in the tunnel under the arena, his ankles gripped by cuffs of iron. A chain linked the cuffs together. He shared the bench with eight other men. They too were cuffed with iron. Guards with spears and swords stood on either side of the bench watching them.

The air in the tunnel was close and smelled strongly of animal excrement. Additional stink arose from animal fear and terror. Echoes of growls and guttural ravings filled the tunnel.

Pate had seen a huge badger and an angry boar behind cage bars when the jailors led him in. From where he sat now, he could look to his right and see a bear claw wrapped around an iron cage bar. More animals on the other side. The tunnel turned sharply beyond the place where they had entered. He could not guess what else lurked in those dark cages.

He wished he could talk to the men next to him beyond just a silent nod. He knew them, naturally. They had been Guardsmen. And the Duke must still fear their strength. Because whatever the men were to fight today, it looked to be with chains on, and without weapons.

The noise of the crowds in the arena found its way

into the tunnel. He wondered what they were expecting to see. What had they been told of today's show? In all his life, Pate had never seen anything gory or bloody in the arena shows. He couldn't even remember one fight.

King Adare had filled the arena with singers, with acrobats, with dramatic plays. Animals, when they had played a part in all this, had nothing to fear. Had Rilken, Elva itself, changed so much since the king's death? Or had the Duke's own mirror given its owner an unthinking unsight as well?

The jailors had not told the men on the bench the part they were to play in today's event. But from the grim look on their faces, the Guardsmen did not believe they would leave it alive.

If Pate had to bet between himself or a hungry badger, he would put ten rills down on the badger without blinking. Unless the badger thought himself an expert on riddles. Then Pate would have a chance. More than a chance. In his present state, he would say the odds would only be two to one against the badger.

A sound drew Pate's attention. The jailors and guards in the tunnel were arguing among themselves, like men unsure of what was supposed to happen. Pate reached down and rubbed an ankle. The argument went on for some time. At last someone won it.

"Look here now!"

Pate raised his head and blinked.

"We're going to take all of you into the arena and leave you in the middle. You won't know which animal will come out first."

The man kept talking in his jeering tone, but Pate stopped listening. Because at that moment, the most unlikely thing of all happened.

A brindled cat walked sedately down the tunnel as if she owned the place.

68

The Duke's Arena

Our eyes took a few moments to adjust to the dimmer light in the stone corridor underneath the arena. Cat seemed to understand this and let out a meow at intervals. Rosie and I made our plans in hurried whispers.

From this moment on, we would play the part of animal trainers sent to help with the show. I would interpret the animals to Rosie, and Rosie would join in with whatever I did. The most important thing was to find Dallen's Bear and free him.

"I'll need to find another way out of this place," I whispered. "The bear can't go up these narrow stairs."

From farther down the tunnel, where Cat was leading us, we could hear the sounds of men talking in stern, bullying tones. A loud grunt blocked out the men's voices for a moment, and tore at my heart.

"That's a boar, Rosie, and he's half-starved." Concern filled me. All kinds of messages were coming down the tunnel. A barrage of complaint and hunger, fear and pain. I grabbed Rosie's arm.

"We have to free *all* the animals, Rosie."

"All right," said Rosie, eagerly.

The passageway turned and we walked by the base of a short ramp that led upward. Light came through the cracks of the tall doors at the top of it. I could see the boots of men stationed by the doors, ready to open them.

"The arena," Rosie said quietly.

I nodded and looked forward.

Rilken's arena had never been meant to showcase wild animals or prisoners, so no bars blocked our way. We soon found ourselves in a wide tunnel that reeked of animal smell. Directly in front of us, flanked by surly guards, a row of men sat on a bench. With a start, I realized I knew them.

Drony was there, and my heart leapt with relief for Zilla. There too were Ben and Coll. Parry and Adam. These men had been Papa's friends. We had often watched their children. This past winter Rosie had taught Adam's daughter every dance she knew.

Fury ignited deep inside me. These men were chained because of lies. Just as my father's memory was chained. I would free them all with Dallen if it took my last breath.

At one end of the bench I recognized someone else.

The old captain's son. Pate. The one we rarely saw in Guardstown because he lived in the castle and served the princes. *What could he be doing here?* Was it as Dallen feared? Had something happened to Ravelin?

I glanced at Rosie and saw the consternation on her face as she eyed the bench. But we had no time to ponder this. One of the guards suddenly looked up and glowered at us.

"What are you doing here?" he yelled. "Get out!" He motioned with his sword.

Rosie stepped forward and glared at the man. "We are here to work with the animals," she said firmly. "And if you want anything to go right this afternoon, you had better let us see to them."

The man lowered his sword, but reached to grab Rosie's arm with his impatient free hand.

"I said, *Get ou—*"

A swirl of ferocious white. The man cried out in pain and dropped his sword with a clatter. The hand that had grabbed Rosie was bleeding profusely, but Squirrel was nowhere to be seen. Rosie stood still as though nothing had happened.

The man backed away, wrapping his hand in the corner of his short cloak. He glanced over his shoulder at another man, one who looked as if he were in charge. This one stepped forward, hastily picking up the dropped sword.

"You don't know a thing," this jailor said. "If we open one cage door, they'll eat you alive." His voice attempted bold assurance, but he glanced nervously at his friend's bleeding hand.

"You have a bear here," I said. "And a badger, a fighting dog, a bull, a boar, and a lion. Am I right? They've had nothing to eat for days. But you did give the lion a small amount of meat this morning because you were afraid of it."

The man narrowed his eyes, but closed his mouth and took a step back.

"Well, let's see how they're doing," I said, in my most competent voice. We walked past him, pretending not to see the men on the bench as we went by, and peered into the first cage.

The bear stood on all fours and lifted its head to look at us. My heart leapt at the sight of him. "There you are," I cried, as if it were a family pet. "We've been *so* worried about you!"

Rosie turned to the jailor. "Is *this* the bear that you are going to send into the arena?"

"Yes," came the defiant answer.

Rosie and I both contrived to look shocked.

I pointed at the bench. "Against those men there?" I stepped closer to the man so he couldn't avoid looking at me. "It's not going to work. This bear is not going to harm those men."

The trumpets sounded. The full call to attention. The audience in the stands above our heads burst into applause. Then shouting. The ceiling seemed to vibrate with the sound.

"Line up those men!" the man called. "Get them waiting by the door!"

The men rose and shuffled toward the ramp. From the look on Drony's face and the quick movement of

Adam's eyes, I knew they had recognized us, but they would not reveal that knowing. They would be stalwart as always. Rosie's hand tightened into a fist, and I knew she would welcome something to throw.

"Look," I said insistently. "We're the ones training this bear. *We're* part of the act."

The man ignored me again. "You there!" he called to someone farther down the tunnel. "Close that gate so the bear doesn't escape."

"He won't escape!" I cried, grabbing the man's arm. "Watch this! Bear, look at me!"

The bear pointed his muzzle directly at me.

"Raise your front right paw."

The bear lifted a furry arm.

"Very good, Bear. Now put that one down and lift the other one. Well done! Now, lie down on your stomach."

The bear did so.

At last, at last, *at last*, I had the man's full attention! He stood beside me gaping. "This is a *tame* bear? But he's as big as a monster!"

He swallowed and pointed to the other cages. "We'll have to start with those," he called out.

"That won't work either." I gave commands as quickly as I could. "Badger, down! Dog, down! Lion, down!" and continued on until every last animal sat in the straw blinking patiently at their jailors.

"What am I going to do?" the man cried. "The Duke will kill me!"

"Not if we give him a great show—" Rosie began.

Trumpets blared above us. The doors to the arena

creaked open and sunlight flooded the passageway beyond. The men were being led into the arena.

I grabbed the man's arm again. "Do you hear that? That is *not* the sound of cheering. They are barely clapping! Now open this cage, attend to your wounded friend, and get out of our way."

The man held out a large key. "The locks are all the same," he said. "We had to make them in a hurry."

I took the key and inserted it into the lock. The cage door unlatched, and I had to decide quickly what I was going to do. The Guardsmen had gone into the arena. The only way to save them was to go into the arena ourselves.

"You ride Bear into the arena, Rosie. I'll send the others after you and make them follow everything you do." Rosie's eyes sparkled.

I turned back to the man. "Just make sure your men stay out of her way. Then we can give the Duke the show he is waiting for."

Rosie stepped into the cage. "Hello, Bear. Let's show this man what we can do. Crouch down so I can climb on your back, just like we practiced." She reached up her hand to her hood. "Hold on tight, Squirrel."

Bear crouched down, and Rosie climbed up while the white squirrel chattered. The man stared in disbelief. Rosie had an exultant look on her face, the kind of look she wore when she climbed on rooftops, or let a stone fly to hit its perfect mark. An unstoppable look.

"Come on, Bear. Let's go to the arena!" she cried.

Bear emerged from the cage, playing his part perfectly, and turned toward the ramp. Rosie called out something to the arena gatekeepers. The jailor took off his cap and mopped his brow. And I went to speak to the badger in the next cage.

THE BRIGHT SPRING sunshine that warmed the arena had also illuminated Kendall's moment of glory. After the trumpets sounded attention, the master tutor had positioned himself near the royal box, and with his strong and melodious voice announced the arrival of each member of the royal family.

All had begun so well. The crowd had been free with their appreciation and applause. They cheered and waved as Lady Petronia and Duchess Olivia took their seats.

But when Kendall announced the arrival of the young prince, that same crowd got to their feet and took up his name, chanting *Ravelin, Ravelin, Ravelin,* over and over as the prince slowly and weakly picked his way to his seat, followed closely by his attendant.

Kendall had waved his arms to get the crowd to stop, but they would not be silenced. *Ravelin! Ravelin! Ravelin!*

Ravelin stood up slowly and raised both arms to the crowd. The people roared even louder. He waved, bowed his head to them, and sat down again. Still, it took some time for the tumult to die down.

And then, Kendall, in his most theatrical voice, announced the name of the majestic Duke with all his many honors and titles. Members of the court cheered wildly at the Duke's entrance.

The response of the rest of the stands? Mere clapping. Sustained, but polite. A glance at the Duke's face showed that he noticed it.

Afterwards, the proclamation of the defeat of Rilken's enemies—a statement that Kendall had spent hours writing with careful words—had been greeted with only a moderate cheer. Too moderate from Kendall's point of view.

Nine prisoners shuffled into the ring, taking painful steps all the way to the center, where they stood in a circle facing outward into the stands.

Enthusiastic applause came only from the courtiers. The rest of the audience fell into awkward silence.

Kendall glanced at the Duke's face. It was a mask of iron.

RAVELIN, too, was very aware of the crowd's response. He knew too well the volatile and dangerous nature of his uncle's pride.

The Guardsmen and Pate stood so bravely in the middle of them all. Did his uncle intend to have them killed before all these watchers—these people of Rilken dressed in their best, sitting with their families, ready for a royal pageant? Was his uncle trying to stir loyalty or abject fear in the crowd?

Ravelin sensed uneasiness in Petronia, seated at his left. Olivia, next to Petronia, had a worried look. Because of the mirror, they could be afraid for different reasons than he guessed, but they were still afraid.

Ravelin did not look past Olivia to the Duke. Instead, he turned his gaze back to the center of the arena. To the brave men standing there. Men he once feared, but now admired. And there was Pate. His lifelong friend. No clever quip could save Pate now.

He had a wild thought that Pate could somehow make it over to him. That he and Wells together could haul him up over the rail to safety.

Safety? Surrounded by a pearl-eyed court and the palace guard?

No, Ravelin told himself, *there is no safety anywhere, anymore.*

His only hope was the crowd. If he could get them to follow him in calling for the rescue of the men, there was a chance his uncle would acquiesce. If only for a few moments. But at least they would have a few moments to use.

The trumpets blared again. He shifted nervously in his seat. The arena doors were thrown open, and Ravelin leaned forward, his eyes wide. For before him was a sight that he never could have imagined.

Rosie heard the crowd gasp at their entrance. She lifted her hand and waved, keeping the other hand firmly gripping the roll of skin like Bear had taught her. It took her one instant to realize she loved this. She loved crowds and people and adventures.

"All right, Bear," she said. "Let's ride all the way

around the arena first, just like the acrobats do. Then we'd better bow at the royal box."

"Hallo! Hallo!" she called as they rode around the arena. "Hallo, good people of Rilken! Surprise! Surprise!"

Laughter and clapping and shouts of *hurrah!* followed her around the arena. Then, as she and Bear approached the royal box, she fixed her eyes on Prince Ravelin.

Sadness smote her. His eyes looked haunted. Like Silvie's did when she woke up from a bad dream, believing she was still in it. She wondered if Bear was seeing those eyes too.

Bear stopped in the perfect spot. He placed his paws on the ground in front of the royal box, with his back to the men who waited in the middle of the arena. Rosie sat up taller.

"All honor to our royal family!" she cried out. She waved her arm and bowed her head briefly as she had seen the acrobats do. Bear bowed too.

"Good people of Rilken, citizens of Elva, what did you expect to see today? Me torn and bleeding under the claws of this bear?"

She pointed to the men behind her. "Some gruesome fate for these poor men? No!" She said the word as loudly as she could. "I do not think that would please our noble prince."

She looked right at Ravelin as she spoke. He was looking back at her, wonderment in his eyes, and Rosie's heart lifted.

"The heart of our prince is good and true! He does not thrill at the torture of animals or men."

The arena doors grated open and a badger stepped uncertainly into the ring. The crowd murmured. "But since you all came to see a show—" Rosie cried. "Follow me, Badger!"

She leaned forward and spoke into Dallen's ear. "Let's do a song, Bear. All the way around the ring. One for Ravelin." She smiled at the crowd again, waved at the royal box, and filled her lungs with air.

Oh, sing me high
And sing me low,
And sing me where
The wind blows.
I'll listen high,
I'll listen low,
And find you where
The wind blows.

The badger was following them around the ring! Obeying her just like Silvie said it would. Rosie was delighted.

Oh, sing me out
And sing me in,
And sing me where
My heart's been.

A lion trotted behind the badger. Out came a boar. It

looked around dazedly for a moment, then followed the lion.

> *I'll listen out*
> *And listen in,*
> *And tell you where*
> *My heart's been.*

A rough-looking dog leapt from the open doorway and barked in time with the song. The crowd laughed and clapped.

> *Oh, sing me near*
> *And sing me far,*
> *And sing me to*
> *A bright star.*

A horned bull came up the ramp, tossed its head from side to side, and followed behind the dog.

> *I'll listen near*
> *And listen far,*
> *And find you at*
> *The bright star.*

Squirrel squeaked loudly just behind her ears. Rosie was enjoying herself immensely. But she had no idea how to end this. Did Dallen? *And where's Silvie?*

Rosie gave the crowd another brilliant smile. "Sing with us this time!" She waved her arm high, and turned to the chained men in the middle of the arena. "Everyone!"

The Guardsmen joined in immediately. In moments, the arena rang with Rilken's old, beloved song.

Oh, sing me high...

69

The Bend in the Tunnel

Out in the streets of the capital city, Tara despaired of ever finding a place for the cart. Every slow turn down every crowded street took her farther from the castle arena. The quarter hour trumpets had long since sounded when she finally found an opening large enough for the inn's horse and cart in front of a cobbler's shop.

"Well, Fox," she said, to the remaining animal in the cart. "This will have to do."

There weren't as many people hurrying by as there had been on the larger streets, but the ones that passed seemed to be heading in the direction of the castle.

She paid the cobbler one rill for allowing her cart and horse to stay there. As he stared at the coin that represented the work of one week to him, he sent a boy immediately to get water for the horse.

Tara thanked him, then she and Fox joined the others who hurried toward the castle, those who knew they would be too late to see the opening, but hoped to find a place in the arena somehow. She heard the roar of the crowd in the distance, and prayed as she ran. *Sender, protect my girls!*

OLIVIA, Duchess of Elva, had never been so afraid. Her husband sat rigidly in the seat next to her, his face immobile, but dark with anger. She glanced nervously at the members of the palace guard that stood around the royal box, ready for Allard's command.

What Allard had feared most, what he had urged others to fear too—this monstrous bear—had actually come into the arena with a young woman on its back. A young woman who couldn't seem to stop...laughing.

To make it worse on her husband, this woman had addressed Ravelin and not Allard—the true king—as she should have. The crowd had also shown its preference for the prince.

Petronia was frowning, but sat silent. Olivia wondered if she were afraid for Allard too.

Ravelin, however, seemed utterly enchanted by the spectacle before him. That was to be expected. The girl on the bear had taken great pains to flatter him. Now the arena was filled with barking, snorting animals, dancing after her like some Galerine conjurer's show.

Olivia felt angry for Allard's sake. This should not be happening! Allard deserved the respect and praise of all Rilken. Of the whole continent of AllHallen! She gave him another glance. His color had darkened even more.

Fear pushed her anger aside. She began to smooth her skirts, first with one hand, then with the other. One, then the other. That revolting girl began to speak again.

SILVIE HADN'T COME YET, and it was the only thing Rosie could think of. The only thing that could be more exciting than a rousing and unexpected song. She held up her hand and called to the crowd. "Would you like to see how fast this bear can run? Would you?"

Cheers and cries of *Yes, yes!* came from the stands. Ravelin nodded approval. With that Rosie's courage flared. She bent down to speak into Dallen's ear.

"Okay, Bear. What if you run slowly around the arena at first, then increase speed until you're going as fast as you can? Then, for a big finish, maybe leap over the heads of the men in the middle and come back here in front of the royal box."

The crowd saw her talk to the bear, saw the bear nod its head and start to walk. Sounds of excitement rippled through the stands.

Bear began to trot around the ring, while Rosie held tight to his roll of fur. The other animals fell in line with him, trotting right behind.

Bear ran faster. So did the others.

He increased his speed a little more.

And more.

Then Rosie felt something change inside of Bear. It was as if joy exploded in his muscles and tendons. She crouched down, put her head against his fur, and she and Squirrel held on for their lives.

RAVELIN MARVELED at the sight before him and gasped along with the crowd. The bear ran faster until he was outrunning all the other animals, leaping over them in his path. As the sun shone down, it picked out hidden colors of gold in the bear's thick brown coat, and in the girl's red hair and green cloak.

Gold. Red. Green.

The colors ran faster and faster, blurring with their speed, until they made Ravelin catch his breath in surprise. The colors of the running threads on his mother's picture were racing before him. And he was the rabbit on the edge of them, watching.

ROSIE HAD to close her eyes, because, honestly, Bear was going so fast she thought she might be sick if she opened them. All at once, she felt a gentle leap, longer than most, and Bear came to rest in front of the royal box.

With that leap came an odd feeling. A feeling that she had been a stone in the hand of the Sender, aimed just so, landing exactly where he had intended.

Rosie lifted her head and sat up again as the crowd sprang to its feet with applause. It was a glorious moment. A moment Rosie drank in. But she had come to the end of her ideas.

Where is Silvie?

THE PAIN and fear that poured from the animal cages, as I worked my way down the row, threatened to overwhelm me. I did my best to calm the beasts, speaking gently to them, and gave each a portion of Ettic's food from my carry bag. But I didn't have much time.

I gave each one clear instructions. Not to fight, not to harm. Only to protect and defend. And to follow and do whatever Rosie and Bear were doing.

The jailor stayed out of my way. He actually stepped into the empty bear cage—the safest place—as each beast raced down the tunnel toward the arena. But I still had to come up with some way to get Dallen's bear out of the arena and to safety.

I had once asked Papa what battle was like, and if he always knew what to do ahead of time. Were there plans that he followed?

There are always plans to follow, he had said. *But plans almost always change the moment the battle begins.*

What do you do then? I asked.

You stay with the principles that you've been trained by. You remember your purpose in the battle. And you follow your leader.

Principles. Purpose. But there was no leader in this underground tunnel.

I came to the last cage and set the bull free. Just beyond, the tunnel bent. Could there be another opening there? A wider one? The animals must have been brought in somehow. If I could find the place, then Rosie and I could lead the animals through this tunnel and out the other end. People would surely move away from us, and we might make it to the city gate safely.

I stepped around the corner and saw what I hoped for. A large opening gaped about forty feet in front of me, a barred gate drawn across it. Was it unlocked? Would my key work? I had to know before I joined Rosie in the arena. I ran to it. The lock released with the key. Relieved, I shoved the door open.

"Silvie! Silvie!" The words echoed in the tunnel.

Prickles rose on my skin. I peered into the shadows of the passage I had just run through.

Another row of cages lined the walls.

As far as I could tell, all were empty but one. A huge bear stood on all fours, his eyes alert, nose lifted. "Silvie!"

It was Dallen's voice.

Which meant *this* was Bear.

Our Bear.

I put the key in the lock with trembling fingers. "Bear! I—I thought I already released you."

"Where's Rosie?" he said, as I turned the key.

"Rosie is in the arena right now, riding on another bear's back."

I swung the cage door open, and Bear sprang out.

Immense and powerful. A true Guardian of Rilken. Just like the other bear. Then I realized. Dallen had known about the other bear.

"But why didn't you open the bars yourself? You're so strong. You didn't have to wait for me!"

He did not answer this, but said, "Climb up, Silvie! Quickly!"

There was no alarm in his voice. No fear or concern over what we were doing. A joyful excitement shimmered around him. He crouched down. I grabbed at his fur and leapt on.

"Strength isn't the only thing with power," he said, remembering my question at last.

I wasn't sure what he meant, but there wasn't time to think. He turned swiftly, eagerly, moving down the main tunnel while the jailors jumped out of our way. I held on as tightly as I could, but my kerchief flew off and my light hair streamed out behind me. What did it matter now? The Guardians of Rilken had come to put Dallen on his throne!

"Open!" I yelled at the men who stood by the arena doors. They barely got them wide enough when we hurtled through.

Rosie and her bear must have just finished some sort of performance, for the crowd was cheering and applauding wildly. All the beasts I had freed stood in a row and bowed before the royal box.

Bear raced over to them. We took our place next to

Rosie and bowed at the same time. The crowd clapped even louder at our arrival.

Rosie grinned at me, looking relieved for just a moment. Then a horrified look came over her face. With one hand she gripped the bear's roll of fur. With the other she made a discreet pointing motion toward it, a question in her wide eyes.

"Guardian," I simply said. There was no danger of anyone overhearing us. Rosie stared down at the fur beneath her. The grin returned and she gave the massive animal a small pat with her hand.

Silvie!

I climbed off and stood by his head so I could hear Dallen better.

"Say these words, Silvie."

I listened closely, while trying to pretend I wasn't listening at all, then held up my arm for silence. The crowd settled down and took their seats again.

"Honored Prince Regent," I began. "Honored Prince Ravelin, honored ladies and gentlemen of the court, and dear people of Rilken. These bears whom you have been seeking so long are presented as a gift to you now from your nephew and brother—Prince Dallen."

The crowd exclaimed at this and cheers swept the stands. I let the cheering go on for a while because my soul rejoiced to hear it. I rested my hand on Dallen's neck and listened long. When I raised my hand for silence again, it took some time to gain it.

"Prince Dallen will be waiting in the Duke's audience chamber and wishes you to bring the bears with you as a sign that you have received his gift in good faith."

My announcement caused distress in the royal box, as I had known it would. Rosie had a sparkle in her eye.

"Should we meet in another room perhaps?" she called out. "Is the chamber not big enough? Should the prince have sent the smaller bears?" These weren't words we had been given to say. Just pure Rosie.

RAVELIN LEANED FORWARD, staring at the scene in front of him. Confusion filled him at the white-haired girl's words. *Dallen alive? And waiting for him?*

The Duke put out his hand toward him as if to halt any movement. But Olivia and Petronia sat between them, and his uncle's hand hovered in the air. "This is an enemy ruse, Ravelin," his uncle cried. "Do *not* listen. We all know Dallen is dead!"

But Ravelin did not hear him. Ravelin was thinking of the picture that hung in his room. And of a rabbit that didn't sit on the side watching, but leapt into the middle of the arena. A rabbit that told a story. His story.

Ravelin nodded politely to his uncle, then grabbed the rail in front of him, and threw himself over.

THE DROP WAS GREATER than it seemed. He stumbled at first, and his hands clutched at the dirt. Cries of dismay came from the crowd. But they cheered when he picked himself up and walked over to the bears. He reached out to pet the muzzles they held out to him. First one. Then the other. Unafraid.

Dallen was alive. Ravelin wasn't afraid of anything now.

He walked between the bears and out to the men in the middle of the ring. His small store of strength began to ebb, but he had to keep going. He had been given the moments he hoped for. Soon he would see if they were enough.

The crowd hushed rapidly when he signaled for silence.

"My dear people!" His voice did not come out as loudly as he wished. He took a deep breath and tried harder. "The royal motto is *Let there be no envy or ill will.*

"The Duke of Elva promised that you would see Rilken's enemies vanquished. Tell your children that *hate* died in the arena today. *Fear* died here too. And all ill will." He looked hard at his uncle. "May it ever be so for my family's house!"

He must not be afraid of collapsing now. *Must* complete what he needed to do.

"Therefore, in the name of my brother King Dallen, I free these men you see standing before you!"

His energy was almost spent. The guards and jailors from under the arena had come out to stand by the gate and watch. He beckoned to them. "Unlock these chains at once!"

I STOOD by Dallen's head and watched the jailors scurry to obey. Saw Ravelin turn to Pate and clasp his hand. Saw all the men bow the knee to the prince. And saw Ravelin begin to slump. Pate reached out an arm to steady him.

The bears were keeping vigilant watch on the royal box and the armed guards in the stands that surged now around the Duke.

"This is too much for your brother, Bear," I said in Dallen's ear. "He is ill."

Bear turned at this. "Mount the men, Silvie. We must go without delay."

Pate helped Ravelin onto the bear behind Rosie, then climbed up himself, followed by Guardsmen. Drony and the remaining Guardsmen joined me on Dallen.

"Aware!" I cried, as we raced toward the arena gates. It was a Guardsman command I had learned from my father. One they cried the moment duty came. A small word that meant so much more to the Guardsmen than to anyone else who heard it.

The crowd roared and cheered, delighted at the show and the prince's part in it. But I thought too that they exulted in the sight of innocent men being set free, and felt the triumph of the men riding away on the very animals that had been meant to kill them.

MAGO AND ALLARD spoke urgently together at her side. Olivia tried to hear what they were saying, but Petronia was close to throwing a fit.

"What is Ravelin doing? He's crazy! What is going on?" she repeated over and over.

Meanwhile, cries of *Dallen, Dallen!* echoed around the ring. The stands began to empty. People ran eagerly toward the entrance, while others imitated Ravelin and dropped into the arena. It looked like there would be a run on the castle by those determined to catch a glimpse of this phantom prince. Dallen somehow back from the dead.

Olivia put a hand on Petronia's shoulder in an attempt to console her, but her daughter shook it off. Petronia stood up and stamped her foot, then turned to leave the royal box. Olivia let her go.

"A bear mishandled can kill anyone, even a prince," Allard was saying to Mago. "We can use that. We have your weapons. And the pearl fire. And, remember, most of the castle will obey only me.

"Do not be alarmed. If Dallen is truly there, we won't let him get away this time. I swear to you, Mago, that when this day is over, *I will be King.*"

70

The Duke's Audience Chamber

Only once did we pause in the tunnel, and that was to order the jailors in the king's name to tend the animals and return them to where they belonged. One instant later, we were in full career, flying through the stone underground of the castle, the bears running one after the other.

When we reached the upper corridors, Bear cleared our way with mighty roars that echoed in the halls. Courtiers and footmen scattered before him. He stopped before a pair of ornately carved doors, plated with gold. Guards in half-armor stood on either side. These did not run from us, but resolutely raised their spears.

"Put those down," Ravelin cried. "In the name of King Dallen!"

The men raised their weapons higher. Their eyes had a strange shimmer, like sun angling off bright stone. They seemed not to hear the prince or be aware of anything else.

Rosie's bear held up one paw. The guards slid down the hallway on either side of us as if thrown. Bear smote the doors with a mighty blow and they flew open.

With one bound, we were inside the Duke's audience chamber.

TARA AND FOX approached the entrance to the arena, then stopped, bewildered. People poured out of its gates, every one of them in a state of unusual excitement. A yip from Fox made her stop and stand back.

"What? What is it?" she cried out to the people running past.

"Dallen is back! King Dallen is here!" They were almost dancing as they sang the words. "He's at the castle!"

A mass of people rushed toward the castle's main hall. *Dallen! Dallen!* they chanted as they ran.

What did this mean? Had they seen Dallen somehow? Had he come out of the bear? Silvie and Rosie must be with Dallen, wherever he was.

"Come, Fox!" She picked up the animal and ran with the main body of people. If they were running toward Dallen, she had to run that way too.

In the middle of the gravel swath before the castle entrance, she passed the mayor of Elva, futilely holding up his hands as if he could stop the onrush. Her eyes met his as she hurried by, and with a shock she realized that he had recognized her.

She pulled her scarf across her nose and mouth and pushed forward. She would have to be more careful in the castle.

Footmen and a handful of guards were trying to keep people from entering, but still the crowd pushed forward. Suddenly, a mighty roar sounded within the castle. A terrifying roar. Rattling the windows and shaking the iron lamp posts on the gravel drive. The crowd's momentum wavered. People on the steps ahead of her began to turn back.

A man's face appeared above the others in the open doorway. "The bears are loose!" he cried out. He plunged down into the crowd.

Tara flattened herself against the balustrade, clutching Fox, as people spun in confusion.

Another roar sounded, louder than the first, and fear convinced the crowd, driving it back down the steps again. Footmen and guards left their posts, joining the flight.

When the steps cleared, Tara lunged through the doors and into the wide entrance hall. Stairways and corridors led from it in all directions. She paused and set Fox down.

"Which way, Fox?"

The animal hesitated. A third roar sounded from the hall at the opposite side of the entrance. Fox gave a yip, and Tara hurried toward it. Soon, no one blocked her way. Servants in palace livery raced down the hall from the opposite direction, panic on their faces. She dodged them, held the scarf across her face with one hand, and pressed on.

WE COULD NOT HAVE ENTERED a place more unlike the arena tunnel. The audience chamber was vast, and I had an instant impression of ivory and gold elegance. On one wall, a giant mirror. On the next, a large fireplace filled with logs burning brightly.

In the back of the room, opposite, but far distant from the mirror, tables covered with white linen held cakes and more. A few aproned workers startled and exclaimed at our entrance, but did not stop their arranging of goblets and bottles of wine.

But I had no time to go beyond these brief impressions. The arena had been only the beginning. Our worst challenge would take place here.

At a gruff bark from Bear, we all dismounted, and the Guardsmen immediately spread throughout the room. I saw them, then I didn't, so quickly had they hidden themselves. I was not to be the general in this battle. Something greater was needed.

I looked around eagerly for the other Guardians, and longed to ask Dallen when the other bears would come. Ravelin's gaze also eagerly searched the room as he slid off the bear.

He leaned heavily on his friend. "Pate, do you see him? Do you see Dallen?"

Instead of answering, Pate cried out to all of us. "Whatever happens, do not look into that mirror, or the Duke will enslave you!" I immediately felt the mirror's pull, but turned my face away. Rosie, by my side, did the same.

Ravelin echoed his friend's urgency. "Don't look at it!"

A concealed door opened in the corner of the hall, between the mirror and the fireplace. The Duke stepped through, followed by many of the palace guard. They took up positions along the mirror wall, spears in hand, tips up. Ready. Others stationed themselves along the fireplace wall, and these put arrows to their strings. Mago, their chief, was not among them.

"How clever of you, Ravelin, to warn them about the mirror," said the Duke. "It is indeed powerful, more powerful than these bears. But still, I don't think you understand."

"Don't look at it, whatever he does!" Ravelin repeated, with energy.

"Now, who will you warn beyond these strange companions of yours?" the Duke continued. "No one in the castle will believe you now. They all believe their minds are their own. Even if I would tell them the truth, they would not believe it." He motioned towards the cooks and assistants among the food tables.

Those servants worked on, heedless of monster bears and broken doors. *Were they real?* I wondered.

How could normal people ignore these things? A chill ran up my back.

"Where's Dallen?" Ravelin cried, turning to me, desperation in his voice.

Before I could begin to answer, the Duke mocked Ravelin's question.

"Yes, where *is* Dallen?" He stepped directly in front of his abominable mirror, trying to force our eyes to look in his direction. I kept my gaze on Ravelin.

"Could it be," the Duke went on, "that Dallen is in fact *truly* dead, as I have told you countless times? Could it be that these rather shocking and ill-dressed women lied to you?

"And as for your speech in the arena, Ravelin, though your words sounded brave in your own ears, you can see now how foolish they were."

A low rumble came from one of the bears.

"Look at me, boy!" the Duke demanded shrilly.

But Ravelin did not turn his head. He gazed at me instead as I mouthed the words. *In the bear.* He shook his head, not understanding.

"Very well then." The Duke raised his hand and gave a small motion with his fingers, a motion that almost looked like a friendly greeting. "Aim for the prince."

Faster than the arrows could fly, the bears shielded us—Ravelin, Pate, Rosie, and me—and by their motions pushed us back against the wall near the door we had come in. The bears knocked the arrows down mid-flight or let them bounce harmlessly off their fur.

But still more arrows flew. And from our position we

could hear the strange, grim song of the bowstrings releasing their darts again and again.

After many sickening moments, the Duke finally gave the command to stop. Rosie and Pate held tight to each of the prince's arms, supporting him as he slumped against the ivory wall behind the shield of bears.

"He's been poisoned," Pate said. His own face looked hollow. "For weeks..." He could not finish for the anguish that contorted his features.

I put my face close to Ravelin's. "I did not lie," I said firmly. "Your brother has been concerned for you these many weeks. He would have died at the hands of the hunters. The Guardians of Rilken kept him safe."

Ravelin raised his head and stared at me. "*Is* he safe?"

I nodded. "*Yes.* And he is here just as he said."

One of the bears raised himself to stand on his hind legs, while the other remained a shield for us. Taller and taller the first grew. Taller and larger than I had ever seen him before. We gazed up at him in wonder.

The bear opened his mouth. The words came in a fearsome growl, yet each one could be clearly heard.

" I. Am. Dallen."

Ravelin and Pate gaped in amazement. But Dallen looked over the Duke's head toward the mirror.

A SHRIEK CAME from the Duke. "You cannot touch this mirror!" he cried. "Nothing can destroy it. Nothing can, I tell you! If you dare harm it, it will kill them."

The private door had opened again, and a small

thicket of people stood in the doorway watching, the Duchess among them.

The Duke's voice mounted higher. "I own them! I own their thoughts, their wills. Don't come near this mirror or they will die!"

Dallen looked down at the Duke from his great height. He dropped to all fours and was still taller than the man. The bear head lowered, ears flattened to its skull. He took one step toward his uncle.

"Mago!" the Duke screamed. "*Mago!*"

TARA HURRIED towards the sound of shouting, to where the rumble of a bear voice came like thunder. She had lost her scarf in a brief collision with a frightened footman, but it didn't matter now. The castle corridor was almost completely empty.

Except.

Coming straight toward her was the one person in all of Elva that she feared. Her steps faltered. She was closer to the open doors than he was. But he was very fast.

Her only hope was to get through the door ahead of him.

"You!" bellowed Mago. Hate filled his eyes. "Why are you here? I swore I'd kill you if you came back!" He drew the short knife from his belt and strode confidently toward her.

Another roar burst into the air around them. Mago's steps slowed.

Tara stared down the man who had cursed Bevan. "Do you hear that, Mago? Truth has come and you can never kill it!" she cried out.

He lunged forward. She turned and ran for the door.

A heavy splat sounded behind her. The sound of a big man having been tripped by a fox. Mago was quick to get back on his feet, but Fox had given her a few steps more. A few moments more.

Moments to enter the audience hall and glimpse Bear.

To hear Rosie cry out.

To feel Mago's hand on her back, grabbing at her hair.

To see Mago fly through the air, knife in hand, and crash into a row of palace guards, knocking them down like a cannonball in a field of wheat stalks, until he came to lie at the Duke's feet.

PATE STOOD STARING. That formidable beast-man. That Mago of nightmares. The arm of the bear had moved in a flash. And Mago flew like a seed tuft in a gale.

Mago's arrival must have injured many of his spearmen. The shouts from the mirror wall were desperate, but determined.

That woman who rushed in. Had she just *confronted* him? *Mago?*

His father's story came back to him. Of a woman in Guardstown that had won his admiration for her bravery. Who dared to challenge Mago's lie. Bevan's wife. A woman with daughters.

He studied the two girls. They were clearly her daughters, and from what he had seen in the arena and since, as brave as their mother. He had no time to think of it further.

Because, at the moment, all the blood seemed to drain from Ravelin's face.

RAVELIN WAS NOT WELL and we could not help him, because to my eyes we were in the worst dilemma. The bears could not move to destroy the mirror that empowered the palace guard because they were protecting us, and especially protecting Ravelin. With the hidden Guardsmen still weaponless, we were in a deadlock.

And yet—curiously—the bears did not signal to the Guardsmen for assistance. Surely there were enough objects and ornaments in the hall that could be used as weapons! Why did the bears not attack the archers and spearmen? Would they do *nothing* but knock the death darts from the air until all arrows had been spent?

I did not understand this battle, not from anything my father had ever told me. I could not sense these bears as I did other animals. But I felt a steady, purposeful calm coming from them. A calm that seemed to point to one thing.

Could it be that this fight did not belong to the hands of mortals? If it did, surely the Guardsmen would have joined in at once. No, this was not a mortal fight.

Something unseen was at war with the Guardians of Rilken.

An eerie twang marked the beginning of another onslaught of arrows. I heard the grunts of men as spears flew from their hands. Though not one passed through the protection of the bears, the point of each seemed to find a mark in Ravelin's soul.

He slid to the floor, while Rosie and Pate did their best to gentle his fall. Mama knelt beside him at once, and cradled his head in her lap, as a mother cradles a fallen son. Pate loosened the tightness of the shirt around the prince's throat. Ravelin was conscious, but without strength.

Rosie crouched at his side and gazed at him with a stricken face. I saw him look up at her. He lifted a weak hand and she took it.

A rumble sounded from deep inside the bears. A thrumming that wavered high and low. Rosie looked up in surprise.

"Silvie," she whispered, "That's the Song of the Hosts!"

For Love of AllHallen. The song Rosie had sung with Harper at the inn.

The bears opened their mouths and out came the song in a majestic roar. Words of sober joy shot into the Duke's audience hall. Words that exulted in melting chains and demolishing a captor's hold. Words of life and courage. And of a powerful Love beyond imagination.

The bears' voices sounded like rapturous thunder while they struck spears from the air. While arrows hit their pelts and fell uselessly to the ground. While color returned to Ravelin's face.

An acrid smell permeated the room. The grunts of men and twang of bowstrings died quickly away amidst a piercing scream. The Duke cried out in agony.

"My mirror! No! No! *Stop!* You can't do this. I own it. It was mine since the day it was born. It can't be destroyed! It can't!"

I peeked through a small gap between the bears. Mago, bleeding from his shoulders, had managed to stand again, unsteadily, at his master's side. The Duke stretched his arms out to the mirror, wailing with a hideous grief. The mirror had gone completely gray and was crumbling in on itself in a billow of smoke.

And still the Song of the Hosts went on.

In the middle of its triumphant chorus, Dallen stepped out from underneath the arm of a bear as naturally as a man emerges from his shelter after a storm.

71

Sight and Unsight

"Uncle," Dallen said. "Your evil is undone."

I heard bold determination in his voice.

At the sound of it, Ravelin sat up. He stared at his brother, eyes full of wonderment.

The Duke turned from his ruined mirror. He, too, stared at the nephew standing before him in travel-stained clothes. But there was no wonderment in his eyes.

The lines of the Duke's face twisted, distorted from emotion. His mouth opened and his lips moved silently. His shoulders heaved. He seemed to be gasping for air.

When he found enough, he pointed at Dallen. "Kill him, Mago! Kill him! Hurry! Now! Do you hear me? *Now!*"

But something else had been happening while the mirror crumbled and the Duke struggled for breath. Some of the palace guard had dropped their bows and grabbed at their eyes. Some drew their knives from their belts slowly with one hand, groping for something in the empty air with the other. One took a step only to stumble and fall, while another struck out at an invisible foe.

"They can't see," I said over my shoulder to the group behind me. "The palace guard has gone blind!"

"If this is the mirror's undoing," Pate replied, "then everyone who has gazed into it must be going blind at this moment."

But terrified men with weapons are deadly. The Guardsmen came cautiously from their concealment.

"Drop your weapons!" Drony called out. "Drop them now or you'll kill each other! Drop them and stay still. We will not harm you!"

Some dropped them, believing the unseen voice. Others gripped their knives more tightly, and when they jostled each other, struck wildly at the imagined threat.

The Duke kept urging Mago to kill Dallen, but Mago was in the same grip of blindness as the others. And more frantic than any. He lashed out at a spearman who stumbled into him and the spearman fell to the ground.

But the Duke would not be gainsaid. He too was in a frenzy, and he pummeled his strong man with fists as well as words.

Mago turned abruptly. His knife met the Duke with force.

"Drop your weapons now!" Drony cried. "You've

killed the Duke! Drop them, in the name of our new king! In the name of King Dallen, drop them at once!"

The last of the weapons clattered to the ground and a hush fell on the room. A hush broken only by the groans of the wounded.

BUT WE WERE NOT to remain in that horrible room. Something of the greatest importance had to be done at once.

The bears ushered us out and down the corridor toward the huge entrance hall of the castle. One of them carried Ravelin on its back, while Dallen walked beside it, talking eagerly with his brother. Mama, Pate, Rosie, and I followed behind.

Cat had found her way to the upper halls of the castle and was sitting watchfully near the foot of a decorative column. Behind her was Fox. His side was badly bruised, and he was terribly sore. I knew at once what he had done to save Mama and scooped him up into my arms.

When we gained the main entrance hall, the bears took Dallen and Ravelin up to the first landing, the broad space before the great staircase split in two. From that place, they turned around to look out over the lower hall.

The bears let out a mighty roar, the kind of which I had never heard before. This was not a roar of warning, the kind that had cleared the corridors before we raced through them. This was a roar that called. That sounded an irresistible call. Not the coercion of evil or fear, but the compelling of anticipation, of the desire for some great good long delayed.

And people came.

The sound of hurrying footsteps in every corridor signaled their approach. Doors along the hallways opened, even hidden servants' doors, and people poured forth. They entered from outside, inside, above us, and below stairs.

They seemed to come from everywhere. The fast and the slower. The seeing and the blind. Some felt their way along the walls, but all came.

The Duchess entered from behind us, her hand held by a lowly maid, and I realized that, in one instance, her blindness was merciful. She would not have seen the death of her husband.

When the room could hold no more, and the hallways themselves were gorged, when the large entrance doors stood open for the sake of the crowd without, the bears roared again and every tongue held still.

From the stair landing above us, Pate cried, "People of Elva, People of Rilken! With great joy, I announce to you that your true king has returned. Dallen, Prince of the Crown, is now King of all Rilken! Give him honor!"

At once, this great mass of people bowed the knee and bowed low, joining in the cry that had greeted kings from the beginning of time. "We hail you as king! As *our* king! We hail you as our king!"

The bears must have lent Ravelin their strength, for after our shouts had died away, he was able to stand, leaning on Pate at the top of the stairs. He called out, "Hear all people! Witness now that I swear loyalty to

Dallen—my brother, my king—with my whole heart, now and for the rest of my days."

Ravelin knelt before Dallen and the crowd erupted in cheers. Cheers that echoed around and around the vast hall, growing in might until the sound was deafening. The hatred of the Duke toward his own brother had brought grief and harm and death to so many. What could the great love and loyalty of a brother do, but mend, recover, and restore?

Tears filled my eyes as Dallen lifted his brother to his feet and clasped him in a strong hug. I thought of the bear that had walked into our clearing so many days ago, of the pain and loneliness of the man he had carried inside, of his weary sojourn. And now here he was. Restored to his rightful place. I was still holding Fox and didn't dare put him down in this crowd, so I bent my head to wipe my eyes on my cloak-covered arm.

Rosie grabbed my other arm, jolting me. "Silvie! Look!"

At first, I was confused and glanced at Mama. She was staring up at the landing, transfixed. Her face the face of one who saw angels.

Then I saw.

A look of great surprise and delight was on Dallen's face. Because between the two great bears, another man had bent the knee to honor Dallen as king. This was a tall, able-bodied man. With the clothing and short hair of a Guardsman. Hair in color like mine.

.   .   .

DALLEN THREW his arms around the man. Hugging him as he had hugged his brother. Then he turned to the crowd who waited below.

"People of Rilken! Dear People of Rilken! I claim your honor for this man. *He* is the one who saved the life of your king! Sweep away what lies you may have believed, and join me in honoring with your whole hearts Bevan the Guardsman!"

King Dallen himself began the cheer. Mama, Rosie, and I clung to each other and bawled as Papa's name was praised in a glorious din. Pate came down the steps, ready to escort us to the landing. He took Fox from my arms and carried him over one shoulder, while taking Mama's hand.

I went up those stairs in a daze. Afraid to take my eyes from Papa, lest he disappear from sight. Mama stepped up onto the landing and Papa wrapped his arms around her. She clung to him, and Rosie and I clung to both of them together. Then Papa's arms encircled us too.

For a moment, I forgot the castle and the crowd that watched us. All I knew in the whole world was that Papa had returned from death itself. And all the longing pain of love could turn to rejoicing again.

I felt a gentle touch on my shoulder, pulling me back to awareness of other things. Pate took my arm and led me to Dallen. Dallen held out his hand to me, and I felt its warmth and strength close around mine.

"Thank you," I said, my whole heart in my eyes. "Thank you so very, very much."

Dallen smiled, then—grasping my hand and Rosie's

—faced the crowd and called out something about the arena. But my mind and heart were too full to attend to what he was saying.

Cheering rolled up from the huge hall below, again and again, echoing all around us. All I could do was look from Papa to Dallen and back to Papa again.

72

Rosabel's Gift

We were given castle apartments of our own —Mama, Papa, Rosie, and I—with a lovely sitting room in the middle, and bedrooms off to the sides. Rosie and I gladly bathed and washed the dirt of the arena and the smell of the tunnel from our hair. Clean clothes were brought for all of us, and trays of food delivered to our door.

Yes, we ate and rested, but mostly we stayed close to Papa. Hugging him, listening to him, openly staring. Our eyes still could not get enough of him, even though night had come and all the candles were lit.

Mama sat at his side on the couch. Rosie and I, wrapped in luxurious robes, our clean hair brushed out to dry, sat on the thick carpet at his feet while he told his story.

He had seen the approach of the palace guard on the forest road, seen the Duke's odd signal, and moved his position to be closer to Dallen. Two Guardsmen had been at the king's side when the king bolted forward, but, like Dallen said, the first blow struck the king from behind. From the Guardsmen at the rear.

Papa could barely say the words.

He pulled Dallen from his horse and blocked the path into the woods. The palace guard shot the Guardsmen and the king's other attendants as they sat on their horses. Then the palace guard turned all their arrows on him.

Arrow after arrow struck his shield. All in a moment. Before he could get into the cover of the trees. The shield broke apart in his hand beneath the onslaught.

"I saw the arrow that was meant to take my life." He spoke slowly and we felt the weight of every word with him. "Saw it release from the bow. It flew as if time had stopped and there was nothing in the world except that arrow and me. I couldn't move. Just watched it come.

"Then something knocked it out of the air. A huge, powerful paw. It knocked down the next arrow, and the next, until the palace guard turned their horses and fled.

"Bodies of the fallen lay all over the road. There was no one alive but me, and I didn't know why I was. I went to the king and carried him to a protected place, under a great tree. When I reached for him, my hands and arms had become the arms and paws of a bear. A bear that stayed at the work in spite of my bewilderment."

Other bears came to help him. After the bodies of the king and his companions were taken to Elva, Papa's bear was sent east, to eastern Rilken. He defended the farms—even Gramma and Grampy's farm—from wolves for a number of days, until the bear took him to Galerine, where he destroyed the workshop of lerin mirrors.

"At that workshop, I learned the danger of these mirrors, how they twisted the mind, and so I learned what must have happened to the Guardsmen. The bear took me into the hills then, to the mine that dug one of the minerals necessary for the mirrors. We scared the miners out and set the mine on fire, destroying the mineral and the mine together."

He paused and looked around at us. "But I feared for you. Feared for my family because of what devilment might be going on in Elva. One morning early, I ran by a Rilken cabbage field. But in this field, roses grew alongside the cabbages. I stopped and stared at it." He took Mama's hand in both of his.

"The colors of the roses, the earth, everything was in the colors of the pouch you made for me, Tara. Peace filled me and I could think clearly again. That was before the bear took me to Galerine."

"But how did you get to the arena, Papa?" Rosie asked.

"After I returned from Galerine, I saw hunting bands combing the towns and farms. I watched them from a distance. It didn't take me long to figure out they were coming for me with their absurd nets. So, one morning, I sat still in a field and let them drape one over me."

"But why?" I asked.

"Because the next part of this battle needed to be fought in Elva." He looked at Rosie and me, pride on his face. "And when I saw the two of you come down that tunnel—"

Rosie reached up and hugged him. "Oh, Papa, if I had known it was *you* racing in the arena—"

"You wouldn't have been able to concentrate on what you needed to do," he replied.

"That's true," I said, leaning my head on his knee. "Neither one of us would."

OUR SLEEP WAS sweet that night, but when we awoke and dressed, Rosie was in a quiet mood. By mid-morning it had not lifted, and I was concerned for her.

"I think I need to get out among the plants, Silvie. Out among the growing green." She had been gazing out the window and turned to look at me. "Does that sound odd?"

"Not at all," I replied. "You still have the Sender's gift. You didn't leave it in the forest. I'm sure you'd be allowed to walk in the palace gardens."

She brightened at this and reached for the new cloak that had been laid out for her. White Squirrel looked up at her imploringly.

"I don't think you should ride on my shoulder anymore, Squirrel," she said in a serious voice. "That might not be castle decorum."

"That cloak has large pockets," I said.

The light green cloak looked beautiful over her pale

gold dress, and White Squirrel fit in the pocket perfectly.

Rosie was almost to the door when she stopped. "Silvie," she said, in the pleading voice of a little sister. "Shouldn't I feel happy now? Papa's alive! The Duke is gone. And—and so much more. Why do I feel so heavy and sad?"

I had been thinking of the same thing. "We've seen a lot of cruelty, Rosie, and those we love have suffered greatly. There is still so much healing needed. So much."

She looked at me with solemn eyes. "His hand was so cold, Silvie. I thought he was dying." A grimace of pain crossed her face, and she left the room.

I knew she was speaking of Ravelin and my heart went out to her.

For my part I was thinking of Dallen.

Last night, Papa left for a short conference with the new king to consider the problem of the mirror-blind. When he returned, he told us that in spite of the Duke's boasts, it was hoped that less than a third of the castle inhabitants had been blinded, but the blinding had affected important portions of the castle community.

Did the evil go farther than just physical blindness? Would the pearl-eyed rise against their king again?

Dallen had ordered that all the blind remain in their rooms for the time being. Papa said the king was baffled at what to do beyond that.

Spring appeared to be in full flower when Ravelin and Wells entered the gardens. Blooms of yellow, white, pink, and purple lit the green of the walks in a cheering way. Wells insisted on pushing Ravelin in the wheeled chair, and Ravelin let him. He never knew from one moment to the next how much strength he would have.

But it felt so good to be able to leave his room without fear. More Guardians had come, and they roamed the halls of the castle. For the first time since his father had left for Tellhaven, the castle was a safe place to live again.

Ravelin took a deep breath of the fresh spring air. "Take this path, if you will, Wells," he said, pointing to one that led to a group of blossoming trees.

"Yes, sir," Wells replied with exuberance. He seemed glad to be outside too.

Ravelin saw Rosabel at once. Her red hair strikingly beautiful beside the white of a flowering apple tree. She was bending to look at a group of plants beneath it, when the sound of their approach made her stand up and look toward them. He saw a look of surprise on her face, then she bowed her head and curtsied.

Ravelin had received such homage all his life, but he felt uncomfortable at this. "After what you've done, I should be bowing to you," he said.

Before she could reply, he asked, "Could we talk for awhile, Rosabel? If Wells would push me over to that bench, you would have a place to sit."

Wells did as he was asked, then withdrew a discreet

distance to a bench of his own. Rosabel sat down and as she did so, Ravelin found himself distracted by the color in her cheeks, the glow of her red hair in the sunlight, the eyes that sparkled with life and looked at him so openly. He forgot what he wanted to say and fell back on a common politeness instead.

"Are you enjoying the gardens?" he asked.

"Very much." She glanced at the colors on either side of them. "So much thought has gone into the beauty and arrangement of your plantings. Your gardeners have done marvelously. The trees and bushes are so grateful."

This last sounded like an odd remark to Ravelin. She must have seen it on his face.

"It's the Sender's gift," she said. "I used to see only color. Now I hear exuberant voices of life. The flowers and bushes—they tell me about themselves."

She pointed to a box tree. "This small tree, so slow-growing and steady? It's name is Faithful. Not a name I gave it, but what it calls itself. It knows you and your brother and is glad to be here in this garden."

His puzzlement increased. Rosabel reddened.

"Does that sound strange, that the plants talk to me?" she asked. "I'm not making it up. It *is* the Sender's gift. I had a hard time believing it myself at first. Is it—is it something *you* can believe?" Concern showed on her face.

"My brother has been a bear," Ravelin replied. "I can believe anything now."

She laughed at this. A delightful laugh. Ravelin smiled, then he turned serious.

"Dallen has always been the best of brothers, but his experience inside the bear has changed him. He's become a deeper, truer version of himself. I've always looked up to him with the pride only a younger brother can feel, I suppose. But now I admire him even more." He leaned forward slightly, resting his elbows on the arms of his chair, and fell silent.

"I asked Papa what it felt like to be inside the bear," she said. "He said it was like wearing living armor. Armor that sometimes followed his movements, but more often led them."

He thought about this. "I can see how that would be. Dallen said the bear spoke to him. Teaching him. Comforting him. Leading him to your family. It was a very hard time for him, and he was grateful to you all."

"It was a very hard time for you." She looked intently at him. "You've been living a nightmare," she said quietly. "I saw it on your face in the arena."

They had come to what he wanted to know, but feared to ask. "Did you mean what you said about me in the arena?" he asked, feeling shy. "Do you remember it?"

"That your heart is good and true?" She still looked at him openly. "I've known it since you were ten years old. Yes, I meant it." Her words carried conviction.

"Rosabel, when you said those things, you changed everything for me. My uncle used my fear to imprison me. You gave me courage to do what I could not have done without you. Seeing you burst into the arena riding on a bear, under the steel of the palace guard, and making everyone sing—I will not forget that moment. Ever."

She smiled, looked embarrassed, and dropped her gaze.

"It reminded me of the Nordian tales of The Fearless. Have you read them?" he asked.

"Countless times," she replied, looking up again. "I always thought my father was one of The Fearless, but he said he was not. Though I think him one of the most fearless people I know."

"Dallen told me everything that happened on the forest road. I owe your father the greatest debt," Ravelin said.

They sat for a few moments in silence, looking around at the flowers and trees.

"I've often thought about The Fearless," Rosabel said. "I'm so curious about them. What do they know that the rest of us don't?" She turned to him as if he knew the answer.

Ravelin's heart leapt. "I've thought much about the same thing!"

"Do you know what they know?" she asked.

He shook his head. "No, but I would love to find out."

"I would too."

They were sitting near the apple tree, and a light breeze dislodged white petals from its branches, wafting them into her lap. She picked one up and turned it over in her hand.

"What is it telling you now?" Ravelin asked. "Some mysteries of the future?"

Rosabel shook her head. "Trees don't know the future." She held up the petal. "This white petal is filled with a glorious happiness." She looked up into the tree. "Every one of them is."

"Dallen told me about the Sender's gifts," he said, "and how every animal does whatever Silvie tells it to. Do the plants do what you tell them also?"

"No. I mean—I don't tell them anything. Plants and animals are so different."

He wanted her to keep talking. He wanted to listen to everything she could possibly say.

"What would you ask the plants to do, if they *could* do it?" he asked.

She stood up, brushed the petals gently from her skirt, and turned her head toward the bushes and flowers, the trees and the stately grasses that surrounded them. He wondered what she saw that he could not.

"I would say," she raised her voice and held out a beckoning arm to the garden. "All those who can, please, heal Ravelin. Heal my prince. Please."

She lowered her arm and turned to him, a depth of meaning in her gaze. "That's what I would say."

The sunlight inflamed the brilliance of her hair. Her eyes glowed with green and hazel and gold. He had rarely seen anything so beautiful in his life. And what were those eyes saying to him?

The loud chittering of a squirrel broke through his thoughts. A small white squirrel was leaping up and down on the path. Astonished, Ravelin realized something was flying through the air.

"Rosabel!" he cried. "Look behind you!"

Leaves and petals detached themselves from the

trees, bushes, and flowers around them. Not just a few, or a dozen.

Hundreds.

A whole sea of green and white, purple, pink, and yellow flew through the air, using the breeze to make their way toward where he sat. They landed softly on his head, his neck, his hands until he was covered with every color of leaf and flower.

As he watched, wide-eyed, the leaves broke themselves apart and sticky salve seeped onto his skin. Some gave a clear, golden fluid. Others a milky white or pale green color.

"What are they doing?" Ravelin exclaimed aloud. The leaves took the opportunity to break themselves on his tongue. Sweetness filled his mouth. Then spicy coolness.

Rosabel took one of Ravelin's hands, and gently rubbed the salve into his fingers, his palms, and his wrists.

"Wells! Come help me!" she cried.

Wells ran to them, and together they rubbed the ointments the plants had given into his neck and across his forehead. Wherever they rubbed, Ravelin felt healing flow into him. Like spring after winter. Like warmth after a long chill. Like hope after despair.

When the salve had all been rubbed in, Rosabel sat down on the bench and leaned forward. Her sparkling eyes studied him. She seemed hesitant to say anything. To ask anything. Wells, too, watched expectantly.

Ravelin looked down at his hands, turning them over. He took a deep breath. Swallowed. Then took another deep breath. The healing warmth had gone completely through him leaving joy in its wake. He couldn't sit still any longer, and got to his feet with ease.

Rosabel stood up too. "How—how do you feel now?" she asked cautiously.

"Whole," he said, wanting to shout with the truth of it. "Wonderful! All the tightness in my chest is gone. My heart beats strong again." He took off his cape, laid it on the chair, and shot a glance at his attendant. "Wells! Watch this!"

Ravelin took a few running steps down the gravel path, leapt into the air, landed on his hands ignoring the sharp rocks, flipped himself over, and landed on his feet. It felt exhilarating!

"Perfect form, sir!" Wells cried.

Ravelin ran back to them. He grabbed Rosabel's hands. "Thank you, Rosabel! Thank you!"

"But I didn't do anything!" she protested.

"You wanted me well. Everything you have done has brought life back to me. You are my bright star! And I have found you!"

She gazed at him, and in her eyes he saw what he had always hoped to see in a woman's eyes. "Your eyes are so clear," she said. "So bright. So alive!"

"Prince Ravelin!" she cried suddenly. *"Your eyes!* What if the gardens hold healing for the mirror-blind too?" She squeezed his hands, then stepped away, turning again toward the long expanse of garden. Again, she held out her arms.

"All who can heal the mirror blindness, come to me!"

The garden stirred itself as in a breeze. Waving back and forth. Circling around. Stirred itself as a cook lovingly, purposefully, stirs her soup.

Rosabel took off her cloak, and Ravelin laid down his cape. Wells took the blanket from the back of the wheeled chair. They spread them out on the grass to capture whatever the plants would send.

In moments, color filled the sky again.

73

Grace from the Sender's Hall

Pate came from the king's study, his heart a turbulent mix of emotion. The news of Dallen's return and his kingship had brought Avelyn and his mother and grandmother to the castle, eager to find him under Dallen's protection. They stayed in the castle now, and his mother joined Rosie in her work to restore the mirror-blind. But his father was gone.

And that crushing loss was not the only weight on Pate's heart.

Several days after Dallen's return, Pate had gone to see Lady Locke. He was tormented by the thought that because he switched Lord Locke's dinner tray with Ravelin's, he had brought about Lord Locke's death. He told Lady Locke what he had done. She lay on a blue couch in her sitting room, staring with sightless eyes toward the ceiling while he asked her forgiveness.

He waited for her reply, but the only answer was silence. After a long time, she merely said, "Leave me now, Pate." He had obeyed.

Avelyn was waiting for him now on a bench in the corridor outside the king's study. She stood up, watching his face closely.

"What did the king say?"

He reached for her hand, but before he could answer, he heard footsteps coming toward them, the sound of heels clipping along on marble floors. Lady Locke came down the hall, wearing her customary light blue brocade gown.

She walked steadily, but without her usual energy. Her step slowed as she approached, and she held her hand out to him with something of her old friendly manner.

"Hello, Pate."

Gratefully, he took her hand and bowed over it. "Good day, Lady Locke. You are out of your room and walking now? May I ask after your health?"

"I've been better. Such headaches and confusion. And the blindness! I lay on that bed for days believing I would never get up again. That I would follow my poor husband to the grave. Then those delightful women came to visit me with salve for the eyes. They come see me every day, and I keep getting better."

"It gladdens my heart to hear that, ma'am. I must tell you that I am so sorry for your loss. The death of your dear husband grieves me beyond measure."

Tears filled her eyes. "Thank you, Pate." Her voice wavered. "I do miss him so. Nothing seems right with him gone."

"How could it?" he replied quietly.

She nodded slowly, then laid her hand on his arm. "I want you to know that I have been thinking about what you said. About the trays. And I believe that Lord Locke would approve of what you did. He loved his king, and his king's sons, and I know that his real and true heart would exult in the knowledge that his sacrifice saved the prince's life."

"Indeed, it did," Pate said solemnly. "He saved Prince Ravelin as surely as if he had held a shield over him."

Lady Locke blinked quickly and nodded. "I've been thinking that the accident may have unwittingly saved my husband too, Pate. What things might he have done for the Duke in his blindness, that would have grieved and haunted him all his life if he had known?"

He looked into her eyes and saw grace, sorrow, and understanding there. "Thank you, Lady Locke."

She nodded towards Avelyn. "And who is this lovely young woman?" she asked, in a brighter voice.

Pate reached out to Avelyn, and she took his hand.

"This lovely young woman is one of the king's greatest artists, soon to become Lady Avelyn."

Lady Locke's face lit up with interest. "Will that be through you, Pate, or on her own merits?"

"Both, I am glad to say. I present to you my future wife."

Lady Locke took Avelyn's hand and patted it with

her other. "I congratulate you, my dear, on your choice of such a quick-witted husband."

"Thank you, my lady," Avelyn said softly.

"I have just found out that I am to be advisor to our king," said Pate. "I will never be as good as Lord Locke, but I will do my best to be useful to His Majesty. And if not that, at least to make him laugh."

Avelyn's eyes glowed at the news. Lady Locke smiled.

"Laughter is very useful, I think. You will do well, Pate. You will do well." She seemed about to continue on her way, then turned back to them.

"Come visit me in my apartments some evening, you and your lady. I am often alone there and would like your company."

"Thank you for your gracious invitation," he replied. "We will most certainly come."

"We will come," Avelyn echoed.

He watched his old friend continue down the hall, and kept watching long after she had turned the corner and disappeared.

NIGHT HAD COME. After hours of trying to sleep, Tara lay awake in bed long past the midnight chime of the castle's tower clock.

Candles still burned in the silver stand on the table by her bed. Several books lay by its base, placed there for the use of guests. But she did not want to read.

She moved out of the way of the candlelight, so it could fall on the man asleep next to her, illuminating the bone of his cheek and the curve of his ears, tracing the outline of his face against the satin pillow. The light caught the glow of that beautiful pale hair that she knew he would ask her to cut again soon.

But it was healing just to look at him. Oh, how dearly lovely he was!

"You're watching me." His lips moved, but his eyes remained shut.

"Yes," she answered.

"Are you never going to sleep?"

"No."

Bevan's eyes opened then. He glanced at the look on her face and raised one eyebrow.

"Never?"

"*Never*," she said, emphatically. She leaned toward him, resting her hand on the side of his face, grateful for the feel of his skin under her fingertips. "I woke up once in the forest, smelling spring in the air. I thought I was in our feather bed and that when I opened my eyes I would see you sleeping peacefully next to me. But you weren't there. And neither was I." Her voice trembled at the memory.

"I dreamt of you so often," she said. "But morning came and the dreams vanished. Sometimes I'd see you in the firelight and I'd watch until you disappeared. When Darrit told me he buried your shield, I knew you were—gone forever."

"I would have thought the same," he said, his voice filled with understanding. "You know the Guardsmen. What else could you have thought?"

"Seeing you at the top of the stairs that day, I

thought I had entered the Sender's Hall. Now I know that some of the grace of the Sender's Hall has come to me here. And I never want to close my eyes to it again."

The light in his eyes intensified. "Neither do I." His arm came out from under the blankets and wrapped around her shoulders, pulling her to him.

"Oh, Tara, my love," he said. "My brave, brave love."

74

A Voice in the Night

Silvie. Silvie!

I woke with a start. The remains of the evening's fire still glowed on the hearth, and in the dim light I could see Fox curled up asleep on his velvet cushion on the floor. Rosie's curls sprawled all over her pillow on her side of the bed. She slept on her stomach, one arm hanging out over the floor. Rosie gave herself wholly to sleep as she gave herself wholly to everything she did.

I sat up and looked beyond her. White Squirrel still slept, curled up on her own satin pillow. The animals, then, had heard nothing to disturb them.

But there had been something so insistent in the voice I had heard, even if it were only a voice in my mind. I moved out of the bed and slid into my warm dressing gown and slippers as silently as I could. Stepping inside the heavy drape of the window, I unlatched it and pulled it open, feeling the cool rush of night air on my face.

The moon had completed much of its journey across the sky, but still reigned over a cloudless night. Beyond its glow, stars salted the darkness. I guessed it to be an hour or so before dawn.

Our window overlooked a portion of the gardens. As I looked down on the shadowy shapes of trees and hedges, I noticed the form of a large bear beneath my window. One of the Guardians of Rilken. I felt instant alarm.

"Bear," I spoke softly into the still night air. "Were you calling me?"

"All is well, Silvie. Put on your cloak and boots, or the night will be too cold for you."

I lit my bedside candle from the remains of the fire, and went at once to the cavernous room off our bedchamber that they called a wardrobe. Our new gowns hung there, but also the clothes we had worn in the forest, which I insisted on keeping. There they were, cleaned and mended, and I quickly donned a skirt Mama had altered for me, along with the layers of underclothing, vest, and blouse that I would need for protection against the night's chill. Stockings. Boots. Cloak.

When I hurried back through our room, Rosie sat up abruptly and blinked at me. "What is it?" she asked in a sleepy voice.

"Bear's at the window."

"Oh," she said. Then, without another question, she pitched back onto her pillow and into deep slumber.

Bear was waiting below. I was about to ask if I should go through the halls and meet him at the doors, when he stood on his hind legs and seemed to grow taller. Enormously tall. As I had seen him grow in the audience hall.

He turned his back to the window and the fur of his shoulders brushed the windowsill.

"Climb onto my back, Silvie. You will not fall."

I obeyed at once. As the bear gently lowered himself to the ground, I could not help speaking my concerns into his ear.

"Is Dallen all right? Is he well?"

The bear did not answer me. When all four of his paws came to rest on the ground, I realized that a man was standing there.

"I am well, Silvie," said Dallen's voice. "I'm coming up on the bear's back too."

Bear lowered to the ground as he had always done for Rosie and me, and Dallen climbed on. He sat in front of me, his hands gripping the roll of fur just as he had once instructed me. I sat behind him, one hand deep in the bear's fur, the other around Dallen's waist, the way Rosie had always situated herself.

"I've never ridden on the *outside* of the bear before," he said. There was a note of adventure in his voice.

"Where are we going?" I asked.

"Someplace very special," he replied. "Is that all right with you?"

I felt strangely happy. "Are we going to gather eggs?"

Dallen laughed and I loved the sound. "I was thinking of fish, actually. Hold on," he said, for Bear had begun to move. Fast.

I lowered my head to Dallen's back and clung to him and to the bear, while the castle gardens blurred to sight. With a bound we were over the ramparts and racing through the dark streets of Elva. In another bound, we hurdled over the city wall. A river sparkled in the remains of the moonlight. Then it vanished and we ran through rolling fields.

The bear ran as though the wind could not catch it. Yet I did not fear falling. Even if I did not have my arm around Dallen, the bear would not lose me and I would not fall. No matter how fast he went.

After a time, the night air began to tell of things that were not fields or forests, towns or cities, and it made me think of the stories of ships on the open sea.

The bear slowed to a walk and then stopped. As we slid from its back, my boots met flat stone, a solid place to stand. I looked around me, making out what I could in the thin gray light.

I was standing on a broad walkway, lined by low bushes. Behind me clustered sweet-smelling trees. Before me, the flat stone led to a structure with a roof, but no walls, and beyond it, a vast emptiness.

It could have been a forlorn place, but birds were waking and calling to each other. Their voices sounded different than the forest birds, but I could hear that they were happy, excited, and eager. And they were thinking about fish.

"Where are we?" I asked Dallen.

"The southeastern boundary of Rilken." His voice sounded excited too. "May I take your hand, Silvie? I want to show you something."

He tucked my arm securely in his, and we walked toward the open building, stepping up into it. It was a large space with a smooth tile floor and half walls that ended in pillars rising to a roof above. Dallen led me across the floor to one of the outer walls. I looked out into the grayness and realized this open room was up very high—a cliff top—and I gasped.

He pointed off to our right, to a large dark mass. "The country of Ardemount lies just over there. And this—" he waved an arm toward the immense grayness in front of us, "—is the Kartan Sea. We are standing in an outdoor ballroom."

I could see it thus. I could easily imagine people dancing in the moonlight or under the stars, while torches lit the pillars, and dozens of lutes and citterns filled the air with music.

"It must be beautiful," I said.

"It is," Dallen replied. "You'll see it when the light returns."

There was a new note in his voice, and I wondered what had made it so. I had heard the sound of his great sorrow, the desperate loneliness, the fear he had for his brother. Then the bold determination as he faced his enemies. This was different from all the rest. His voice carried the hope of joy, and it stirred my heart.

The waves crashed against the rocks at the base of the cliff in a majestic rhythm. Dallen stepped back from the view, bowed, and held his hand out to me with a flourish.

"Are you asking me to dance?" I almost laughed at the absurdity of it.

Dallen did not seem to think it absurd at all. "Why do you think we are here?"

I was too aware of my worn boots, the long braid down my back that I tied merely to control my hair for sleep, the mended cloak.

"I don't know if I'm fit for a king," I said.

Dallen grasped my hand. "I don't know if I'm fit for a king either," he said lightly.

He led me to the center of the floor and, with a smile that the dimness could not hide, bowed again while I made the appropriate curtsey. He held up one hand, palm toward me, and I knew which dance he wished to do. I pressed my hand into his.

Two small steps toward each other. Two steps back. A change of hands then steps again. We repeated the steps with hands pressed together, dancing slowly, measuring each fourth step in time with the waves.

I held one arm up into the air. He caught my hand over my head and turned me, while in my heart I heard lutes and citterns pick up the song of the waves. Another turn followed. All the while, I could not take my eyes from his. The light in his eyes seemed to come from great depths.

After the dance, he led me over to the edge of the ballroom, and we looked out again. Early light began to silver the sea, and I could make out crystal white rows of waves. Far to the east, rose streaked the sky, and gray faded to azure.

"It's magnificent!" I cried.

Dallen gazed out at the sight. "When I was seven years old, I thought this the most beautiful place in the world."

"I understand why," I replied.

"Although lately I discovered the amazing beauty one can see on a hilltop in the forests of Rilken, golden in the early morn."

I turned to look at him. He reached out a hand and touched my forehead, tracing the side of my face. "Your hair is so beautiful, so luminous in the half-light." He had not let go of my other hand since the dance. I hoped he never would.

"Silvie, when I was young I made myself a promise. That when the time came to ask a woman to be my wife, I would do it here. I want no woman by my side but you.

"In the forest I was hidden inside a frightening animal. Yet you looked past that, searching for me. I saw it in your eyes again and again. Even now, I see life in your eyes. I have loved you from the first, Silvie, and for some time I dared to hope I saw love in your eyes too."

"Yes," I whispered, unsure of my voice. "You saw rightly. It is there. So much love."

"Dearest Silvie, will you be my wife and my queen?"

I am love for my Love, the King. "Yes, Dallen. Yes."

The sun could linger no more. Its first rays streaked across the surface of the sea and touched Dallen's grey eyes with the light of dawn. He put strong and gentle hands on either side of my face. I tasted joy on his lips.

OLIVIA SAT on the small couch in her room, facing the broad fireplace. She wore her dressing gown, a blanket spread on her lap, and stared at the fire.

What had been only darkness, over time had transformed into a blur of light. Today, distinct and individual flames leapt and danced around the logs. As sight returned, her headaches eased. The sharp thorns that had challenged her every thought, dulled, then diminished. Yet numbness filled her soul.

She had sent her maids away, because now that she could see again, she wanted simply to be left alone. Left alone in a land where she could gaze at a fire and not think of anything at all. Not struggle. Not decide. Not respond. Not remember.

A knock sounded. The door opened and Petronia came in. She was wearing a simple, unadorned gown of sage-colored linen, and her long dark hair hung loosely down her back. She almost looked like a young girl again.

Instead of taking the chair opposite the couch, the one by the fireside, a place she often sat to question or debate or challenge Olivia, Petronia came over to the couch and sat down quietly beside her. She, too, seemed to become absorbed in the dancing flames. After a time, she spoke.

"Mother, I don't know who I am anymore." The words came hesitantly. "I barely trust what I think or see."

Petronia didn't usually like to be answered, often

rebelled against any attempt to console or encourage, so Olivia waited to hear more.

"I feel like my mind has been away for a long time and it has returned a stranger."

Olivia watched her daughter silently. Time hung still in the quiet room.

"What will happen to us now?" Petronia turned toward her mother, as if she wanted an answer to this question, and Olivia saw apprehension in her eyes.

"I don't know," she replied. "We'll wait to see what the king will do."

"Will—will Dallen punish us for—for what Father did?" The words came haltingly, as if fear threatened to choke each one.

Olivia didn't know how to answer. Her hands smoothed the blanket on her lap. Then some of the grayness in her mind lifted, and a thin layer of memory appeared.

A memory of the royal ballroom in Falland, glowing with thousands of candles. The slippered feet of royalty and nobility from every country in AllHallen pounding the gleaming wood floor. The man she was contracted to marry, turning aside to ask someone else to dance.

Dozens of staring eyes following her while she painfully retreated to the wall. Then—after a nightmare of agony—smiles appearing on the staring faces. Scorn turning to admiration as they stepped aside. The king of Rilken approaching.

Adare bowing and his gracious smile. *Come, my new sister. This is good music for dancing.* She heard again the applause that came when he swirled her onto the ballroom floor.

"No, Petronia," Olivia said, reaching for her daughter's hand. "Dallen will not punish us. He will be good. Just like his father."

EPILOGUE

A Forest Promise

Dallen and I were wed in the Hall of the King at Elva Castle, on the day of our coronation, six months after the fall of the mirror. Mama spent those months happily embroidering our coronation and wedding robes, creating pictures of moons and roses, mighty bears and noble rabbits, oaks and acorns —every symbol of Rilken. During the ceremony, they glowed on our shoulders like living things. Even Duke John of Nordia exclaimed in wonder.

"This marriage is the very best thing for Rilken right now," he told Mama.

"Yes," she agreed. "Silvie is her father's daughter, with the loyalty, strength, and love of the Guardsmen.

And Dallen is his father's son, with all the goodness and grace of the best of kings."

THE HEALING of the mirror-blind continued. People who did not live in the castle, yet had somehow gazed into the mirror, came to be healed from their blindness. A woman requested the healing salve on behalf of her brother, a man who had to leave the king's service because of winter fever. One afternoon he suddenly went blind. Her brother turned out to be Captain Hurd, the man my father replaced for that tragic journey.

The Guardians of Rilken stayed with us for a long time, until after Ravelin married Rosie. The bears secured our kingdom until the numbers of the new Guardsmen could be built up again.

My father and the eight Guardsmen who had survived came to be called the Nine. From those Nine came an even greater company of Guardsmen. Darrit returned, bringing Tike with him, joining the others who trained to pass the Guardsman tests that Pate's father had set up long ago.

The Guardsmen adopted a new insignia, a rose of white and red petals set in an oval, a memory of their salvation in the arena. The palace guard was disbanded, and the new Guardsmen became both the palace guard and the king's elite, guarding his castle and his person all at once.

Dallen—hungry for wisdom in the middle of all these changes—invited Master Redmond to the castle to advise him. Redmond came and was as delighted to have a ruler listen to him as Dallen was delighted to hear.

Professor Redmond became a great favorite in Elva, which Mama said she could have predicted. He went from inn to inn throughout the city, listening to everyone and engaging them in conversation. He read the mood of the people accurately and, as a result, advised Dallen very well.

Guardstown never again housed the Guardsmen. Instead, they lived in homes spread throughout the city. As a result, Elva became the safest city in all of AllHallen. It was said that a woman could walk from one end of Elva to the other in the middle of the night carrying a large purse, and she would reach her destination in safety. My father says he still would not recommend it. But Elva, having nearly lost them, loved and honored her Guardsmen more than ever.

The Grumpy Rabbit was gratified to find itself the destination for a royal visit. A wide-eyed Ettie saw her sovereign sitting in her kitchen on Mama's old stool, sampling one of her freshly made rolls.

"You have your father's gift," I told Dallen afterwards. "His gift of loving people. It's yours as well."

In the inn, Ravelin saw a picture of the rabbit that had appeared on the wall of his bedroom. The embroidery picture has been reframed and hangs in his study. We still marvel at the story it told.

Dallen turned the hunting station into a small but beautiful royal hunting lodge, with Jarlath as caretaker. The rosebushes still bloom year round by the door. Nothing was ever done to disturb them. Rosie's garden flourishes. Jarlath says he can't keep up with how fast things grow in it.

At Ravelin's request, Dallen arranged a marriage treaty with Ophria. Petronia wed the son and heir of the Duke of Ophria and moved into that lovely palace on the lake she had so admired. Olivia left Rilken to live in Ophria with her daughter. Both brothers hoped that their aunt and cousin might at last be happy.

Ravelin's own happiness was apparent. He and Rosie walked in the gardens together hand-in-hand, every day. Dallen said he had never seen his brother smile so much. I felt the same about my sister.

In the midst of all this, there was one place above all the others that needed the Sender's special healing. One place my dear husband could never see again, and one place Ravelin would never go. The site on the northwest road where their father had been killed.

It took several years of work, and I was close to the birth of our first child, but at last came time for the opening ceremony at a new woodland park.

"It's a gift," I told Dallen one evening as Rosie and I sat with our husbands. "Truly a gift from your people to you. Many have worked hard on this because they love you."

"They say it has been healing for them," Rosie added. "They hope it will be healing for you."

Dallen and Ravelin agreed, but I knew from Dallen's face what a struggle the day would be for him.

We left Elva that morning in a procession of

carriages and coaches. Even if I hadn't known where the location was, I would have been able to tell by the way Dallen reached out to hold my hand when we approached. And by the tightness of his grip.

"Wait!" he cried suddenly. "The road turns here. Why is it going straight?" Dallen leaned forward, looking intently around him.

"We're almost there," I replied gently.

Master Redmond and a group of gardeners, woodsmen, and artists waited to greet us. "To our dear King Dallen and Queen Silvia," Redmond began, "and to our dear First Prince Ravelin and First Princess Rosabel. To you and to all, we humbly present these gardens. They are called *The King's Peace*."

The old section of the road, the road that had brought death, had been completely removed and given a new route. The forest trees had been thinned. Light now poured into what had been a dark place.

Gravel paths wandered among the trees, leading to statues and monuments, all of which were graced with exquisite plantings that exuded peace. A rippling stream, crossed by an elegantly carved footbridge, poured into a small lake.

Rosie and Ravelin took their own slow route through the garden while Dallen and I took ours. Mama and Papa wandered under the trees as well, while other Guardsmen watched dutifully. And here, Lady Avelyn's outstanding sculptures touched the hearts of all of us.

There was a superb statue of Pate's father, standing tall in full Guardsman attire. Pate and his mother stood weeping before it, Avelyn's arms around them both.

King Adare's beloved queen sat on a chair as if ready to welcome a young son into her lap. And there was King Adare himself, whole again, a warm and lively expression on his face.

Dallen's heart was too full for words. We sat on a bench across from the statue of his father and looked up at it without speaking for a long time.

"It has been done," he said at last. "The evil is gone from this place."

"I feel that too," I replied softly. "The gardeners did not start their work until the trees told Rosie it was time."

He helped me to my feet, and we took a path that lined the garden edge.

"Silvie." His voice quiet, but urgent. "Look there."

He pointed into the trees. A bear, standing tall on its back legs, watched us. Not an ordinary bear. But a bear of the kind Dallen knew well.

I released his hand, and he left the path and took several paces through the trees toward it. The bear did nothing but gaze at him, at this hard-working and heart-sore young king, yet I felt it was speaking with him the way it must have when it carried him.

They communed in silence together for some time. When Dallen returned to the path, the glow of a new peace was upon him.

Redmond presided at a large banquet in the manor house nearby, and at the end of it, Dallen stood up to speak. He thanked everyone from his heart, everyone from the smallest gardener to the grandest artist.

Then he said, "You have called this place *The King's*

Peace. A true and right name. So it will be to us and to those who come after. But the Guardians of Rilken know it by another name."

Curious eyes stared at him. Rosie shot me a questioning glance.

"The Guardians call it *The Sender's Promise*," Dallen said. "The promise to one day restore everything that was lost, and heal everything that was broken."

Redmond raised his goblet of wine. "The Sender's Promise," he said with solemn dignity.

"The Sender's Promise," we echoed back.

SONGS AND POEMS OF RILKEN AND ALLHALLEN

Sing Me High
(A Rilken Folk Song)

Oh, sing me high
    And sing me low,
    And sing me where
The wind blows.
I'll listen high,
I'll listen low,
And find you where
The wind blows.

Oh, sing me out
    And sing me in,
    And sing me where
My heart's been.
I'll listen out

And listen in,
And tell you where
My heart's been.

Oh, sing me near
  And sing me far,
  And sing me to
  A bright star.
  I'll listen near
  And listen far,
  And find you at
  The bright star.

~

Motto of the Ruling House of Rilken

Absit invidia.
Let there be no envy or ill will.

~

Oath of the Guardsmen
I am valor for my Valor, the King.
I am strength for my Strength, the King.
I am truth for my Truth, the King.
I give my life for my Life, the King.

~

Pate's Doggerel

Oh, what a devious thing is wine
It has such might and power.
O'er all who drink without a care
It rules within the hour.

For Love of AllHallen
(The Song of the Hosts)

ON THE HEIGHTS a blazing fire glows
  Held in the Hosts' right hand.
  Their horses bold race to the foe,
  Who quaking make their stand.
  Love and strength race on before them,
  Melting monsters as they sing.
  Swift they ride, Light their weapon,
  And make the Northlands ring:

      O AllHallen land,
      See to the good.
      Bring not the evil in.
      Live in beauty strong,
      And sing the song
      Of Love that will not end.

Sing of Strength that shatters darkness,
Of Truth that can't be turned.
Sing of Love that strikes the prowling ones,

Of Fear it will not learn.
Love that searches, with compassion,
Finds and rescues, triumphs long.
Binds the darkness with great Joy,
And gives to Night this song:

> *O AllHallen land,*
> *See to the good.*
> *Bring not the evil in.*
> *Live in beauty strong,*
> *And sing the song*
> *Of Love that will not end.*

AUTHOR'S NOTE

If you are a fairy tale aficionado, you may have recognized the seeds from which *The Last Guardsman* came. This novel is a retelling and reimagining of *Snow White and Rose Red* by the Brothers Grimm, a completely different story with completely different characters than the more famous story of a Snow White surrounded by seven dwarves. And a story that I've always liked better.

I found great satisfaction in making the tale grow up, bringing out the parts that I found most intriguing—especially the loyalty and friendship between two very unlike sisters—and in deleting the parts that detracted from what I saw as the truth of the tale. Thank you so much for sharing the experience with me. I hope you enjoyed *The Last Guardsman* as much as I did.

And as for that other fairy tale, the one with so many dwarves? It also has a place in my world of AllHallen, but several other stories are begging to be reimagined first.

ACKNOWLEDGMENTS

To the following dear people, my sincere and deepest gratitude:

My test readers, for your time, willingness, and enthusiasm for this project: Bonita Krupp, Laura Eckhardt, Caleb Eckhardt, and Dave Wood. I owe you so very, very much.

Jenn, my editor, for your incomparable sense of story, your generosity, and your commitment to this book.

Kristen, my graphic designer, for using your skill to give readers something beautiful to hold in their hands.

Tami Lange and her daughter Elizabeth, for so much generous time at your stables teaching me about the behavior of horses. Bjorn Olson, for a long phone call discussing the behaviors of fighting men. All errors and misunderstandings are clearly my own.

Jillian Wood; Jared and Sarah Stone; David and

Jamie Moldenhauer; and Joe, Meg and the rest of the Monday night community group, for providing additional support and encouragement on parts of this project.

My daughter Adrienne, for singing the Song of the Hosts over the phone to me.

My husband Dale, for loving this project so much.

And to the Lord Jesus Christ, the true Love that will not end. *All glory forever.*

ABOUT THE AUTHOR

Rhonda Chandler was born in California and spent her childhood traveling with her family in Asia Minor, Europe, and all across the United States. In 1979, she graduated from Concordia College, Nebraska (now Concordia University) with degrees in education and history.

After teaching at the high school level for several years, she left to devote her time to her husband and daughters, and to writing.

She now lives with her family in southern Illinois, where on Saturday mornings they make breakfast, brew coffee, and talk for hours about all the important things in life.

Rhonda writes historical, contemporary, and fantasy fiction with spiritual and historical overtones. To find out what's new, visit her at rhondachandler.com and subscribe to her mailing list.

If you enjoyed this book and found it valuable, please leave a review on Goodreads and on Amazon, Barnes &

Noble, Kobo, or wherever else you purchased it. In today's world, reviews are very important in helping people like you find this book. Thank you so much.

www.ingramcontent.com/pod-product-compliance
Lightning Source LLC
Chambersburg PA
CBHW021239200726
48288CB00014B/16